Always & Forever

Debbie Macomber is an American writer born in the state of Washington, where she still lives with her husband and four children. Debbie's successful writing career actually started in childhood, when her brother copied—and sold!—her diary. She's gone on to a considerably wider readership since then as a prolific and popular author whose books have been published around the world.

Jasmine Cresswell's writing career began when she finally decided to stop writing research papers and try her hand at a novel. Born in England, Jasmine has lived and worked all over the world. She met her husband, another expatriate Britisher, in Rio de Janeiro. They're currently living in the United States in Ohio. Jasmine is the mother of three daughters and one son.

Bethany Campbell, an English major and textbook consultant, calls her writing world her 'hidey-hole', that marvellous place where true love always wins out. Her hobbies include writing poetry. Bethany Campbell is the winner of two RITA awards, and her many romances have delighted readers everywhere.

Always & Forever

THE MAN YOU'LL MARRY
by Debbie Macomber

LOVE FOR HIRE
by Jasmine Cresswell

THE LADY AND THE TOMCAT
by Bethany Campbell

MILLS & BOON

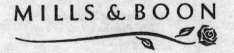

*MILLS & BOON and the Rose Device are trademarks of the publisher.
Harlequin Mills & Boon Limited,
Eton House, 18-24 Paradise Road, Richmond, Surrey TW9 1SR.
This edition published by arrangement with Harlequin Enterprises B.V.*

ALWAYS AND FOREVER © Harlequin Enterprises B.V. 1995

THE MAN YOU'LL MARRY © 1992 by Debbie Macomber
LOVE FOR HIRE © 1992 by Jasmine Cresswell
THE LADY AND THE TOMCAT © 1993 by Bethany Campbell

ISBN 0 263 79288 9

98-9506-C

*Printed in Great Britain by
BPC Paperbacks Ltd*

CONTENTS

CONTENTS

THE MAN YOU'LL MARRY
by Debbie Macomber

FOR JENNY AND KEVIN

CHAPTER ONE

JILL MORRISON caught her breath as she stared excitedly out the airplane window. Seattle and everything familiar was quickly shrinking from view. She settled back comfortably and sighed with pure satisfaction.

This first-class seat was an unexpected gift from the airline. The booking agent had made a mistake and Jill turned out to be the beneficiary. Not a bad way to start a long-awaited vacation.

She glanced, not for the first time, at the man sitting next to her. He looked like the stereotypical businessman, typing industriously on a lap-top computer keyboard, his brow furrowed with concentration. She couldn't tell exactly what he was doing, but noticed several columns of figures. He paused, and something must have troubled him, because he reached for the phone located on the seat between them and punched out a long series of numbers. He turned away from her to speak briskly into the receiver. When he'd finished, he returned to his computer. He seemed impatient and restless, as though he begrudged this traveling time. Not a good sign, Jill mused, when the flight to Honolulu was scheduled to take five hours.

He wasn't the talkative sort, either. In her enthusiasm before takeoff, Jill had made a couple of attempts at light conversation, but both tries had been met with the most minimal responses possible, followed by cool silence.

Great. She was stuck sitting next to this grouch for the start of a vacation she'd been planning for nearly two years. A vacation that Jill and her best friend, Shelly Hansen, had once dreamed of taking together. Only Shelly wasn't Shelly Hansen anymore. Her former college roommate was married now. For an entire month Shelly Hansen had been Shelly Brady.

Even after all this time, Jill had problems taking it in. For as long as Jill had known Shelly, her friend had been adamant about making her career as a video producer her highest priority. Men and relationships would always remain a distant second in her busy life, she'd vowed. For years Jill had watched Shelly discourage attention from the opposite sex. From college onward, Shelly had rigidly avoided any hint of commitment.

Then it had happened. Her friend met Mark Brady and the unexpected became a reality. To Shelly's way of thinking, her mother's Great-Aunt Millicent—known to everyone in the family as Aunt Milly—was directly responsible for her present happiness. She'd met her tax-accountant husband immediately after the elderly woman had mailed Shelly a "magic" wedding dress. The same dress Milly had worn herself fifty years earlier.

Both Shelly and Jill had insisted there was no such thing as magic, especially associated with a wedding dress. Magic belonged to wands or fairy godmothers, not wedding dresses. To fairy tales, not real life.

They'd steadfastly denied the ridiculous story that went along with the gown. Both refused to believe what Aunt Milly had written in her letter; no one in her right mind, they told each other, could possibly take the sweet old woman seriously. *Marry the next man you meet?* Preposterous.

Personally, Jill had found the whole story hilarious. Shelly hadn't been laughing though. Shelly, being Shelly, had overreacted, fretting and worrying, wondering if there wasn't some small chance that Milly could be right. Shelly hadn't *wanted* her to be right, but there it was—the dress arrived one day, and the next she'd fallen into Mark Brady's arms.

Literally.

The rest, as they say, is history and Jill wasn't laughing any longer. Shelly and Mark had been married in June and from all appearances were blissfully happy.

Four weeks after the wedding, Jill was jetting off to Hawaii. Not the best month to visit the tropics, but that couldn't be helped. Her budget was limited and July offered the most value for her money.

The businessman in the seat beside her leaned back and sighed deeply, pinching the bridge of his nose. Whatever problem he'd encountered earlier had persisted, Jill guessed. She must have been right, because no more than ten seconds later, he reached for the phone again and made four calls in a row. Jill had the impression this man never stopped working; even during their meal he continued his calculations. Not a moment of their flight time was wasted. If he wasn't on the phone, he was studying papers from his briefcase or typing more columns of figures into his portable computer.

An hour passed. Jill had hoped her seatmate would be the friendly sort. A couple of times, almost against her will, she found herself watching him. Although she assumed he was somewhere in his mid-thirties, he seemed older. No, she corrected, not older, but... experienced. His face managed to be pleasing to the eye despite his rugged, uneven features. She wondered fleetingly how he would assess her appearance. Except that he hadn't looked directly at her once. It was as if he was totally unaware there was someone in the seat next to him. His eyes were gray, she'd noted earlier, the color of polished steel. There was nothing soft about him. Nothing gentle, either, Jill wagered.

This was obviously a man who had it all—hand-tailored suits, Italian leather shoes, gold pen and watch. She'd bet even his plastic was gold! No doubt he lived the way he flew—first class. He was the type who had all the answers, too. The type of man who didn't question his own attitudes and beliefs....

He reminded Jill of her father, long dead, long grieved. He, too, had been an influential businessman who'd held success in the palm of his hand. Adam Morrison had fought off middle age on a gym floor. Energy was his trademark and death was an eternity away. Only it was just around the corner, and he didn't know it.

Ironic that she should be sitting next to him thirteen years after his death. Not her father, but someone so much like him it was all Jill could do not to ask when he'd last seen his family.

He must have felt her scrutiny, because he suddenly turned and stared at her. Jill blushed guiltily, bowing her head over her book, reading it with exaggerated fervor.

"Did you like what you saw?" he asked her boldly.

"I—I don't know what you mean," she said in a small voice, moving the paperback ridiculously close to her face.

For the first time since he'd taken the seat next to her, the stranger grinned. It was an odd smile, off center and unpracticed, as if he didn't often find anything to smile about.

The remainder of the flight was uneventful. Jill held her breath during the descent, until the tires bumped down on the runway in Honolulu. She wished again that Shelly was taking this trip, too. With or without her best friend, though, Jill intended to have the time of her life. She had seven glorious days to laze in the sun. Seven days to shop to her heart's content and to go sight-seeing and to swim and relax and eat glorious meals.

For months Jill had dreamed of the wonders she would see and experience. Tranquil villages, orchid plantations—oh, how she loved orchids. At night, she'd stroll along lava-strewn beaches and by day there'd be flower-cloaked canyons to explore, tumbling waterfalls and smoldering volcanoes all waiting for her. Hawaii was going to be a grand adventure, Jill could feel it in her bones.

The man beside her was on his feet the instant their plane came to a standstill. He removed his carry-on bag from the storage compartment above the seat with an efficiency that told her he was a seasoned traveler. The smiling flight attendant handed him a garment bag as he strode off the plane.

Jill followed him, watching for directions to the baggage pickup. Her seatmate's steps were crisp and purposeful. It didn't surprise her; this was a man on the go, always in a rush to get somewhere. Meet someone. Make a deal. No time to stop and smell the roses for her friend the grouch.

Jill lost sight of him when she stopped to purchase a lei at a concession stand. She draped the lovely garland of orchids around her neck and fingered the delicate string of flowers, marveling at their beauty.

Once again the reminder that adventures awaited her on this tropical island moved full sail across her heart. She wasn't the fanciful sort, nor did she possess an extravagant imagination. Not like Shelly. Yet Jill felt something deep inside her stir to life....

Shelly had become a real believer in magic, Jill mused, smiling as she bought herself a fresh slice of pineapple. For that matter, even she—ever the practical one—found herself a tiny bit susceptible to the claims of a charmed wedding dress. Just a tiny bit, though.

Jill's pulse quickened the way it did whenever she thought about what had happened between Shelly and Mark. It was simply the most romantic thing she'd ever known.

Romance had scurried past Jill several times. Currently she was dating Ralph, a computer programmer, but it was more for companionship than romance, although he'd been hinting for several months that they should start "getting serious." Jill assumed he meant marriage. Ralph was nice, and so far Jill had been able to dissuade him from discussing anything about a long-term relationship. She didn't want to hurt his feelings, but she just wasn't interested in marrying him.

However, Jill fully intended to marry someday. There'd never been any question of that. The only question was *who*. She'd dated frequently in college, but there hadn't been anyone special. Then, when she'd been hired as a pharmacist for PayRite, a drugstore chain with several outlets in the Pacific Northwest, the opportunities to meet eligible men had dwindled dramatically.

Prospects weren't exactly crowding the horizon, but Jill had given up worrying about it. She'd done a fair job of pushing the thought of a husband and family to the far reaches of her mind—until she'd made one small mistake.

She'd tried on Aunt Milly's wedding dress.

Shelly had hung the infamous dress in the very back of her closet. Out of sight, out of mind—only it hadn't worked that way. Not a minute passed that Shelly wasn't keenly aware of the dress and its alleged powers.

On an impulse, Jill had tried it on herself. To this day she didn't know what had prompted her to slip into the beautiful hand-sewn wedding dress. It was so elegant, so beautiful, with row upon row of pearls and delicate lace layered over satin.

That it fit as though it had been specifically designed for her had come as much of a surprise to

Shelly as it had to Jill. Shelly had seemed almost giddy with relief, insisting her aunt had made a mistake and the dress was actually meant for Jill. But by that time, Shelly had already met Mark....

No, Aunt Milly hadn't made a mistake—the wedding dress had been meant for Shelly all along. Her marriage to Mark proved it. Besides, given the choice, Jill preferred to find her husband the old-fashioned way! And really, she'd have to attribute Shelly's meeting and marrying Mark to the power of suggestion, the power of expectation. She shook her head and hurried off to retrieve her luggage.

Then she headed outside, intent on grabbing a taxi. As the driver loaded her bags, she simply stood for a moment, savoring the warm breeze, enjoying the first sounds and sights of Hawaii. She couldn't wait to get to her hotel. Through a friend who was a travel agent, Jill had been able to book a room in one of the most exclusive places on Oahu at a ridiculously low rate.

The hotel was everything the brochure had promised and more. Jill had to pinch herself when she got to her room. The first thing she did was walk to the sliding-glass doors that led to the lanai, a balcony overlooking the swimming-pool area. Beyond that, the Pacific Ocean thundered against the sandy shore. The sight was mesmerizing, the beauty so keen, it brought tears of appreciation to Jill's eyes.

She quickly tipped the bellhop, who'd carted up her luggage, and returned to the view. If she never went beyond this room, Jill would have been satisfied. She stood at the railing, the breeze riffling her long hair about her face.

The hotel was U-shaped, and something—a movement, a figure—caught her eye. A man. Jill glanced across the swimming pool, across the tiki-hut roof of the bar until her gaze found what she was seeking. The grouch. In a lanai directly across from her. At least she thought so. He wore the same dark suit as the man with whom she'd spent five of the most uncommunicative hours of her life.

Shelly didn't know what prompted her, but she waved. After a moment, he waved back. He stepped farther out onto the lanai and she knew beyond a doubt. Their rooms were in different sections of the hotel, but they were on the same floor, their lanais facing each other.

He held a portable phone to his ear, but he slowly lowered it.

For several moments they simply stared at one another. After what seemed like an embarrassingly long time, Jill tried to pull herself away and found she couldn't. Unsure why, unsure what had attracted her attention to the man in the first place, unsure of everything, Jill looked away.

A knock at the door distracted her.

"Yes?" she asked, opening her door. A bellhop in a crisp white uniform stood before her with a large wrapped box.

"This arrived by special courier for you earlier today, Ms. Morrison," he explained politely.

When he'd left, Jill studied the package, reading the Seattle postmark and the unfamiliar block printing. She carried it to the bed, still puzzled. She had no idea who would be mailing her anything from home. Especially since she'd only left that morning.

Sitting on the edge of the bed, she carefully unwrapped the package and lifted the lid. Her hands froze. Her heart froze. Her breath jammed in her throat. When she was able to move again, she inhaled sharply and closed her eyes.

It was Aunt Milly's wedding dress.

A letter rested on top of the tissue-wrapped dress. With trembling hands, Jill reached for it.

Dearest Jill,
Trust me, I know exactly what you're feeling. I remember so well my own emotions when I opened this very box and found Aunt Milly's wedding dress staring up at me. As you know, my first instinct was to run and hide. Instead I was fortunate enough to find Mark and fall in love.

I suppose you're wondering why I'm mailing this dress to you in Hawaii. Why didn't I simply give it to you before you left Seattle? Good question, and if I had a reasonable answer I'd be more than happy to explain.

One thing I've learned these past few months is that there's precious little logic when it comes to understanding any of this—love, fate, the magic within Aunt Milly's wedding dress. Take my advice and don't even try to make sense of it.

I suppose I should tell you what prompted me to give you the dress in the first place. I was sitting at the table the other morning, with my first cup of coffee. I wasn't fully awake yet. My eyes were closed. Suddenly you were in my mind, standing waist-deep in the blue-green water. There was a waterfall behind you and lush beautiful plants all around. It had to be Hawaii. You looked happier than I can ever remember seeing you.

There was a man with you, and I wish I could describe him. Unfortunately, he was in shadow. Read into that whatever you will. There was a certain look about you, a look I've only seen once before—the day you tried on the wedding gown. You were radiant.

This all happened a week ago. I talked to Mark about it that evening. He seemed to feel the same way I did—that the dress was meant for you. I phoned Aunt Milly and told her. She said by all means to make you the dress's next recipient.

I should probably have given you the dress then, but something held me back. Nothing I can put into words, but a feeling it would be too soon, I suppose. So I'm mailing it to you now.

My wish for you, Jill, is that you find someone to love. Someone as wonderful as Mark. Of the two of us, you've always been the sensible one. You believed in logic and common sense. But you also believed in love, long before I did. I was the skeptic there. Something tells me the man you'll marry is just as cynical as I once was. You're going to have to teach him about love, the same way Mark's taught me.

Call me as soon as you get back. I'll be waiting to hear what happens. In my heart I already know it's going to be wonderful.

Love,
Shelly

Jill read the letter twice. Her pulse quickened as her eyes lifted and involuntarily returned to the lanai directly across from her own.

The frantic pace of her heart slowed to normal.

The grouch was gone.

Jill recalled Aunt Milly's letter to Shelly. "When you receive this dress," she wrote, "the first man you meet is the man you'll marry."

So it wasn't the grouch, it was someone else. Not that she really believed in any of this. Still, her knees went unaccountably weak with relief.

After unpacking her clothes, Shelly showered and lay down for a few moments, closing her eyes. She hadn't intended to fall asleep, but when she awoke, a rosy dusk had settled. Flickering fires from the bamboo poles that surrounded the pool sent shadows dancing on her walls.

She'd seen him, Jill realized. While she slept. Her hero, her predestined husband. But try as she might, she wasn't able to bring him into clear focus. Naturally it was her imagination. Fanciful thinking. Dreams gone wild. Jill reminded herself stoutly that she didn't believe in the power of the wedding dress any more than she believed in the Easter Bunny. But it was rather nice to fantasize now and again, to pretend.

Unquestionably, there was a certain amount of anticipation created by the delivery of the wedding dress and Shelly's letter. But unlike her friend, Jill didn't expect anything to come of this. Both Jill's feet were firmly planted on the ground. She wasn't as whimsical as Shelly, nor was she as easily influenced by outside forces.

True, at twenty-eight, Jill was more than ready to marry and settle down. She knew she wanted children eventually, too. But when it came to marrying the man of her dreams, she'd prefer to find him the old trial-and-error way. She didn't need a magic wedding dress gently guiding her toward him!

Initially, Shelly had had many of the same thoughts herself, Jill remembered, but she'd married the first man she'd met after the dress arrived.

The first man you meet. She was thinking about that while she changed into a light cotton dress and sandals. She was still thinking about it as she rode the elevator down to the lobby to have a look around.

There must have been something in the air. Maybe it was because she was on vacation and feeling free of her usual routines and restraints; Jill didn't know. But for some unknown reason she found herself glancing around, wondering what man it could possibly be.

The hotel was full of possibilities. A distinguished gentleman sauntered past. An ambassador perhaps? Hmm, that might be nice, she mused. Or a politician.

Naw, she countered silently, laughing at herself. She wasn't interested in politics. Furthermore she didn't see herself as an ambassador's wife. She'd probably say the wrong thing to the wrong person and inadvertently cause an international incident.

A guy who looked like a rock star strolled her way next. Now, there was an interesting prospect, although Jill had a minor problem picturing herself married to a man who wore his hair longer than she did. He was cute, though. A definite possibility—*if* she were to take Shelly's letter seriously.

A doctor would be ideal, Jill decided. With her medical background, they were sure to have a lot in common. She scanned the lobby area, searching for someone who looked as if he'd feel at home with a stethoscope around his neck.

No luck. Nor, for that matter, did she seem to be generating much interest herself. She might as well be invisible. So much for that! These speculations were all in jest anyway....

Swallowing an urge to laugh, she headed out the back of the hotel toward the pristine beach. A lazy evening stroll among swaying palms sounded just the thing.

She walked toward the ocean, removed her shoes and held them by the straps as she wandered ankle-deep into the delightfully warm water. She wasn't paying much attention to where she was going, thinking, instead, about her hopes for a family of her own. Thinking about the few truly happy memories she had of her father. The Christmas when she was five and a camping trip two years later. A picnic, once. But by the time she was eight, his success had overtaken him. It wasn't that he didn't love her or her mother, she supposed, but—

"I wouldn't go out much farther if I were you," a deep male voice called from behind her.

Jill's pulse soared at the unexpectedness of the intrusion. The silhouette of a man leaning against a palm tree captured her attention. In the darkness she couldn't make out his features, yet he seemed vaguely familiar.

"I won't," she said, trying to see who'd spoken. Whoever it was stayed stubbornly under the shadows of the tree.

From the distance Jill noted that he had the physique of an athlete. She happened to appreciate wide, powerful shoulders on a man. She stepped closer, attempting to get a better look at him without being obvious. Although his features remained hidden, his chin was tilted at an arrogant angle.

A dash of arrogance in a man was a nice touch, too.

"I wondered if you were planning to go swimming at night. Only a fool would do that."

Jill bristled. She had no intention of swimming. For one thing, she wasn't dressed for it. Before she could defend herself, however, he continued, "You look just like one of those helpless romantics who can't resist testing the water. Let me guess—this is your first visit to the islands?"

Jill nodded. She'd ventured far enough onto the beach to actually see him now. Her heart sank—no wonder he'd seemed vaguely familiar. No wonder he was vaguely insulting. For the second time in a twenty-four-hour period she'd happened upon the grouch.

"I don't suppose you took time to eat dinner, either."

"I . . . had something earlier. On the plane."

He snickered softly. "Plastic food."

"I don't know what concern it is of yours."

"None," he admitted, shrugging.

"Then my going without dinner shouldn't bother you." She bristled again at the intense way he was studying her. His mouth had twisted into a faint smile, and he seemed amused by her.

"Thank you for all your advice," she said stiffly, turning away from him and heading back toward the water.

"You're not wearing the lei."

Jill's fingers automatically went to her neck as she stopped midstep. She'd left it in her room when she changed clothes.

"Allow me." He stepped forward, removing the one from his own neck, and draped it around hers. Since this was her first visit to the islands, Jill didn't know if giving someone a lei had any symbolism attached to it. She didn't really want that kind of connection with him. Just in case.

"Thank you." She hoped she sounded adequately grateful.

"I might have saved your life, you know."

That was a ridiculous comment. "How?"

"You could have drowned."

Jill couldn't help it. She laughed. "Not very likely. I had no intention of swimming."

"You can't trust the tides here. Even this close to shore, the waves are capable of jerking your feet out from under you. You might easily have been swept out to sea."

"That's absurd."

"Perhaps," he agreed, amicably enough. "I was hoping you'd realize you're in my debt."

Ah, now they were getting somewhere. This man wasn't given to generosity. She'd bet a month's wages that he'd initiated the conversation for his own purposes. He'd had plenty of time on their flight from Seattle to advise her about swimming.

No, he was after something.

Jill should have been suspicious from the first. "What is it you want?"

He grinned that cocky, unused smile of his and nodded. Apparently this was high praise of her finely honed intuitive skills.

"Nothing much. I was hoping you'd agree to attend a small business dinner with me."

"Tonight?"

He nodded again. "You did mention you hadn't eaten."

"Yes, but..."

"It'll only take an hour or so of your time." He sounded a bit impatient, as if he'd expected her to agree to his scheme without question.

"I don't even know who you are. Why would I want to attend a dinner party with you? I'm Jill Morrison, by the way."

"Jordan Wilcox," he said abruptly. "All right, if you must know, I need a woman to come with me so I won't be forced to offend someone I can't afford to alienate."

"Then don't."

"He's not the one I'm worried about. It's his daughter. She's apparently set her sights on me and she doesn't seem capable of taking a hint."

"Well, then, it sounds as though you've got yourself a problem." Privately Jill wondered at the woman's taste.

He frowned, shoving his hands into the pockets of his formal dinner jacket. He'd changed clothes, too, but he hadn't substituted something more casual for his business suit. Quite the reverse. But then, that shouldn't have surprised her. It was always business, never pleasure, with people like him.

"I don't know what it is about you women," he said plaintively. "Can't you tell when a man's not interested?"

"Not always." Jill was beginning to feel a bit cocky. She swung her shoes at her side. "In other words you need me as a bodyguard."

Clearly he didn't approve of her terminology, but he let it pass. "Something like that."

"Do I have to pretend to be madly in love with you?"

"Good heavens, no."

Jill hesitated. "I'm not sure I brought along anything appropriate to wear."

He reached inside his pocket and pulled out a thick wad of cash. He peeled away several one-hundred dollar bills and stuffed them into her hand. "Buy yourself something. The shop in the hotel's still open."

CHAPTER TWO

"I'LL PAY for the dress myself," Jill insisted for the tenth time. She couldn't believe she'd agreed to attend this dinner party with Jordan. Not only didn't she know the man, she didn't even like him.

"I'll pay for the dress," he replied, also for the tenth time. "It's the least I can do."

They were in the ultraexpensive dress shop located off the hotel lobby. Jill was shifting judiciously through the rack of evening gowns. Most were outrageously priced. She found a simple one she thought might flatter her petite build, ran her hand down the sleeve until she reached the white tag, then sighed. The price was higher than any of the others. Grumbling under her breath, she dropped the sleeve and continued her search.

Jordan glanced impatiently at his watch. "What's wrong with this one?" He held up an elegant cocktail dress. The bodice was covered with bright green sequins, and the dark green skirt was straight and slim. Lovely indeed, but hardly worth a week's salary.

"Nothing's wrong with it," she answered absently as she flipped through the row of dresses.

"Then buy it."

Jill glared at him. "I can't afford five-hundred dollars for a dress I'll probably only wear once."

"I can," he returned between clenched teeth.

"I *won't* allow you to pay for my dress."

"The party's in thirty minutes," he reminded her sharply.

"All right, all right."

He sighed with obvious relief and reached for the dress. Jill's hand on his forearm stopped him.

"Obviously nothing here is going to work. I'll check what I brought along with me. Maybe what I have is more suitable than I thought."

Groaning, he followed her to the elevator. "Wait in the hall," she instructed as she unlocked her door. She wasn't about to let a strange man into her hotel room. She stood by the closet and rooted through the dresses she'd unpacked that afternoon. The only suitable one was an antique white shirtwaist with large gold buttons and a wide gold belt. It wasn't exactly what one would wear to an elegant dinner party, but it was passable.

She raced to the door and held it up for Jordan. "Will this do?"

The poor man looked exasperated. "Hell, I don't know."

Leaving the door open, Jill raced back to scan her closet. "The only other dress I have is Aunt Milly's wedding gown," she muttered.

"You packed a wedding dress?" His gray eyes lit up with amusement. It seemed an effort not to laugh

THE MAN YOU'LL MARRY

outright. "You apparently have high hopes for this vacation."

"I didn't bring it with me," she informed him primly, sorry she'd even mentioned it. "A friend had it delivered."

"You're getting married?"

"Not exactly. I— Oh, I don't have time to explain."

Jordan eyed her as if he had plenty of questions, but wasn't completely sure he wanted to ask them.

"Wear the one you showed me, then," he said testily. "I'm sure it'll be fine."

"All right, I will." By now Jill regretted agreeing to attend this dinner party. "I'll only be a minute." She closed the door again, but not before she got a glimpse of the surprised look on Jordan's face. It wasn't until she'd slipped out of her sundress that she realized he probably wasn't accustomed to women who left him waiting in the hallway while they changed clothes.

Although she knew Jordan was impatient, Jill took a few extra minutes to freshen her makeup and run a brush through her shoulder-length brown hair. Using a gold clip, she pinned it up in a simple chignon. Despite herself, she couldn't help feeling excited about this small adventure. There was no telling whom she might meet tonight.

Drawing in a deep breath to calm herself, she smoothed the skirt of her dress, then walked slowly to the door. Jordan was waiting for her, his back against the opposite wall. He straightened when she appeared.

"Will this do?"

His gaze narrowed assessingly. His scrutiny made Jill feel uncomfortable, and she held herself stiff and straight. At last he nodded.

"You look fine," was all he said.

Jill heaved a sigh of relief, returned to her room long enough to retrieve her purse, and then joined Jordan. She tested the door to be sure it was locked.

The dinner party, as Jordan had explained earlier, was in a private room in one of the hotel's restaurants. Jordan led the way to the elevator, his pace urgent.

"You'd better explain what you want me to do," she said.

"Do?" he repeated with a frown. "Hell, just do whatever it is you women do to let one another know a certain man is off-limits, and make sure Suzi understands." He hesitated. "Only do it without fawning all over me."

"I wouldn't dream of it," Jill said, gazing up at him in mock adoration and fluttering her long lashes.

Jordan's frown deepened. "None of that, either."

"Of what?"

"That thing with the eyes." He motioned with his hand, looking annoyed.

"Should I know something about who's attending the party?"

"Not really," he answered impatiently.

"What about you?" He shot her a puzzled look, and Jill elaborated. "If I'm your date, it makes sense

I'd know who you are—something beyond your name, I mean—and what you do."

"I suppose it does." He buried his hands in his pockets. "I'm the CEO for a large development company based in Seattle. Simply put, we develop projects, gather together the financing, arrange for the construction, and then once the project is completed, we sell."

"That sounds interesting." If you thrived on tension and pressure, that is.

"It can be," was his only response. He looked her over once more, but his glance revealed neither approval nor reproach.

"I didn't like you when we first met." Jill didn't know why she felt obliged to explain this. In fact, she still didn't like him, though she had to admit he was a very attractive man indeed. "I sat next to you during the flight, and I thought you were most unfriendly," she continued.

"I take it your opinion of me hasn't changed?" He cocked one brow with the question, as if to suggest her answer wouldn't trouble him one way or the other.

Jill ignored him. "You don't like women very much, do you?"

"They have their uses."

He said it in such a belittling, negative way that Jill felt a flash of hot color invade her cheeks. She turned to look at him, feeling almost sorry for a man who had everything yet seemed so empty inside. "What's made you so cynical?"

He glanced at her again, a bit scornfully. "Life."

Jill didn't know what to make of that response, but luckily the elevator arrived just then.

"Is there anything else I should know before we arrive?" she asked once they were inside. Her role, Jill understood, was to protect him from an associate's daughter. She wasn't sure how she was supposed to manage that, but she'd think of something when the time came.

"Nothing important," he answered. He paused, frowning. "I'm afraid the two of us might arouse a bit of curiosity, though."

"Why's that?"

"I don't generally associate with ... innocents."

"Innocents?" He made her sound like one of the pre-school crowd. No one she'd ever known could insult her with less effort. "I'm over twenty-one, you know!"

He laughed outright at that, and Jill stiffened, regretting—probably not for the last time—that she'd ever agreed to this.

"I think you're wonderful, too," she said sarcastically.

"So you told me before."

The elevator arrived at the top floor of the hotel, where the restaurant was located. Jordan spoke briefly to the maître d', who led them to the dinner party.

Jill glanced around the simple, elegant room, and her heart did a tiny somersault. All the guests were executive types, the men in dark suits, the women in sophisticated dresses that could all have been bought from that little boutique downstairs. Everyone had an aura of prosperity and power.

Jill's breath came in shallow gasps. She was miles out of her league. These people had money, real money, whereas she'd spent months just saving for this vacation. Her money was invested in panty hose and frozen dinners, not property and office towers and massive stock portfolios.

Jordan must have felt her unease, because he turned to her and smiled briefly. "You'll be fine."

It amazed Jill how three little words from him could give her an immeasurable boost of confidence. She smiled her appreciation and drew herself up as tall and proud as her five-foot-three-inch frame would allow.

Waiters carried trays of delicate hors d'oeuvres and narrow etched-glass champagne flutes filled with sparkling, golden liquid. Jill reached for a glass and took her first sip, widening her eyes in surprise. Never had she tasted anything better.

"This is excellent."

"It should be, at a hundred and fifty dollars a bottle."

Before Jill could comment, an older, distinguished-looking gentleman detached himself from a younger colleague and made his way from across the room toward them. He was probably close to fifty, but could have stepped off the pages of *Gentlemen's Quarterly*.

"Jordan," he said in a hearty voice, extending his hand, "I'm delighted you could make it."

"I am, too."

"I trust your flight was uneventful."

Jordan's gaze briefly met Jill's. "Very pleasant. I'd like you to meet Jill Morrison. Jill, Dean Lundquist."

"Hello," she said pleasantly, extending her hand.

"Delighted," Dean said again, turning to smile at her. He took her hand and held it considerably longer than good manners required. Jill had the impression she was being carefully inspected and did her utmost to appear composed.

Finally, he released her hand and nodded toward the entrance. "If you'll both excuse me a moment, Nicholson's just arrived."

"Of course," Jordan agreed politely.

Jill waited until Dean Lundquist was out of earshot. Then she leaned toward Jordan and whispered, "Suzi's dad?"

Jordan made a wry face. "Smart girl."

Not really, since few other men would have had cause to inspect her so closely, but Jill didn't discount the compliment. She wasn't likely to receive that many, at least not from Jordan.

"Who was that standing with him?" She inclined her head in the direction of a tall, good-looking young man. Something about him didn't seem quite right. Nothing she could put her finger on, but it was a feeling she couldn't shake.

"That's Dean, Junior," Jordan explained.

Jill noticed the way Jordan's mouth thinned and the thoughtful, preoccupied look that came briefly into his eyes. "He's being groomed by Daddy to take my place."

"Junior?" Jill studied the younger man a second time. "I don't think you'll have much of a problem."

"Why's that?"

She shrugged, not sure why she felt so confident of that. "I can't picture you losing at anything."

His gaze swept her warmly. "I have no intention of giving Junior the opportunity, but the time's fast approaching when I'm going to have one hell of a fight on my hands."

"Just a minute," Jill said, tapping her finger against her lower lip. "If Suzi is Dean, Senior's daughter, then wouldn't a marriage between you two secure your position?" It wouldn't exactly be a love match, but she couldn't envision Jordan marrying for something as commonplace as love.

Jordan gave her a quick, unreadable look. "It'd help, but unfortunately I'm not the marrying kind."

Jill had guessed as much. She doubted there was time in his busy schedule for love or commitment, just for work, work, work. Complete one project and start another. She knew the pattern.

Jill couldn't imagine herself falling in love with someone like Jordan. And she couldn't picture Jordan in love at all. As he'd said, he wasn't the marrying kind.

"Jordan." A woman's shrill voice sent a chill up Jill's spine as a beautiful blonde raced past her and straight into Jordan's unsuspecting arms, locking him in a tight embrace.

"This must be Suzi," Jill said conversationally from behind the woman who was squeezing Jordan for all she was worth.

Jordan's irate eyes found hers. "Do something!" he mouthed.

Jill was enjoying the scene far too much to interrupt Suzi's passionate greeting. While Jordan was occupied, Jill reached for a hors d'oeuvre from a nearby silver platter. Whatever it was tasted divine, and she automatically reached for two more. She hadn't realized how hungry she was. Not until she was on her third cracker did she realize she was sampling caviar.

"Oh, darling, I didn't think you'd ever get here," Suzi said breathlessly. Her pretty blue eyes filled with something close to hero worship as she gazed longingly up at Jordan. "Whatever took you so long? Didn't you know I'd been waiting hours and hours and hours for you?"

"Suzi," Jordan said stiffly, disentangling himself from the blonde's embrace. He straightened the cuffs of his shirt. "I'd like you to meet Jill Morrison, my date. Jill, this is Suzi Lundquist."

"Hello," Jill said before reaching for yet another cracker. Jordan's look told her this was not the time to discover a taste for Russian caviar.

Suzi's big blue eyes widened incredulously. She really was lovely, but one glimpse and Jill understood Jordan's reluctance. Suzi was very young, twenty at most, and terribly vulnerable. She had to admire his tactic of putting the girl off without being unnecessarily rude.

Jordan had made Dean Lundquist's daughter sound like a vamp. Jill disagreed. Suzi might be a vamp-in-training, but right now she was only young and head-strong.

"You're Jordan's date?" Suzi asked, fluttering her incredible lashes—which were almost long enough to create a draft in the room, Jill decided.

She smiled and nodded. "We're very good friends, aren't we, Jordan?" She slipped her arm in his and gazed up at him, ever so sweetly.

"But I thought—I hoped..." Suzi turned to Jordan who'd edged himself closer to Jill, draping his arm across her shoulders as though they'd been an item for quite some time.

"Yes?"

Suzi glanced from Jordan to Jill and then back to Jordan. Tears brimmed in her bright blue eyes. "I thought there was something special between us...."

"I'm sorry, Suzi," he said gently.

"But Daddy seemed to think..." She left the rest unsaid as she slowly backed away. After three short steps, she turned and dashed out of the room. Jill popped another cracker into her mouth.

Several people were looking in their direction, though Jordan seemed unaware of it. Jill, however, keenly felt the interested glances. Not exactly a comfortable feeling, especially when one's mouth was full of caviar.

After an awkward moment, conversation resumed, and Jill was able to swallow. "That was dreadful," she muttered. "I feel sorry for the poor girl."

"Frankly, so do I. But she'll get over it." He turned toward Jill. "A lot of help you were," he grumbled. "You were stuffing down crackers like there was no tomorrow."

"This is the first time I've tasted caviar. I didn't know it was so good."

"I didn't bring you along to appraise the hors d'oeuvres."

"I served my purpose," Jill countered. "But I'm not happy about it. She's not a bad kid."

"Believe me," Jordan insisted, his face tightening, "she *will* get over it. She'll pout for a while, but in the end she'll realize we did her a favor."

"I still don't like it."

Now that her mission was accomplished, Jill felt free to examine the room. She wandered around a bit, sipping her champagne. The young man playing the piano caught her attention. He was good. Darn good. After five years of lessons herself, Jill knew talent when she heard it. She walked over to the baby grand to compliment the pianist, and they chatted briefly about music until she noticed Jordan looking for her. Jill excused herself; their meal was about to be served.

Dinner was delicious. Jill was seated beside Jordan, who was busy carrying on a conversation with a stately looking gentleman on his other side. The man on her right, a distinguished gentleman in his mid-sixties, introduced himself as Andrew Howard. Although he didn't acknowledge it in so many words, Jill realized he was the president of Howard Pharmaceuticals, now retired. Jill pointed out that PayRite

Pharmacy, where she worked, carried a number of his company's medications, and the two of them were quickly involved in a lengthy conversation. By the time dessert was served Jill felt as comfortable with Mr. Howard, as if she'd known him all her life.

Following a glass of brandy, Jordan seemed ready to leave.

"Thank you so much," she told Mr. Howard as she slid back her chair. "I enjoyed our conversation immensely."

He stood with her and clasped her hand warmly. "I did, too. If you don't mind, I'd like to keep in touch."

Jill smiled. "I'd enjoy that. And thank you for the invitation."

Then she and Jordan exchanged good-nights with her dinner companion and headed for the elevator. Jordan didn't speak until they were inside.

"What was that all about with Howard?"

"Nothing. He invited me out to see his home. Apparently it's something of a showplace."

"He's a bit old for you, don't you think?"

Jill gave him an incredulous look. "Don't be ridiculous. He assumed you and I knew each other. He just wanted me to feel welcome, I suppose." She didn't mention that Jordan had spent the entire dinner talking with a business associate. He seemed to have all but forgotten she was with him.

"Howard invited you to his home?"

"Us, actually. You can make your excuses if you want, but I'd really like to take him up on his offer."

"Andrew Howard and my father were good friends. My father passed away several years back, and Howard likes to keep track of the projects I'm involved with. He's gone in on the occasional deal."

"He's a sweet man. Did you know he lost his only son to cancer? It's the reason his company has done so much in the field of cancer research. His son's death changed the course of his life."

"I had no idea." Jordan was obviously astounded that he'd known Andrew Howard for so many years and not realized he'd lost a child. "You learned this over dinner?"

"Good grief, dinner lasted nearly two hours." She sighed deeply and pressed her hands to her stomach. "I'm stuffed. I'll never sleep unless I walk off some of this food."

"It would've helped if you hadn't eaten half the hors d'oeuvres by yourself."

Jill decided to ignore that comment.

"Do you mind if I join you?" Jordan surprised her by asking.

"Not in the least, as long as you promise not to make any more remarks about hors d'oeuvres. *Or* lecture me about the dangers of swimming at night."

Jordan grinned. "You've got yourself a deal."

They walked through the lobby and out of the hotel toward the beach. The surf thundered against the shore, slapping the sand, then retreating. Jill found the rhythmic sounds relaxing.

"What sort of project do you have planned for Hawaii?" she ventured after a few minutes.

"A shopping complex."

Although he'd answered her question, his expression was preoccupied. "Why the frown?" she asked.

He shot a quick glance her way. "The Lundquists seem to have some sort of hidden agenda," he said.

"You said Daddy's grooming Junior to take your place," Jill prompted.

"It looks like I'm headed for a proxy fight, which is an expensive and costly proposition for everyone involved. For now, I have the controlling interest, but by no means do I have control."

"This trip to Hawaii . . . ?"

"It's strictly business. I just wish I knew what the hell was going on behind my back."

"I wish you the best." This was a world far removed from Jill's.

"Thanks." He grinned, and suddenly seemed to leave his worries behind.

They strolled for several minutes in companionable silence. The breeze was warm, the moon full and bright, and the rhythm of the ocean waves went on and on.

"I suppose I should go back," Jill said reluctantly. She had a full day planned, beginning first thing in the morning, and although she didn't feel the least bit tired, she should think about getting some sleep.

"Me, too."

They altered their meandering course in the direction of the hotel, their shoes sinking into the moist sand.

"Thanks for your help with Suzi Lundquist."

"Anytime. Just say the word and I'll be there, especially if there's caviar involved." She felt guilty, however, about the young and vulnerable Suzi. Jordan had been gentle with her; nevertheless, Jill's sympathy went out to the girl. "I can't help feeling bad for Suzi."

Jordan sighed. "The girl just won't take no for an answer."

"Do you?"

"What do you mean?"

Jill stopped a moment to collect her thoughts. "I don't understand finance, but it seems to me that you'd never get anywhere if you quit at the first stumbling block. Suzi takes after her father and brother. She saw what she wanted and went after it. Rather an admirable trait, I guess. I suspect you haven't seen the last of her."

"Probably not, but I won't be here more than a few days. I should be able to avoid her in that time."

"Good luck." She hesitated when they reached the pathway, bordered by vivid flowering shrubs, that led to the huge lighted swimming pool.

Jordan grinned. "What with one thing and another, I have the feeling I'm going to need it."

The night couldn't have been more perfect. It seemed such a shame to waste these warm romantic moments, but Jill finally forced herself to murmur a good-night.

"Here," Jordan said just as she did.

Jill was startled when he presented her with a single lavender orchid. "What's this for?"

"In appreciation for all your help."

"Actually, I should be the one thanking you. I had a wonderful evening." It beat the heck out of sitting in front of her television and ordering dinner from room service, which was exactly what she'd planned. She held the flower under her nose and breathed in the delicate scent.

"Enjoy your stay in Hawaii."

"Thank you, I will." Her itinerary was full for nearly every day. "I might even see you...around the hotel."

"Don't count on it. I'm headed back to Seattle in two days."

"Goodbye, then."

"Goodbye."

Neither moved. Jill didn't understand why. They'd said their good-nights—there seemed nothing left to say. It was time to leave. Time for her to return to her room and sleep off the effects of an exceptionally long day.

She made a decisive movement, but before she could turn away, his hand at her shoulder stopped her. Jill's troubled gaze met his. "Jordan?"

He captured her chin, his touch light but firm.

"Yes?" she whispered, her heart in her throat.

"Nothing." He dropped his hand.

Jill was about to turn away again when he stepped toward her, took her by the shoulders and kissed her. Jill had certainly been kissed before, and the experience had always been pleasant, if a bit predictable.

Not this time.

Exciting, unfamiliar sensations raced through her. Jordan's mouth feasted on hers with practiced ease while his hands roved her back, caressing slowly, confidently.

Jill was breathless and weak when he finally broke away. He stared down at her with a perplexed look, as if he'd shocked himself by kissing her. As if he didn't know what had come over him.

Jill didn't know, either. There was a sinking feeling in the pit of her stomach, and then she remembered something Shelly had told her—the overwhelming sensation she'd experienced the first time Mark had kissed her. From that moment on, Shelly had known her fate was sealed.

Jill had never felt anything that even came close to what she'd just felt in Jordan's arms. Was it possible? *Could* there be something magical about Aunt Milly's wedding dress? Jill didn't know. She didn't want to find out, either.

"Jill?"

"Oh, no," she moaned as she looked up at him.

"Oh, no," Jordan echoed, apparently amused. "I'll admit women have reacted when I've kissed them, but no one's ever said that."

She barely heard him.

"What's wrong?"

"The dress . . ." Jill stopped herself in time.

"What about the dress?"

Jill knew she wasn't making any sense. The whole thing was preposterous. Ridiculous. Unbelievable.

"What about the dress?" he repeated.

"You wouldn't understand." She had no intention of explaining it to him. She could just imagine what someone like Jordan Wilcox would say when he heard about Aunt Milly's wedding dress.

CHAPTER THREE

JILL GLARED at Jordan. He had no idea how devastating she'd found his kiss. And the worst of it was, *she* had no idea why she was feeling this way.

"Jill?" he said, eyeing her suspiciously. "What's my kissing you got to do with a dress?"

She squeezed her eyes shut, then opened them. "It hasn't got anything to do with it," she blurted without thinking, then quickly corrected herself. "It's got everything to do with it." She knew she was overreacting, but she couldn't seem to help herself. Good grief, all he'd done was kiss her! There was no reason to behave like a fool. She had a good excuse, however. It had been a long and unusual day compounded by Shelly's letter and the arrival of the wedding dress. Who wouldn't be flustered? Who wouldn't be confused—especially in light of Shelly's experience?

"You're not speaking too clearly," Jordan reminded her.

"I know. I'm sorry."

"Could you explain yourself?" he added patiently.

Jill didn't see how that was possible. Jordan, so much a man of the world, wouldn't understand a matter of the heart. Not only that, he was cynical and scornful. The man who owned the keys to yuppie-dom, who placed power and profit above all else, would laugh at something as absurd as the story about this wedding dress.

She drew in an unsteady breath. "There's nothing I can say."

"Was my kiss so repugnant to you?" It didn't appear that he was going to graciously drop the matter, not when his male ego was on the line.

Forcing her voice to sound light and carefree, Jill placed a hand on his shoulder and looked him square in the eye. "I'd think a man of your vast experience would be accustomed to having women crumple at his feet."

"Don't be ridiculous." His habitual frown snapped into place.

"I'm not," she countered smoothly. Best to keep Jordan in the dark, otherwise he might misread her intentions. Besides, he wouldn't be any more enthusiastic about a romance between them than she was. "The kiss was very nice," she admitted grudgingly.

"And that's bad?" He rubbed a frustrated hand along his blunt, determined-looking jaw. "Perhaps you'll feel better once you're in your room."

Jill nodded eagerly. "Thank you. For dinner," she added, remembering her manners.

"Thank you for joining me. It was...a pleasure meeting you."

"You, too."

"I probably won't see you again."

"That's right," she agreed resolutely. No reason to tempt fate. She was beginning to like him and that could be dangerous. "You'll be gone in a couple of days, won't you? I'm here for the week." She retreated a couple of steps. "Have a safe trip home, and don't work too hard."

They parted then, but before she walked into the hotel, Jill turned back to see Jordan strolling in the opposite direction, away from her.

JILL AWOKE LATE the following morning. It was rare for her to sleep past eight-thirty, even on weekends. The tour bus wasn't scheduled to leave the hotel until ten, so she took her time showering and dressing. Breakfast consisted of coffee, an English muffin and slices of fresh pineapple, which she ate leisurely on her lanai, savoring the morning sunlight.

Out of curiosity, she glanced over at Jordan's room to see if the draperies were open. They were. From what she could discern, he was sitting at a table near the window, talking on his phone and working with his computer.

Business. Business. Business.

The man lived and breathed it, just the way her father had. And, in the end, it had killed him.

Dismissing Jordan from her thoughts, she reached for her purse and hurried down to the lobby where she was meeting the tour group.

The sight-seeing expedition proved excellent. Jill visited Pearl Harbor and the U.S.S. *Arizona* memorial and a huge shopping mall, returning to the hotel by three o'clock.

Her room was cool and inviting. Jill took a few minutes to examine the souvenirs she'd purchased, a shell lei and several colorful T-shirts. Then, with a good portion of the day still left to enjoy, she decided to spend the remaining afternoon hours lazing around the pool. Once again she glanced across the way to Jordan's room, her action almost involuntary. And once again she saw that he was on the phone. Jill wondered if he'd been talking since the morning.

Changing into her bathing suit, a modest one-piece in a—what else—Hawaiian print, she carried her beach bag, complete with three different kinds of tanning lotion, down to the swimming pool. With a large straw hat perched on her head and sunglasses protecting her eyes, she stretched out on a chaise longue to absorb the sun.

She hadn't been there more than fifteen minutes when a waiter approached carrying a dome-covered platter and a glass of champagne. "Ms. Morrison?"

"Yes?" Jill sat up abruptly, knocking her hat askew. "I...I didn't order anything," she said uncertainly as she reached up to straighten the hat.

"This was sent compliments of Mr. Wilcox."

"Oh." Jill wasn't sure what to say. She twisted around and, shading her eyes with her hand, looked up. Jordan was standing on his lanai. She waved, and he returned the gesture.

"If that will be all?" the waiter murmured, stepping away.

"Yes...Oh, just a moment." Jill scrambled in her beach bag for a tip, which she handed to the young man. He smiled his appreciation.

Curious, she balanced the glass of champagne as she lifted the lid—and nearly laughed out loud. Inside was a large array of crackers topped with caviar. She glanced up at Jordan a second time and blew him a kiss.

Something must have distracted him then. He turned away, and when Jill saw him again a few minutes later, he was pacing the lanai, phone in hand. She was convinced he'd completely forgotten about her. It was ironic, she mused, and really rather sad; here he was in paradise and he'd hardly ventured beyond his hotel room.

Jill drank her champagne and savored a few of the caviar-laden crackers, then decided she couldn't stand his attitude a minute longer. Packing up her things, she looped the towel around her neck and picked up the platter in one hand, her beach bag in the other. Then she headed back inside the hotel. She knew she was breaking her promise to herself by seeking him out, but she couldn't stop herself.

Muttering under her breath, she rode the elevator up to Jordan's floor, calculated which room was his and knocked boldly on the door.

A long moment passed before the door finally opened. Jordan, still talking on his phone, gestured her inside. He didn't so much as pause in his conversation, tossing dollar figures around as casually as other people talked about the weather.

Jill sat on the foot of his bed and crossed her legs, swinging her foot impatiently as Jordan strode back and forth across the carpet, seemingly oblivious to her presence.

"Listen, Rick, something's come up," he said, darting a look in her direction. "Give me a call in five minutes. Sure, sure, no problem. Five minutes. This shouldn't take any longer. See if you can contact Raymond, get these numbers to him, then call me back." He disconnected the line without a word of farewell, then glanced at Jill.

"Hello," he said.

"Hi," she returned, holding out the platter to offer him an hors d'oeuvre.

"No, thanks."

She took one herself and chewed it slowly. She could almost feel his irritation.

"Something I can do for you?"

"Yes," she stated calmly. "Sit down a minute."

"Sit down?"

She nodded, motioning toward the table. "I have a story to tell you."

"A story?" He didn't sound particularly charmed by the idea.

"Yes, and I promise it won't take longer than five minutes," she added pointedly.

He was obviously relieved that she intended to keep this short. "Go on."

"As I've mentioned before, I don't know a whole lot about the world of high finance. But I'm well aware that time has skyrocketed in value during the last fifteen or so years. I also realize that the value of any commodity depends on its availability.''

''Does this story have a point?''

''Actually I haven't got to the story yet, but I will soon,'' she announced cheerfully.

''Can you do it in—'' he paused and glanced at his watch ''—two and a half minutes?''

''I'll hurry,'' she promised, and drew a deep breath. ''I was nine when my mother signed me up for piano lessons. I could hardly wait. The other kids dreaded having to practice, but not me. From the time I was in kindergarten, I loved to pound away at the old upright in our living room. My heart and soul went into making music. It was probably no coincidence that one of the first pieces I learned was 'Heart and Soul.' I hammered out those notes like machine-gun blasts. I overemphasized each crescendo, cherished each lingering note. Van Cliburn couldn't have finished a piece with more pizazz than I did. My hands would fly into the air, then flutter gently to my lap.''

''I noticed you standing by the piano at the dinner party. Are you a musician?''

''Nope. For all my theatrical talents, I had one serious shortcoming. I could never master the caesura—the rest.''

''The rest?''

''You know, that little zigzag thingamajig on sheet music that instructs the player to do nothing.''

''Nothing,'' he repeated slowly.

''My impatience was a disappointment to my mother. I'm sure I frustrated my piano teacher no end.

As hard as she tried, she couldn't make me understand that music was always sweeter and more compelling after a rest.''

"I see." His hands were buried deep in his pockets as he studied her.

If Jordan was as much like her father as she suspected, she doubted he really did understand. But she'd told him what she'd come to say. Mission accomplished. There wasn't any other reason to stay, so she got briskly to her feet and reached for her beach bag.

"That's it?"

"That's it. Thank you for the caviar. It was a delightful surprise." With that she moved toward his door. "Just remember what I said about the rest," she said, glancing over her shoulder.

The phone pealed sharply just then and Jill grimaced. "Goodbye," she mouthed, grasping the doorknob.

The phone rang again. "Goodbye." Jordan hesitated. "Jill?"

"Yes?" The way he said her name seemed so urgent. She whirled around, hope surging in her heart. Perhaps he didn't intend to answer the ring!

The phone went a third time, and Jordan's eyes, dark gray, smoky with indecision, traveled from Jill to the telephone.

"Yes?" she repeated.

"Nothing," he said harshly, reaching for the phone. "Thanks for the story."

"You're welcome." With nothing left to say, Jill walked out of his room and closed the door. Even before the lock slid into place she heard Jordan rhyming off lists of figures.

Her room felt less welcoming than when she'd returned earlier. Jill slipped out of her swimsuit and showered. She was vain enough to check her reflection in the mirror, hoping to have enhanced the slight tan she'd managed to achieve between Seattle's infamous June cloudbursts. It didn't look as though her sojourn in the tropics had done anything but add a not-so-fetching touch of pink across her shoulders.

She dressed in a thick terry robe supplied by the hotel and had just wrapped a towel around her wet hair when her phone rang.

"Hello," she said, breathlessly, sinking onto her bed. Her stomach knotted with anticipation.

"Jill Morrison?"

"Yes." It wasn't Jordan. But the voice sounded vaguely familiar, though she couldn't immediately place it.

"Andrew Howard. I sat next to you at the dinner party last night."

"Yes, of course." Her voice rose with delight. She'd thoroughly enjoyed her chat with the older man. "How are you?"

He chuckled. "Just fine. I tried to phone earlier, but you were out."

"I went on a tour first thing this morning."

"Ah, that explains it. I realize it's rather short notice, but would you be free for dinner tonight?"

Jill didn't hesitate. "Yes, I am."

"Good, good. Could you join me around eight?"

"Eight would be perfect." Normally Jill dined much earlier, but she wasn't hungry yet, thanks to an expensive snack, compliments of Jordan Wilcox.

"Wonderful." Mr. Howard seemed genuinely pleased. "I'll have a car waiting for you and Wilcox out front at seven-thirty."

And Wilcox. She'd almost missed the words. So Jordan had accepted Mr. Howard's invitation. Perhaps she'd been too critical; perhaps he'd understood the point of her story, after all, and was willing to put business aside for one evening. Perhaps he was as eager to spend time with her as she was with him.

"I WONDERED if you'd be here," Jordan announced when they met in the lobby at the appointed time. He didn't exactly greet her with open enthusiasm, but Jill comforted herself with the observation that Jordan wasn't one to reveal his emotions.

"I wouldn't miss this for the world," he added. That was when she remembered he was hoping to have the older man invest in his shopping-mall project. Dinner, for Jordan, would be a golden opportunity to conduct business, elicit Mr. Howard's support and gain the financial backing he needed for the project.

Realizing all this, Jill couldn't help feeling disappointed. "I'll do my best not to interrupt your sales pitch," she said, a little sarcastically.

"My sales pitch?" he echoed, then grinned, apparently amused by her assumption. "You don't have to worry. Howard doesn't want in on this project, which is fine. He just likes to keep tabs on me, especially since Dad died. He seems to think I need a mentor, or at least some kind of paternal adviser.''

''Do you?''

Jordan hesitated. ''There've been one or two occasions when I've appreciated his wisdom. I don't need him holding my hand, but I have sometimes looked to him for advice.''

Remembering her dinner conversation with the older man, Jill said, ''In some ways, Mr. Howard must think of you as a son.''

Jordan shrugged. ''I doubt that.'' Then he scowled, muttering, ''I've known him all this time and not once did he ever mention he'd lost a son.''

''It was almost thirty years ago, and as I told you, it's the reason his company's done so much cancer research. Howard Pharmaceuticals makes several of the leading cancer-fighting medications.'' When Andrew Howard had told her about his son's death, a tear had come to his eye. Although Jeff Howard had succumbed to childhood leukemia a long time ago, his father still grieved. Andrew had become a widower a few years later, and he'd never fully recovered from the double blow. Jill was deeply touched by Mr. Howard's story. During their conversation, she'd shared a little of the pain she had felt at her own father's death, something she rarely did, even with her mother or her closest friend.

''What amazes me,'' Jordan continued, ''is that I've worked on different projects with him over the years. We've also kept in touch socially. And not once, *not once,* did he mention a son."

"Perhaps there was never a reason."

Jordan dismissed that idea with a shake of his head.

"Mr. Howard's a sweet man. I couldn't help liking him," Jill asserted.

"Sweet? Andrew Howard?" Jordan grinned, his eyes bright with humor. "I've known alligators with more agreeable personalities."

"Apparently there's more to your friend than you realized."

"My friend," Jordan repeated. "Funny, I'd always thought of him as my father's friend, not my own. But you're right—he *is* my friend and— Oh, here's the car." With a hand on her arm, he escorted her outside.

A tall, uniformed driver stepped from the long white limousine. "Ms. Morrison and Mr. Wilcox?" he asked crisply.

Jordan nodded, and the chauffeur ceremoniously opened the back door for them. Soon they were heading out of the city toward the island's opposite coast.

"Do you still play the piano?" Jordan asked unexpectedly.

"Every so often, when the mood strikes me," Jill told him a bit ruefully. "Not as much as I'd like."

"I take it you still haven't conquered the caesura?"

"Not yet, but I'm learning." She wasn't sure what had prompted his question, then decided to ask a few of her own. "What about you? Do you think you might be interested in learning to play the piano?"

Jordan shook his head adamantly. "Unfortunately, I've never had much interest in that sort of thing."

Jill sighed and looked away.

Nearly thirty minutes passed before they reached Andrew Howard's oceanside estate. Jill suspected it was the longest Jordan had gone without a business conversation since he'd registered at the hotel.

Her heart pounded as they approached the beautifully landscaped grounds. A security guard pushed a button that opened a huge wrought-iron gate. They drove down a private road, nearly a mile long and bordered on each side by rolling green lawns and tropical-flower beds. At the end stood a sprawling stone house.

No sooner had the car stopped when Mr. Howard hurried out of the house, grinning broadly.

"Welcome, welcome!" He greeted them expansively, holding out his arms to Jill.

In a spontaneous display of affection, she hugged him and kissed his cheek. "Thank you so much for inviting us."

"The pleasure's all mine. Come inside. Everything's ready and waiting." After a hearty handshake with Jordan, Mr. Howard led the way into his home.

Jill had been impressed with the outside, but the beauty of the interior overwhelmed her. The entryway was tiled in white marble and illuminated by a sparkling crystal chandelier. Huge crystal vases of vivid pink and purple hibiscus added color and life. From there, Mr. Howard escorted them into a massive living room with floor-to-ceiling windows that overlooked the Pacific. Frothing waves crashed against the shore, bathed in the fire of an island sunset.

"This is lovely," Jill breathed in awe.

"I knew you'd appreciate it." Mr. Howard reached for a bell, which he rang once. Almost immediately the housekeeper appeared, carrying a tray of glasses and bottles of white and red wine, sherry and assorted aperitifs.

They were sipping their drinks when the same woman reappeared. "Mr. Wilcox, there's a phone call for you."

It was all Jill could do not to gnash her teeth. The man was never free, the phone cord wrapped around his neck tighter than a hangman's noose.

"Excuse me, please," Jordan said as he left the room, his step brisk.

Jill looked away, refusing to watch him go.

"How do you feel about that young man?" Mr. Howard asked bluntly when Jordan was gone.

"We met only recently. I—I don't have any feelings for him one way or the other."

"Well, then, what do you think of him?"

Jill's gaze remained stubbornly focused on her wine. "He works too hard."

Sighing, the old man nodded and rubbed his eyes. "He reminds me of myself more than thirty years ago. Sometimes I'd like to take him by the shoulders and shake some sense into him, but I doubt it'd do much good. That boy's too stubborn to listen. Unfortunately, he's a lot like his father.''

Knowing so little of Jordan and his background, Jill was eager to learn what she could. At the same time, a saner part of her insisted she was better off not hearing this. The more she knew, the greater her chances were of caring.

Nevertheless, Jill found herself asking curiously, "What made Jordan the way he is?"

"To begin with, his parents divorced when he was young. It was a sad situation." Andrew leaned forward and clasped his wineglass with both hands. "It was plain as the nose on your face that James and Gladys Wilcox were in love. But, somehow, bitterness replaced the love, and their son became a weapon they used against each other."

"Oh, how sad." Just as she'd feared, Jill felt herself sympathizing with Jordan.

"They both married other people, and Jordan seemed to remind his parents of their earlier unhappiness. He was sent to the best boarding schools, but there was precious little love in his life. Before he died, James tried to build a relationship with his son, but..." He shrugged. "And to the best of my knowledge his mother hasn't seen him since he was a teenager. I'm afraid he's had very little experience of real love, the kind that gives life meaning. Oh, there've been women, plenty of them, but never one who could teach him how to love and bring joy into his life—until now." He paused and looked pointedly at Jill.

"As I said before, I've only known Jordan a short while."

"Be patient with him," Mr. Howard continued as though Jill hadn't spoken. "Jordan's talented, don't get me wrong—the boy's got a way of pulling a deal together that amazes just about everyone—but there are times when he seems to forget about human values, like compassion. And the ability to enjoy what you have."

Jill wasn't sure how to respond.

"Frankly, I was beginning to lose faith in him," Mr. Howard said, grinning sheepishly. "He can be hard and unforgiving. You've given me the first ray of hope."

Jill took a big swallow of wine.

"He needs you. Your warmth, your gentleness, your love."

Jill wanted to weep with frustration. Mr. Howard was telling her exactly what she didn't want to hear. "I'm sure you're mistaken," she mumbled.

Mr. Howard chuckled. "I doubt that, but I'm an old man, so indulge me, will you?"

"Of course, but—"

"There's a reason you've come into his life," he said, gazing intently at her. "A very important reason." Andrew closed his eyes. "I feel this more profoundly than I've felt anything in a long while. He needs you, Jill."

"No...I'm sure he doesn't." Jill realized she was beginning to sound desperate, but she couldn't help it.

The old man's eyes opened slowly and he smiled. "And I'm just as sure he does." He would have continued, but Jordan returned to the room then.

From the marinated-shrimp appetizer to the homemade mango-and-pineapple ice cream, dinner was one of the most delectable, elegant meals Jill had ever tasted. They lingered over coffee, followed by a glass of smooth brandy. By the end of the evening, Jill felt mellow and warm, a dangerous sensation. Jordan had been wonderful company—witty, charming, fun. He seemed more relaxed, too. Apparently the phone call had brought good news; it was the only thing to which she could attribute his cheerfulness.

"I can't thank you enough," she told Andrew when the limousine arrived to drive her and Jordan back to the hotel. "I can't remember a lovelier evening."

"The pleasure was all mine." The older man hugged Jill and whispered close to her ear, "Remember what I said." Breaking away, he extended his hand, gripping Jordan's elbow as the two exchanged meaningful looks. "It was good of you to come."

"I'll be in touch again soon," Jordan promised.

"Good, good. I'll look forward to hearing from you. Let me know what happens with this shopping-mall project."

"I will," Jordan promised.

The car was cool and inviting in the warm night. Before she realized it, Jill found her head resting on Jordan's broad shoulder. "Oh, sorry," she mumbled through a yawn.

"Are you sleepy?"

She smiled softly to herself, too tired to fight the powers of attraction—and exhaustion. "Maybe a little. Wine makes me sleepy."

Jordan pressed her head against his shoulder and held her there. His hand gently stroked her hair. "Do you mind telling me what went on between you and Howard while I was on the phone?"

Jill went stock-still. "Uh, nothing. What makes you ask?" She decided it was best to pretend she didn't know what he was talking about.

"Then why was Howard wearing a silly grin every time he looked at me?" Jordan demanded.

"I—I don't know, you'll have to ask him." She tried to straighten up, but Jordan wouldn't allow it. After a moment she gave up, too relaxed to put up much of a struggle.

"I swear there was a twinkle in his eye from the moment I returned from the telephone call. It was like I'd been left out of a joke."

"I'm sure you're wrong."

Jordan seemed to ponder that. "I don't think so."

"Hmm." She felt sleepy, and leaning against Jordan was strangely comforting.

"I've been thinking about what you said this afternoon," he told her a few minutes later. His mouth was against her ear, and although she might have been mistaken, she thought his lips lightly brushed her cheek.

"My sad but true tale," she whispered on the end of a yawn.

"About your trouble with the musical rest."

"Ah, yes, the rest."

"I'm flying back to Seattle tomorrow," Jordan said abruptly.

Jill nodded, feeling inexplicably sad, then surprised by the intensity of her reaction. With Jordan in Seattle, they wouldn't be bumping into each other at every turn. Wouldn't be arguing, bantering—or kissing. With Jordan in Seattle, she wouldn't confuse him with the legacy behind Aunt Milly's wedding dress. "Well...I hope you have a good flight."

"I have a meeting Tuesday morning. It would be impossible to cancel at this late date, but I was able to change my flight."

"You changed your flight?" Jill prayed he wouldn't hear the breathless catch in her voice.

"I don't have to be at the airport until early evening."

"How early?" It shouldn't make any difference to her, yet she found herself wanting to know. Needing to know.

"Eight."

Jill was much too dazed to calculate the time difference, but she knew it meant he'd arrive in Seattle sometime in the early morning. He'd be exhausted. Not exactly the best way to arrive at a high-powered meeting.

"I was thinking," Jordan continued. "I've been to Hawaii a number of times but other than meetings or dinner engagements, I haven't seen much of the islands. I've never explored them."

"That's a pity," she said, meaning it.

"And," he went on, "it seemed to me that sight-seeing wouldn't be nearly as much fun alone."

"I enjoyed myself this morning." Her effort to refute him was weak at best.

His fingers were entwined in her hair. "Will you come with me, Jill?" he asked, his voice a husky murmur. "Share the day with me. Let's discover Hawaii together."

CHAPTER FOUR

"I CAN'T," was Jill's immediate response. She'd already lowered her guard—enough to be snuggling in his arms. So much for her resolve not to become involved with Jordan Wilcox, she thought with dismay. So much for steering a wide course around the man.

"Why not?" Jordan asked with the directness she'd come to expect from him.

"I've...already made plans," she stammered. Even now, she could feel herself weakening. With his arm tucked around her and her head nestled against his shoulder it was difficult to refuse him.

"Cancel them."

How arrogant of him to assume she should abandon her plans because the almighty businessman was willing to grant her some of his valuable time.

"I'm afraid I can't do that," she answered coolly, her determination reinforced. She'd already paid for the rental car as part of her vacation package, she rationalized, and she wasn't about to let that money go to waste.

"Why not?" He sounded surprised.

Isn't spending time with him what you really want? The question stole into her mind, and Jill wanted to scream out her response. A resounding NO. Jordan Wilcox frightened her. It was all too easy to envision them together, strolling hand in hand along sun-drenched beaches. He'd kissed her that first time, that only time, on the beach, and the memory stubbornly refused to go away.

"Jill?"

At the softness in his voice, she involuntarily raised her gaze to his. Their eyes held for the longest time. Jill hadn't expected ever to see tenderness in Jordan, but she did now, and it was nearly her undoing. Her feelings for him were changing, and she found herself more strongly attracted than ever. She remembered the first time she'd seen him, the way she'd been convinced there was nothing gentle in him. He'd seemed so hard, so untouchable. Yet now, this very moment, he'd made himself vulnerable to her. For her.

"You're trembling," he said, running his hands down the length of her arm. "What's wrong?"

"Nothing," she denied quickly, breathlessly. "I'm . . . a little tired, I guess. It's been a long day."

"That's what you said last night when I kissed you. Remember? You started mumbling some nonsense about a dress, then you went stiff as a board on me."

"Nothing's wrong," she insisted, breaking away from him. She straightened and lowered her hand to her skirt, smoothing away imaginary creases.

"I don't buy that, Jill. Something's bothering you."

She wished he hadn't mentioned the dress, because it brought to mind, uninvited and unwanted, Aunt

Milly's wedding dress, which was hanging in her hotel-room closet.

"You'd be shaking, too, if you knew the things I did," she exclaimed, instantly regretting the impulse.

"You're afraid of something?"

She stared out the window, then slowly her lower lip began to tremble with the effort to restrain her laughter. She was actually frightened of a silly dress! She wasn't afraid to fall in love; she just didn't want it to be with Jordan.

"For a woman who drags a wedding dress on vacation with her, you're not doing very much to encourage romance."

"I did not bring that dress with me."

"It was in the room when you arrived? Someone left it behind?"

"Not exactly. My friend Shelly, uh, enjoys a good laugh. She mailed it to me."

"It never occurred to me that you might be engaged," he said slowly. "You're not, are you?"

"No." But according to her best friend, she soon would be.

"Who's Shelly?"

"My best friend," Jill explained, "or at least she used to be." Then, impulsively, her heart racing, she added, "Listen, Jordan, I think you have a lot of potential in the husband category, but I can't fall in love with you. I just can't."

A stunned silence followed her announcement.

He cocked his eyebrows. "Aren't you taking a few things for granted here? I asked you to explore the island with me, not bear my children."

She'd done it again, blurted out something totally illogical. Worse, she couldn't make herself stop. Children were a subject near and dear to her heart.

"That's another thing," she wailed. "I bet you don't even like children. No, I just can't go with you tomorrow. Please don't ask me to...because it's so hard to say no." It must be the wine, Jill decided; she was telling him far more than she should.

Jordan relaxed against the leather upholstery and crossed his long legs. "All right, if you'd rather not go, I'm certainly not going to force you."

His easy acceptance astonished her. She glanced at him out of the corner of her eye, feeling almost disappointed that he wasn't trying to convince her.

Something was drastically, dangerously, wrong with her. She was beginning to like Jordan, really like him. Yet she couldn't allow this attraction to continue. She couldn't allow herself to fall in love with a man so much like her father. Because she knew what that meant, what kind of life it led to, what kind of unhappiness it engendered.

When the limousine stopped in front of the hotel, it was all Jill could do to wait for the chauffeur to climb out of the driver's seat, walk around and open the door for her.

She didn't wait for Jordan, but hurried inside the lobby, needing to breathe in the fresh air of reason. Wait for sanity to catch up with her heart.

She paused in front of the elevators and pushed the button, holding her thumb against the plate, hoping that would hurry it along.

"Next time, keep your little anecdotes to yourself," Jordan said sharply from behind her, then walked leisurely across the lobby.

Keep her little anecdotes to herself? The temptation to rush after him and demand an explanation was strong, but Jill forced herself to resist it.

Not until she was in the elevator did she understand. This entire discussion had arisen because she'd told him her story about the caesura and her lack of real musical talent. And now he was turning her own disclosure against her! She allowed the righteous anger to build in her heart.

But by the time Jill was in her room and ready for bed, she felt wretched. Jordan had asked her to spend a day with him, and she'd reacted as if he'd insulted her.

The way she'd gone on and on about his potential as a husband was bad enough, but then she'd dragged the subject of children into their conversation. That mortified her even more. The wine could be blamed for only so much.

She cringed, too, as she recalled what Andrew Howard had said, the faith he'd placed in her. Jordan needed her, he'd insisted, apparently convinced that Jordan would never know love if she didn't teach him. She hated the thought of disappointing Andrew Howard, and yet . . . and yet . . .

It didn't surprise Jill that she slept poorly. By morning she wasn't feeling the least bit enthusiastic about picking up her rental car or viewing the sights on the north shore.

She reviewed the room-service menu, ordered coffee and toast, then stared at the phone for several minutes before conceding there was one thing she still had to do. Anxious to get it over with, Jill rang through to Jordan's room.

"Hello," he answered gruffly on the first ring. He was definitely a man who never ventured far from his phone.

"Hello," she said with uncharacteristic meekness. "I'm ... calling to apologize."

"Are you sorry enough to change your mind and spend the day with me?"

Jill hesitated. "I've already paid for a rental car."

"Great, then I won't need to order one."

Jill closed her eyes. She knew what she was going to say, had known it the night before. In the same heartbeat, she realized she'd regret it later. "Yes," she whispered. "If you still want me to join you, I'll meet you in the lobby in half an hour."

"Twenty minutes."

She groaned. "Fine, twenty minutes, then."

Despite her misgivings, Jill's spirits lifted immediately. "One day won't hurt anything," she said bracingly to herself. What could possibly happen in so short a time? Certainly nothing earth-shattering. Nothing of consequence.

Who was she kidding? Not herself, Jill admitted.

She thought she understood why a moth ventured close to the fire, enticed by the light and the warmth. Against her will, Jordan was drawing her dangerously close to him. She knew even as she came nearer that she'd walk away burned. And yet she didn't hesitate.

He was waiting for her when she stepped out of the elevator and into the lobby. He stood, grinning, his look almost boyish. This was the first time she'd seen him without a business suit. Instead, he wore white slacks and a pale blue shirt, with the sleeves rolled up.

"You ready?" he asked, taking her beach bag from her.

"One question first." Her heart was pounding because she had no right to ask.

"Sure." His eyes held hers.

"Your portable phone—is it in the hotel room?" Jordan nodded.

"What about your pager?"

He pulled an impossibly tiny device from his shirt pocket. Jill stared at it for several moments, feeling the tension work its way down her neck and back. Her father had always carried a pager. All family outings, which were few and far between, had been subject to outside interference. Early in life, Jill had received a clear message: business was more important to her father than she was. In fact, almost everything had seemed more significant than spending time with those who'd loved him.

Jordan must have read the look in her eyes because he said, "I'll leave it at the front desk," and then promptly did so. Stunned, Jill watched as he handed it to the hotel clerk. Bit by bit, her muscles began to relax.

While he was busy at the hotel desk, Jill filled out the necessary paperwork for the rental car. She was waiting outside by the economy model when Jordan appeared. He paused, staring at the vehicle with narrowed eyes as if he wasn't sure it would make it to the end of the street, let alone around the island.

"I'm on a limited budget," Jill explained, hiding a smile. The car suited her petite frame perfectly, but for a man of Jordan's stature it was a little like stuffing a rag doll inside a pickle jar, Jill thought, enjoying the whimsical comparison.

"You're sure this thing runs?" he muttered under his breath as he climbed into the driver's seat. His long legs were cramped below the steering wheel, his head practically touching the roof.

"Relatively sure." Jill remembered reading that this particular model got exceptionally good gas mileage—but then it should, with an engine only a little bigger than a lawnmower's.

To prove her right, the car roared to life with a flick of the key.

"Where are we headed?" Jill asked once they'd merged with the flow of traffic on the busy thoroughfare by the hotel.

"The airport."

"The airport?" she repeated, struggling to hide her disappointment. "I thought your flight didn't leave until eight."

"Mine doesn't, but ours takes off in half an hour."

"Ours?" What about the sugarcane fields and watching the workers harvest pineapple? Surely he didn't intend for them to miss that. "Where is this plane taking us?"

"Hawaii," he announced casually. "The island of. Do you know how to scuba dive?"

"No." Her voice was oddly breathless and high-pitched. She might have spent the past twenty-odd years in Seattle—practically surrounded by water—but she wasn't all that comfortable *under* it.

"How about snorkeling?"

"Ah..." She jerked her thumb over her shoulder. "There are pineapple fields on the other side of this island. I thought you'd want to see those."

"Another time, perhaps. I'd like to try my hand at marlin fishing, but we don't have enough time today."

"Snorkeling," Jill said as though she'd never heard the word before. "Well...it might be fun." In her guidebook Jill remembered reading about green beaches of crushed olivine crystals and black sands of soft lava. These were sights she couldn't expect to find anywhere else. However, she wasn't entirely convinced she wanted to view them through a rubber mask!

A small private plane was ready for them when they arrived at Honolulu Airport. The pilot, who apparently knew Jordan, greeted them cordially. After brief introductions and a few minutes' chat, they were on their way.

Another car, considerably larger than the one Jill had rented, was waiting for them on the island of Hawaii. A large, white wicker picnic basket sat in the middle of the back seat.

"I hope you're hungry."

"Not yet."

"You will be," Jordan promised.

He drove for perhaps half an hour until they reached a deserted inlet with a magnificent waterfall. He parked the car, then got out and opened the trunk. Inside was everything they'd need for snorkeling in the crystal-clear aquamarine waters.

Never having done this before, Jill was uncertain of the procedure. Jordan patiently answered her questions and waded into the water with her. He paused when they were waist-deep, gave her detailed instructions, then clasped her hand. Being linked with him lent her confidence, and soon she was investigating an undersea world of breathtaking beauty. Swimming out of the inlet, they happened upon a reef, with colorful fish slipping in and out of white coral caverns. After what seemed like only minutes, Jordan steered them back toward the inlet and shore.

"I don't think I've ever seen anything more beautiful," she breathed, pushing the mask from her face.

"I don't think I have, either," he agreed as they stepped out of the water.

While Jill ran a comb through her hair and put on a shirt to protect her shoulders from the sun, Jordan brought out their lunch.

He spread the blanket in the shade of a palm tree. Jill joined him there, kneeling down to open the basket. Inside were generous crab-salad sandwiches, fresh slices of papaya and pineapple and thick chocolate-chip cookies. She removed two cold cans of soda and handed one to Jordan.

They ate, then napped with a cool, gentle breeze whisking over them.

Jill awoke before Jordan. He was asleep on his back with his hand thrown carelessly across his face, shading his eyes from the glare of the sun. His features were more relaxed than she'd ever seen them. Jill studied him for several moments, her heart aching for the man she'd loved so much, so long ago. Her father. The man she'd never really had the chance to know. In certain ways, Jordan was so much like her father it pained her to be with him, and at the same time it thrilled her. Not only because in learning about Jordan she was discovering a part of her past, of herself, she'd assumed was gone, but because she'd rarely felt so *alive* in anyone's company.

As she recognized this truth, a heaviness settled on her heart. She didn't want to fall in love with him. She was so afraid her life would mirror her mother's. Elaine Morrison had grown embittered. She'd been a young woman when her husband died, but she'd never remarried; instead she'd closed off her heart, not wanting to risk again the pain that loving Jill's father had brought her.

Sitting up, Jill brushed her now-dry hair from her face. She wrapped her arms around her bent legs and pressed her forehead to her knees, gulping in breath after breath.

"Jill?" His voice was soft, husky. Gentle.

"You shouldn't have left your pager behind, after all," she told him, her voice tight. "Or your phone." Without them, he was a handsome, compelling man who appealed to all her senses. Without them, she was defenseless against his charm.

"Why not?"

"Because I like you too much."

"That's a problem?"

"Yes!" she cried. "Don't you understand?"

"Obviously not," he said with such tenderness she wanted to vault to her feet and yell at him to stop. "Maybe you'd better explain it to me," he added.

"I can't," she whispered, keeping her head lowered. "You'd never believe me. I don't blame you—I wouldn't believe me, either."

Jordan hesitated. "Does this have something to do with your reaction the first time I kissed you?"

"The only time!"

"That's about to change."

Her head shot up at the casual way in which he said it, as though kissing her was a foregone conclusion.

He was right.

His kiss was gentle. Jill resisted, unwilling to grant him her heart, knowing what became of women who loved men like this. Men like Jordan Wilcox.

It happened again, only now it was much more potent than that first night. His touch somehow transcended the sensual. Jill could think of no other way to describe it. His fingers brushed her temple. His lips moved across her face, grazing her chin, her cheek, her eyes. She moaned, not from pleasure, but from fear, from a pain that reached deep inside her.

"Oh, no..."

"It's happening again, isn't it?" he whispered.

She nodded. "Can you feel it?"

"Yes. I did the first time, too."

Her eyes drifted slowly open. "I can't love you."

"So you've told me. More than once."

"It isn't anything personal." She tried to break free without being obvious about it, but Jordan held her firmly in his embrace.

"Tell me what's upsetting you so much."

"I can't." Looking into the distance, she focused on the smoky-blue outline of a mountain. Anything to keep her gaze away from Jordan.

"You're involved with someone else, aren't you?"

It would be so easy to lie to him. To tell him about Ralph as though the friendship they shared was one of blazing passion, but she found she couldn't make herself do it.

"No," she wailed, "but I wish I was."

"Why?" he demanded gruffly.

"What about you?" she countered with a question of her own. "Why did you seek out my company? Why'd you ask me to attend the dinner party with you? Surely there was someone else, someone far more suitable."

"I'll admit no other woman reacts to my kisses the way you do," he confessed.

"But I've been rude."

"Actually, more amusing than rude."

"But why?" she asked. "What is it about me that interests you? We're about as different as two people can get. We're strangers—strangers with nothing in common."

Jordan was frowning, his eyes revealing his own lack of understanding. "I don't know."

"See what I mean?" She spoke as if it were the jury's final decree. "The whole thing is a farce. You kiss me and ... and I feel a certain ... feeling."

"Feeling? Is that all you can say about it? Sweetheart, I've seen electrical storms unleash less energy than when I take you in my arms."

Suddenly Jill found it nearly impossible to breathe. Jordan couldn't possibly be affected by the wedding dress and its so-called magic—could he? Jill swore the minute she arrived in Seattle she was returning it to Shelly and Mark. She wasn't taking any chances!

"You remind me of my father," Jill said, refusing to meet his eyes. Even talking about Adam Morrison produced a pain in her heart. "He was always in a hurry to get somewhere, to meet someone, to make a deal. We took a family vacation when I was ten. We saw California in one day, Disneyland in an hour. Do you get the picture?" She didn't wait for a response. "He died of a heart attack when I was fifteen. We were wealthy by a lot of people's standards, and after his death my mother didn't have to work. There was even a fund set aside for my college expenses."

An awkward moment passed. When Jordan didn't comment, Jill glanced at him. "You don't have anything to say?"

"Not really, other than to remind you I'm not your father."

"But in a way you are. I recognized it the first minute I saw you." She leapt to her feet, grabbed her towel and crammed it into her beach bag.

Jordan reluctantly stood, and while she shook the sand off the blanket and folded it, he loaded their snorkeling gear into the trunk of the car.

They were both quiet during the drive back to the airport, the silence strained and unnatural. A couple of times, Jill glanced in Jordan's direction. The hardness was back. The tightness in his jaw, the harsh, almost grim expression . . .

Jill could well imagine what he'd be like in a board meeting. No wonder he didn't seem too concerned about the threat of a takeover. He would withstand that, and a whole lot more, in the years to come. But at what price? Power demanded sacrifice; prestige didn't come cheap. There was a cost, and Jill could only speculate what it would be for Jordan. His health? His happiness?

She found it intolerable to think about. Words burned on her heart. Words of caution. Words of appeal, but he wouldn't listen to her any more than her father had heeded the tearful pleas of her mother.

As the airport came into view, Jill knew she couldn't let their day end on such an unhappy note. "I did have a wonderful time. Thank you."

"Mmm," he replied, his gaze focused on the road ahead.

Jill stared at him. "Is that all you can say?"

"What do you want me to say?" His voice was crisp and emotionless.

"Like, I don't know, that you enjoyed yourself, too."

"It was interesting."

"Interesting?" Jill repeated.

They'd had a marvelous adventure! Not only that, he'd actually *relaxed*. The lines of fatigue around his eyes were gone. She'd bet a year's wages this was the first afternoon nap he'd had in years. Possibly decades. It was probably the longest stretch of time he'd been away from a telephone in his adult life.

All he'd admit was that their day had been "interesting"?

"What about the kissing?" she demanded, "was *that* interesting?"

"Very."

Jill seethed silently. "It was . . . interesting for me, too."

"So you claimed."

Jill tucked a long strand of hair behind her ear. "I was only being honest with you."

"I admit it was a fresh approach. Do you generally discuss marriage and children with a man on a first date?"

Color exploded in her cheeks, and she looked uncomfortably away. "No, but you were different . . . and it wasn't an approach."

"Excuse me, that's right, you were being honest." The cold sarcasm in his voice kept her from even trying to explain.

They'd almost reached the airport when she spoke again. "Would you do one small favor for me?" She nearly choked on the pride she had to swallow, hating to ask him for anything.

"What?"

"Would you... The next time you see Mr. Howard, would you tell him something for me? Would you tell him I'm sorry?" He'd be disappointed in her, but Jill couldn't risk her own happiness because a dear man with a romantic heart believed she was Jordan Wilcox's one chance at finding love.

Jordan hesitated, then stopped the car abruptly and turned to glare at her. "You want me to apologize to Howard?"

"Please."

"Sorry," he said without a pause. "You'll have to do that yourself."

CHAPTER FIVE

FOUR DAYS LATER, Jill stepped off the plane at Sea-Tac Airport in Seattle. Her skin glowed with a golden tan, accentuated by the bold pink-flower print of her slacks and matching blouse. She hadn't expected anyone to meet her, but was pleasantly surprised to see Shelly and Mark. Shelly waved excitedly when she located Jill.

"Welcome home," Shelly said as she rushed forward, exuberantly throwing her arms around Jill. "How was Hawaii? My goodness, your tan is gorgeous. You must have spent hours in the sun."

"Hawaii was wonderful." A slight exaggeration. She'd hardly slept since Jordan's departure.

"Tell me everything," Shelly insisted, gripping Jill's hands. "I'm dying to find out who you met after we mailed you the wedding dress."

"Honey," Mark chided gently, "give her a chance to breathe."

"Are you with someone?" Shelly asked, looking around expectantly. "I mean, you know, you're not married, are you?"

"I'm not even close to being married," Jill informed her friend dryly.

Mark collected the large beach bag Jill had brought home with her, stuffed full of souvenirs and everything else she couldn't fit inside her suitcase. She removed one of the three leis she was wearing and looped it around Shelly's neck. "Here, my gift to you."

"Oh, Jill, it's beautiful. Thank you," Shelly said, fingering the fragrant lei made of pink orchids. They were walking toward the baggage-claim area, and Shelly slipped her arm through Jill's. "I don't think I can wait a moment longer. Tell me what happened after the dress arrived. I want to hear every detail."

Jill had been dreading this moment, but she hadn't expected to face it quite so soon. "I'm afraid I'm going to have to return the dress."

Shelly stared at her as if she hadn't heard correctly. "I beg your pardon?"

"I didn't meet anyone."

"You mean to tell me you spent seven days in Hawaii and you didn't speak to a single man?" Shelly asked incredulously.

"Not exactly."

"Aha! So there was someone."

Jill swallowed a groan. "Sort of."

Shelly smiled, sliding one arm around her husband's waist. "The plot thickens."

"I met him briefly the first day. Actually I don't think he counts...."

"Why shouldn't he count?" Shelly demanded.

"We sat next to each other on the plane, so technically we met *before* I got the wedding dress, so I'm sure he's not the one." Jill had decided to play along with her friend's theory, pretend to take it more seriously than she actually did. Logical objections, like this mistake in timing, should convince Shelly—but probably wouldn't.

"In fact," she continued, "I've been thinking about that dress lately, and I'm convinced you and your Aunt Milly are wrong—it's not for me. It never was."

"But it fit you. Remember?"

Jill didn't need to be reminded. "That was a fluke. I'm sure if I were to try it on now, it wouldn't."

"Then try it on! Prove me wrong."

"Here?" Jill laughed.

"When you get home. Anyway, never mind that now. Just tell me about this guy you met. You keep trying to avoid the subject."

"There's nothing to tell," Jill insisted, sorry she'd said anything. She'd tried for the past few days to push every thought of Jordan from her mind, with little success. He'd haunted her remaining time on the islands, refusing to leave her alone. If she did sleep, he invaded her dreams.

"Start with his name," Shelly said. "Surely you know his name."

"Jordan Wilcox, but—"

"Jordan Wilcox," Mark repeated. "He doesn't happen to be a developer, does he?"

"I think he does something along those lines."

Mark released a low whistle. "He's one of the big boys."

"Big boys," Shelly echoed disparagingly. "Speak English. Do you mean he's tall?"

"No." Mark's smiling eyes briefly met Jill's. "He's a well-known corporate giant. I've met him a few times. If I understand it correctly, he puts together commercial projects, finds backers for them, works with the designer and the builders, and when the project's complete, he sells. He's made millions in the last few years. He's damn good at it."

"He was in Hawaii to put together financial backing for a shopping mall," Jill explained.

"Well," Shelly said, eyeing her closely, "what did you think of him?"

"What was there to think? I sat next to him on the plane and we stayed in the same hotel, but that was about it." It was best not to mention the other incidents; Shelly would put far too much stock in a couple of dinners and a day on the beach. Heaven help Jill if Shelly ever found out they'd exchanged a few kisses!

"I'm sure he's the one," Shelly announced gleefully. Her eyes fairly sparkled with delight. "I can *feel* it. He's our man."

"No, he isn't," Jill argued, knowing it was futile, yet compelled to try. "I already told you—I met him before the dress arrived. Besides, we have absolutely nothing in common."

"Do Mark and I?" Shelly glanced lovingly at her husband. "And I'm crazy about him."

At first, Jill had wondered what Mark, a tax consultant with orderly habits and a closetful of suits, could possibly have in common with her zany, creative, unconventional friend. The answer was simple. Nothing. But that hadn't stopped them from falling in love. Jill couldn't be in the same room with them without sensing the powerful attraction they felt for each other.

However, there was little similarity between Shelly's marriage to Mark and Jill's dealings with Jordan. Jill understood him; in many ways they were alike. But she'd learned from her father's life—and death—the value of bringing a balance into her life. Although her career mattered to her, it didn't define her life or occupy every minute of her time.

"In this case I think Jill might be right," Mark said, his voice low and thoughtful. "A man like Jordan Wilcox eats little girls like Jill for breakfast."

"He's the one," Shelly insisted for the second time.

"I've met the man," Mark went on to say. "He's cold and unemotional. If he does have a heart, it was frozen a long time ago."

"So?" Ever optimistic, Shelly refused to listen. "Jill's perfect for him, then. She's warm and gentle and caring."

Right now Jill didn't feel any of those things. Listening to Mark describe Jordan, she had to fight the urge to defend him, to tell them what Andrew Howard had told her. Yes, Jordan was everything Mark said, but there was another side to him, one Jill had briefly encountered. One that was so appealing it had frightened her into running away, which was exactly what she'd done that day on the beach. He'd kissed her and she'd known immediately, intuitively, that she'd never be the same. But knowing it didn't alter her resolve. She couldn't love him because the price would be too high. He would give her all the things she craved, a husband and family, wealth beyond her imagination. But eventually she'd end up like her mother, lonely and bitter.

"I just can't imagine Jordan Wilcox married," Mark concluded.

"I can," Shelly interrupted with unflinching enthusiasm. "To Jill."

"Shelly," Mark said, grinning indulgently, "listen to reason."

"When has falling in love ever been reasonable?" She fired the question at her husband, who merely shrugged, then turned back to Jill. "Did you tell him about Aunt Milly's wedding dress?"

"Good heavens, no!"

"All the better. I'll bet you really threw the guy for a loop. Was he on this flight?"

"No, he returned four days ago."

"Four days ago," Shelly echoed slowly, suspiciously. "There's something you're not telling us. Come on, Jill, 'fess up. You did a whole lot more than sit next to this guy on the plane. And Mark and I want to know what."

"Uh . . ." Jill was tired from the flight and her resistance was low. Under normal circumstances she would have sidestepped the issue. "It isn't the way it sounds," she said weakly. "We talked a couple of times, that's all."

"Did you kiss?" The question came out in a soft whisper. "The first time Mark kissed me was when I knew. If you and Jordan kissed, there wouldn't be any doubt in your mind. You'd know."

Sooner or later Shelly would worm it out of her. By telling the truth now, Jill thought she might be able to avoid a lengthy inquisition later. "All right, if you insist—yes, we did kiss. A couple of times."

Even Mark seemed surprised by that.

"See?" Shelly cried triumphantly. "And what happened?"

Jill heaved an exaggerated sigh. "Nothing. I want to return the wedding dress."

"Sorry," Shelly said, her eyes flashing with excitement, "it's nonreturnable."

"I don't plan on ever seeing him again," Jill said adamantly. She'd more or less told Jordan that, too. He was in full agreement; he wanted nothing to do with her, either. "I insist you take back the wedding dress," Jill repeated. Shelly and Mark's eyes met. Slowly they smiled, as if sharing a private joke.

But Jill wasn't laughing.

THE FIRST PERSON Jill called when she got home was her mother. Their conversation was friendly, and she was relieved to find her mother less vague and self-absorbed than she'd been recently. Jill shared a few anecdotes, described the island and the hotel, but resisted telling her mother about meeting Jordan.

She was strangely reluctant to call Ralph, even though she knew he was waiting to hear from her. He was terribly nice, but unfortunately she found him…a bit dull. She put off calling; two days later, he called her, leaving a message on her answering machine.

They'd kissed a few times, and the kisses were pleasant enough, but for her there wasn't any spark. When Jordan took her in his arms it felt like a forest fire compared to the placid warmth she experienced with Ralph.

Jordan. Forgetting him hadn't become any easier. Jill had assumed that once she was home, surrounded by everything that was familiar and comfortable, she'd be able to put their brief interlude behind her.

It hadn't happened.

Wednesday afternoon, Jill returned home from work, put water on for tea and began reading the evening paper. Normally she didn't glance at the financial section. She wasn't sure why she did now. Skimming the headlines, she idly folded back the page—and saw Jordan's name. It seemed to leap at her.

Jill's heart slowed, then vaulted into action as she read the article. He'd done it. The paper was reporting Jordan's latest coup. His company had reached an agreement with a land-management outfit in Hawaii, and construction on the shopping mall would begin sometime in the next three months.

He must be pleased. Although he hadn't said much, Jill knew Jordan had wanted this project to fly. A hundred questions bombarded her. Had he heard from Andrew Howard? Had the older man joined forces with Jordan, after all? Had he asked Jordan about her, and if so, what had Jordan told him? What could he possibly tell Mr. Howard about her now?

Jill had thought of writing Mr. Howard a note, but she didn't have his address. She didn't have Jordan's, either, but that didn't stop her.

Before she could determine the wisdom of her actions, she scribbled a few lines of congratulation, wrote Jordan's name on the envelope, along with the name of the building listed in the news article, and the next morning, mailed the card. She had no idea if it would even reach him.

Two days later when Jill returned home from work, she noticed a long luxury car parked in front of her apartment building. Other than giving it an inquisitive glance, she didn't pay any attention. She was shuffling through her purse searching for her keys when she heard someone approach from behind.

Tossing a look over her shoulder, she nearly dropped her purse. It was Jordan. He looked very much as he had the first time she'd seen him. Cynical and hard. Detached and unemotional. His smoky-gray eyes scanned her without revealing a hint of his thoughts. There was nothing to indicate he was glad to see her, or if he'd spared her a moment's thought since they'd parted. Nothing but cool indifference.

"Hello, Jill."

She was so flustered that the newspaper, which she'd tucked under her arm, fell to the floor. Stooping, she retrieved it, then clutched it against her chest as she straightened. "Jordan."

"I got your note."

"I—I wanted you to know how happy I was for you."

He was staring pointedly at her door.

"Um, would you like to come inside?" she asked, unlatching the door with fumbling fingers. "I'll make some tea if you like. Or coffee..." She hadn't expected this, nor was she emotionally prepared for seeing him. She hadn't anticipated him to do anything but read the card and then drop it into his wastebasket.

"Tea sounds fine."

"I'll just be a minute," she said as she hurried into the kitchen. Her heart was rampaging, pounding against her ribs. "Make yourself at home," she called out, holding the tea kettle under the faucet.

"You have a nice place," he said, standing in the doorway between the kitchen and the living room.

"Thank you. I've lived here for three years now." She didn't know why she'd told him that. It didn't matter to him how long she'd lived there.

"Why'd you send me the card?" he asked while she was setting out cups and saucers. She didn't feel comfortable using the mugs she did for everyday; she had a couple of lovely china cups her mother had given her and she'd decided on those instead. She paused at his question, frowning slightly. "To congratulate you."

"The real reason."

"That was the real reason. This shopping mall was important to you and I was happy to read that everything had finally come together. I knew you worked hard to make it happen. That was the only reason I wrote the note." Her cheeks warmed at his implication. He seemed to believe something she hadn't intended—or had she?

"Andrew Howard decided to invest in the project at the last minute. It was his support that made the difference."

Jill nodded. "I was hoping he would."

"I have you to thank for that."

Nothing in his expression indicated he was grateful for any assistance she might unwittingly have given him. His features remained cold and hard. The man who'd spent that day on the beach with her wasn't the harsh, unrelenting businessman who stood before her now.

"If I played any part in Mr. Howard's decision, I'm sure it was small."

"He seemed quite taken with you."

"I was quite taken with him, too."

A flicker of emotion passed through Jordan's eyes, one so fleeting, so transitory, she was sure she'd imagined it.

"I'd like to thank you, if you'd let me," he said.

She was dropping tea bags into her best ceramic teapot. "Thank me? You already have."

"I was thinking more along the lines of dinner."

Jill's first thought was that she didn't have anything appropriate to wear. Not to an elegant restaurant, and of course she couldn't imagine Jordan dining anywhere else. He wasn't exactly the kind of man who ate in a burger joint.

"Unless you already have plans..."

He was offering her an escape, and his eyes seemed to challenge her to take it.

"No," she said, almost gasping. Jill wasn't sure why she accepted so readily, why she didn't even consider declining. "I don't have anything planned for tonight."

"Is there a particular place you'd like to go?"

She shook her head. "You choose."

Jill felt a surge of excitement. She felt almost light-headed with happiness and anticipation. Trying to keep her voice steady, she added, "I'll need to change clothes, but that shouldn't take long."

He looked at her skirt and blouse as if seeing them for the first time. "You look fine just the way you are," he said, dismissing her concern.

The kettle whistled and Jill quickly removed it from the burner, pouring the scalding water into the teapot. "This should steep for a few minutes." She backed out of the kitchen, irrationally fearing that he'd disappear if she let him out of her sight.

She chose the same outfit she'd worn on the trip home—the Hawaiian print shirt with the hot pink flowers. The slacks weren't particularly dressy so she stepped into high heels. She put on the shell lei she'd purchased the first day she'd gone touring. Then she freshened her makeup and brushed her hair.

Jordan had poured the tea and was adding sugar to his cup when she entered the kitchen. His gaze didn't waver or change in any way, yet she could tell he liked her choice.

The phone rang. Jill darted a look at it, willing it to stop. She didn't know who would be phoning her now, but guessed it was probably Ralph. The man seemed to have an incredibly bad sense of timing.

"Hello," she said, hoping her voice didn't convey her lack of welcome.

"Jill, it's Shelly. How are you? I haven't heard a word from you since you got home. Are you all right? I've been worried. You generally phone once or twice a week. It's not like you to—"

"I'm fine."

"You're sure?"

"Positive." Talk about timing, Jill mused. Shelly's was worse than Ralph's!

"You sound preoccupied. Am I catching you at a bad time? Is Ralph there? Maybe he'll take the hint and go home. Honestly, Jill, I don't know why you continue to see that guy. I mean, he's nice, but he's about as romantic as mold."

"Uh, I have company."

"Company," Shelly echoed. "Who? No, let me guess. Jordan Wilcox!"

"Bingo."

"Talk to you later. Bye." The drone of the disconnected line sounded in her ear so fast that Jill was left holding the receiver for several seconds before she realized her friend had hung up.

No sooner had Jill replaced it when the phone rang again. She cast an apologetic glance toward Jordan and snatched up the receiver. "Hello."

"This is Shelly again. I want it understood that you're to give me a full report later."

"Shelly!"

"And don't you dare try to return that wedding dress. He's the one, Jill. Quit fighting it. I'll let you go now, but just remember, I want details, so be prepared." She hung up as quickly as she had the first time.

"That was my best friend."

"Shelly?"

Jill couldn't remember mentioning her to Jordan, but obviously she had. "She's married to Mark Brady." She waited, wondering if Jordan would recognize the name.

"Mark Brady." He tested it, as though saying it aloud would jar his memory. "Is Mark a tax consultant? I seem to remember hearing something about him not long ago. Isn't he the head of his own firm?"

"That's Mark." The story of how Shelly and Mark met nearly slipped out, but Jill stopped herself in the nick of time. Jordan knew about the wedding dress—though not its significance—because Jill had inadvertently let it slip that first night.

"And Mark's married to your best friend?"

"That's right." She took a sip of her tea. "When I mentioned I'd met you, Mark knew who you were right away."

"So you mentioned me." He seemed pleasantly surprised.

He could have no idea how much he'd been in her thoughts the past couple of weeks. She'd tried, heaven knew she'd tried, to push every memory of him from her mind. But it hadn't worked. She couldn't quite explain it, but somehow nothing was the same anymore.

"You're ready?" he asked after a moment.

Jill nodded and carried their empty cups to the sink. Then Jordan led her to his car, opening the door and ushering her inside. When he joined her, he reached for his ever-present phone, punched out one number, then asked that his calls be held.

"You don't need to do that on my account," she told him.

"I'm not," he said, his smile tight, almost a grimace. "I'm doing it for me." With that he started the engine.

Jill hadn't a clue where they were going. He took the freeway and headed north, exiting into the downtown area of Seattle. There were any number of four-star restaurants within a five-block area. Jill was curious, but she didn't ask. She'd know soon enough.

When Jordan pulled into the underground garage of a luxury skyscraper, Jill was momentarily surprised. But then several of the office complexes housed world-class restaurants.

"I didn't know there was a restaurant here," she said conversationally.

"There isn't."

"Oh."

"I live in the penthouse."

"Oh."

"Unless you object?"

"No...no, that's fine."

"I phoned earlier and asked the cook to prepare dinner for two."

"You have a cook?" Oddly, that fact amazed her, though she supposed it shouldn't have, considering his wealth.

He smiled, his first genuine smile since he'd shown up at her door. "You're easily impressed."

He made it sound as though everyone employed a cook, the way most people had a newspaper-delivery boy.

They rode a private elevator thirty floors up to the penthouse suite. The first thing that greeted Jill as the doors glided open was a breathtaking view of Puget Sound.

"This is beautiful," she whispered, stepping out. She followed him through his living room, past a white leather sectional sofa and a glass-and-chrome coffee table that held a small sculpture. She wasn't too knowledgeable when it came to works of art, but this looked like a collector's item.

"That's a Doug Graham piece," Jordan said matter-of-factly.

Jill nodded, hoping he wouldn't guess how ignorant she was.

"White wine?"

"Please." Jill couldn't take her eyes off the view. The waterways of Puget Sound were dotted with white-and-green ferries. The islands—Bainbridge, Whidbey and Vashon—were jewellike against the backdrop of the Olympic mountains.

"Nothing like Hawaii, is it?" Jordan asked as he handed her a long-stemmed wineglass.

"No, but just as beautiful in its own way."

"I'm headed back to Oahu next week."

"So soon?" Jill was envious.

"It's another short trip. Two or three days at most."

"Perhaps you'll get a chance to go snorkeling again."

Jordan shook his head. "I won't have time for any underwater adventures this trip," he told her.

Jill perched on the edge of the sofa, staring down at her wine. "I don't think I'll ever be able to separate you from my time in Oahu," she said softly. "The rest of my week seemed so...empty."

"I know what you mean."

Her heartbeat quickened as his gaze strayed to her mouth. He sat beside her and removed the wine goblet from her unresisting hand. Next his fingers curved around her neck, ever so lightly, brushing aside her hair. His eyes held hers as if he expected resistance. Then slowly, giving her ample opportunity to pull away if she wished, he lowered his mouth to hers.

Jill moaned in anticipation, instinctively moving closer. Common sense shouted in alarm, but she refused to listen. Just once she wanted to know what it was like to be kissed with real passion—to be cherished by a man. Just once she wanted to know what it meant to be adored. Her heart filled with a delirious joy. Her hands slid up his chest to his shoulders, as she clung to him. He kissed her again, small, nibbling kisses, as though he were afraid of frightening her with the strength of his need. But he must have sensed her receptiveness, because he deepened the kiss.

Suddenly it came to her. The same thing that had happened to Shelly was now happening to her. The phenomenon Aunt Milly had experienced fifty years earlier was coming to pass a third time.

The wedding dress.

Abruptly, she broke off the kiss. Panting, holding both hands over her heart, she sprang to her feet. Her eyes were wide and incredulous as she gazed down at a surprised Jordan.

"It's you!" she cried. "It really is you."

CHAPTER SIX

"WHAT DO YOU MEAN, it's me?" Jordan demanded. When she didn't answer, he asked, "What's wrong, Jill?"

"Everything," she cried, shaking her head.

"I hurt you?"

"No," she whispered, "no." She sobbed quietly as she wrung her hands. "I don't know what to do."

"Why do you have to do anything?"

"Because...oh, you wouldn't understand." Worse, she couldn't tell him. Every time he looked at her, she became more and more convinced that Shelly had been right. Jordan Wilcox was her future.

But she *couldn't* fall in love with him, because she knew what would happen to her if she did—she'd become like her mother, lonely, bitter and unhappy. If she was going to marry, she wanted a man who was safe and sensible. A man like...Ralph. Yet the thought of spending the rest of her life with Ralph produced an even deeper sense of discontent.

"I'm not an unreasonable man," Jordan said. Then he added, "Well, generally I'm not. If there's a problem you can tell me."

"It's not supposed to be a problem. According to Shelly and her Aunt Milly, it's a blessing. I know I'm talking in riddles, but . . . there's no way you'd understand!"

"Try me."

"I can't. I'm sorry, I just can't."

"But it has something to do with my kissing you?"

She stared at him blankly. "No. Yes."

"You seem rather uncertain about this. Perhaps we should try it again and see what happens."

"That isn't necessary." But even as she spoke, Jordan was reaching for her, pulling her down onto his lap. Jill willingly surrendered to his embrace, greeting his kiss with a muffled groan of welcome, a sigh of defeat. His arms held her close, and not for the first time, Jill was stunned by the effect he had on her. It left her feeling both unnerved and overwhelmed.

His lips, gentle and caressing, moved over her face. Jill felt as though she'd been swept into a whirlpool, and if she didn't do something to save herself it would soon be too late.

"Better?" he asked a moment later in a remarkably steady voice.

Unable to answer, Jill closed her eyes, then nodded. Better, yes. And worse. Every time he touched her, it confirmed what she feared most.

"I thought so." He seemed reassured, but that did little to comfort Jill. For weeks she'd played a silly game of denial. They'd met, and from that moment forth, nothing had been the same.

She didn't, couldn't, believe in the power of the wedding dress; she scoffed at the implausibility of its legend. Yet even Mr. Howard, who knew nothing about Aunt Milly and the old story, had felt compelled to explain Jordan's past to her, had seen Jill as his future.

She'd spent only three days with Jordan, but she knew more about him than she knew about Ralph, whom she'd been dating for months. Their day on the beach and the dinner with Andrew Howard had given her an insight into Jordan's personality. Since then Jill had found it more difficult to accept what she saw on the surface—the detached, cynical male. The man who wore his I-don't-give-a-damn attitude like an elaborate mask.

Perhaps she understood him because he was so much like her father. Adam Morrison had lived for the excitement, the risks, of the big deal. He poured his life's blood into each business transaction because he'd never really accepted the importance of family, emotion, human values.

Jordan wouldn't, either.

Dinner was a strained affair, although Jordan made several efforts to lighten the mood. As he drove her home, Jill sensed he wanted to say something more. Whatever it was, he left unsaid.

"Have a safe trip," she told him when he escorted her to her door. Her heart was pounding, not with excitement, but with trepidation, wondering if he planned to kiss her again. Fearing he did, praying he would.

"I'll call you when I get back," he told her. And that was all.

"THERE'S A SPECIAL fondness in my heart for this place," Shelly said as she slipped into a chair opposite Jill. They were meeting for lunch at Patrick's, a restaurant in the mall where Jill's branch of PayRite was located. Typically, she was ten minutes late. Marriage to Mark, who was habitually prompt, hadn't altered Shelly's tardiness. Jill often wondered how they managed to keep their love so strong when they were so different.

Patrick's had played a minor role in Shelly's romance with Mark. Jill recalled the Saturday she'd met her friend there for lunch, and how amused she'd been at Shelly's crazy story of receiving the infamous wedding dress.

Funny, that was exactly the way Jill felt now— frantic, frightened, confused. And strangely excited ...

"So tell me everything," Shelly said breathlessly.

"Jordan stopped by. We had dinner. He left town this morning on a business trip," she explained dispassionately. "There isn't much to tell."

Shelly's hand closed around her water glass, her eyes connecting with Jill's. "Do you remember when I first met Mark?"

"I'm not likely to forget," Jill said, smiling despite her present mood.

"Any time you or my mother or anyone else asked me about Mark, I always said there wasn't anything to tell. Remember?"

"Yes." Jill remembered how Shelly's face would close, her voice grow abrupt, whenever anyone mentioned Mark's name.

"When I told you nothing was happening, I was stretching the truth a bit," Shelly continued. "A whole lot was going on, but nothing I felt I could share. Even with you." She raised her eyebrows. "You, my friend, are wearing the same look I did. A great deal has taken place between you and Jordan. So much that you're frightened out of your wits. Trust me, I know."

"He kissed me again," Jill admitted.

"It was better than before?"

"Worse!"

Shelly apparently found Jill's answer amusing. She tried to hide her smile behind the menu, then lowered it to say, "Don't count on your feelings becoming any less complicated. They won't."

"He's going to be away for a few days. Thank goodness, because it gives me time to think."

"Oh, Jill," Shelly said with a sympathetic sigh, "I wish there was something I could say to help you. Why are you fighting this so hard?" She grinned sheepishly. "I fought it, too. Be smart, just accept it. Love isn't really all that terrifying once you let go of your doubts."

"Instead of talking about Jordan, why don't we order lunch?" Jill suggested a little curtly. "I'm starved."

"Me, too."

The waitress arrived at their table a moment later, and Jill ordered the split-pea soup and a turkey sandwich.

"Just a minute," Shelly interrupted, motioning toward the waitress. She turned to Jill. "You don't even *like* split-pea soup. You never order it." She gave Jill an odd look, then turned back to the waitress. "She'll have the clam chowder."

"Shelly!"

The waitress wrote down the order quickly, as though she feared an argument was about to erupt.

"You're more upset than I realized," Shelly said when they were alone. "Ordering split-pea soup—I can't believe it."

"It's soup, Shelly, not nuclear waste." Her friend definitely had a tendency to overreact. It drove Jill crazy, but it was the very thing that made Shelly so endearing.

"I'm going to call Jordan Wilcox myself," Shelly announced suddenly.

"You're going to *what?*" It was all Jill could do to remain in her seat.

"You heard me."

"Shelly, no! I absolutely forbid you to discuss me with Jordan. How would you have felt if I'd called Mark?"

Shelly's frown deepened. "I'd have been furious."

"I will be, too, if you say so much as one word to Jordan about me."

Shelly paused, her eyes wide with concern. "But I'm afraid you're going to mess this up."

Nothing to fear there—Jill already had. She reached for a package of rye crisps from the bread basket, as Shelly frowned. It wasn't until then that she realized she wasn't any fonder of rye crisps than she was of split-pea soup.

"Promise me you'll stay out of it," Jill pleaded. "Please," she added for extra measure.

"All right," Shelly muttered. "Just don't do anything stupid."

"THIS IS A PLEASANT surprise," Jill's mother said as she opened the front door. Elaine Morrison was in her mid-fifties, slim and attractive.

"I thought I'd bring over your gift from Hawaii," Jill said, following her mother into the kitchen where Elaine automatically poured them tall glasses of iced tea. Jill set the box of chocolate-covered macadamia nuts on the counter.

"I'm glad your vacation went so well."

Jill pulled out a bar stool and sat at the counter, trying to look relaxed when she was anything but. "I met someone while I was in Hawaii."

Her mother paused, then smiled. "I thought you might have."

"What makes you say that?"

"Oh, there's a certain look about you. Now tell me how you met, what he's like, where he's from and what he does for a living."

Jill couldn't help laughing at the rapid-fire questions.

Elaine added slices of lemon to their tea and started across the kitchen, a new excitement in her step. Finally, after fifteen years, her mother was beginning to overcome the bitterness, the sense of loss, her husband's obsession with business had created. She was finally coming to terms with her grief over his neglect, and his death.

Jill was relieved and delighted by the signs of her mother's recovery, but she had to say, "Frankly, Mom, I don't think you'll like him."

Her mother looked surprised. "Whyever not?"

Jill didn't hesitate, didn't pause. "Because he reminds me of Daddy."

Her mother's eyes widened with shock, and tears sprang to her eyes. "Jill, no. For the love of heaven, no."

"I'VE BEEN GIVING some thought to your suggestion," Jill said to Ralph a few hours later. Her nerves were in turmoil. The clam chowder sat like a dead weight in the pit of her stomach, and her mother's dire warnings had badly shaken her.

Ralph wasn't tall and strikingly handsome like Jordan, but he was a comfortable sort of man. He made a person feel at ease. In fact, his laid-back manner was a blessed relief after the high-stress, high-energy hours she'd spent with Jordan, few though they were.

Jordan Wilcox could pull together a deal for an apartment complex before Ralph stepped out of the shower in the morning. Ralph's idea of an exhilarating evening was doing the newspaper crossword puzzle.

Everything about Jordan was complex. Everything about Ralph was uncomplicated; he was a straightforward, honest man who'd be a good husband and a loving father.

"Are you saying what I think you're saying?" Ralph prompted when she didn't immediately continue.

Jill cupped her water glass. "You said something not long ago about the two of us giving serious consideration to making our relationship permanent and...and I wanted you to know I was...I was giving some thought to that myself lately."

Ralph didn't reveal any emotion. He put down his hamburger, looked her way and asked casually, "Why now?"

"Uh...I'm going to be twenty-nine soon." She was outwardly calm, but her heart was pounding like a sledgehammer.

She was the biggest coward who ever lived. But what else could she do? Her mother had become nearly hysterical when Jill had told her about Jordan. Her own heart was filled with trepidation. On one hand there was Shelly, so confident Jordan was the man for Jill. On the other was her mother, adamant that Jill would be forever sorry if she got involved with a workaholic.

Jill was trapped somewhere in the middle, frightened and unsure.

Ralph relaxed against the red vinyl upholstery. The diner was his favorite place to eat, and he took her there every time they dined out. "So you think we should seriously consider marriage?"

It was the subject Jill had been leading up to all evening, yet when Ralph directly posed the question, she hesitated. If only Jordan hadn't kissed her. If only he hadn't held her in his arms. And if only she hadn't spoken to her mother.

"I missed you while you were away," Ralph said, his gaze holding hers.

Jill knew this was about as close to romance as she was likely to get from Ralph. Romance was his weakest suit, dependability and steadiness his strongest. Ralph would always be there by his wife's side. He'd make the kind of father who played catch in the backyard with his son. The kind of father who would bring his wife and daughter pretty pink corsages on Easter morning. He was a rock, a fortress of permanence. If only she could fall in love with him....

Jordan might have a talent for making millions, but all the money in the world couldn't buy happiness.

"I missed you, too," Jill said softly. She'd thought of Ralph, had wondered about him. A few times, anyway. Hadn't she mailed him a postcard? Hadn't she brought him back a book on volcanoes?

"I'm glad to hear that," Ralph said, and then clearing his throat, added, "Jill Morrison, will you do me the honor of becoming my wife?"

The question was out now, ready for her to answer. A proposal was what she'd been hinting for all evening. Now that Ralph had asked, Jill wasn't sure what she felt. Relief? No, it wasn't even close to that. Pleasure? Yes—in a way. But not a throw-open-the-windows-and-shout kind of joy.

Joy. The word hit her like an unanticipated punch. Joy was what she'd experienced the first time Jordan had taken her in his arms. A free-flowing joy and the promise of so much more.

The promise she was rejecting out of fear. Ralph might not be the love of her life, but he'd care for her and devote his life to her. It was enough. She could live with enough.

"Jill?" he prompted.

She tried to smile, tried to look happy and excited. Ralph deserved that much. "Yes," she whispered, stretching her hand across the table for him to take. "Yes, I'll marry you."

"WHAT DO YOU MEAN you're engaged to marry Ralph?" Shelly demanded. Her voice had risen to such a high pitch that Jill held the telephone receiver away from her ear.

"He asked me tonight and I've accepted."

"You can't *do* that!" her friend shrieked.

Jill ignored her outrage. "Of course I can."

"What about Jordan?" Shelly asked next.

"I'd already decided not to see him again." Jill was able to keep her composure, although she found it difficult.

"If marrying Ralph is typical of your recent decisions, then I'd like to suggest you talk to a mental-health professional."

Jill laughed despite herself. Her decision had been based on maintaining her sanity, not destroying it.

"I don't know what's so funny. I just can't believe you'd do something like this! What about Aunt Milly's wedding dress? Doesn't that mean anything to you? Don't you care that Mark, Aunt Milly and I all felt the dress should go to you next? You can't ignore it. Something dreadful might happen."

"Don't be ridiculous."

"I'm not," Shelly insisted resolutely. "You're playing with fire here. You can't reject the man destiny has chosen for you without serious consequences." Shelly's voice was growing more solemn by the second.

"You don't know that Jordan's the man," Jill said with far more conviction than she was feeling. "We both know a wedding dress can't dictate who I'll marry. The choice is mine—and I've chosen Ralph."

"You're honestly choosing Ralph over Jordan?" The question had an incredulous quality.

"Yes."

There was a moment's silence.

"You're running scared," Shelly went on, "frightened half out of your wits because of everything you feel. I know, because I went through the same thing. Jill, please, think about this before you do something you'll regret the rest of your life."

"I have thought about it," she insisted. She'd thought of little else since her last encounter with Jordan. Since her talk with Shelly. Since her visit to her mother's. She'd carefully weighed her options. Marrying Ralph seemed the best course.

"You have no intention of changing your mind, do you?" Shelly cried. "Do you honestly expect me to stand by and do nothing while you ruin your life?"

"I'm not ruining my life. Don't be absurd." Her voice grew hard. "Naturally I'll return your Aunt Milly's wedding dress and—"

"No," Shelly groaned. "Here, talk to Mark before I say something I shouldn't."

"Jill?" Mark came on the line. "What's the problem?"

Jill didn't want to repeat everything. She was tired and it was late and all she wanted to do was go to bed. Escape for the next eight hours and then face the world again. Jill hadn't intended to tell Shelly and Mark her news quite so soon, but there had been a telephone message from them when she arrived home. She'd decided she might as well let Shelly know of her decision. Jill wasn't sure what she'd expected from her friends, but certainly not this.

"Just a minute," Mark said next. "Shelly's trying to tell me something."

Although Shelly had given the phone to her husband, Jill could hear her friend's frantic words as clearly as if she still held the receiver. Shelly was pleading with Mark to talk some sense into Jill, begging him to try because she hadn't been able to change Jill's mind.

"Mark," Jill called, but apparently he didn't hear her. "Mark," she tried again, louder this time.

"I'm sorry, Jill," he said politely, "but Shelly's upset, and I'm having a hard time figuring out just what the problem is. All I can make out is that you've decided not to see Jordan Wilcox again."

"I'm marrying Ralph Emery, and I don't think he'd take kindly to my dating Jordan."

Mark chuckled. "No, I don't suppose he would. Frankly, I believe the decision is yours, and yours alone. I know Jordan, I've talked to him a couple of times and I share your concerns. I can't picture him married."

"He's already married," Jill stated unemotionally, "to his job. A wife would only stand in the way."

"That's probably true. What about Ralph—have I met him?"

"I don't think so," Jill returned stiffly. "He's a very nice man. Honest and hardworking. Shelly seems to think he's dull, and perhaps he is in some ways, but he…cares for me. It isn't a great love match, but we're both aware of that."

"Shelly thinks I'm dull, too, but that didn't stop her from marrying me."

Mark was so calm, so reassuring. He was exactly what Jill needed. She was so grateful she felt close to tears. "I want to do the right thing," she said, sucking in a small breath. Her voice wavered and she bit her lower lip, blinking rapidly.

"It's difficult knowing what's right sometimes, isn't it?" Mark said quietly. "I remember how I felt the first time I met Shelly. Here was this completely bizarre woman announcing to everyone who'd listen that she refused to marry me. I hadn't even asked— didn't even know her name. Then we stumbled on each other a second time and a third, and finally I learned about Aunt Milly's wedding dress."

"What did you think when she told you?"

"That it was the most ridiculous thing I'd ever heard."

"I did, too. I still do." She wanted a husband, *but not Jordan*.

"I'm sure you'll make the right decision," Mark said confidently.

"I am, too. Thanks, Mark, I really appreciate talking to you." The more she grew to know her friend's husband, the more Jill realized how perfectly the two suited each other. Mark brought a wonderful balance into Shelly's life, and she'd infused his with her warmth and wit. If only she, Jill, could have met someone like Mark.

No sooner had she hung up the phone when there was a loud knock on her door. Since it was late, close to eleven, Jill was surprised.

Peering through the peephole in the door, she gasped and drew away. Jordan Wilcox.

"I thought you were in Hawaii," she said as she opened the door.

"I was." His eyes scanned her hungrily. "This morning I had the most incredible feeling something was wrong. I tried to phone, but there wasn't any answer."

"I . . . was out for most of the day."

He gripped her shoulders and then, before she could protest, dragged her into his arms.

"Jordan?" She'd never seen him like this, didn't understand why he seemed so disturbed.

"I just couldn't shake the feeling something was terribly wrong with you."

"I'm fine."

"I know," he said, inhaling deeply. "Thank God you're safe."

CHAPTER SEVEN

"OF COURSE I'M SAFE," Jill insisted, as surprised as she was bewildered. Jordan's arms were tight around her and he buried his head in the curve of her neck, his breathing hard.

"I've never experienced anything like this before," he said, loosening his hold. His hands caressed the length of her arms as he moved back one small step. He studied her, his gaze intimate and tender. "I hope nothing like this ever happens to me again." Taking her hand, he led her to the sofa.

"You're not making any sense."

"I know." He momentarily closed his eyes, then gave a deep sigh. Gripping her fingers with his own, he raised them to his lips and gently kissed the back of her hand.

"It was the most unbelievable thing," he continued, with a small shrug of his shoulders. "I awoke with this feeling of impending doom. At first I tried to ignore it, pretend it didn't exist. But as the day wore on I couldn't shake it. All I knew was that it had something to do with you.

"I thought if I talked to you I could assure myself nothing was wrong, that this feeling would go away. Only I wasn't able to get hold of you."

"I was out most of the day," she repeated unnecessarily.

Jordan rubbed a hand down his face. "When I tried to phone and couldn't get an answer, I panicked. I booked the next flight to Seattle."

"What about your business in Hawaii?"

"I canceled one meeting and left what I could with an assistant. Everything's taken care of." He sighed once more and sagged against the back of her sofa. "I could do with a cup of coffee."

"Of course." Jill immediately stood and hurried into her compact kitchen, starting the coffee and assembling cups and saucers in a matter of minutes. She was arranging everything on a tray when Jordan stepped up behind her.

He slid his arms around her waist and kissed the side of her neck. "I don't know what's happening between us."

"I . . . don't know that anything is."

Jordan chuckled softly, the sound a gentle caress against her skin. "I'm beginning to think you've cast a spell over me."

Jill froze. "Spell" and "magic" were words she'd rather not hear. A lump the size of Texas filled her throat. Even the smallest hint that the wedding dress was affecting him wouldn't change what she'd done. She'd made her decisions. The dress was packed away in the box Shelly had mailed her, ready to be returned.

"I've never experienced anything like this before," Jordan said again, sounding almost uncertain.

Jill should have been shocked. Jordan Wilcox had probably never felt confused or doubtful about anything in his adult life. She speculated that his emotions had been buried so deep, hidden by pride for so long, that he barely recognized them anymore.

"I think I'm falling in love with you."

Jill gasped and closed her eyes. She didn't want to hear this, didn't want to deal with a declaration of love. Not now. Not when she'd settled everything in her own mind. Not when she'd reconciled herself to never seeing him again.

"That's not true," Jordan countered evenly, twisting her around and into his arms. "I can't live without you. I've known that from the first moment we kissed."

"Oh, no..."

The sound of his amusement filled her small kitchen. "You said the same thing that night, too. Remember?" The smile faded as he gazed at her upturned face. His eyes, so gray and intense, seemed to sear her with a look of such power it was all Jill could do not to cry out and break off his embrace. She glanced away, chewing nervously on her lower lip, willing him to free her, willing him to leave before she changed her mind.

His hands cupped her face, his thumbs stroking her cheeks. "You feel it, too, don't you?" he whispered.

"You have from the very first. Neither one of us can deny it."

She meant to tell him then, to blurt out that she was engaged to Ralph, but she wasn't given the chance. Before she could utter a word, before she could even begin to explain, Jordan captured her mouth with his own.

His lips were hard and desperate as they claimed possession of hers, firing her senses to life. She moaned, not from pleasure, although that was keen, but from regret.

Ralph had kissed her that night, too. Jill had tried so hard to reassure herself their marriage would work. She'd put her heart and her soul into their good-night kiss and hadn't experienced even a fraction of what she did with Jordan.

It was so unfair, so wrong. She was marrying Ralph, her mind shouted. But her heart, her foolish, romantic heart, refused to listen.

Nothing Jordan could say was going to change her plans, she decided, forcing herself to think of Ralph and the commitment they'd made to each other only a few hours earlier.

If only Jordan would stop kissing her. *Oh, please stop,* she begged silently as frustration brought burning tears to her eyes. If only he'd leave, walk out of her life forever so she could start forgetting.

But she had to push him out of her arms before she could push him out of her life. Yet here she was clinging to him, her arms, her traitorous arms, curved around his neck. And she was holding on as though her life depended on it.

Jordan obviously felt none of her hesitation, none of her doubts. He went on numbing her senses with his kisses and soon, far too soon, Jill was returning them with equal fervor. Raw emotion overwhelmed her until she was so weak she slumped against him, needing his support to remain upright. Her breath came in shallow gasps as his lips trembled against hers.

"Oh, Jill," he breathed, his voice a husky caress. "The things you do to me. I've frightened you, haven't I?"

"No." He had, but for none of the reasons he knew. She was terrified by the things he made her feel. Terrified by the rush of need and love that crowded her heart.

She buried her face in his shoulder, wanting to escape his arms even as she submerged herself in them.

"I never knew love could be like this," Jordan said hoarsely. "I've never been in love, never experienced it before you." He rested his jaw alongside her cheek in a gesture of tenderness that moved her deeply.

Jill swallowed against the tightness blocking her throat and blinked through a wall of tears. "Please..." She had to say something, had to let him know before he spoke again, before he convinced her to love him. She'd set her mind, her will, everything within her, to resist him and found she couldn't.

"I realize we haven't known each other long," Jordan was saying. "Yet it seems as if you've always been a part of my life, always will be."

"No..."

"Yes," he countered softly, his lips grazing the side of her face. "I want to marry you, Jill. Soon. The sooner the better. I need you in my life. I need you to teach me so many things. Loving me isn't going to be easy, but—"

"No!" Abruptly she broke away from him, although it demanded every ounce of energy she possessed. "Please, no." She buried her face in her hands and began to sob.

"Jill, what is it?" He tried to comfort her, tried to bring her back into his embrace, but she wouldn't let him.

"I can't marry you." The words, born of frustration and anger, were meant to be shouted, but by the time they passed her lips they were barely audible.

"Can't marry me?" Jordan repeated as though he was sure he'd misunderstood. "Why not?"

"Because..." Saying it became nearly an impossible task, but she forced herself. "Because...I'm already engaged."

She saw and felt his shock. His eyes narrowed with disbelief and pain as the color drained from his face, leaving him pale beneath his tan.

"You're making it up."

"No, it's true." She held herself stiff, braced for the backlash her words were sure to bring.

"When?" he demanded.

She heaved in a breath and squared her shoulders. "Tonight."

A shudder went through him as his eyes, dark and haunting, raked her face. Jill's throat muscles constricted at his tortured look, and she couldn't speak, couldn't explain.

It took Jordan a moment to compose himself. But he did so with amazing dexterity. All emotion fled from his face. For a breathless moment he just stared at her.

"I'm sure," he said finally, without any outward hint of regret, "whoever it is will make you a far better husband than I would have."

"His name is Ralph."

Jordan grimaced, but quickly rearranged his features into a cool mask. "I wish you and…Ralph every happiness."

With that, he turned and walked out of her life.

EARLY THE NEXT MORNING, after an almost sleepless night, Jill carted the infamous wedding dress to her car and drove directly to Shelly and Mark's. The curtains were open so she assumed they were up and about. Even if they weren't, she didn't care.

Keeping the wedding dress a moment longer was intolerable. The thing was an albatross around her neck. The sooner she was rid of it, the sooner her life would return to normal.

Jill locked her car and carried the box to the Bradys' front door. Her steps were crisp and impatient. If Shelly wasn't home, Jill swore she'd leave the wedding gown on the front steps rather than take it back to her apartment.

A few minutes passed before the door opened. Shelly stood on the other side, dressed in a long robe, her hair in disarray and her hand covering her mouth to hide a huge, shoulder-raising yawn.

"I got you out of bed?" That much was obvious, but Jill was in no state for intelligent conversation.

"I was awake," Shelly said, yawning again. "Mark had to go into the office early this morning, but I couldn't make myself get up." She gestured Jill inside. "Come on in. I'm sure Mark made a pot of coffee. He knows I need a cup first thing in the morning."

Jill set the box down on the sofa and followed Shelly into the kitchen. Clearly her friend wasn't fully awake yet, so Jill walked over to the cupboards and collected two mugs, filling each with coffee, then bringing them to the table where Shelly was sitting.

"Oh, thanks," she mumbled. "I'm impossible until I've had my first cup."

"I seem to remember that from our college days."

"Right," Shelly said, managing a half smile. "You know all my faults. Can you believe Mark loves me in spite of the fact that I can't cook, can't tolerate mornings and am impossibly disorganized?"

Having seen the love in Mark's eyes when he looked at his wife, Jill could well believe it. "Yes."

"I'm glad you're here," Shelly said, resting her head on her arm, which was stretched across the kitchen table.

"You are?" It was apparent that Shelly hadn't guessed the reason for this unexpected visit, hadn't realized Jill intended to return the wedding dress.

Half-asleep as she was, she obviously hadn't noticed the box.

"Yes, I'm *delighted* you're here," Shelly said as her eyes drifted shut. "Mark and I had a long talk about you and Ralph. He seems to think I'm overreacting to this engagement thing. But you aren't going to marry Ralph—you know it and I know it. This engagement is a farce, even if you don't recognize that yet. I know you, Jill. In some ways I know you as well as I do myself. Getting Ralph to propose is the only way you can deal with what's happening between you and Jordan. But you'd never go through with it. You're too honest. You won't let yourself cheat Ralph—because if you marry him, that's exactly what you'll be doing."

"He knows I don't love him."

"I'm sure he does, but I'm also sure he believes that in time you'll feel differently. What he doesn't understand is that you're already in love with someone else."

A few hours earlier, Jill would have adamantly denied loving Jordan, but she couldn't any longer. Her heart burned with the intensity of her feelings. Still, it didn't change anything, didn't alter the path she'd chosen.

"Ralph doesn't know about Jordan, does he?"

"No," Jill said reluctantly. If she was forced to, she'd tell Ralph about him. Difficult as it was to admit, Shelly was right. Jill would never be able to marry Ralph unless she was completely honest with him.

Shelly straightened and took her first sip of coffee. It seemed to revive her somewhat. "I should apologize for what I said last night. I didn't mean to offend you."

"You didn't," Jill was quick to assure her.

"You frightened me."

"Why?"

"I was afraid for you, afraid you were going to ruin your life. I don't think I could stand idly by and allow you to do it."

"I fully intend to marry Ralph." Jill didn't know for whose benefit she was saying this—Shelly's or her own. The doubts were back, but she did her best to ignore them.

"I'm sure you do intend to marry Ralph...now," Shelly continued, "but when the time comes, I have every confidence it won't happen. So does Mark."

"That isn't what he said when we talked." Mark had been the cool voice of reason in their impassioned discussion the night before. He'd reassured her and comforted her, and for that Jill would always be grateful.

"What he said," Shelly explained between giant yawns, "was that he was sure you'd make the right decision. And he is. I was, too, after he calmed me down."

"I've made my choice. There's no turning back now."

"You'll change your mind."

"Perhaps. I don't know. All I know right now is that I agreed to marry Ralph." No matter how hard she tried, she couldn't keep the breathless catch from her voice.

Shelly heard it, and her eyes slowly opened. "What happened?" Her gaze sharply assessed Jill, who tried not to say or do anything that would give her away.

"Tell me," she said when Jill hesitated. "You know I'll get it out of you one way or another."

Jill sighed. Hiding the truth would do little good. "Jordan stopped in late last night."

"I thought you said he was in Hawaii."

"He was."

"Then what was he doing at your place?" The question was sharp, insistent.

"He said he felt there was something wrong—and he flew home."

"There *is* something wrong!" Shelly cried. "You're engaged to the wrong man."

Wrong. Wrong. Wrong. Unexpectedly, Jill felt defeated. She'd hardly slept the night before, and the tears she'd managed to hold at bay refused to be held back any longer. They brimmed in her eyes, spilling onto her cheeks, cool against her flushed skin.

"I'm not engaged to the wrong man," she said once she was able to speak coherently. "I happen to love the wrong one."

"If you're in love with Jordan," Shelly said, "and I believe you are, then why in heaven's name would you even consider marrying Ralph?"

It was too difficult to explain, too difficult to put into words. Rather than make the effort, she merely shook her head and stood, almost toppling her chair in her eagerness to escape.

"Jill." Shelly stood, too.

"I have to go now..."

"Jill, what's wrong? My goodness, I've never seen you like this. Tell me."

Jill shook her head again and hurried into the living room. "I brought back the wedding dress. Thank your Aunt Milly for me, but I can't...wear it."

"You brought back the dress?" Shelly sounded as though she was about to break into tears herself. "Oh, Jill, I wish you hadn't."

Jill didn't stick around to argue. She rushed out the front door and to her car. Her destination wasn't clear until she reached Ralph's apartment. She hadn't planned to go there and wasn't sure what had directed her there. For several minutes she sat outside, collecting her thoughts, gathering her courage.

When she'd composed herself, blown her nose and dried her eyes, she walked to his front door and rang the doorbell. Ralph answered, looking pleased to see her.

"Good morning. You're out and about early. I was just about ready to leave for work."

She forced a smile. "Have you got a minute?"

"Sure. Come in." He paused and seemed to remember that they were now an engaged couple. He leaned forward and lightly brushed his lips across her cheek.

"I should have phoned first."

"No. I was just thinking that this afternoon might be a good time for us to look at engagement rings."

Jill guiltily dropped her gaze and her voice trembled. "That's very sweet." She could barely say the

words she had to say. "I should explain . . . the reason
I'm here—"

Ralph motioned her toward a chair. "Please, sit
down."

Jill was grateful because she wasn't sure how much
longer her legs would support her. Everything seemed
so much more difficult in the light of day. She'd been
so confident before, so sure she and Ralph could make
a life together. Now she felt as though she were walking around in a heavy fog. Nothing was clear, and
confusion greeted her at every turn.

She took a deep breath. "There's something I need
to explain."

"Sure." Ralph sat comfortably across from her.

She was so close to the edge of the chair she was in
danger of slipping off. "It's only fair you should
know." She hesitated, thinking he might say something, but when he didn't, she continued, "I met a
man in Hawaii."

He nodded gravely. "I thought you must have."

His intuition surprised her. "His name . . . Oh, it
doesn't matter what his name is. We went out a couple of times."

"Are you in love with him?" Ralph asked outright.

"Yes," Jill whispered slowly, regretfully. It hurt to
admit, and for a moment she dared not look at Ralph.

"It doesn't seem like a lot of time to be falling in
love with a man. You were only gone a week."

Jill didn't tell him Jordan was in Hawaii only three
days. Nor did she mention the two brief times she'd

seen him since. She couldn't see that it would do any good to analyze the relationship. It was over. She'd made certain of that when she told him she was marrying Ralph. She'd never hear from Jordan again.

"Love happens like that sometimes," was the only answer Jill had.

"If you're so in love with this other guy, then why did you agree to marry me?"

"Because I'm frightened and, oh, Ralph, I'm so sorry. I should never have involved you in this. You're a wonderful man and I care for you, I honestly do. You've been a good friend and I've enjoyed our times together, but I realized this morning that I can't marry you."

For a moment he said nothing, then he reached for her hand and held it gently between his own. "You don't need to feel so guilty about it."

"But I do." She was practically drowning in guilt.

"Don't. It took me about two minutes to realize something was troubling you last night. You surprised me completely when you started talking about getting married."

"I surprised you?"

"To be honest, I assumed you were about to tell me you'd met someone else and wouldn't be seeing me any longer. I've known for a long time that you don't love me."

"But I believed that would've changed," Jill said almost desperately.

"That's what I figured, too."

"You're steady and dependable, and I need that in my life," she said, although the rationale sounded poor even to her own ears. True, if she married Ralph she wouldn't have the love match she'd always dreamed about, but she'd told herself that love was highly overrated. She'd decided she could live without love, live without passion—until Jordan showed up on her doorstep. And that morning, Shelly had told her what she already knew. She couldn't marry Ralph.

"You're here because you want to call off the engagement, aren't you?" Ralph asked.

Miserably, Jill nodded. "I didn't mean to hurt you. That's the last thing I want."

"You haven't," he said pragmatically. "I figured you'd call things off sooner or later."

"You did?"

He grinned sheepishly. "You going to marry this other man?"

Jill shrugged. "I don't know."

"If you do..."

"Yes?" Jill reluctantly raised her eyes to his.

"If you do, would you consider subletting your apartment to me? Your place is at least twice as big as mine, and your rent's cheaper."

Jill started to laugh. She didn't know where she found the energy, but the humor bubbled up inside her like fizz in a flute of champagne. Leave it to Ralph, ever practical, ever sensible, to brush off a broken engagement and ask about subletting her apartment.

THE WEEK THAT FOLLOWED was one of the worst of Jill's life. She awoke every morning feeling as though she hadn't slept. She was depressed and lonely. Several times she found herself close to tears for no apparent reason. She'd be reading a prescription and the words would blur and misery would grip her heart with such intensity she'd be forced to swallow a sob.

"Jill," her supervisor called early Friday afternoon, walking into the back room where she was taking her lunch break. "There's someone out front who wants to talk to you."

It was unusual for anyone to visit her at work. She immediately feared it was Jordan, but she quickly dismissed that concern. She knew him too well. She was out of his life. The instant she'd told him she was engaged to Ralph, he'd cut her out, surgically removed all emotion for her. It was as if she no longer existed for him.

But as she'd been so often lately, Jill was wrong. Jordan stood there waiting for her. His gaze was as hard as flint. Something flickered briefly in the smoky-gray depths, but whatever emotion he felt at seeing her was too fleeting for Jill to identify.

She'd had far less practice at hiding her own feelings, and right now, they were wreaking havoc with her pulse. With great effort she managed to remain outwardly composed. "You wanted to speak to me?"

A nerve twitched in his jaw. "You might be more comfortable if we spoke elsewhere," he said stiffly.

Jill glanced at her watch. She had only fifteen minutes of her lunch break left. Time enough, she was sure, for whatever Jordan intended. "All right."

Wordlessly, he walked out of the drugstore, obviously expecting her to follow, which she did. He paused in front of his car, then turned to face her. A cool, disinterested smile slanted his mouth.

"Yes?" she said after an awkward moment. She folded her arms defensively around her middle. If only he didn't look compelling, so wonderfully male.

"I need you to explain something."

She nodded. "I'll try."

"Your friend Shelly Brady was in to see me this morning."

Jill groaned inwardly. She hadn't talked to Shelly since the morning she'd dropped off the wedding dress. Her friend had phoned several times and left messages, but Jill hadn't either the energy or the patience to return the calls.

"How she managed to get past my secretary and my two assistants is beyond me."

It was a nightmare come true. "What did she say?" As if Jill needed to know.

"She rambled on about how you were making the worst mistake of your life and how I'd be an even bigger fool if I let you. But, you know, if you prefer to marry Roger, then that's your prerogative."

"His name is Ralph," she corrected.

"It doesn't make much difference to me."

"I didn't think it would," she said, keeping her gaze lowered to the black asphalt of the parking lot.

"Then she started telling me this ridiculous story about a legend behind a certain wedding dress."

Jill's eyes closed in frustration. "It's a bunch of foolishness."

"It certainly didn't make too much sense, especially the part about the dress fitting her and her marrying Mark. But she insisted that I realize the dress also fits you."

"Don't take Shelly seriously. She seems to put a lot of credence in that dress. Personally, I think the whole thing's a fluke. You don't need to worry about it."

"*Then* she told me this ridiculous tale about a vision she had of you in Hawaii and how happy you looked. It didn't make any more sense than the rest."

"I don't think you need to worry. Shelly means well, but she doesn't understand. The wedding dress is beautiful, but it isn't meant for me. The whole thing is ridiculous—you said so yourself, and I agree with you."

"That's what I thought—at first. A magic wedding dress makes about as much sense as a talking rabbit. I don't believe in such nonsense."

"Then why are you here?"

"Because I remembered something. You had a wedding dress with you in Hawaii. When I asked you about it, you said a friend had mailed it to you. Then, this morning, Shelly arrived and started explaining why she'd sent you the dress. She told me the story about her Aunt Milly and how she'd met her husband. She also explained how Milly had mailed the dress to her and she'd fallen into Mark Brady's arms."

"Did she leave anything out?" Jill asked sarcastically.

He ignored her question. "In the end I phoned Mark and asked him about it. I don't know Brady well, but I figured he'd be able to explain matters a little more rationally."

"Shelly does tend to get a bit dramatic."

"She's your friend."

"Yes, I know. It's just that I wish she hadn't said anything to you."

"I imagine you do," he remarked dryly.

"What did Mark say?"

"We talked for several minutes. By this time Shelly was weeping and nearly hysterical, convinced she was saving us both from a fate worse than death. Mark was kind enough to inject a bit of sanity into the discussion. What it boiled down to is this."

"What?" Jill wasn't purposely being obtuse.

"Me confronting you. I'm here to ask you about Aunt Milly's wedding dress."

He could ask her what he wanted, but she didn't have any answers.

"Jill?"

She heaved a sigh. "I returned the dress to Shelly."

"She explained that, too. Said you'd brought it back the morning after my visit."

"It wasn't meant for me."

"Not true, according to Shelly and Mark." He remained standing where he was, hard and unyielding, unwilling to divulge his own feelings.

"So you're going to go ahead and marry Roger."

"Ralph."

"Whoever," Jordan snapped.

"No!" she shouted, furious with him, furious with Shelly and Mark, too.

A moment of shocked silence followed her announcement. Several feet separated Jill from Jordan, and although neither of them moved, they suddenly seemed much closer.

"I know," he said after a moment.

"How could you possibly know?" Jill hadn't told anyone yet. Not Shelly and certainly not Jordan.

"Because you're marrying me."

CHAPTER EIGHT

ALL JILL'S DEFENSES came tumbling down. She'd known they would from the moment Jordan had first kissed her. Known from the moment she'd walked out of the lunchroom and confronted him. Known in the very depths of her soul that he would eventually have his way. She hadn't the strength to fight him any longer.

He must have sensed her acquiescence because he moved toward her, pausing just short of taking her in his arms. "You will marry me, won't you?" The words were gentle yet insistent, brooking no argument.

Jill nodded. "I don't want...don't want to love you."

"I know." He reached for her then, drawing her into his embrace as though he were comforting a child.

It should have eased her mind that settling into his arms felt more natural than anything she'd done in the past week. A feeling of welcome. A feeling of rightness. And yet there was fear.

"You're going to break my heart," she whispered.

"Not if I can help it."

"Why do you want to marry me?" The answer evaded her. A man like Jordan could have his pick of women. He had wealth and prestige and a dozen other attributes that attracted far more sophisticated and far more beautiful women than Jill.

The air between them seemed to pulse for long moments before Jordan answered. "I've done some thinking about that myself. You're intelligent. Insightful. You feel things deeply and you're sensitive to the needs of others." He traced a finger along the line of her jaw, his touch light, feather-soft. "You're passionate about the people you love."

She should have been reassured that he seemed to know her so well after such a short acquaintance, but she wasn't. Because she knew that for a time she'd be a welcome distraction. Their marriage would be like a toy to him, then gradually as the newness wore off, she'd be put on a shelf to look pretty and brought down when it suited his purposes. His life, his love, his personality, would be consumed by the drive to succeed, just the way her father's had been. Everything else faded into the background, to eventually disappear. Love. Family. Commitment. All that was important to her would ultimately mean nothing to him.

"I want us to marry soon," Jordan whispered as his chin stroked the crown of her head.

"I—I was hoping for a long engagement."

Jordan's eyes were adamant. "I've waited too long already."

Jill didn't understand what he meant, but she didn't question him. She knew Jordan was an impatient man and always had been. When he wanted something, he went after it with relentless determination. Now he wanted her—and heaven help her, she wanted him.

"A bride should be happy," he said, tucking his hand under her chin and raising her face to his. "Why the tears?"

How could she possibly explain her fears? She loved him, although she'd fought it with everything she had. She'd been willing, for a time, to consider marrying Ralph in her effort to drive Jordan from her life. Yet even then she'd known it was useless and of course so had Ralph. Nothing could save her. Her heart had been on a collision course with Jordan's from the moment she'd been assigned the seat next to his on the flight to Hawaii.

"I'll be happy," she murmured, and then silently added *for a while*.

"So will I," Jordan said, his chest expanding with a breath and then a sigh that seemed to come all the way from his soul.

THE SMALL PRIVATE wedding took place three weeks later in Hawaii at the home of Andrew Howard. Shelly was Jill's matron of honor and Mark stood up for Jordan. Elaine Morrison, was there, too, weeping through the entire ceremony. But these weren't tears of joy. Her mother, like Jill, recognized Jordan's type and feared what it meant for her daughter's life, her happiness.

"Jill," Elaine had pleaded with her earlier that morning, before the wedding. Her eyes were filled with concern. "Are you sure this is what you want?"

Jill had nearly laughed aloud. With all her heart, with all her being, she longed to be Jordan's wife. And yet, if the opportunity had availed itself, she would have backed out of the marriage.

"He needs me." Repeatedly over the past few weeks, Jill had been reminded of how much Jordan did need her. He didn't realize it himself, of course, not on a conscious level, but something deep inside him had acknowledged his need. And in her own way, Jill needed him.

Andrew Howard had recognized the fact that they belonged together. He'd been the first one to point it out to Jill. From the time he'd been a child, Jordan's life had been devoid of love, devoid of emotion. As an adult he'd closed himself off from both, refused to allow himself to become vulnerable. That he should experience something as powerful as love for her in so short a time was something of a miracle. But then, Jill was becoming accustomed to miracles.

"All I want is your happiness," her mother had gone on to say, her eyes, so like Jill's, blurred with tears. "You're my only child. I don't want you to make the same mistakes I did."

Could loving someone ever be a mistake? Jill wondered. Her mother had loved her father, sacrificed herself for him even though, as the years went on, he'd barely seemed to reciprocate her love. And when he died prematurely, without warning, she'd become lost and miserable.

Jill knew she loved Jordan enough to put aside her fears and agree to become his wife, to bind herself in a relationship that might ultimately cause her pain. But she vowed she wouldn't lose her own identity. She wouldn't, couldn't, allow Jordan's personality to swallow her own.

He hadn't understood that in the beginning, despite her attempts to explain it. To him, Jill's desire to continue working after their marriage seemed utterly foolish. For what purpose? he'd asked. She didn't need the income; he'd made certain of that, lavishing her with gifts and more money than she could possibly spend. Her insistence on continuing her job resulted in their first real argument. But in the end Jordan had reluctantly agreed.

Andrew Howard had gone to a great deal of trouble to arrange their wedding, warming Jill's heart with his efforts. More and more she understood that the older man looked upon Jordan as the son he'd lost. He was more than a mentor, far more than a friend. He was the only real family Jordan had—until now.

Flowers filled every room of Andrew's oceanfront home, their fragrance sweet in the summer air. An archway of orange blossoms stood outside on the lush green lawn that overlooked the roaring ocean. A small reception and dinner were to follow. Tables laid with white linen tablecloths were placed around the patio.

The warm wind whispered over Jill as Andrew Howard came to escort her into the sunshine where

Jordan was waiting. Andrew paused when he saw her, his eyes vivid with appreciation. "I've never had a daughter," he said softly, "but if I did, I'd want her to be like you."

Tears of love and gratitude filled her eyes. Her mother, fussing about Jill, arranged the long, flowing train of the dress, then slowly straightened. "He's right," Elaine said softly, stepping back to examine Jill. "You've never looked more beautiful."

It was the dress, Jill realized. The dress and its magic. She ran her glove along the bodice with its Venetian lace and row upon row of delicate pearls. The high collar was adorned with pearls, too, each one stitched on by hand. The skirt flared from her waist, the hem accentuated with a flounce of lace and wide satin ribbons.

Andrew Howard stood beside her mother as the minister asked Jordan and Jill to repeat their vows. Jill's gaze met Jordan's as she made her promises. Her voice, although low, was steady and confident. Jordan's eyes held hers with a look of warmth, of tenderness.

A magic wedding dress? The scenario seemed implausible. Yet here they were, standing before God, their friends and family, declaring their love for one another.

"You look so beautiful," Shelly told Jill shortly after the ceremony. "Even more beautiful than the day you first tried on the dress."

"My hair wasn't done and I didn't have on much makeup and I—"

"No," Shelly interrupted, squeezing Jill's fingers, "it's more than that. You hadn't met Jordan yet. It's complete now."

"What is?"

"Everything," Shelly explained with characteristic ambiguity. "Aunt Milly's wedding dress, you and Jordan. Oh, Jill," she whispered, her eyes brimming with tears, "you're going to be so happy."

Jill wanted to believe that—how she wanted to believe that!—but she was afraid. So very afraid of what the future held for her and Jordan.

"I know what you're thinking," Shelly said, dabbing her eyes. "I loved Mark when I married him. I'd loved him for months, but deep down I wondered how long a marriage between us would last. We're so different."

Jill smiled to herself. Shelly was right; she and Mark were different, but they were perfectly matched, balancing each other's strengths.

"I was sure my lack of domestic skills would drive Mark to distraction, and at the same time I was convinced the way he organizes everything would kill our relationship. Did you know that man makes lists of lists? Even before I walked to the altar, I was worried that this marriage was doomed."

"It's been all right, though, hasn't it?"

Shelly smiled. "It's been so easy—love does that, you know. It takes something that's difficult and makes it feel so effortless. You'll understand what I mean in a few months."

Unfortunately Jill shared little of her friend's confidence. She was delighted that things had worked out between Shelly and Mark, but she didn't expect the same kind of happiness for her and Jordan.

"When you stop to think about it, it's not all that surprising," Shelly had gone on to say. "Take Aunt Milly and Uncle John for example. She's educated and idealistic, and John, bless his heart, was a realist and a mechanic with barely a grade-school education. Yet he was so proud of her. He loved her until the day he died."

"Mark will always love you, too," Jill said, running her hand down the satin of the wedding dress.

"Jordan feels the same way about you."

Jill's heart stopped. It hit her then, for perhaps the first time—Jordan loved her. His love was what had guided Jill through her uncertainties. It had helped her understand what had led her to this point, helped her look past her mother's tears and her own doubts.

The small reception and dinner held immediately after the ceremony featured a light, elegant meal and a warm atmosphere. Jill met several of Jordan's business associates, who seemed both surprised and pleased for them. Even the Lundquists put in a jovial appearance, although Suzi was absent.

When it came time for them to leave, Jill kissed Andrew Howard's cheek and thanked him once more. "Everything's been wonderful."

"I lost my only son," he reminded her, his eyes momentarily aged and sad. "For years I've hungered for a family. After my wife died, and before, too, I shut myself away, locked in my grief and watched the world go on without me.''

"You're being hard on yourself," Jill told him. "Your work—"

"True enough," he said, cutting her off. "For a while I was able to bury myself in my company, but two years ago I realized I'd wasted too much of my life struggling with this grief. Soon afterward I decided to retire.'' His gaze wandered away from Jill and toward her mother, and he smiled softly. "I think the time might be right for me to make other changes, take the next step. What do you think, my dear?''

Jill smiled. Her mother needed someone like Andrew. Someone to bring the sparkle back to her eyes, to teach her that love didn't always mean pain.

"I'd forgotten what it was like to be young," he said, now smiling easily. "I've known Jordan nearly all his life. I've watched him build a name for himself and admired his cunning. He's good, Jill, damn good. But he's a man without a family, and I suspect I see a lot of myself in him. The thought of him growing old and disillusioned with life troubled me. I want him to avoid the mistakes I made.''

Funny how her mother had said basically the same thing to Jill a few hours earlier. "There are certain mistakes we each have to make," Jill returned softly. "It's the only way we seem to learn, painful as it is.''

"How smart you are," Andrew said, chuckling. "Much too clever for your years.''

"I love him." Somehow it was important Mr. Howard know that. "I don't know if my love will make a lot of difference, but..."

"Ah, that's where you're wrong. It will change him. Love does that, my dear, and he needs you so badly."

"How can you be sure I'll have any influence over Jordan's life? I'm marrying him because I love him, but I don't expect anything to change."

"It will. Just wait and see."

"How do you know that?"

His smile came slowly, transforming his face, brightening his eyes and relaxing his mouth. "Because, my child," he said, gripping her hand in his own, "because it once transformed my life, and I'm hopeful that it will again." He glanced at her mother as he spoke, and Jill leaned over to give him another quick kiss. "Good luck," she whispered.

"Jill," Jordan called then, approaching her. "Are you ready?"

She looked at her husband of less than two hours and nodded. He was referring to their honeymoon trip, but she... she was thinking about their lives together.

"HMM," JILL MURMURED as the first light of dawn crept into their hotel room. She raised her arms high above her head and yawned.

"Good morning, wife," Jordan said, kissing her ear.

"Good morning, husband."

"Did you sleep well?"

Eyes still closed, she nodded.

"Me, too."

"I was exhausted," Jill told him, smiling shyly.

"Little wonder."

Although her eyes remained closed, Jill knew Jordan was smiling. Her introduction to the physical aspect of marriage had been incredible, wonderful. Jordan was a patient and gentle lover. Jill had felt understandably nervous, but he'd been tender and reassuring.

"I didn't know it could be so good," she said, snuggling in her husband's arms.

"I didn't, either," he surprised her by saying. His lips were in her hair, his hands exploring her soft skin. "It's enough to make a husband think about wasting away the morning in bed."

"Wasting?" Jill teased, a smile lifting the corners of her mouth. "Surely I misunderstood you. The Jordan Wilcox I've met wouldn't know how to waste time."

"It all has to do with the musical rest," he said seductively. "The all-important caesura. Who would ever have guessed something so small could change a man's entire life?" He kissed her then with a hunger that moved her, then made love to her with a need that humbled her.

It was noon before they left the hotel room and one o'clock when they returned.

"Jordan," Jill said, blushing when he reached for her the moment they were alone. "It's the middle of the day."

"So?"

"So . . . it's indecent."

"Really?" But as he spoke, he was lowering his mouth to hers. The kiss was intoxicating, and any resistance Jill might have felt vanished like ice in the sun.

Her hands sought his neck, and she rested her palms against the corded contours of his shoulders as he kissed her again and again.

Unable to stop herself, Jill moaned softly.

Dragging his mouth from hers, he trailed kisses down the side of her neck. "There's that sight-seeing trip you wanted to take," he reminded her. "To see the pineapple and sugarcane fields."

"It's not important. We could see them another time," she offered breathlessly.

"That's not what you claimed earlier."

"I was just thinking . . ." She didn't get the opportunity to finish. Jordan's kiss absorbed her words and scattered the thought.

"What did you think?"

"That married people should occasionally be willing to change their plans," she managed.

Jordan chuckled, and lifting her gently into his arms, carried her to the bed. "I'm beginning to think married life is going to agree with me." His mouth found hers and gentleness gave way to urgency.

FIVE DAYS LATER, when Jordan and Jill returned to the mainland, their honeymoon over, Jill was so deeply in love with her husband she wondered why she'd ever hesitated, why she'd fought so hard against marrying him.

The first person she called when they arrived at the penthouse was Shelly. Jordan had arranged to have her things moved there while they were away. Ralph lived at her old apartment now and was elated with the extra space.

"Have you got time to meet an old friend for lunch?" Jill asked without preamble.

"Jill!" Shelly cried. "When did you get back?"

"About an hour ago." Although he hadn't said as much, she knew Jordan was dying to get to his office. "I thought I'd steal away for a few minutes and meet you."

"I'd love to see you. Just name the place and time."

Jill did, then kissed Jordan on the cheek while he was talking to his secretary on the phone in his study. He broke away, covered the mouthpiece with his hand and gave her a surprised look. "Where are you headed?"

"Out for lunch. You don't mind, do you?"

"No." But he didn't sound all that sure.

"I thought you'd want to go to the office," she explained.

"I do," he said, wrapping his arm around her waist and bringing her close to his side.

"I know, so I thought I'd meet Shelly."

He grinned, kissed her lightly and returned to his telephone conversation as though she'd already left. Jill lingered at the door, waiting for the elevator to arrive. Part of her longed to stay with him, to hold on to the happiness before it escaped, before it was dispersed by everyday tensions and demands.

"Well," Shelly said a half hour later as she slid into the restaurant booth across from Jill, "how are the newlyweds?"

"Wonderful."

"I thought you'd be more tanned."

Jill blushed; Shelly laughed and reached for her napkin. "It was the same with Mark and me. I swear we didn't leave that hotel room for three days."

"We made several short trips," Jill said, but she didn't elaborate on exactly how short their sight-seeing ventures had been.

"Married life certainly seems to agree with you."

"It's only been a week," Jill reminded her friend. "That's hardly time enough to tell."

"I knew after the first week," Shelly said confidently, her face animated by a smile. "I figured if Mark and I survived the honeymoon, our marriage had a chance. Mark wanted to honeymoon at Niagara Falls, remember?"

"And you suggested a rafting trip through the Grand Canyon." Jill smiled at the memory. Mark was looking for tradition and Shelly was seeking adventure, but in the end, they'd learned what she and Jordan had already discovered. All that mattered was their marriage, their love for each other.

"We couldn't agree," Shelly continued. "I was seriously worried about it. If we were at odds over a honeymoon site, then what on earth would happen

when it came to dealing with the really important issues?''

Jill understood what Shelly meant. She loved Jordan; of that there could be no doubt. Now she had to
place her trust in their love, hope that it was strong
enough to withstand day-to-day reality. She was still
fearful, but ready to fight for her marriage, to keep it
safe.

Suddenly Shelly set aside the menu, pressed her
hand against her stomach and slowly exhaled.

''Shell, what's wrong?''

Shelly briefly closed her eyes. ''Nothing bad. I just
can't stand to read about food.''

''About food?'' That made absolutely no sense to
Jill.

''I'm two months pregnant.''

''Shelly!'' Jill was so excited she nearly toppled her
water glass. ''Why didn't you say something sooner?
Good grief, I'm your best friend—I'd think you'd
want me to know.''

''I do, but I couldn't tell you until I knew, could I?''

''You just found out?''

''Not exactly.'' Shelly reached for a small packet of
soda crackers, tore away the cellophane wrapper and
munched on one. ''I found out just before your wedding, but I didn't want to say anything then.''

Jill appreciated Shelly's considerateness, her wish
not to compete with Jill's important day.

''Actually, it was Mark who told me. Imagine a
husband explaining the facts of life to his wife. I'm

such a scatterbrain—I miscalculated and didn't even know it.''

As far as Jill was concerned, this baby certainly wasn't a mistake, and from Shelly's happy glow, her friend felt the same way.

''I was a bit afraid Mark might be upset. Naturally we'd talked about starting a family, but neither of us planned to have it happen so soon.''

''He wasn't upset, though, was he?'' Jill would have been very surprised if Mark had been anything but thrilled.

''Not in the least. When he first told me what he suspected, I just laughed.'' She shook her head in mock consternation. ''You'd think I'd know better than to question a man who sleeps with his Daily Planner by his side!''

''I'm so excited for you.''

''Now that I've adjusted to it, I can't wait. I have to admit, though, this baby's a real surprise.''

After the waitress had taken their order, Jill relaxed against the banquette cushion. ''It happened just the way you said it would,'' she said.

''What did?''

''Loving Jordan.'' Jill felt a little shy talking so openly about something so intimate. Although she and Jordan were married and deeply in love with each other, they never spoke of their feelings. Jordan was still uncomfortable with expressing emotion. But he didn't need to tell Jill he loved her, not when he went about proving it in every way he knew how. She'd never pressured him, never demanded the words.

"The day we were married you told me love makes the difficult things seem effortless. Remember?"

Ever confident, Shelly grinned. "You're going to be so happy..." She paused, swallowed and reached for her napkin, dabbing her eyes. "I get so emotional these days, I can't believe it. The other night I found myself weeping at a stupid television commercial."

"You?"

"If you think that's bad, Mark's got a terrible case of morning sickness."

Jill laughed at her friend's teasing. Laughter came easily since her marriage; it was all the happiness in her heart brimming over, spilling out. She'd never felt so carefree or laughed at so many silly things before.

When Jill returned from lunch two hours later, Jordan was gone. Exhausted from the flight and the excitement of the past week, she crawled into bed and slept, waking when it was dark.

Rolling onto her back, she stretched luxuriously under the weight of the blanket and smiled, musing how thoughtful it was of Jordan to let her sleep.

She kicked aside the blanket and blindly sent her feet searching for her shoes. Yawning, she walked into the living room, surprised to find it dark.

"Jordan?" she called.

She was greeted by silence.

Turning on the lights, Jill was shocked to discover it was after nine. Jordan must still be at the office, she supposed, her stomach knotting. Could it be happening so soon? Could he have grown tired of her already?

No sooner had the thought formed when the elevator doors opened and Jordan appeared. She didn't fly into his arms, although that was her first instinct.

"Hello," she greeted him, a bit coolly.

He was loosening his tie. "What time is it?"

"Nine-fifteen. Are you hungry?"

He paused, as though he needed to think about it. "Yeah, I guess I am. Sorry I didn't call. I didn't have a clue it was this late."

"No problem."

He followed her into the kitchen and slid his arms around her waist while she investigated the contents of the refrigerator.

"It won't be like this every night," he said, his words sounding very much like a promise her father had once made to her mother.

"I know," Jill said, desperately trying to sound as though she believed him.

SHE COULDN'T SLEEP that night. Perhaps it was the long nap she'd taken in the middle of the afternoon; at least that was what she tried to tell herself. More likely, though, it was the gnawing fear that Jordan's love for her was already faltering. She tried to push the doubts aside, tried to convince herself she was overreacting. He'd been away from his office for a week. There must have been all kinds of important issues that demanded his attention. Was she expecting too much?

In the morning, she promised herself, she'd talk to him about it. But when she awoke, Jordan had already left for the office. At least that was where she assumed he'd gone.

Frowning, she dressed and wandered into the kitchen for a cup of coffee.

"Morning." Jordan's cook, Mrs. Murphy, a middle-aged woman with sparkling blue eyes and a wide smile, greeted her. Jill smiled back, although her cheerfulness felt a little strained.

"Hello, Mrs. Murphy, it's nice to see you again," she said, helping herself to coffee. "Uh, what time did Mr. Wilcox leave this morning?"

"Early," the cook said with a disappointed sigh. "I was thinking Mr. Wilcox would stop working so hard once he was married. He hasn't even been home from his honeymoon twenty-four hours and he's already at the office at the crack of dawn."

Jill hated to disillusion the woman, but this wasn't Jordan's first trip to his office. "I'll see what I can do to give him some incentive to stay home," Jill said, savoring the first sip of her coffee.

Mrs. Murphy chuckled. "I'm glad to hear it. That man works too many hours. I've been telling my George for some time now that Mr. Wilcox needs a wife to keep him home at night."

"I'll do my best," Jill promised, but she had the distinct feeling her efforts would make little difference. Checking her watch, she quickly drank the rest of her coffee and hurried into the bedroom to shower.

Within half an hour she was dressed and ready for work.

"Mrs. Murphy," she told the cook, "I'll be at work—PayRite Pharmacy—if Jordan happens to call. Tell him I'll be home a little after five." Jill wished she'd had the chance to talk to him herself; she was more than a little distressed that within a week of their wedding she was communicating with her husband through a third party.

Despite everything, Jill enjoyed her day, which was busier than usual. The pharmacy staff took her out for a celebration lunch, and dozens of customers came by to wish her well. Many of the people whose prescriptions she filled regularly had become friends. In light of how her married life was working out, Jill was thankful she'd decided to keep her job.

By five she was eager to return home, eager to share her day with Jordan and hear about his. She was met by the aroma of cheese, tomato sauce and garlic, and followed it into the kitchen, where she found Mrs. Murphy untying her apron.

"Whatever you're cooking smells sinfully delicious."

"It's my lasagna. Mr. Wilcox's favorite."

Jill opened the oven door and peeked inside. She was famished. "Did Jordan phone?" she asked, her voice rising on a note of longing.

"About fifteen minutes ago. I told him you'd be home a bit after five."

No sooner were the words out than the phone rang. Jill was licking spicy tomato sauce from her fingertip when she answered.

"This is Brian Macauley, Mr. Wilcox's assistant," a crisp male voice informed her. "He's asked that I let you know he won't be home for dinner."

CHAPTER NINE

"Jill."

Her name seemed to come from a long way off. Someone was calling her, but she could barely hear.

"Sweetheart." The voice was louder now.

She snuggled into the warmth, ignoring the persistent sound. After hours and hours of forcing herself to stay awake, she'd finally given up the effort and succumbed to the sweet seduction of sleep.

"Honey, if you don't wake up, you'll get a crick in your neck."

"Jordan?" Her eyes instantly flew open to find her husband kneeling on the carpet beside her chair. She straightened and stared at him as though seeing him for the first time. "Oh, Jordan," she whispered, wrapping her arms around his neck. "I'm so glad you're home."

"With this kind of reception, I'll have to stay away more often."

Jill decided to ignore that comment. "What time is it?"

"Late," was all he said.

She kissed him, needing him, savoring the feel of his arms around her. He looked dreadful. He hadn't been home for dinner in well over a week and spent all hours of the day and night at his office.

Although she'd asked him several times, Jordan's only explanation was that a project he'd been working on had gone wrong. A project. For this he was willing to send both their lives into tumult; for this he was willing to place their marriage at risk. The upheaval had all but ruined the memory of their brief idyllic honeymoon. They'd been back in Seattle two weeks now, and Jill hadn't been allotted a single uninterrupted hour of Jordan's time.

"Are you hungry?" She doubted he'd eaten a decent meal in days.

He shook his head, then rubbed his face wearily. "I'm more tired than anything."

"How much longer is this going to continue?" she asked, keeping her voice as steady as she could. She'd gone into this marriage with her eyes wide open. From the moment she'd met Jordan, she'd known how stiff the competition would be, how demanding his way of life was. She'd always known how difficult keeping their marriage intact was going to be. But she'd figured their love would hold the edge for at least the first couple of years.

Unfortunately she'd figured wrong. If anything, she'd underestimated the strength of his obsession with business and success. Jordan loved her; he might rarely have told her that, but Jill didn't need the words. What she did need was some of his time, some of his attention.

"I've barely seen you all week," she reminded him. "You're gone before I wake up in the mornings. Heaven only knows what time you get home at night."

"It won't be much longer," Jordan said stiffly, standing. "I promise."

"Would it be so terrible if this project folded?"

"Yes," he returned emphatically.

"One failure isn't the end of the world, you know."

Jordan smiled wryly, and his condescension angered her.

"It's true," she answered softly. "Did I ever tell you about trying out for the lead in the high-school play during my senior year?"

Jordan frowned. "No, but is this another story like the one about your piano-playing?"

Jill tucked her legs under her and rested one elbow on the chair arm. "A little."

Jordan sank down on the leather sofa across from her, leaned his head back and closed his eyes. "In that case, why don't you move directly to the point and skip the story?"

He wasn't being rude, Jill told herself, only practical. He was exhausted and in desperate need of rest. He didn't have the energy to wade through her mournful tale in search of a moral.

"All right," she agreed amicably enough. "You've probably already guessed I didn't get the lead. But I'd been so sure I would. I'd played major roles in several plays. In fact, I'd gotten every part I'd ever tried out for. Not only didn't I get this part, I wasn't even in the play, and damn it all, even now I think I would have done a really good job of playing Helen Keller.''

He grinned. "I'm sure you would have, too."

"What I learned most from that experience was not to fear failure. I survived not playing Helen Keller, and later, in college, when I was awarded a wonderful role, it heightened my appreciation of that success." When Jordan didn't immediately respond, she added, "Do you understand what I'm saying, or are you asleep?"

His eyes were closed but his mouth lifted in a gentle smile. "I was just mulling over the sad history of your musical and acting careers."

Jill smiled, too. "I know it sounds ludicrous, but failure liberated me. My heart and soul went into my audition for that role, and when I lost, I felt I could never act again. It took me a long time to regain my confidence, to be willing to hazard another rejection, but eventually I was stronger for it. When I decided to try out for a play in my freshman year of college, I felt as though I was somehow protected, because failure wasn't going to rock me the way it had earlier."

"So you wanted to be an actress?"

"No, I'm not much good at waiting tables."

It took Jordan a moment to catch her joke, but when he did, he laughed out loud.

"You know what they say about hindsight being twenty-twenty? In this case it's true. If failure hadn't taught me to appreciate success when I had it, I might have fallen into a nasty trap."

"What was that?"

"Thinking I deserved it, believing I was so talented, so incredibly gifted, so good that I'd never lose."

Jordan fell silent. Jill waited a moment, then said, "Mr. Howard told me something . . . about the shopping-mall project. I didn't say anything to you at the time because . . . well, because I wasn't sure he wanted me to."

She had Jordan's full attention now.

He straightened, his eyes searching hers. "What did he say?"

"He hasn't often gone in on a construction project with you, has he?"

"Only a handful of times."

"There's a reason for that."

"Oh?"

"You've never failed."

Jordan's head came up sharply. "I beg your pardon?"

Jill realized Jordan found such thinking preposterous. If anything, his successes should have been an inducement to his financial supporters.

"Mr. Howard explained that he doesn't like to deal with a man until he's been devastated financially at least once."

"That makes no sense," Jordan returned irritably.

"Perhaps not. Since my experience in the financial world is limited to balancing my checkbook, I wouldn't know," Jill admitted.

"Who's going to lend money to someone who's failed?"

"Apparently Andrew Howard," Jill said with a grin. "He told me the man who's lost everything is much more careful the next time around."

"I didn't realize you and Howard talked business."

"We didn't." She did her best to appear nonchalant. "Mostly we discussed you."

This didn't please Jordan, either. "I'd prefer to think I owe my success to hard work, determination and foresight. I certainly couldn't have come as far as I have without them."

"True enough," Jill agreed willingly, "but..."

"Is there always going to be a but?"

She nodded, trying to hold back a laugh. Actually she was enjoying this, while her tired husband was left to suffer the indignities of her insights.

"Well," he said shortly, "go on, knock my argument all to hell."

"Oh, I agree your intelligence and dedication have played a large role in your success, but others have worked just as hard, been just as determined and shown just as much foresight—and lost everything."

Jordan scowled. "My, you're full of good cheer, aren't you?"

"I just don't want you to put so much store in this one project. If it falls apart, so what? You're beating yourself to death with this." She didn't mention what it was doing to their marriage; that went without saying.

He considered her words for a few seconds, then his face tightened. "I won't lose. I absolutely, categorically, refuse not to succeed."

"How much longer?" Jill asked when she could disguise the defeat and frustration she was feeling.

He hesitated, then massaged the back of his neck as though to ease away a tiredness that stretched from the top of his head to the bottom of his feet. "A week. It shouldn't take much longer than that."

A week. Seven days. She closed her eyes, because looking at him, seeing him this exhausted, this spent, was painful. He needed her support now, not her censure.

"All right," she murmured.

"I don't like this any better than you do." Jordan stood and wrapped her securely in his embrace, burying his face in the warm curve of her neck. "I'm a newlywed, remember. There's no one I want to spend time with more than my wife."

Jill nodded, because it would have been impossible to speak.

"I wish you hadn't waited up for me," he said, lifting her into his arms and carrying her into their bedroom. Without turning on the light, he settled her on the bed and lay down beside her, placing his head on her chest. Jill's fingers idly stroked his hair.

Words burned in her throat, the need to unburden herself, but she dared not. Jordan was exhausted. This wasn't the right time. Would it ever be the right time?

There had been so many lonely evenings, so many empty mornings. Every night Jill went to bed alone, and only when Jordan slipped in beside her did she feel alive. Only when they were together did she feel whole. And so she waited night after night for a few precious minutes, knowing they were all he had to spare.

The even sound of Jordan's breathing told her he'd fallen asleep already. The weight on her chest was growing uncomfortable, yet she continued to stroke his hair for several minutes, unwilling to disturb his rest.

She'd always known it would come to this; she just hadn't expected it to happen so soon. A week. He'd promised her it would be over within a week.

And it would be—until the next time.

JILL AWOKE EARLY the following morning, amazed to find Jordan asleep beside her. At some point during the night he'd rolled away from her and covered them both with a blanket. He hadn't bothered to undress.

Jill wriggled toward him and playfully kissed his ear. She knew she ought to let him sleep, but she also knew he'd be annoyed if he was late for the office.

Slowly he opened his eyes, looking surprised to find her there with him.

"Morning," she whispered, with a series of tiny, nibbling kisses.

"What time is it?" he asked.

"Somewhere around eight, I'd guess." She looped her arms around his neck and smiled down at him.

"Hmm. An indecent hour."

"Very indecent."

"My favorite time of day." His fingers were busy unfastening the opening of her pajama top and his eyes blazed with unmistakable need.

"Jordan," she said a bit breathlessly, "you'll be late for work."

A smile coaxed his mouth. "I fully intend to be," he said, directing her lips to his.

"IT'S HAPPENING ALREADY, isn't it?" Elaine Morrison said bluntly the following Saturday. She stood in Jill's living room, holding a china cup and saucer and staring out the window. The view of the Olympic Mountains was spectacular, the white peaks jutting against a backdrop of bright blue sky as fluffy clouds drifted past.

Jill knew precisely what her mother was saying. She responded the only way she could—truthfully. "Yes."

Elaine turned, her face pale, haunted with the pain of the past, the pain she saw reflected in her daughter's life. "I feared this would happen."

Until recently, Jill had found communicating with her mother difficult. After her husband's death, Elaine had withdrawn from life, hidden herself away in her grief and regrets. In many ways, Jill had lost her mother at the same time as she had her father.

"Mom, it's all right," Jill said in an attempt to reassure her. "It's only for the next little while. Once this project's under control everything will be different."

Jill knew better. She wasn't fooling herself, and she sincerely doubted she'd be able to fool her mother.

"I warned you," Elaine said, walking to the white leather sofa and sitting tensely on the edge. Placing the cup and saucer on a nearby table, she turned pleading eyes to Jill. "Didn't I tell you? The day of the wedding—I knew then."

"Yes, Mother, you warned me."

"Why didn't you listen?"

Jill exhaled slowly, praying for patience. "I'm in love with him, just like you loved Daddy."

It seemed unfair to drag her father into this, her much-grieved father, but it was the only way Jill knew to explain.

"What are you going to do about it?"

"Mother," Jill sighed. "It's not as though Jordan's having an affair."

"He might as well be," Elaine replied heatedly. "Here it is, Saturday afternoon and he's working. One look at him told me he had the same drive and ambition, the same need for power, as your father."

"Mother, please . . . It isn't like that with Jordan."

The older woman's eyes were infinitely sad as she gazed at her daughter. "Don't count on that, Jill. Just don't count on it."

HER MOTHER'S VISIT had unsettled Jill. Afterward, she tried to relax with a book, but found her concentration wandering. The phone rang at six, just as it had every night that week. Jordan's secretary or assistant had called to let her know Jordan wouldn't be home for dinner.

One ring.

Walking over to the phone, Jill stood directly in front of it, but she didn't lift the receiver.

Two rings.

Drawing in a deep breath, she flexed her fingers. Twice in the past couple of weeks, Jordan had phoned himself. Maybe he'd be on the other end of the line, inviting her to join him for dinner. Maybe he was phoning to tell her he'd unscrambled the entire mess and he'd be home within the next half hour. Perhaps he was calling to suggest they take a few days off and vacation somewhere exotic, just the two of them.

Three rings.

Jill could feel her pulse throbbing at the base of her throat. But still she didn't answer.

Four rings.

Five rings.

The phone went silent.

Her entire body was trembling when she turned away and walked toward the bedroom. She sat on the bed and covered her face with both hands.

The phone began to ring again, the sound reverberating loudly through the apartment. Jill slapped her hands over her ears, unable to bear it. Each ring tormented her, pretending to offer her hope when there was none. It wouldn't be Jordan, but his assistant, and his message would be the same one he'd relayed every night that week.

Making a rapid decision, Jill reached for her jacket and purse and hurried toward the penthouse elevator.

Not having anywhere in particular to go, she wandered downtown until she found a movie theater. The movie wasn't one that really interested her, but she bought a ticket, anyway, willing to subject herself to a B-grade comedy if it meant she could escape for a couple of hours.

Actually the movie turned out to be quite entertaining. The plot was ridiculous, but there were enough humorous moments to make her laugh. And if Jill had ever needed some comic relief, it was now.

On impulse she stopped at a deli and picked up a couple of sandwiches, then flagged down a taxi. Before she could change her mind, she gave the driver the address of Jordan's office.

She had a bit of trouble convincing the security guard to admit her, but eventually, after the guard talked to Jordan, she was allowed in the building.

"Jill," he snapped when she stepped off the elevator, "where have you been?"

"It's good to see you, too," she said, ignoring the irritation in his voice. She kissed his cheek, then walked casually past him.

"Where were you?"

"I went out to a movie," she said, strolling into his office. His desk, a large mahogany one, was littered with folders and papers. She noted dryly that he was alone. Everyone else had taken the weekend off, but he hadn't afforded himself the same luxury.

"You were at a movie?"

She didn't bother to answer. "I thought you might be hungry," she said, neatly stacking a pile of folders in order to clear one small corner of his desk. "I stopped in at Griffin's and bought us both something to eat."

"I ate earlier."

"Oh." So much for that brilliant idea. "Unfortunately, I didn't." She plopped herself down in the comfortable leather chair and pulled a turkey-on-rye from the sack, along with a cup of coffee, setting both on the small space she'd cleared.

Jordan looked as though he wasn't sure what to do with her. He leaned over the desk and shoved several files to one side.

"I'm not interrupting anything, am I?"

"Of course not," he answered dryly. "I was staying late for the fun of it."

"There certainly isn't any reason to hurry home," she returned just as dryly.

Jordan rubbed his eyes, and his shoulders slumped. "I'm sorry, Jill. These past couple of weeks have been hard on you, haven't they?"

He moved behind her and grasped her shoulders. His touch had always had a calming effect on Jill, and she wanted to fight it, wanted to fight her weakness for him.

"Jill," Jordan whispered. "Let's go home." He bent down then and kissed the side of her neck. A shiver raced down her body and Jill breathed deeply, placing her hands on his.

"Home," she repeated softly, as if it was the most beautiful word in the English language.

"JILL," SHELLY CRIED, her eyes widening when she opened the front door, one evening a few weeks later. "What's wrong?"

"Wrong," Jill repeated numbly.

"You look awful."

"How kind of you to point it out."

"I've got it," Shelly said excitedly, tapping her fingers against her lips, "you're pregnant, too."

"Unfortunately, no," she said, passing Shelly and walking into the kitchen. She took a clean mug from the dishwasher and poured herself a cup of coffee. "How are you feeling, by the way?"

"Rotten," Shelly admitted wryly, then added with a smile, "Wonderful."

Jill pulled out a kitchen chair and sat down. If she spent another evening alone, she was going to go crazy. She probably should have phoned Shelly first rather than dropping in unannounced, but driving over here gave her an excuse to leave the penthouse. This evening she badly needed an excuse. Anything to get away. Anything to escape the loneliness. Funny, she'd lived on her own for years, yet she'd never felt so empty, so alone, as she had in the past two months. Even the conversation with Andrew Howard earlier in the evening had only momentarily lifted her spirits.

"Where's Mark?"

Shelly grinned. "You won't believe it if I tell you."

"Tell me."

"He's taking a carpentry class."

"Carpentry? Mark?"

Shelly's grin broadened. "He wants to make a cradle for the baby. He's so sweet I can barely stand it. You know Mark, he's absolutely useless when it comes to anything practical. Give him a few numbers and he's a whiz kid, but when he has to change a light bulb, he needs an instruction manual. I love him dearly, but when he announced he was going to build a cradle for the baby, I couldn't help it, I laughed.''

"Shelly!''

"I know. It was a rotten thing to do, so Mark's out there proving how wrong I am. This is his first night, and I just hope to heaven the instructor doesn't kick him out of class.''

Despite her unhappiness, Jill smiled. It felt good to be around Shelly, to laugh again, to have reason to laugh.

"I haven't talked to you in ages,'' Shelly remarked, stirring her coffee. "But then I shouldn't expect to, should I? You and Jordan are still on your honeymoon, aren't you?''

Tears sprang instantly to Jill's eyes, blurring her vision. "Yes,'' she lied, looking away, praying that Shelly, who was so happy in her own marriage, wouldn't notice how miserable Jill was in hers.

"Oh, before I forget,'' Shelly said excitedly, "I heard from Aunt Milly.''

"What did she have to say?''

"She asked me to thank you for your letter, telling her about meeting Jordan and everything. She loves a good romance. Then she said something odd.''

"Oh?''

"She felt the dress was meant to be worn one more time.''

"Again? By who?''

Shelly leaned forward, cupping her mug with both hands. "I realize you and Jordan were too wrapped up

in each other on your wedding day to notice, but your mother and Mr. Howard got along famously. Milly wouldn't have known that, of course, but . . . it's obviously meant to be."

"My mother." Now that she recalled her conversation with Andrew at the wedding, it made sense. In the weeks since their return from Hawaii, she'd forgotten about it. He'd phoned Jill twice since the wedding, but he hadn't mentioned Elaine; nor had her mother mentioned him.

"What do you think?"

"My mother and Mr. Howard?" Jill felt an immense sense of rightness.

"Isn't that incredible?" Shelly positively beamed. "Wonderful?" Until recently—the arrival of the wedding dress, to be exact—Jill hadn't realized what a complete romantic her friend was.

"But Mom hasn't said a word."

"Did you expect her to?"

Jill shrugged. For a lot of reasons, Shelly was right. Elaine would approach romance and remarriage with extreme caution.

"Wouldn't it be fabulous if your mother ended up wearing the dress?"

Jill nodded and, placing her fingertips to her temple, closed her eyes. "A vision's coming to me now..."

Shelly laughed.

"I think we should call my mom and tell her that we both had a clear vision of her standing in the dress next to a distinguished-looking older man."

Once again, Shelly giggled. "Oh, that's good. That's really good." She sighed contentedly. "The dress definitely belongs with your mother, you know. We'll have to do something about that soon."

Jill pretended her tears were ones of mirth and dashed them away with the back of one hand.

But the amusement slowly faded from Shelly's eyes. "Are you going to tell me what's wrong, or are you going to make me torture it out of you?"

"I—I'm fine."

"No, you're not. Don't forget I know you. You've been my best friend for years. You wouldn't be here if something wasn't wrong."

"It's that crazy wedding dress again," Jill confessed.

"The wedding dress?"

"I should never have worn it."

"Jill!" Shelly exclaimed, then frowned. "You're not making any sense."

"It clouded my judgment. I was always the romantic one, remember? Always a sucker for a good love story. When Milly first mailed you the dress, I thought it was the neatest thing to happen since low-fat ice cream."

"Not true! Remember how you persuaded me—"

"I know what I said," Jill interrupted. "But deep down inside I could hardly wait to see what happened. When you and Mark decided to marry, I was thrilled. Later, after I arrived in Hawaii and you had the wedding dress delivered to me, I kind of allowed myself to play along with the fantasy—until I met

Jordan, that is. I've wanted to get married for a long time. I'd like to have several children."

"Jill," Shelly said, looking puzzled, "I'm not sure I follow you."

"I think I might have even felt a little bit . . . jealous that you got married before I did. I was the one who wanted a husband, not you, and yet here you were so deeply in love with Mark. Somehow it just didn't seem fair." The tears slipped down her cheek and she absently brushed them aside.

"But you're married now and Jordan's crazy about you."

"He was for about a week, but that's worn off."

"He loves you!"

"Yes, I suppose in his own way he does." Jill hadn't the strength to argue. "But not enough."

"Not enough?"

"It's too difficult to explain," she said, swallowing the tears that clogged her throat. "I came over to tell you I've made a decision." As hard as she tried, she couldn't keep herself from sobbing, "I've decided to leave Jordan."

CHAPTER TEN

SHELLY'S EYES NARROWED with disbelief. "You can't
possibly mean that!"

Leaving Jordan wasn't a decision Jill had made
lightly. She'd agonized over it for days. Unable to answer her friend, she pushed back her hair with hands
that refused to stop shaking. Her stomach was in
knots. "It just isn't going to work. I need some time
away from him to sort through my feelings. I don't
want to leave, but I'm afraid I'll just fall apart if I stay
any longer."

Shelly never had been one to disguise her feelings.
Anger flashed from her eyes like blue fire. "You
haven't even given the marriage a decent chance. It
hasn't even been two months."

"I know everything I need to know. Jordan isn't
married to me, he's married to his company. Shelly,
you're my best friend—but there are things you don't
know, things I can't explain about what's happening
between me and Jordan. Things that go back to my
childhood and being raised the way I was."

"You love him."

Jill closed her eyes and nodded. She did love Jordan, so much her heart was breaking, so much she

didn't know if she'd survive leaving him, so much she doubted she'd ever love this deeply again.

"I don't expect you to understand," Jill continued, choking over the words. "I wanted you to know...because I'm going to be living with my mother for a while. Just until I can sort through my feelings and make a decision."

"Have you told him yet?" Shelly's voice sounded less sharp.

"No." Jill had delayed that as long as possible, not knowing what to say or how to say it. This wasn't a game, or an attempt to manipulate Jordan into devoting more time to her and their marriage. She refused to fall into that trap. If she was going to make the break, she wanted it to be clean. Decisive. Not cluttered with threats.

"You *are* going to tell him?"

"Of course." She could never be so cowardly as to move out while Jordan was at the office. Besides, the sorry truth was that she might be gone for days before he noticed.

Confronting him wasn't a task she relished. She knew Jordan well and could predict his reaction—he'd be furious with her, more than she'd probably ever seen him. Jill was prepared for that. But in the end he would let her go as if she meant nothing to him. His pride would demand that.

"When do you plan to tell him?" Shelly asked softly, seeming to understand for the first time Jill's torment. A true sign of the strength of their friendship was that Shelly didn't ply her with questions, but accepted Jill's less-than-satisfactory explanation.

"Tonight." She hadn't packed her things yet, but she intended to do that when she got back home.

Home.

The word echoed in her mind. Although the penthouse was so distinctly marked with Jordan's personality, it did feel like home. She'd only lived there a short while, but in the long, lonely weeks following her honeymoon with Jordan, she'd become intimately acquainted with every room. She was going to miss the solace she gained from looking out over Puget Sound and the jagged peaks of the Olympics. And Mrs. Murphy had become a special friend, almost like a second mother, who fretted over her and worried about the long hours Jordan worked. Jill would miss her, too. Although Jill hadn't mentioned leaving to the cook, she guessed that Mrs. Murphy wouldn't be surprised.

"You're sure this is what you want?" Shelly asked regretfully.

Leaving Jordan, even for a short time, was the last thing Jill wanted. Yet it had to be done—and soon, before it was too late, before she found it impossible to go.

"Don't answer that," Shelly whispered. "The pain in your eyes says everything I need to know."

Jill stood and searched in her purse for a tissue. The tears were rolling freely down her cheeks now. She had to compose herself before she encountered Jordan.

Had to draw on every bit of inner strength she possessed.

Shelly hugged her, and once again Jill was grateful for their friendship. They were as close as sisters, and Jill had never needed family more than she did right then.

The penthouse echoed with an empty silence when she arrived home. Jill stood in the middle of the living room, then slowly moved around, skimming her hand over each piece of furniture. Her gaze gravitated toward the view, and she walked toward the window, staring into the night. Far below, lights flashed and glowed, but she was far removed from the brilliance. Far removed from the light...

Reluctantly, she entered the bedroom she shared with Jordan. Her breath came in shallow, pain-filled gasps as she dragged out her suitcases and set them on top of the bed. Carefully, she folded her clothes and one by one deposited them inside.

Several times she was forced to stop, clenching an article of clothing in her hands, crushing the fabric, until she composed herself enough to continue. Tears stung her eyes, but she refused to succumb to them. If ever there was a time she needed to be strong, it was now.

"Jill?"

Her hands froze. Her heart froze. She hadn't expected Jordan to come home for several hours yet. They'd barely seen one another all week, barely spoken.

"Where are you going?" he asked calmly.

Pulling herself together, Jill turned to face him. Jordan stood on the other side of the room, but he might as well have been half a world away. He held himself stiffly, his gaze perplexed.

"My mother's," she finally answered.

"Is she ill?"

"No..." Drawing a deep breath, hoping it would calm her frantic heart, she forged ahead. "I'm leaving for a while. I—I need to sort through my feelings...make some important decisions."

The fire that leapt into his eyes was filled with anger. "You plan to divorce me?" he demanded incredulously.

"No. For now, I'm just moving in with my mother."

"Why?"

Jill could feel her own anger mounting. "That you even have to ask should be answer enough! Can't you see what's happening? Don't you care? At this rate our marriage isn't going to last another month." She paused to gulp a much-needed breath. "My instincts told me this would happen, but I was so much in love with you that I chose to ignore what was obvious from the first. You don't need a wife. You never have. I don't understand why you wanted to marry me because—"

"When did all this come on?" he growled.

"It's been coming on, as you say, from the minute we got home from our honeymoon. Our marriage has to be one of the shortest on record. One week. That's all the time you allotted to it. I need more than five minutes at the end of the day when you're so exhausted you can hardly speak. I wish I were stronger, but I'm not. I need more from you than you can give me.''

''You might have said something to me earlier.''

''I did a hundred times.''

''When?'' he barked.

''I'm not going to get involved in a shouting match with you, Jordan. I refuse to sit by and watch you work yourself to death over some stupid project. You'd said ages ago that it'd be finished in a week. I was stupid enough to believe you. If it's so important to you that you're willing to risk everything to keep it from folding, then fine, it's all yours.''

''When did you tell me?'' he demanded a second time.

''Do you remember our conversation last night?'' she asked starkly.

Jordan frowned, then shook his head.

''I didn't think you had.''

The previous afternoon, Jill had been so terribly lonely that she'd reached for the phone, planning to call Ralph to invite him to a movie. She'd nearly dialed his number before she remembered she was married. The incident had had a profound effect upon her. She didn't *feel* married. She felt abandoned. Forgotten. Unimportant. If she was going to live her life alone, then fine, she could accept that. But she refused to be a pretty bird locked in a cage and brought out and stroked when it was convenient.

This time apart would help her gain perspective, show her what she needed to do. Explaining it to Jordan was impossible, though. But in time, a week perhaps, she might be able to tell him all that was in her heart.

"What was it you said last night?" Jordan wanted to know, clearly confused.

Jill neatly folded a silk blouse and put it inside the suitcase. "I told you how I almost called Ralph to ask him if he wanted to see a movie ... and you laughed. Remember? You found it humorous that your wife would forget she was a married woman. What you apparently didn't understand was what had led me to the point of wanting to call an old boyfriend."

"You're not making a damn bit of sense."

"No, I suppose not. I'm sorry, Jordan. I wish I could explain it better. But as I already told you, I need more from our relationship than you can give me..."

"I've explained that this project would be settled soon. I'll grant you it's taking longer than I'd thought, but if you'd just be patient for a little longer... Is that so much to ask? You'd think..." He hesitated, then jammed his hands in his pockets and marched to the other side of the room. "These past few weeks haven't been a picnic for me, either. You'd think a wife would be more willing to lend her husband support, instead of bullying him into doing what she wants with threats."

It didn't surprise Jill that Jordan assumed her leaving was merely a ploy. He didn't understand how serious she was.

"I can't live like this. I just can't!" she cried. "Not now, not ever. I want my children to know their father! My own was a shadow who passed through my life, and I couldn't bear my children to suffer what I did."

"This is a fine time for you to figure it all out," Jordan growled, his hold on his frustration and anger obviously precarious.

"If I could go back and change everything, I would...I would." Hurrying now, she closed her suitcases.

"Are you pregnant?" The question came at her like a bolt of lightning.

"No."

"You're sure?"

"Of course."

A moment of silence followed as she collected her purse and a sweater.

"Nothing I can say is going to change your mind, is it?"

"No." She reached for the handles of the two suitcases and dragged them both across the bed. "If...if there's any reason you need to get hold of me, I'll be at my mother's."

Jordan just stood there, his back toward her, his spine ramrod stiff. "If you're so set on leaving, then just go."

"JILL, SWEETHEART." Her mother knocked lightly, then walked into the darkening bedroom. Jill sat on the padded window seat, her knees tucked under her chin, staring out the bay window to the oak-lined street below. Often as a child she'd sat there and reflected on her problems. But now her problems couldn't be worked out by staring out her bedroom window or by pounding on a piano for an hour or two.

"How are you feeling?"

"Fine." She wasn't ready to talk yet.

"I've made dinner," Elaine told her, her voice gentle and sympathetic. There was a radiant glow about her these days. Andrew Howard had called almost daily since Jill had been living with her mother, although he knew nothing of her separation from Jordan. Jill had sworn her mother to secrecy. The last Jill heard, Andrew planned to fly to the mainland early the next month so that he and Elaine could spend some time together. Jill was delighted for her mother and for Andrew. Her own situation, though, was bleak.

"Thanks, Mom, but I'm not hungry."

Her mother didn't argue, but sat on the edge of the cushion and leaned forward to hug Jill. The unexpected display of affection moved Jill to tears.

"You haven't eaten anything to speak of all week."

"I'm fine, Mom." Jill didn't want her mother fussing over her just now, and she was grateful when her mother seemed to realize it. Elaine lovingly brushed the hair from Jill's face and got to her feet.

"If you need me..."

"I'm fine, Mom."

Her mother hesitated. "Are you going back to him, Jill?"

Jill didn't answer. Not because she didn't want to, but because she didn't know. She hadn't heard from Jordan at all in the week she'd been gone. A concerned Shelly had dropped by twice, unobtrusively leaving the wedding dress, in its original mailing box, on Jill's window seat. Even Ralph had called. But she hadn't heard from Jordan.

She shouldn't miss him this much. Shouldn't feel so empty without him, so lost. Jill had hoped this time apart would clear her thoughts. It hadn't. If anything they were more confused than ever. Her musings were like snagged fishing lines, impossible to untangle, frustrating her more by the hour.

She hadn't really expected him to get in touch with her, but deep down she'd hoped. Foolishly hoped. Although if he had, Jill didn't know how she would have reacted.

The doorbell chimed in the distance. A few moments later Jill heard her mother talking with another woman. The voice wasn't familiar and Jill pressed her forehead to her knees, suddenly weary. Part of her had wanted the visitor to be Jordan. Fool that she was, Jill prayed that he'd be willing to put aside his pride enough to come after her, to convince her they could make their marriage work. Her heart ached for the sight of him. Obviously, though, any move would have to come from her. But Jill wasn't ready. Not yet. Not when her heart was in such turmoil.

"Jill?" Her mother knocked lightly again on her bedroom door and opened it a crack. "There's someone here to see you. A Suzi Lundquist. She says it's important."

"Suzi Lundquist?" Jill repeated incredulously.

"She's waiting for you in the living room," her mother said.

Jill hadn't the slightest idea why Suzi would want to see her. Jordan had used her to ward off the younger woman's affections. Perhaps Suzi still loved Jordan and intended to rekindle the fire. But in that case, she wasn't likely to announce her plans to Jill.

Slipping into a fresh sweater, Jill came out of her room. Suzi was pacing the living room, smoking a long filtered cigarette. She smashed the butt in an ashtray when Jill appeared.

"I hope you're happy."

Jill blinked. "I beg your pardon?"

"He's done it, you know, and it's all because of you."

"Done what?"

"Given up the fight." Suzi was staring at her as though Jill was completely and utterly dense.

"I hate to seem ignorant, but I honestly don't know what you're talking about."

"You're married to Jordan, aren't you?"

"Yes." They stood several feet apart from one another, like duelists preparing to choose their weapons.

"Jordan's handed control of the firm to my father and brother," Suzi explained impatiently.

"Isn't this rather sudden? When did all this happen?" Surely if Jordan was in a proxy fight, he would have said something to her. Surely he would have let her know. She'd only been away for a week. Nothing could have threatened his hold on the company in that short a time, could it?

"This proxy battle's been going on for months," Suzi snapped. "It all started while you and Jordan were on your honeymoon. He couldn't have chosen a worse time to leave. He knew it, too—that's what was so confusing. By the time he returned from Hawaii, he had a full-fledged revolt on his hands. Dad used that time against Jordan, buying shares until he controlled as large a percentage of the company as Jordan did. He wanted Jordan out as CEO and my brother in."

"What happened?"

"After months of gathering supporters, of buying and selling stock, of doing everything humanly possible to forestall a proxy fight," Suzi continued, "Jordan up and handed everything over to my father, who'll hand it all to my brother on a silver platter. You met Dean, and we both know he doesn't have the leadership or the maturity to be a CEO. Within five years, he'll wipe out everything Jordan's spent his life building."

Jill didn't know what to say. Her immediate reaction was to argue with Suzi. Jordan would never willingly have surrendered control of his company. She didn't need the younger woman to tell her that Jordan had worked his entire adult life to build the company; he'd invested everything in it—everything.

Although it seemed a long time ago, she remembered that he'd told her about buying the controlling shares. He'd also said that he'd soon be forced to battle to remain in power. Jill remembered what she'd said to him. She'd told him she couldn't imagine him losing.

"Jordan's resigned?" she repeated, breathless with disbelief.

"This morning, effective immediately."

"But why?"

"You should know," Suzi said harshly, reaching for a second cigarette and lighting it. Snapping her gold lighter shut, she blew a stream of smoke at the ceiling. "Because he's in love with you."

"What has that got to do with anything?"

"Apparently he felt it was either you or the company. He chose you."

"He sent you here to tell me?" That didn't sound like something Jordan would do. He preferred to do his own talking.

Suzi gave a short, humorless laugh. "You've got to be joking. He'd have my hide if he knew I was anywhere within a mile of you."

"Then why are you here?"

Suzi took another drag of her cigarette. "Because I fancied myself in love with him not long ago. He was pretty decent about it. He could have used me to his own advantage if he'd wanted, but he didn't. Beneath that surly exterior is a real heart. You know it, too, otherwise you'd never have married him.''

''Yes . . .'' Jill agreed softly.

''He needs you. I don't know why you left him, but I figure that's between you and Jordan. He's not the type of man to be unfaithful, so I doubt there's another woman involved. If anything, he's too damn honorable. If you don't realize what you've got, you're a fool.''

Jill's emotions were playing havoc with her. Jordan had resigned! It was too much to take in. Too much to believe.

''Are you going to him?'' Suzi demanded.

Jill hesitated. ''I, uh . . .''

Suzi inhaled on her cigarette, then stabbed it out in the ashtray. ''If pride's stopping you, then I don't think you have much to worry about. Eventually Jordan will come to you. It may take a while, though, if you're determined to wait him out.''

''I'm going to him.'' Recovering somewhat, Jill looked to Suzi, struggling for the ability to speak. ''I can't thank you enough for coming. I owe you so much.''

''Don't thank me. I just hope to high heaven you appreciate what he's done,'' Suzi muttered as she picked up her purse, tucking it under her arm.

''I do,'' Jill assured her, leading the way to the front door. No sooner had Suzi left than Jill went looking for her mother.

She found her in the kitchen. "I heard," Elaine said before Jill could explain the purpose of the other woman's visit. "It might not last, you know."

"I'm going to him."

Her mother's eyes searched Jill's face before she nodded. "I knew that, too."

As they embraced briefly, Jill whispered, "There's a box in my room, Mom. Shelly brought it over for you—and for Andrew Howard."

The drive into downtown Seattle seemed to take forever. It was rush-hour and the only parking space she could find was a loading zone. Without a qualm, she took it, then hurried toward Jordan's office building. Luck was with her, for the building hadn't been locked yet, but she was waylaid by a security guard. Fortunately, he was the same man she'd met earlier, and he permitted her to stay.

"Has Mr. Wilcox left yet?" she asked.

"Not yet."

"Thank you," she said, sighing with relief.

She hurried to the elevator. Jordan's office was on the top floor. When the elevator doors opened, she ran down the wide corridor to the outer office where his assistants and his secretary worked. The double doors leading into Jordan's massive office were open. He was packing the things from his desk into a cardboard box.

Jill froze. She stared at Jordan for a long moment, unable to move or speak. He looked haggard, as though he hadn't slept in the week she'd been gone.

Dark stubble shadowed his face, and his hair, ordinarily neat and trim, looked rumpled.

He must have sensed her presence because he paused in his task, his eyes slowly meeting hers. His hands went still. The whole world seemed to come to a sudden halt. In that unguarded moment she read his pain and it became hers.

"You can't do it!" she cried, choking on a sob. "You just can't."

Jordan's face hardened and he seemed to clamp down on his emotions. He ignored her and continued packing away the objects from his desk. A smile, one that spoke more of sadness than of joy, came into his eyes. "Your husband is unemployed as of five o'clock this afternoon."

"Oh, Jordan, why would you do such a thing? For me? Because I left you? But you never told me... Not once did you explain, even when I pleaded with you. Didn't you trust me enough to tell me what was happening?" That was what hurt most of all, that Jordan had kept everything to himself. Not sharing his burden, carrying it alone.

"It was a mistake not to tell you," he admitted, the regret written clearly across his face. "I realized that the night you left. By nature, I tend to keep my troubles to myself."

"But I'm your wife."

He grinned at that, but again his smile was marked with sadness. "I'm new to this marriage business. Obviously I'm not much good at it. The one thing I was hoping to do was keep my business life separate from my personal life. I didn't want to bring my company problems home to you."

"But, Jordan, if I'd known, if you'd explained, I might have been able to help."

"You did, in more ways than you know."

Tears blurred Jill's eyes. She would have given everything she owned for Jordan to take her in his arms, but he stood so far away, so alone.

Jordan picked up a small photograph, one of their wedding day. He stared at it for several moments, then tucked it into the box. "I loved you almost from the moment we met. Don't ask me to explain it, because I can't. After that first night, when we kissed on the beach, I knew my life would never be the same."

"Oh, Jordan."

"Being with you was like standing in the sun. I never knew how lonely I was, how my heart ached for love, how much I longed to share my life with someone..."

Tears ran unashamedly down Jill's face.

"The day we were married," he went on, "I swear I've never seen a more beautiful bride. I couldn't believe you'd actually agreed to be my wife. I swore then and there I'd never do anything to risk what I'd found."

"But to resign..." Trembling a little, nervous and unsure, Jill moved across the room to Jordan's side. He tensed at her approach, his expression a blend of undisguised longing and hope.

"I can't lose you."

"But to walk away from your life's work?" What he'd done remained incomprehensible to Jill.

"I have a new life," he said, gently pulling her into his arms. He buried his face in her hair and inhaled deeply. "None of this means anything without you. Not anymore."

"But what are you going to do?"

"I thought we'd take a year off and travel. Would you like that?"

Jill nodded through her tears.

"And after that, I'd like to start our family."

Once again Jill nodded, her heart pounding with love and excitement.

"Then, when the time's right, I'll find something that interests me and start again, but I'll never allow work to control my life. I can't," he said quietly. "You're my life now."

"You're sure this is what you want?" He'd given up so much.

She felt him smile against her hair. "Without a doubt. I don't need a business to fill up the emptiness in my life. Not when I have you."

"Oh, Jordan," she whispered, her throat tight. "I love you so much." She squeezed her eyes closed and murmured a prayer of thanksgiving for the wonderful man she'd married.

"Shall we go home, my love?" he asked her.

Jill nodded and slipped her hand into his. "Home," she repeated softly. With her husband. The man she loved. The man she'd married.

LOVE FOR HIRE
by Jasmine Cresswell

CHAPTER ONE

JULIE GRIPPED the office phone so tightly that her fingers ached, but by some miracle of self-control she managed to inject a note of happiness into her voice.

"That's wonderful news, Mother." The lie didn't come easily and she hurried on, afraid the silence might somehow betray her. "I never imagined John would marry again so soon—and to my little sister! When's the wedd—" The word stuck obstinately in her throat and she swallowed hard. "Have Alice and John set a date for the wedding?"

"A week Saturday." Mrs. Marshall's reply bubbled over the long-distance wires between Chipping Hill and Chelsea. Even the faint crackle of interference couldn't hide her good cheer. "There's really no reason for them to wait. Poor little Vickie needs a new mother as soon as possible after all she's been through, and Alice would like to move into John's house without stirring up a lot of gossip. We all agreed the sooner they tie the knot the better." She chuckled. "Now your father's medical practice is really going to be all in the family."

And I'll be more of an outsider than ever. Julie shook off the self-pitying thought. She was twenty-four years old, which meant that it was way past time to stop berating herself because she didn't share the rest of her family's talent for healing the sick. "Alice plans to carry on with her nursing, then?'' she asked with careful politeness.

''At least for a while, but she and John are hoping to have a baby quite soon. Vickie would like a brother or sister, and you know how wonderful Alice is with children. I expect they'll eventually have a big family.''

Pain sliced through Julie with renewed sharpness. ''Alice has lots of patience. She'll be a terrific mother.'' Somehow Julie produced the appropriate phrases, although her lungs felt as if they were being squeezed by a pair of steel hands. She had believed she was cured of her teenage infatuation for John Farringdon. Too late, she realized that she had never entirely excised him from her heart.

Julie drew a deep breath, forcing herself to confront the fact that her sister would soon marry the only man Julie had ever loved. A week from Saturday, Alice would become Mrs. John Farringdon.

''That's just eight days from now!'' Julie whispered, not realizing she had spoken aloud until her mother answered.

''Well, we're planning a quiet wedding, you know.'' For the first time, Mrs. Marshall sounded a touch defensive. ''They can't have the traditional church service, of course, because of John's divorce. Although how anybody could blame him for legally ending the marriage after the way his wife ran off and left him, and not for the first time, either—''

''But the vicar is willing to bless their marriage?'' Julie asked hastily. She didn't want to discuss the past misdeeds of John's former wife. That brought back far too many humiliating memories of Julie's own folly.

"Yes, thank goodness. So we're planning a simple church service and some champagne for the family right after the ceremony. In the circumstances, your father thought anything more elaborate might not be in the best of taste."

Since John's divorce from his first wife had been finalized a scant three weeks ago, some people would probably find even the quietest of weddings a bit scandalous, but Julie didn't point this out. When she was with her family, she spent a great deal of time not saying what she was actually thinking. Her parents and sister were all good, kind people. It was worrying to consider how rarely she found herself in harmony with them.

But this wasn't the moment to attempt to mend a relationship that had been strained for years. This was the moment for making sure neither her parents nor her sister ever learned the truth about her feelings for John. And especially the moment to make sure they never found out the real reason she had left home in such a hurry three years ago.

"I'll take the usual train, so I'll be home by lunchtime on Friday," she said. "I'll bring one of my raspberry tortes."

"Wonderful. That's your father's favorite. And of course we're counting on you for the wedding cake, dear. We thought four tiers would be about right, although five would look rather splendid if you could manage that many."

Unexpectedly, Julie actually felt herself smile. Cooking and catering had never been her mother's forte. "Mother, four tiers would provide enough wedding cake for a hundred and fifty guests!"

"Well, dear, it's always a good idea to be prepared, isn't it?"

Mrs. Marshall sounded suspiciously vague, and Julie recognized the warning signs at once. "Mother, just how many people are you planning to invite to this small, quiet wedding?"

"There's no need to sound so aggressive, Julie. I've warned you a dozen times about how unfeminine you sound when you take that antagonistic attitude. I'm doing my best to keep this wedding simple, but John has such an enormous family. Three brothers and seven aunts and uncles before we start counting the cousins and nieces and nephews. And then there are Alice's friends from nursing school, and your father's colleagues from the hospital, and my ladies from the church—"

"Mother, please give me a straightforward answer! How many people are coming to this wedding?"

"Not many more than a hundred," Mrs. Marshall said quickly. "Four tiers will be quite big enough for the cake, Julie dearest, and you needn't worry about the rest of the food. I've hired some excellent local caterers and we've decided to have a buffet. We'll have a marquee in the garden, so we'll be snug and dry even if it rains."

Mrs. Marshall was well and truly launched into the wedding plans, which seemed extraordinarily far advanced for a marriage that had been decided on only yesterday. Julie leaned back against the wall of her tiny office, murmuring occasionally to indicate she was listening to her mother's rapturous description of Alice's ivory satin wedding gown, the gladioli chosen from the garden to decorate the altar, and the pale blue organdy selected for five-year-old Vickie's dress.

The familiar smell of bread coming out of the ovens tickled Julie's nose, and over the clatter of baking trays she heard the ping of the cash register. She glanced at her watch. Four o'clock. Late afternoon was always a busy time of day in the shop, which meant—thank heaven—that she had a valid reason to cut short her mother's call. There was a limit to how long she could pretend enthusiasm. *Face up to the truth,* she told herself grimly. *You've been hoping John would come and see you ever since you heard about his divorce.*

Gritting her teeth, Julie took a firmer grip on her self-control. "Mother, I'm sure Vickie will look as pretty as a picture. But I really have to go now. I can see half a dozen people in the shop, and one of my bakers is away with a cold. I need to go and help out with the serving—"

"Honestly, Julie, that bakery is an absolute obsession with you! I don't believe you've heard a word I said in the last few minutes. I asked if you're bringing Robert Donahue to the wedding. He *is* your fiancé, for heaven's sake, and since you've been dating him for over a year now, your father and I think it's about time for us to meet him. Alice is dying to meet him, too. And John, of course."

Robert Donahue. They wanted to meet Robert! If Julie's heart hadn't already been beating in double time, the mention of Robert's name would surely have sent it rocketing into overdrive. She fought back a sudden gasp of hysterical laughter.

"Oh, I don't think Robert could possibly make it on such short notice," she said hurriedly, the familiar excuse sounding thin even to her own ears. "You know what these American business tycoons are like—"

"No, we've no idea," her mother said with unusual acidity. "We keep hoping we'll find out, but every time we suggest a meeting with Robert you come up with a different excuse."

"He's very busy."

"Ha! I know that! He was in New York for your father's fiftieth birthday. He flew to Australia at Christmas, and he took you with him to Paris at Easter. Then last month when we all came to London he was tied up with a cabinet minister the whole weekend. Honestly, Julie, we were delighted when you finally started dating somebody so glamorous after all those years of living like a nun-in-training, but we're beginning to think you must be ashamed of us. And you never come home anymore. I think dating Robert has made you bored by what goes on in an ordinary, middle-class family."

"Mother! That's not the way it is! Not at all!"

Mrs. Marshall swept on, totally ignoring Julie's interruption. Her anger and hurt had obviously been building for several months and were now exploding. "Your father may not be a millionaire, but he's a good man and a wonderful doctor. I only hope your rich and important tycoon is half as kind and caring. If he is, he'll *want* to come with you next week to your sister's wedding, and he'll rearrange his schedule so that he can. After all, Alice is the only sister you have, and John is one of your oldest and dearest friends, as well as your father's partner. It's not as if we have a family wedding every month." A tremor of tears entered Mrs. Marshall's voice. "And you have nothing to be ashamed of, Julie, nothing at all. Just because this wedding's going to strain our budget doesn't mean we're planning to cut corners—"

"Mother, honestly, you've totally misunderstood!" Julie finally managed to get a word in edgewise, horrified at the wrong interpretation her family had put on her repeated excuses for the nonappearance of Robert Donahue. In other circumstances, their misconceptions might almost have been funny.

"Robert would love to meet you," she said hastily. "He's commented a dozen times on how much he would like to spend some time with you, and I'm more than anxious for us all to get together. But you know how hectic Robert's schedule has been. And then with my long hours at the bakery... Well, so far things just haven't worked out."

"Then make sure they work out for your sister's wedding." Mrs. Marshall's voice remained acerbic, tearful—and ominously final. "Alice will call you tonight when she finishes work, and your father and I will look forward to seeing you next Friday. With the wedding cake *and* Robert."

"Yes, Mother. Robert will do his best to come, I'm sure, but I can't promise anything—"

"Tell him not to invent a convenient case of the flu, because we won't believe it."

The hum on the wires told Julie that the call had been disconnected. Not quite sure whether to give way to floods of tears or gales of horrified laughter, she sat paralyzed at her desk. Sometimes she wondered if that wasn't the story of her life: not knowing which course of action to choose, so ending up choosing neither.

With a sigh, she reached up to make sure her fly-away blond hair was still in its chignon. Everything felt smooth and neat. Outside it seemed that she was still in one piece, but inside, she felt shredded. She hung up the phone, rose to her feet and left the office. When her emotions got out of hand, she had learned to take refuge in her work. Baking provided a multitude of comforts.

Even in this moment of crisis, she felt a spurt of pride and pleasure as she entered the front of the store and glanced around the bakery. As always The Crusty Corner was pleasantly crowded with customers waiting their turn to purchase gourmet fresh-fruit pastries, or the light, crisp-crusted breads for which the shop had become locally famous. Pam, one of her assistants, said goodbye to a customer, then greeted Julie with a smile of relief.

"Phew, thank goodness you're here! On Friday afternoons I sometimes wonder if the whole population of Chelsea stops to buy something at this shop."

"If you knew how much money I still owe on those fancy ovens we have in the back, you'd be hoping they did! Anyway, I'll take over at the cash register so Laura can help you behind the counter."

For the next half hour, Julie had time only for her customers, but as six o'clock approached, the crowd unexpectedly thinned.

"Just as well," Pam remarked. "We don't have a single cottage loaf left. Got any raspberry cream tartlets in your display case, Laura? I'm feeling peckish."

The other assistant searched along the nearly empty shelves. "We're down to our last one," she said.

"And that one's sold!" interjected a cheerful American voice. "Sorry, ladies, but it's only the thought of a raspberry cream tart that's kept me going for the past three miles."

"Why, hello, Mr. Baxter!" Pam, a happily married mother of two children, blushed like a schoolgirl as she met the newcomer's eyes. Tall, dark and spectacularly built, he was the sort of man likely to cause a flutter in the heart of any woman still actively breathing.

"We wondered if you'd be in today," Pam continued. "Been jogging again? You'll wear out the pavement!"

Laura gave up all pretense of rearranging the bread and stared with unabashed appreciation at the sweat-dampened T-shirt clinging to Mr. Baxter's enticing set of pectorals. "It's hot for running today," she said.

He grinned ruefully. "It sure is. Humid, too. And if I don't dredge up some willpower and stop coming in here for cream puffs, I'll have to start pounding out an extra mile every day. I can't go on much longer pretending all my trousers shrank at the dry cleaners!"

Pam laughed as she handed over the raspberry tartlet. "You don't look as if you've gained any weight, Mr. Baxter. All I can see is muscle."

He sucked in his nonexistent stomach and puffed out his chest with exaggerated pleasure as he tossed the two assistants a wink. "You've inspired me with new hope," he said in a loud stage whisper. "I'm going to approach the Ice Maiden at the cash register and ask her for a date. I dreamed about her again last night and in the dream she smiled at me. What do you think? Is it an omen? Is it going to be my twentieth time lucky?"

"Who knows? Nothing ventured, nothing gained," Laura replied with a little giggle. The Crusty Corner was at the end of Mr. Baxter's jogging route, and he had been coming into the shop three or four times a week for almost two months. For the past couple of weeks, he had routinely asked Julie for a date each time he saw her. Equally routinely, she had turned him down, just as she turned down most opportunities to date. After her experience with John Farringdon, Julie had decided that life was much simpler without men.

Mr. Baxter's original suggestion that Julie might like to join him at the theater had probably been intended seriously, but ever since her initial turndown, his invitations had become more extravagant with each passing day. Julie, entering into the spirit of the game, had become equally extravagant in her refusals. Recently she had found herself waiting for him to come into the shop and looking forward to their silly exchanges. She missed their few minutes of banter on the days he didn't jog.

Today, however, she was much too tense to enjoy the prospect of playing games. She didn't know what to worry about first: John Farringdon's approaching marriage to her sister or the fact that her mother wanted Robert Donahue to attend the wedding. Why in the world had she given her "fiancé" that particular name? And why, for heaven's sake, had she chosen to make him American? She could always announce that she'd broken off her engagement, of course, except that the news might ruin her mother's enjoyment of Alice's wedding day.

Absorbed in her personal dilemma, Julie watched with less than half her attention as Mr. Baxter rummaged in the pocket of his tracksuit and pulled out a pound note with a triumphant flourish. Her assistants were right, she reflected absently. He was an exceptionally good-looking man—a powerful-looking man. Her stomach lurched, giving an odd little leap of excitement before she smothered the feeling with an impatient shrug. Good grief, she had better things to worry about today than Mr. Baxter and his aura of power.

Twirling an imaginary mustache, Mr. Baxter handed his pound note to Julie to pay for his tartlet. Almost before her eyes he was transformed into a caricature of every wicked vaudeville seducer who had ever stomped the boards.

"Miss Julie, ma'am, I'd be exceedingly honored if you'd agree to fly with me to the Casbah some time this weekend. I could arrange my private jet to take off at your convenience. The champagne and caviar are already on ice, and you may rest assured your honor would be safe with me."

Cupping his mouth with his hand, he turned in a faked aside to his appreciative audience of Pam and Laura. "Little does the poor innocent know that I plan to ply her with hard liquor and work my wicked seductive wiles on her the moment the plane is in the air."

The two shop assistants chuckled. Although they had told Julie on numerous occasions that she was insane to miss out on a date with such an attractive man, they had given up trying to change her mind and now simply enjoyed the lighthearted repartee. They raised expectant faces toward Julie, looking forward to hearing her latest turndown.

Julie returned their gaze, although she scarcely saw either of them. In truth, she had barely heard Mr. Baxter's invitation over the sudden roaring in her ears. She certainly had no witty rejection quivering on the tip of her tongue. A dozen conflicting thoughts tumbled about in her head. None of them seemed to make much sense, least of all the insistent drumbeat that kept pounding out the message. *Mr. Baxter is an American.* In her shop, right under her nose, she had somebody asking her for a date. And he was an American.

Julie felt her eyes grow huge. She fixed her gaze on the man, absorbing—really absorbing—the details of his appearance for the first time. Tall, at least six feet. Body along the lines of a slimmed-down Arnold Schwarzenegger. Very dark hair and a tanned complexion. But blue eyes, she noticed with a little quiver of excitement, and straight white teeth. He also had a nice smile, friendly and sexy at the same time, as Pam and Laura had often pointed out. Her assistants seemed to consider him God's most exciting gift to the women of the world. Would he make an equally good impression on her mother?

Julie hurriedly closed the door on that crazy thought. Mr. Baxter was pleasant and friendly, but there was no reason he would agree to help her. Besides, she had no idea what he did for a living. He might not be able to conduct a halfway intelligent conversation, let alone a conversation about international finance. And that would be essential for the mythical Robert Donahue. She was insane even to be thinking along these lines. Just because she'd sensed a hint of disciplined power lurking behind the easygoing manners, that didn't mean Mr. Baxter could play the role of a millionaire international financier. Even if he wanted to.

Julie stared at Mr. Baxter, totally tongue-tied, afraid to open her mouth in case some of the wild ideas whirling around in her mind spilled out into words.

Mr. Baxter didn't need to be very perceptive to see that her reaction to his invitation wasn't following the usual pattern. He looked at her for no more than a moment, his expression faintly quizzical, but Julie had the oddest sensation that he was seeing a great deal more of her turmoil than she would have wished.

Acutely aware of their interested audience, she was relieved when he chose to remain in the character of a vaudeville seducer. Clasping his hand to his chest, he said teasingly, "Don't keep me in suspense, Miss Julie. This unexpected hesitation has raised my hopes. Does it mean—could it mean—that your stony heart has melted at last?"

If only he knew! Far from being stony, at this moment her heart was giving an excellent imitation of an active volcano. *I could pay him,* she thought wildly. *We could make it a business arrangement. Five hundred pounds for the weekend.* Drawing in a deep breath, she opened her mouth, then snapped it shut. Good grief, she was insane even to think such a thing! Her mother's phone call had unhinged her reason.

Mr. Baxter came a little closer to the cash register. "My plane's very comfortable," he said softly. "And I've heard great things about the Casbah. Or we could go to dinner right here in London if you're too busy to fly to Morocco."

Julie finally regained the use of her tongue. "Your name's Robert, isn't it?" she asked, then felt a hot blush of embarrassment rush into her cheeks. For heaven's sake, that was exactly the kind of remark she'd been trying not to make!

Mr. Baxter made no comment on the oddness of her question. "Yes," he said. "Is that good or bad?"

"I...don't know. I, um, think maybe it's good."

On the edge of her vision she saw Pam and Laura exchange astonished glances. As well they might, she thought wryly. They had no way of knowing how badly she needed a Robert by next weekend.

Sanity struck before she could wade any deeper into the quagmire opening in front of her. She needed Robert *Donahue* next weekend, not just any old Robert who came along. Stress was undoubtedly causing a dangerous softening of her brain. Better to send Mr. Baxter on his way before she did something she would surely live to regret.

"I'm sorry," she said, avoiding his inquiring gaze. "I appreciate the invitation, but I'm really busy this weekend." Over the sound of Pam's and Laura's sighs, she scooped up some change and handed it to him. "Here you are, Mr. Baxter. I hope we'll see you again next week. I'm working on a new recipe for blackberry and fresh-cream layer cake."

"Sounds sinfully tempting. I might as well resign myself to running four miles instead of three, starting tomorrow." He took the change and dropped it carefully into a pocket. "Would you like to come and have a drink while we discuss the possibility of flying away to the Casbah the weekend after next? Or anything else you might want to talk about?" His voice suddenly sober, he added, "I've been told I'm a great listener."

Julie felt a fatal hesitation. Would there be any harm in just asking him if he'd like to go to a wedding? He was American, his name was Robert and he had dark hair. Surely when the fates sent such obvious signs, a person would be foolish not to pay attention. Julie clasped her hands tightly in her lap, trying to conceal their sudden shaking. He even had the requisite blue eyes. She'd always been super careful to avoid any precise descriptions of Robert Donahue, but on one harassing occasion she'd slipped up and told her parents that he had dark hair and blue eyes. Julie sneaked another quick, silent glance at the man in front of her. To sum up her situation in a nutshell, Robert Baxter was about as close to a gift from the gods as she was likely to get in this lifetime.

She stood, shutting the drawer of the cash register with a decisive snap. "Robert and I are going for a drink," she said to her goggle-eyed assistants. "Pam, you have the keys. Could you lock up, please?"

With a visible start, Pam pulled herself together. "Don't worry, Julie. We'll take care of everything. You two have fun."

Robert Baxter touched his hand to Julie's elbow and a curious spark of electricity shot through her arm. He turned and looked down at her, his normally laughing expression tinged with a hint of seriousness.

"I don't think Julie knows how to have fun," he said, his voice soft. "But I'll try to teach her."

Silence enveloped the bakery for a moment. Then, with a return of his familiar grin, Robert put the raspberry tart he'd bought onto the counter. "A present for you, ladies. Now that Julie's agreed to come out with me, I no longer need to drown my frustration in calories. Enjoy your snack!''

Pam's and Laura's laughing words of thanks followed Julie out of the bakery. ''Since I'm wearing a tracksuit, we don't have too many choices,'' Robert said. ''We could go back to my apartment, which is just around the corner from here. Or we could go to Chez Tibi. That's nearby, and they serve decent wine and great cheese fondue.''

''Chez Tibi sounds fine,'' Julie said.

He smiled ruefully as they began walking toward the restaurant. ''I was afraid you'd say that.''

Julie felt a twinge of guilt, even though she suspected somebody as personable as Robert Baxter rarely had difficulty finding dates. ''Robert, perhaps I shouldn't have come out with you,'' she said. ''The truth is, I've accepted your invitation under false pretenses.''

''You're married.'' The flat statement was tinged with cynicism.

''No, of course not! How could you possibly think such a thing?''

''Quite easily, believe me.''

Julie couldn't pretend shock at his words. She had encountered that attitude many times before. In any case, she was in no position to cast moral stones. If her own sense of right and wrong hadn't been so shaky three years ago, she wouldn't be in such a painfully silly situation today. Obviously the sooner she told Robert what she wanted, the better it would be for both of them. What she needed was to get their relationship onto the proper business footing as quickly as possible. Grasping her courage in both hands, she spoke before too many doubts could crowd in and silence her.

"The fact is, Robert, I have a problem I hoped you could help me with.... I have a proposition to put to you, a business proposition. That's the only reason I agreed to come out with you this evening."

"A business proposition?"

"Yes."

For a moment she sensed a rigidity in him, a resistance. Then he looked at her again, his eyes revealing nothing more than mild curiosity, and she wondered if she had been mistaken.

"I'm always interested in a good proposition," he said. "Let's hear yours."

CHAPTER TWO

CHEZ TIBI WAS already crowded with people celebrating the arrival of the weekend, but the manager recognized Robert, and a corner booth was soon cleared for them.

Robert took his seat on the padded bench a polite few inches away from Julie. She was grateful for his consideration, reassured that he didn't seem compelled to push for intimacy. Unfortunately she wasn't sure that she wanted him to be too sensible and considerate. A sensible man was likely to run screaming from the booth when she told him her scheme. Julie began to reconsider, relieved that she hadn't yet gone into the embarrassing details.

Robert leaned back against the seat and smiled at the restaurant manager. "Thanks, Dave, I owe you one. What'll you have to drink, Julie?"

"White wine, please. Chablis, if they have it by the glass."

"Bring us a bottle of the St. Cyr, Dave, and a pot of your famous cheese fondue when you have a moment. We're not in any rush." He looked at Julie across the table as the manager left. "Are we?"

"I don't want to keep you if you have plans...."

"Nothing that can't wait. Have you tasted Tibi's fondue? It's excellent. Not quite in the same class as your cream puffs, but getting there."

"No, I've never been here before. I don't eat out very often." Julie twisted her fingers nervously together.

"You don't like other people's cooking?"

"If it's good, I love it. But I don't have much free time. The bakery keeps me busy. I purchase my own supplies, including fruit from the market in summer. And creating successful new recipes takes many more hours than you'd imagine. How about you, Robert? Do you enjoy eating out? How have you found the London restaurants?"

"Expensive," he said with a return of his familiar grin. "Very expensive."

It was the opening she needed. "I've heard that most things in London are expensive for Americans," she said. "What line of work are you in?"

"I'm over here to make a movie for Titan Studios. They're on a tight budget, but despite that, the pay isn't bad."

"How exciting! What do you do?"

He smiled wryly. "Actually, I'm one of their actors."

"An actor!" Her mind raced. How perfect! No wonder he had always made Laura and Pam laugh as he hammed his way through those crazy invitations. Even today, when her mind had been almost entirely on other matters, she had noticed how effectively he transformed himself from plain Robert Baxter into the mustache-twirling villain of melodrama. The fates could hardly have sent her a clearer message. She needed an American millionaire financier by Friday, and she was sitting opposite one of the few men in England who could portray that role with conviction.

Robert's voice broke into her reverie. "Is there something about actors in general that stuns you into silence, or is it me in particular?"

She blinked, then realized she was staring at him with her mouth hanging open. She snapped her lips together and swallowed hard. "Oh, no, I was just surprised. And interested." Heaven knew, *that* was the truth. "I've never met an actor before. Is this your first film?"

"Not exactly."

A horrible thought occurred to Julie. "Oh, Lord! Are you a world-famous film star and I didn't recognize you? I'm sorry. I don't go to the cinema very often."

He looked hurt. "You don't? You mean you've never heard of Sylvester Stallone. I thought everyone had heard of Sylvester Stallone."

Julie paled. "You mean *you're* . . . No, you couldn't be . . ." she gulped. "You're surely not Sylvester Stallone?"

His blue eyes danced with amusement. "No, I'm not. I just asked if you'd ever heard of him."

She grimaced with mock indignation and Robert's mouth curved into a smile. She sensed some indefinable relaxation in his manner as he stretched across the table and lightly touched her hand.

"You're safe, Julie. Even a movie buff wouldn't recognize me. I'm not a famous actor. I'm not even a nearly famous actor. I did some TV commercials when I was in college, but the ad agency decided the dog acted so much better than I did they dispensed with my services. I was crushed, I can tell you, but I nursed my shattered ego back to health and managed to survive. I've worked for a film-production company ever since, but this is the first time any casting director's been kind enough to put me in front of the camera since Fido upstaged me fifteen years ago.''

''But still, you're a trained, professional actor!''

''You sound ecstatic. Are you sure actors don't have some special significance in your life?''

Julie looked down at Robert's hand, which rested casually on the table alongside her own. An odd shiver of anticipation rippled through her and she realized that her mind was made up. Robert might have been upstaged by a dog when he was in college, but if he was a good-enough actor for an American movie company to ship him all the way to London, he must be good enough to play the role of an international financier for a group of uncritical, unsuspicious wedding guests. She only needed him for one weekend. Once Alice and John were married... Her mind skittered at that thought, but she brought it firmly back on track. Once Alice and John were married, she'd call her mother and announce that the great romance had ended. She would say that Robert Donahue's work and travel schedule made their relationship impossible. The whole horrible mess she'd gradually talked herself into would be over.

The restaurant manager returned and placed a bubbling pot of fondue in front of them, together with a basket of bread and a set of special, long-handled serving forks. With swift expertise, he opened the wine and poured a little for Robert to taste.

The interruption gave Julie's common sense plenty of time to return to active duty, so she should have been glad of the brief respite. Instead, she found herself wishing that the waiter would hurry up and leave.

When they were alone, Robert raised his wineglass in a toast. "Here's to a great Friday night," he said. "And to your proposition. Are you going to tell me why you finally accepted one of my invitations?"

Julie took a sip of her wine, then another. If her stomach hadn't been trying to do back flips, she thought the wine might have tasted good. She drew a fortifying lungful of air. "I want you to come with me to my sister's wedding next weekend." There, she'd said it, and it hadn't been so difficult.

Robert's face expressed comical disappointment. "Good grief, where I come from that's not a proposition. It's scarcely even a date. Asking a man to a family wedding is one notch down from asking him to escort you to the church social."

She laughed, although she wouldn't have thought anything connected with Alice and John's wedding could inspire laughter. "Where do you come from, Robert?"

"New York. Right in the center of Manhattan. My parents and most of my cousins still live there, although my brother's moved out west to Colorado, and my thirty-year-old 'baby' sister has defected with her new husband to Boston."

"I'll pay you to come with me to the wedding," she blurted out. "Five hundred pounds from Friday morning until Sunday lunch."

He looked at her for a long moment. "Five hundred pounds is a lot of money," he said eventually. "Almost a thousand dollars. I'd have come for free."

Julie quelled a momentary flare of hope. "You haven't heard the whole story, Robert. The thing is, I don't want you to come as yourself. I want you to play a part."

"A part? As in acting a role?"

She nodded. "I want you to pretend to be my fiancé." As soon as the words were out, she buried her nose in her glass and gulped down the remainder of the wine. It helped to blur the sharp edge of her embarrassment just a little.

His face expressionless, Robert poured her more wine. Then he wedged a piece of bread onto one of the forks, dipped it into the fondue and handed the result to Julie. He repeated the procedure for himself before speaking.

"What's the real problem, Julie?" he asked. "You're young and single. You have a great body, a beautiful face, and so far I've seen no signs that you turn into a vampire when the sun goes down. All of which being the case, why in the world do you need to *pay* a virtual stranger five hundred pounds to escort you to your sister's wedding? If it's important to have an escort—even a fake fiancé—you must have half a dozen friends you can call on."

"I want an American," she said, glad that she didn't need to reveal how pitifully short of male acquaintances she really was.

"And you don't know any Americans apart from me?"

She shook her head. "A few Americans come into the bakery, but they're nearly always women."

He sighed. "All right, I'll buy into this ridiculous conversation. Why specifically do you need an American fiancé?"

"Because I told a tiny little lie one day when I was desperate, and the lie's been snowballing ever since."

Interestingly enough, he didn't immediately ask about the lie. "What were you desperate about?" he said.

"Placating my family. Stopping them from worrying about me." She grimaced. "No, that isn't entirely true. I wanted them to leave me alone to lead my own life. I was tired of justifying why I wanted to stay in London."

"So you lied."

She nodded. "It was this time last year, and I'd had a wonderful offer from a big food company to buy out the bakery. My parents were really keen for me to sell the shop and go back to Chipping Hill to live with them. I didn't know how to explain that I loved them, but I couldn't bear the prospect of living with them on a daily basis. They couldn't understand that I had my own plans for the bakery." She stared with fierce concentration at the bubbling cheese, trying not to remember the hurt and bewilderment in her mother's voice, trying not to remember how much she had wanted to give in to the temptation of going back to Chipping Hill and being close to John Farringdon.

"In other words, you needed an excuse not to go home, so you invented a lover?"

"It seemed so simple at the time," she said apologetically. "I told my family I'd met this fabulous

American multimillionaire and we wanted to spend as much time together as we could."

"Why American?"

"I picked the first foreign nationality that came into my head. I couldn't choose an Englishman in case they started asking which company he worked for, or what school he'd been to, and where he lived. America sounded far enough away to make the lies manageable."

"And the millionaire part?"

Julie felt herself blush. "I decided that if I was going to lie, I might as well go all the way. I never planned to keep up the story, but Robert Donahue turned out to be so convenient—"

"Robert Donahue? Your American millionaire is called *Robert Donahue?*"

"It's an amazing coincidence, isn't it? You both have the same first name."

"It is amazing. Some people might think 'incredible' was a better word."

Julie was too caught up in the rush of her story to consider any possible significance to the dry, sarcastic note in his voice. "The details about Robert just kept growing," she confided. "Every time I needed an excuse not to go home, 'Robert' was there, the perfect alibi. My mother stopped nagging me about when I was going to find a nice young man and settle down. My father stopped worrying about whether I could meet the payments on my expensive new bakery ovens. It was wonderful. Gradually I realized that I'd built my nonexistent relationship with Robert Donahue into the love affair of the century."

"Why didn't you quit while you were ahead? Before you really needed to produce your Mr. Donahue?"

Because John's wife left him again, and I realized he was falling in love with my sister. "You're right," she said, avoiding Robert's gaze. "I should have stopped lying months ago. But by the time I realized what I'd done, it was too late. My parents have been waiting to meet this wonderful international financier for the past three months. Now they're beginning to think I'm keeping Robert hidden away because I'm ashamed of them. My mother will be really hurt if I turn up at my sister's wedding without an American millionaire in tow."

Robert took his time preparing and eating another forkful of fondue. "Tell your parents you and Mr. Donahue broke up," he said at last.

"No." The denial came out too harshly and much too laden with emotion. "No," she repeated, striving for calm. "I need a fiancé this weekend, Robert. I must have one."

He was quick to pick up on her tension. "Don't you think it's time to tell me the real story behind all this?" he asked quietly. "Somehow I'm quite sure it's more than a desire to avoid hurting your parents' feelings."

He was proving much too perceptive for Julie's peace of mind, but if he was going to help her, perhaps she owed him a small slice of honesty. "I need a fiancé for protection," she admitted finally. "I'm in love with a man I can't marry."

"And he'll be at the wedding?"

"Yes."

"Why can't you marry him? Is he married already?"

"Not exactly."

"Married is a yes-or-no kind of thing, Julie. If he's telling you he'll get a divorce soon, wise up to reality. He won't."

Julie felt the humiliation close in a hard fist around her stomach. "He's not married," she said evenly. "It's not what you think, Robert, so please could we stick to the point? I promise you nobody is going to be harmed if you agree to come with me to my sister's wedding. In fact, a lot of people are going to have a much happier day. Just think of it as a strictly professional assignment. Three days of acting, except not in front of a camera. Everybody benefits. You'll have five hundred pounds to spend on eating out at your favorite restaurants, or on a weekend in Paris. And I'll have..."

"What will you have, Julie?"

"Peace of mind," she said quietly. Or as close to peace as she could hope to achieve when she watched John Farringdon marry her sister.

Robert leaned back. "Tell me how you plan to set this up."

"You mean you'll do it?" Julie couldn't keep the squeak of astonished relief out of her voice.

"I'm thinking about it at least. Tomorrow morning I'll probably wake up with several other signs of raging insanity."

"You might have fun," she interjected quickly. "It's a chance for you to see a typical English wedding, and the countryside around my parents' home is very beautiful."

"Where do they live?"

"In a village called Chipping Hill, which is about a hundred miles from London and fifteen miles from Bath. The village has a thousand people, one church and two pubs. The 'new' pub was built in the early eighteen hundreds. The 'old' one dates from the reign of Charles II in the seventeenth century. They still serve the beer warm in both places."

"And that's supposed to be an inducement to come?" Robert's nose wrinkled. "Assuming that sanity doesn't strike within the next few days, I'm going to need a rundown on your family history, not to mention a few details about Robert Donahue's past. Let's start with your sister. Who's she marrying?"

"My sister's name is Alice. She's twenty-three, eighteen months younger than me, and very pretty. Fair hair—"

"Like yours?"

"No, a bit darker, and curly. Her husband-to-be is John Farringdon. He's recently divorced, with a young daughter." Julie was proud of the cool indifference with which she managed to say John's name. But then, she'd had a lot of experience at sounding indifferent when her heart was silently breaking. "John came to the village four years ago as the junior partner in my father's medical practice—"

"You're father's a doctor?"

"Yes. And my mother was a nurse and my sister, Alice, is a fully qualified midwife."

"No brothers?"

"No."

"How did you manage to escape the family medical tradition?"

He spoke casually. Little did he know how accurate Julie found his choice of words. "Escape wasn't easy," she said with a credible lightness. "My parents were very disappointed when I went to a catering school in Brussels instead of nursing school in Bristol."

"That's all changed now, I guess. They must be very impressed with the success you've made of your bakery."

She smiled. She was good at smiling. Almost as good as she was at sounding indifferent. "I don't think they understand why I waste my time baking bread rather than saving lives, but they're glad I've managed to make a profitable career for myself, of course."

"Translation: Your parents don't have the faintest idea what makes you tick, and you feel guilty about their inadequacies."

She wasn't going to let him probe beneath the surface of her feelings. Probing was dangerous, because it ruffled the image she had worked so hard to perfect over the past three years. Her smile simply widened.

"Parents aren't supposed to understand their children, Robert. They're just supposed to love them, and mine do that wonderfully." *Or at least to the best of their ability.*

His look was a great deal more assessing than she liked, but fortunately he didn't pursue the topic. "Tell me about Robert Donahue," he said. "How did he get to be a millionaire? Does he eat failing companies for breakfast, or did he make his fortune in computer chips? How about selling car engines to the Japanese?"

"I've no idea," she confessed. "Honestly, Robert, my parents can barely keep their own bank account straight, let alone cope with the intricacies of international finance. They've never asked me any questions about how Robert Donahue made his money, and they'll believe almost any story you care to spin them."

"I'm surprised they haven't been more curious."

"Once you've met them, you'll understand. My father's totally dedicated to curing the sick and keeping the healthy from getting sick. My mother's totally dedicated to making her home perfect. 'International finance' are just words to them. So you can invent whatever you want, and they won't question the details."

"Maybe I inherited it."

"No," she said. "Too easy. They'd like to think you made it by the sweat of your own brow."

"International financiers don't sweat. The first money they make, they buy air conditioners."

She bit back a gurgle of laughter. "Please be serious, Robert."

He thought for a moment. "How about the movie industry?" he suggested. "I know something about film finances, so I could talk about that without making a total ass of myself."

"That's a great idea." Almost as soon as she had spoken, her enthusiasm waned. "But people who make money in films are all famous actors or directors, aren't they? Even my parents will be suspicious, since nobody's ever heard of anybody called Robert Donahue."

He gave her an odd look, then laughed with obvious amusement. "The movie world has as many reclusive gnomes and wizards as any other industry. The biggest profits in Hollywood are being made by people who spend a fortune keeping their names *out* of the papers and off the TV screens. Financial backers can make millions on a single big project. And then, on a smaller scale, there's always money to be made on low-budget movies for the home-video market."

He sounded as though churning out profits in the movie industry was as simple as cutting out biscuits from a roll of dough. Julie, with three years of practical experience under her belt, knew that making even a small profit wasn't nearly as easy as it looked. But Robert was an actor, and from everything she'd read about actors, they pursued their profession with such single-minded devotion it was unlikely he knew very much about the snares and pitfalls of the business world.

"Don't make it sound too easy to make money," she cautioned. "I'm sure real financiers take their money-making very seriously."

"Didn't anyone ever tell you it's only the first million that's difficult?" Robert's eyes widened with teasing innocence. "After I'd scrounged and begged and pleaded to get the funds to bankroll my first horror movie, I never had another difficult moment."

"What movie was that?" she asked, then laughed at her own foolishness. "You *are* a good actor, Robert. For a second there you had me playing right along."

"Thanks for the compliment," he said. "I'll tell my director. Yesterday I had the impression he was about to bring back Fido and give him my role."

"Which is ... ?"

He paused for a moment, then grinned. "This is our night for incredible coincidence. Would you believe I'm playing an international financier? Crooked, of course.''

Julie didn't laugh. A tiny shiver of foreboding rippled its way down her spine. The fates weren't just providing a few bizarre coincidences; they were positively drowning her in them. The interweaving of fantasy and reality was becoming uncomfortable. Once again Robert picked up on her shift of mood with disconcerting promptness.

"Having second thoughts?" he queried softly.

"And third and fourth," she admitted.

"Lies usually don't work out," he said. "I'm sure my granddaddy told me that, and he's the wiliest old bird I've ever met. Why not consider the wedding as a time to make a clean break and start telling the truth?

Great advice—except that she was a coward, Julie thought. Even if she could face her parents, there was no way in the world she could travel home and spend forty-eight hours laughing and joking while John married her sister. She was going to need something major to occupy her mind. A set of lies to worry about so that she wouldn't think about John taking Alice's hand as he repeated his vow to love and cherish her. A strong arm to cling to as she walked out of the church behind Alice and John. A human barrier between herself and her too deep emotions. And face it, she told herself ruefully, you've got your darn pride. You want a fiancé to fling in the teeth of all that neighborly and family curiosity. Not to mention Alice. When your baby sister asks what you've been doing with yourself in the big city, you don't want her to guess at the lonely, pitiful truth.

Julie took a final sip from her glass, which had somehow become nearly empty again. "I want you to come with me," she said. "If five hundred pounds isn't enough, I'll pay you six hundred."

The pause before he replied was infinitesimal. "All right," he said coolly. "I'd like three hundred up front, and three hundred when I've completed the assignment to your satisfaction. Cash, please. Preferably fifties."

She hadn't expected his sudden capitulation, or the calculated crispness of his terms. Obscurely hurt, she tried to match his briskness. "I'll have the advance money for you on Friday," she said. "Where shall I pick you up? At your flat?"

"Let's do it the other way around. Give me your home address and I'll pick *you* up."

"I was going to take the train," she said. "I always do. I planned to stop by your flat in a cab on the way to the station."

"Do multimillionaires travel by train?"

"When they're in London on a flying visit, they travel by train," she replied firmly. "Robert, I can't afford anything else."

He gave a grimace of regret. "There goes another daydream! I thought I might finally get to ride in a chauffeur-driven Rolls."

"Sorry, just plain old British Rail. Robert, about your clothes..."

"No problem. Wardrobe's provided me with a natty selection of sober designer suits for this movie. Do you want me to bring one to the wedding?"

"That would be perfect," she said with undisguised relief.

"Afraid I only had sweatpants and T-shirts to my name?" he asked. "Don't worry, Julie, I can dress the part."

"But can you play it?" The words shot out before she could bite them back.

He turned around on the seat, the amusement in his eyes darkening to some other, more powerful, emotion. In total silence, he reached for her hand and held it lightly. His eyes, burning with what Julie would have sworn was intense emotion, locked with hers, refusing to release her gaze. She knew he was only acting, but suddenly heat flared in the pit of her stomach, and her hand trembled in his clasp.

"You are the most beautiful yet unawakened woman I've ever seen," he said, his voice deep and faintly husky. He carried her hand to his lips and pressed the lightest of kisses against each of her fingertips. "When are you going to come into my arms so that I can show you what it's like to fall in love?"

The heat burning inside her intensified, flaming along her veins and melting her bones. That must be why she was incapable of movement, Julie decided. Oddly enough, her hands felt icy cold even though the rest of her was burning hot. Only the very tips of her fingers were warm, pulsing with a rhythmical tingle where Robert's mouth had touched them.

Slowly he raised his head and gently returned her hand to its original resting spot on the table. "Did I do that right?" he asked, sounding slightly anxious as he leaned back against the padded seat. "Love scenes have never been one of my strong points."

Julie closed her eyes and drew several deep breaths. "I told you..." Her voice sounded very strange. She stopped, drew another deep breath and tried again. "Love scenes aren't necessary, Robert. My parents want to meet a solid citizen, good husband material. Not a passionate lover."

He wasn't smiling at all when he spoke. "You know, Julie, it sounds to me as if you and your parents are both laboring under a major misconception. Unless a man loves his wife passionately, he's never going to be any good as a husband, however many millions of dollars he might have. And if you don't understand that, you may end up learning your lesson the hard way."

CHAPTER THREE

WISDOM HAD SET IN by dawn on Saturday morning. If Julie could have reached Robert then, or at any time during the ensuing week, she would have canceled the planned masquerade without a moment's hesitation. But despite calling the phone number Robert had given her, at all hours of the day and night, she didn't manage to get in touch with him.

Robert's usual visits to the bakery also stopped. Gritting her teeth, Julie endured her assistants' interested questions, alternating between relief that the wretched man had been scared off and fury that he hadn't been courageous enough to admit outright that her scheme was crazy and he wanted no part of it.

Fortunately she had so much extra work to do in order to bake four layers of traditional, rich fruit wedding cake and then to decorate each layer that she had little time for brooding. The cakes had to be baked late at night when the ovens weren't in use for the shop, and it was midnight three days in a row before she got home to bed.

By Friday morning, overwork and undersleep had reduced her to a state of numbness. The thought of John and Alice now produced no more than a flicker of pain. Oddly enough, if any emotion at all surfaced through her fatigue, it was regret that she wasn't going to have Robert as a shield that weekend.

She retained a vivid image of Robert's smile. It flashed in front of her inner eye at the strangest moments, causing her cheeks to flame with inexplicable heat. His smile, she realized, was one that most women would find irresistible. She would have enjoyed seeing its effect on some of her elderly aunts and gossipy neighbors.

Such petty satisfactions were obviously going to be denied her, along with others of far greater importance. But the weekend still had to be lived through with as much dignity as she could muster. Breakfast finished, Julie called the cab company, and the dispatcher promised to send a car without delay. She methodically emptied the coffeepot, wiped the counter and watered her row of plants. She was proud of being able to afford a flat of her own, even if it was tiny, and she took pleasure in keeping the small rooms neat and attractive.

She checked for a second time to make sure all the windows were shut, planning what she should say to her parents about the nonappearance of her fiancé. Robert's suggestion might be best. She would pretend she had broken up with ''Mr. Donahue,'' unable to reconcile his demanding schedule and constant travel with her desire for a speedy marriage. It was as good an explanation as any and provided an excuse for the dark shadows under her eyes and the lingering lines of tension around her mouth.

The ringing of the telephone broke the silence. ''Damn!'' she muttered. ''That wretched cab company is going to let me down again.'' She grabbed the receiver. "Hello!" she snapped. "What's your excuse this time?"

"I didn't know I needed one. Is that friendly greeting specially for me, or does everybody get the same warm welcome?"

"Robert?" Her heart thudded and her mouth went suddenly dry. She spoke quickly, trying to disguise the crazy little rush of pleasure his voice had produced. "Where in the world have you been all week?"

"Working."

"I've been nearly frantic trying to reach you!"

"I didn't know we'd committed to daily heart-to-hearts, just to a weekend of deception. I'm sorry."

He was right, and she hastened to pull her wayward emotions under control. "No, I'm the one who should apologize. I'm not being very rational this morning."

"I guess you're not a morning kind of person," he said, a thread of laughter entering his voice. "Too bad! I'm at my best before breakfast."

"That's a shame," she said tersely. "I'm a night person myself."

"Don't worry, Julie." This time the laughter was unmistakable. "I'm sure we'll find some way to reconcile our differences once we're married. When *are* we getting married, by the way? That's a date I should have firmly fixed in mind before I meet your family."

"I told my parents we hadn't set the date yet."

"No wonder, dearest, if you're always this grouchy in the morning."

"I'm not grouchy!" she yelled. "I'm in a wonderful mood!" She realized to her surprise that this was almost true. Her fatigue and her anger had mysteriously vanished, and something close to excitement pulsed through her veins.

"Good, because I need your advice. I'm sitting here staring at my suits, and I can't make up my mind whether I should wear executive-style navy blue pinstripe, or cautiously festive gray-on-gray plaid. Which would your family prefer?"

"Gray-on-gray plaid," she answered absently. "Save the pinstripe for the wedding ceremony tomorrow. Robert, were you filming out on location or something? I've been phoning all week and there's never been any answer."

"Missing me, huh?"

In a strange sort of way, she *had* missed him. "Of course not!" She denied her own thoughts as much as his question. "But we had business to discuss."

"I thought we took care of all our business last Friday at Chez Tibi. First sign of millionaire quality, Julie. Never waste time going over a simple set of arrangements twice."

"These arrangements aren't simple. They're very complicated, for heaven's sake! For a start, I have the three hundred pounds I owe you sitting in my handbag."

His voice lost its teasing edge. "Julie, you sound really upset. Has your family been difficult?"

"They're feeling the pressure of the wedding, naturally. It's important that everything go smoothly."

"Translation from polite English into practical American: they've been driving you nuts. I'm sorry I couldn't be there for you."

Absurdly, he sounded so sincere that Julie had to remind herself he was an actor, preparing himself to play a part. "I'm glad you're back," she astonished herself by saying. "It'll make the weekend so much easier for me."

There was a split-second silence before he spoke again. "I didn't answer the phone all week because I had to make an unexpected trip to New York. My agent wanted me to...audition for an upcoming play that might make it to Broadway."

"Oh, Robert, how wonderful! Maybe this film here in London is going to be a turning point in your career." Julie was surprised at how pleased she felt about Robert's success.

She could almost hear his grin. "Somehow I don't think Robbie Redford has to start worrying just yet."

"But how about Fido?" she teased.

"Now that's another matter. He might be in trouble. Revenge for my college humiliation at last."

Julie laughed. Incredible as it seemed, she was really looking forward to seeing Robert again. She'd thought her numb feelings wouldn't allow such a positive emotion to seep through.

"There's the doorbell," she said hurriedly. "Must be the cabdriver. It'll take me a good ten minutes to load the wedding cake, but I should be at your flat in less than half an hour, unless the traffic's worse than usual."

"Take your time," he said. "I just got back from running, so right now I'm wearing nothing but a towel."

Fortunately he hung up the phone before Julie's silence could become too obvious. Then she shrugged, impatient with herself. It was ridiculous for a twenty-four-year-old woman to blush because a man casually

mentioned he was undressed. And her blush had nothing at all to do with the sudden picture of an almost
naked Robert that flashed through her mind. Nothing
at all.

THE ADDRESS Robert had given her turned out to be a
pleasant residential square, built around an iron-fenced
private garden. Number 26, like its neighbors, was a
freshly painted nineteenth-century town house in im-
maculate repair. Land values in London had soared,
and nowadays this type of house rented for astronom-
ical sums. Even if Robert lived in the attics or the
basement, his film company was doing him proud.

He must have been watching for the taxi, because he
was out the door before she had a chance to walk up
the short front path, much less ring the bell. As she'd
suggested, he wore the gray suit, which he'd teamed
with a linen shirt so white and starched it seemed to
gleam in the pale morning sunshine. His tie was exactly the same gray as his suit, a discreet maroon stripe
giving it a touch of color. Julie found herself drawing
in a breath and holding it. If she'd ever seen Robert
dressed like this, she acknowledged, she would never
have found the courage to put her crazy proposition to
him. In jogging pants and tattered T-shirt he had
seemed like a pleasant, easygoing sort of person. In this
formal outfit he looked distinguished, successful—almost predatory. Amazingly like a millionaire international financier, in fact.

Julie swallowed a tiny gasp of hysterical laughter. He
heard the sound and turned to look straight at her. Any
impulse to laugh died then; Robert wasn't smiling, and
up close he seemed even more intimidating than at a

distance. His eyes were as blue and bright as Julie remembered, but for a disconcerting moment they seemed to speak of power and ruthless tenacity rather than lightheartedness and teasing good humor. Then he grinned, and the daunting illusion faded. He flicked a casual finger to his tie.

"Impressive, don't you think? Looks like I'm about to take on Wall Street and the Bank of England before lunch. And win."

"Before breakfast even." Shyly she reached out and touched his arm. "Thank you for making the effort to look the part, Robert. I really appreciate it."

His gaze was quizzical as he pocketed the door key. "It wasn't that difficult, you know. I've worn the occasional suit and tie before this." He didn't give her time to reply. "Come on! We don't want to miss the train."

Robert paid for the taxi when they arrived at Paddington Station and managed to summon a porter with no more than a casually raised hand and a brief nod.

"You do that so well," Julie teased once the boxes of wedding cake were safely stowed on the cart.

"What? Oh, you mean getting a porter." For a moment, he looked disconcerted, then he smiled. "These clothes make excellent props. I feel more like a millionaire with each passing minute. By the time we get to your parents' home, I'll probably be complaining because I had to leave my valet behind in London."

She laughed. "Remember I told my family you're a *nice* millionaire."

He bared his teeth. "There's no such animal. Millionaires come in only one model—ruthless."

It didn't seem possible that she should be giggling as she got on the train taking her to John and Alice's wedding, but she was. In honor of her fiancé's supposed millionaire status, Julie had sprung for two first-class tickets, and they had the carriage to themselves. Robert kept her laughing as they trundled through the gray-slate and redbrick suburbs and out into the green and leafy countryside. He couldn't have been doing it deliberately, of course, but somehow he managed to keep all thoughts of the dreaded weekend at bay until they were past Oxford. The change in conversation started harmlessly enough.

"Aren't you worried about the wedding cake getting spoiled?" Robert asked, glancing up at the luggage rack. "How in the world will the frosting survive this jostling?"

"It's not that brittle," Julie said. "We have special containers at the bakery and I kept the design low and simple, so nothing should break."

"Icing doesn't break. It smooshes."

"Smooshes?" She smiled at the word, then remembered a recipe from her catering-school days. "Wedding cakes in America are made of sponge cake and covered with soft butter cream, aren't they? But in England, we make a dark fruit cake that's rich and spicy, and we ice the cake over a layer of marzipan with a spun-sugar mixture that turns hard and crunchy when it's set. Cakes like this may be heavy to transport, but they won't melt if it gets hot."

"That's a relief. I was afraid your reputation as a baker was about to go down the tubes. Tell me some more about your sister and her husband-to-be. How long has John been divorced?"

"Not very long." Julie rushed on before he could ask any awkward questions. "But Sally—that was John's first wife—has run off and left him twice before. This time, when she left, John started divorce proceedings right away."

"It's unusual that he should have sole custody of his daughter, even in this day and age."

"Sally isn't very maternal."

"But your sister is?"

"Alice loves children." Try as she might, Julie couldn't keep her voice entirely neutral. Robert must have picked up on the underlying note of tension, because he looked at her with sudden concern. "Are you worried in case John is marrying your sister just to provide a mother for his little girl?"

Something snapped inside Julie. "I've no idea why John is marrying Alice," she said harshly. "He never seemed to have the least interest in her, and I should know." She stopped, turning quickly to stare out of the window, appalled at what she had almost revealed.

She couldn't see Robert, but her awareness of his cool scrutiny added to her discomfort. He spoke quietly, without much inflection. "John could hardly express interest in Alice or any other woman when he was married. Presumably all his emotions were consumed by his failing marriage."

"You're quite right of course." With a supreme effort, Julie turned back from the window and produced a smile. "I'm being silly, but that's a woman's privilege when her baby sister gets married. When I left home, Alice was still a college student, squabbling with my parents about how late she could stay out on Saturday night."

"Three years is a long time, Julie. People grow up, even baby sisters. Especially when they fall in love with the right man."

Robert's words sliced into Julie's consciousness with the sharpness of a surgical scalpel. *But John isn't the right man for Alice,* she wanted to cry out. *He's the right man for me.* She bit her lip, holding the petulant words back with an effort that was almost physical. Gradually the truth she had tried to push to the side of her consciousness marched onto center stage. Alice and John *were* ideally suited. John was a dedicated, obsessively hardworking doctor, just like Julie's father. And Alice was a skillful, sympathetic nurse, just like Julie's mother. Alice, perhaps, was less willing than her mother to sacrifice her career to become a permanent, full-time homemaker, but that was a generational difference, rather than a difference in basic personality. In many important ways, Alice and John were duplicates of Barbara and Derek Marshall.

Julie didn't like the trend of her thoughts at all, and she searched for a casual remark to set the conversational ball rolling in a different direction. A spark flickered in the darkness of her thoughts. Robert had a sister, too. She could ask about his family.

"Didn't you say your baby sister recently moved to Boston? Is she happy there?"

"Mollie? She's wildly in love with her husband, so I guess she'd be happy anywhere provided he was with her. But Boston is a bonus because she loves the city. They're both teaching at Harvard."

"I'm impressed. What do they teach?"

"Mollie's a botanist and a very junior member of the biology department. Her husband's older, and he's well on his way to becoming American's leading authority on ancient languages.''

''Latin and Greek, you mean?''

He grinned. ''You're about a thousand years too modern. Try Sanskrit and Aramaic.''

Julie's dark mood lifted slightly, and she asked with genuine interest, ''How about your brother? Is he married, too?''

''Very much so. Matt's a year younger than me. He runs a resort hotel out in Colorado, and his wife runs him. They have three impossibly precocious children who spend most of their time eating and skiing, both of which they do brilliantly.''

''With your sister and brother safely married off, do your parents keep nagging you to get married as well?''

''They've given up,'' he said. His eyes twinkled. ''My mother was recently driven to the sorry state of suggesting I find myself a nice girl and live with her, since the idea of marriage seemed to reduce me to a state of shaking incompetence.''

Somehow, Julie couldn't imagine Robert as either shaking or incompetent, although she could believe he didn't want to get married. She suspected he was having far too much fun as a bachelor. ''How did you answer her?'' she asked.

He opened innocent blue eyes. ''Naturally I told her I was shocked to the core. Mothers aren't supposed to suggest that their children live in sin.''

''She was suggesting a long-term relationship, Robert, not a life of sin.''

''Long-term relationships take up too much time,'' he said dryly. ''And far too much emotional energy.

My schedule has no room for any more commitments."

"Are actors that short of time? I thought they spent most of their lives hanging around, waiting for a part."

"They spend most of their lives waiting, all right. Waiting on tables, that is. Or washing cars, or delivering pizza. Anything, so that they can eat until they find their next job. Being a movie star may be fun, although I have my doubts. Being an unknown, unemployed actor is as close to hell on earth as I would care to come."

"Then why do so many people want to become actors? Why do you?"

"I can't answer for other people," he said after a moment. "But I'm not really an actor, Julie. Like I told you, I work in production, and that keeps me employed full-time. This movie role here in London is a special situation for me. A time-out-of-the-real-world sort of situation."

She would have liked to ask more about the exact nature of his work, but a glance out the window showed her they were almost in Bath. Her stomach lurched. In a few minutes she would see John again. John and Alice.

"We're five minutes early," she said. "There's the station just ahead." She stood up and reached for the smallest box of wedding cake, glad of an excuse to turn her burning cheeks away from Robert's gaze.

"Here, let me help." He came easily to his feet and stood alongside her. The train lurched as it slowed, and Julie stumbled. Determined to protect the cake, she found herself catapulted into Robert's outstretched arms.

For a moment—surely it was no more than a moment—she felt a tingle of excitement as her face rested against the solid wall of his chest. The steady beat of his heart thudded against her cheek. The smell of clean, starched linen tickled her nose. Quickly she pulled herself upright, clutching the cake box.

"Let me take that." Robert gestured to the box with one hand. His other remained strong and supportive around her waist.

"No, no, that's all right. I have it safe." She juggled the weight of the box from side to side until she had it balanced, looking and sounding every bit as flustered as she felt.

Without saying anything, he braced himself against the side of the carriage and took the box out of her hands. He placed it gently on the seat, then straightened and looked down at her. The silence was so loud she could hear it beating against her ears.

He crooked his finger under her chin and tilted her face gently upward. "You're a very beautiful woman, Julie."

"Th-thank you." She suddenly had no idea what to do with her hands, so she clenched them by her sides, fingernails digging into her palms. He brushed his thumb lightly across her mouth, and her lips trembled in response.

He smiled then, an odd, self-mocking sort of smile. "Do you have any idea how long I've been wanting to kiss you?"

"H-how long?"

He glanced at his watch. "About six weeks, three days, two hours and thirty-five minutes." He bent his head until his mouth was only a breath away from hers.

"In other words, ever since the first moment I saw you."

"That's a long time," she whispered.

"Too long."

Julie knew she couldn't have been the one who closed the infinitesimal gap between their lips. She had been in love with John for so long she'd forgotten how to feel attracted to any other man. Of course she didn't want to kiss Robert. But somehow his mouth was covering hers, and she was leaning toward him, curving with a sense of inevitability into the refuge provided by his strong arms and powerful body.

His kiss was expert, seeking, sensual and oddly tender. For a second or two, Julie felt nothing at all, her mind and nerve endings equally numb with shock. For three years, she had cut herself off from even the most tentative emotional contact with a man. Now, in Robert's arms, she was beginning to feel again. She felt Robert's hand, firm on the small of her back, his fingers splayed toward her hips. She felt his chest, broad and muscled and hard against her breasts. She felt his mouth, gentle and possessive against her lips. For the first time in three years, she felt alive.

Julie closed her eyes. Blind to the sunlight streaming in through the carriage window, deaf to the noise of carriage doors banging open, Julie drowned slowly, pleasurably, in a rushing wave of sensation.

It was Robert who finally ended the kiss, but he continued to hold her within the protective circle of his arms. "Is this the end of the line for the train?" he asked.

Julie blinked, trying to return her dazed brain and dazzled senses to functioning order. "I think it goes on

to Bristol," she said. Even to her own ears, her voice
sounded distinctly odd—husky and disoriented.

Robert dropped a light kiss on the end of her nose.
"Then we'd better let this porter know that we'd appreciate his services. I think the departure whistle's
about to blow."

Julie whirled around to face the porter's appreciative grin. "Sorry to break up the clinch, luv." At a nod
from Robert, he piled their two small cases and the
cake boxes onto his trolley. "Where do you want me to
take this lot, then? Somebody meetin' you out the
front?"

"Yes, thank you." Robert stepped from the carriage and turned back to assist Julie. She would have
liked to spurn his outstretched hand, but her knees were
wobbling so much that she needed his support.

She stared past Robert, avoiding his eyes with fierce
determination. They followed the porter out of the
station, and a tall, handsome man hurried forward.

"Julie!" he said, his voice less deep than she remembered. "You're here at last."

Her entire body went rigid with the effort of retain-
ing control. The warmth Robert's kiss had aroused
vanished as if it had never been. Icy cold, she held out
her hand and produced a smile. "Hello, John. How are
you?"

He took her hand and bent to kiss her cheek, but she
pulled her head away quickly, and his lips barely
brushed her skin. So many conflicting emotions were
churning inside her she was afraid she might be sick.

Robert finished paying off the porter, and when he
dropped his arm around her shoulder in a brief hug,
she turned to him almost gratefully. He gazed down at

her, his eyes alight with an emotion she could have sworn was anger. Before she could say anything, he bent his head and brushed a quick, possessive kiss across her astonished mouth. "Are you feeling okay, Julie? You look pale."

"I'm ... I'm fine." She worked to produce another smile. "Too many late nights this past week."

"You always work too hard." Robert gave her arm a reassuring squeeze. "I'll have to take special care of you tonight. See if I can't find a way to put some color back into your cheeks."

She gazed up at him in mute astonishment and he said, "I'm your fiancé, remember? It's my job to take care of you."

She had needed the reminder. Good Lord, what was the matter with her? She could usually put on a better facade than this.

John viewed the little scene in silence. Obviously uncomfortable, he held out his hand to Robert. "How do you do? I'm John Farringdon. You must be Julie's fiancé. You're ... just as she described you."

"Yes, I'm Robert Donahue. I'll resist the temptation to ask how Julie described me." Robert shook John's hand, offering him a bland smile. "Congratulations on your upcoming wedding. Julie is very excited for you and her sister."

John glanced swiftly toward Julie, then away again. "Thank you. Alice and I think we can make a very good life together, and we thought it would be best for Vickie if we got married as soon as possible. Naturally she doesn't quite understand why her home is being broken up."

"Children can adapt to most things with enough love and attention," Robert replied.

"And Alice is wonderful with her," John said, sounding more cheerful. He looked around anxiously. Outside his consulting rooms, he tended to be overwhelmed by the details of life. "Perhaps I should go and get the car. There was nowhere to park and I had to leave it around the corner."

"That would be best," Robert agreed. "The wedding cake would be difficult to carry more than a few yards."

"Well, I'll be off," John said. "See you in a few minutes. I'm driving the old Ford, Julie. Do you remember? The car, I mean."

She closed her eyes against the humiliating memory of her own youthful infatuation. "Yes, I remember," she said curtly.

John hurried off, his long stride loping. Robert barely waited until he was out of earshot before he grabbed Julie's shoulders and swung her around to face him. His expression was light-years away from its normal, easygoing smile.

"Why didn't you tell me?" he demanded.

"Tell you wh-what?"

"You know damn well. Why didn't you tell me that John Farringdon was your lover?"

CHAPTER FOUR

JULIE'S DENIAL came a fraction of a second too late to be convincing. "Of course John isn't my lover," she said. "I doubt if I've seen him half a dozen times since I moved to London." She was telling the literal truth, but the knowledge that she had once been very much in love with him tinged her reply with guilt.

"Never try to earn your living in the movies," Robert said, with no trace of his usual good humor. "You make a lousy actress, Julie."

"Then it's fortunate I'm an excellent baker, isn't it?" she snapped. "You're supposed to be the actor, Robert, not me. I hired you to play a part, not to make moral judgments, and I'm paying you well. Please don't forget why you're here."

His smile was sardonic. "Don't worry, I never renege on a business deal. I plan to give you full value in exchange for your six hundred pounds. You hired a fiancé for the weekend, and you're going to get the best damn fiancé who ever danced at a family wedding." He shrugged. "It's none of my business if you're in love with the man your sister's marrying."

"You're right," Julie said, proud of her cool smile. "My feelings are none of your business."

His reply mocked her prim words. "I see you believe in the hallowed British tradition of hypocrisy.

Never display the family's dirty linen if you have a shred of clean cloth to use as a cover."

"I suppose you think the American habit of spilling intimate secrets on national television is better."

"Not at all," he said. "I'm a great believer in keeping necessary secrets."

Something about his tone of voice set Julie's alarm system jangling. "Do you have secrets?" she asked.

"Of course," he replied smoothly. "Lots of them. Don't we all?" He shoved his hands into the pockets of his trousers and jingled the loose change. "There's no need to look so worried, Julie. I'm a decent actor, a card-carrying member of Equity. You can have faith in your hired hand."

"How do I know that? I've never seen you perform."

Robert's expression lost some of its hard edge. "Let's not exaggerate the skill I'm going to need. Playing the role of your fiancé doesn't require an Oscar-winning performance."

"I suppose not." Julie gave him a quick sideways glance, relieved to feel her mental equilibrium beginning to return. "But then most actors don't lose their first starring role to a dog."

Robert groaned, but his eyes gleamed with laughter. "Darn it, I've ruined my reputation with you! I knew I should never have admitted the truth about Fido. That wretched animal has haunted my career."

Julie smiled. "Shh, don't say anything more." She pointed to the ancient Ford estate car that had appeared at the end of the line of traffic. "Here comes John."

John drew up at the curb and got out of the car. "Sorry to have kept you waiting," he said, his voice sounding a little abstracted. "The traffic always builds up near the station."

"Where would you like me to put the cake boxes?" Robert asked briskly.

John's handsome features twisted into a vaguely worried frown, and Julie felt an unexpected spurt of irritation. It was his wedding, for heaven's sake, and his car. Couldn't he even decide where to stow the cake?

"How about wedging the boxes in the back here?" Robert suggested, lifting the boxes into place as he spoke.

John looked relieved to have the decision taken out of his hands. "Be careful, won't you, old chap? Mustn't damage the wedding cake or the ladies will be furious with us."

"I wouldn't dream of damaging something Julie worked so hard to produce," Robert said. "It's taken her hours of work late at night to bake these layers of cake for you and her sister."

"Well, of course, we certainly appreciate all her effort—"

"I'm sure you do," Robert interjected. "Julie's bakery is such a tremendous success I expect her family bores you to tears boasting about how well she's done. The Crusty Corner is a landmark in Chelsea, you know. It's been written up in the local papers a couple of times, and one of the Sunday newspapers recommended her fruit desserts as the best in London."

John and Julie both stared at Robert in astonishment; Julie because of the research Robert had obviously conducted into her background, John presumably because—in common with the rest of the Marshall family—he had never given a second's thought to Julie's career. If someone wasn't a doctor or a nurse, or at least a medical technician, John and his future in-laws scarcely registered the fact that they were gainfully employed.

Robert's blue eyes darkened with amusement as he caught Julie's gaze. Suddenly she found herself hiding a gurgle of laughter as she watched John absorb the amazing fact that her bakery wasn't some quaint little hobby but a profitable commercial venture that had required skill, flair and a lot of business acumen to get off the ground.

"Er...um...of course we're all very proud of Julie and her little shop," John said finally.

"You should be." Robert tucked the last box into the back and strode around to open the car door for Julie. "Hop in, darling. How far did you say it was to Chipping Hill?"

"Sixteen miles, give or take a few curves in the road."

"Less than half an hour," John commented, slamming the rear door. "The traffic isn't too bad once we're out of town."

"Half an hour can sometimes seem like a very long time," Robert murmured, catching Julie around the waist as she leaned forward to step into the car. "I definitely need a kiss for the road."

Julie ignored the glow of excitement that coursed through her as she felt the solid strength of Robert's arm against her midriff. Nerves, and seeing John again, must be doing something strange to her hormones. Her system seemed to be disastrously con-

fused, sending adrenaline racing every time Robert
came near her and provoking irritation every time she
looked at John.

She soon realized this was not the moment to be
contemplating her errant hormones. Robert, his entire
body taut with mischief, waited for her kiss, while John
looked on with fascinated attention. Julie gritted her
teeth. She wouldn't make a fuss now, she decided, but
as soon as she and Robert were alone, she'd make it
clear that he wouldn't receive the remainder of his
money unless he stopped this ridiculous byplay. Kissing and hugging had definitely not been part of their
original deal. She turned, still within the circle of
Robert's arms, glared daggers at him and dropped a
sisterly kiss onto his cheek.

"There, *darling*," she said with pointed brightness.
"That should keep you going."

He tightened his hold on her waist and smiled a
predatory smile. "Not by a long shot, *darling*. I'm in
a serious state of deprivation after a week away from
you in New York." Before she could protest, he pulled
her against him in a way that melded every inch of her
body into the rock-hard contours of his. His hand slid
up her throat to hold her face still as his mouth de-
scended in a long, searching kiss.

As soon as their lips met, it happened again, just as
it had on the train. Julie felt the uncoiling of a sensation she recognized as intense physical desire. It had
been a long time since she had let a man kiss her, and
she was a normal woman, with all the normal female
instincts. Her body was informing her in no uncertain
terms that it had been starved of male attention for
much too long.

In a minute, she reassured herself. In just a minute she would stop this ridiculous kiss. But right now, the touch of Robert's mouth against hers felt wonderful. Unbidden, her hands wound themselves in the thick, springy darkness of his hair. Desire prickled her skin with heat and made the blood thrum in her ears. She allowed herself to sink into the warmth and protection of his embrace.

Julie had no idea how long she might have continued kissing Robert before coming to her senses. Her resolution was never put to the test. Suddenly she felt herself lifted away from him and eased gently into the front seat of the car.

"Julie, darling, that was spectacular, but I'm afraid we're holding up traffic," Robert murmured, his words tinged with rueful amusement. "Later, sweetheart," he whispered. "We can continue this later when we're alone."

Fortunately she couldn't speak for a crucial few seconds, or she probably would have agreed to his ridiculous proposition. Drunk on the heady effects of his kiss, she gazed deep into Robert's eyes. Exceptionally attractive eyes, they rested on her with warm masculine appreciation, and some other emotion. Sympathy, she realized, gathering her scattered wits. Amused, patronizing *sympathy*. Good grief, the wretched man was sorry for her! And no wonder—she'd melted in his arms like a sex-starved spinster. Which, she realized with a humiliating flash of insight, was exactly what she was.

John cleared his throat. "You two nearly sizzled a hole in the pavement," he said, sounding embarrassed.

"Sorry," Robert replied, sounding anything but. He got into the back seat of the Ford and gave John a cheerful smile. "Julie and I tend to get carried away when we've been separated for a while, don't we, darling?"

For a minute, Julie was furious with him. Then the absurdity of the whole situation brought an unexpected smile to her lips. "Yes," she said, turning around to look at Robert and letting him see the exasperation mingled with her amusement. "I certainly think we got carried away."

Robert's gaze flickered over her flushed cheeks before coming to rest on her mouth. Julie felt her smile fade and heat blossom in the pit of her stomach. "I always knew it would be like that between us," he said softly. "But we can wait. We have the whole weekend ahead of us." Then he leaned back against the faded upholstery and stared with seeming consuming interest at a passing porter.

Julie glanced nervously at John, wondering if he'd noticed the oddness of her "fiancé's" comments. Fortunately it appeared he hadn't, for he put the car into gear and eased into the stream of traffic.

"We'd better get going," he said, clearing his throat. "My goodness! Half-past twelve already. Your parents will be wondering what's happened to us all."

Had John always had this aggravating habit of coughing or clearing his throat before he made a simple remark? Julie dismissed the thought as disloyal. John was a serious-minded man, dedicated to the wellbeing of his fellow human beings. Robert could afford to be witty and charming and obnoxiously cheerful. After all, he had no ambition to be anything other than an entertainer. John carried the burden of life-and-death decisions each minute of his working day. No wonder he sometimes seemed too abstracted to cope with the problems of everyday living.

"How are my parents?" Julie asked him, when they were safely on the road to Chipping Hill. "And Alice, too? They must be exhausted with all the last-minute arrangements."

"They're bearing up pretty well," John said. "Your mother actually seems to be enjoying herself, although I'll be relieved when the fuss is over and we can settle down quietly at home. I've done all this before, you see."

"But not with Alice," Robert pointed out, his voice cool.

John flushed. "No, of course not. I didn't mean that remark the way it sounded. I'm just not good at parties and family reunions and that sort of thing." He gave another of his embarrassed laughs. "I seem to be much better at talking to people who feel sick than people who are feeling well and happy."

Julie waited for Robert to make some sharp comeback, but it never came. He merely said, "The ability to make sick people feel at ease must be a tremendous asset for a doctor."

"It helps a lot," John agreed, sounding more confident now that the subject was his profession. "Even today, with all the advances in drugs and technology, convincing the patient he's going to get well is often more than half the battle in getting him on his feet again."

They stopped at a crossroads marked by a pub, a tiny church, and four or five thatched cottages. "Take away the telegraph poles and television aerials, and I don't suppose this scene has changed much in two hundred years,'' Julie commented.

Robert looked out the car window with obvious interest. ''This is exactly how I imagined England when I was growing up,'' he said. ''Dreaming of being a great Shakespearean actor, striding the boards at Stratford-on-Avon.''

''You wanted to be an actor?'' John asked, surprised. ''Then how in the world did you end up as an international financier?''

Julie didn't turn around, but she could literally feel Robert's grin. *Please don't let him tell that ridiculous story about Fido,* she thought.

''Oh, I discovered right after college that I wasn't cut out for the life of a thespian,'' Robert said. ''Every time I got cast in some minor part, I'd get fired right away for explaining to the producer how it would be more cost effective to organize things my way, rather than his. It took me a while, but in the end, I figured out it was a lot easier for me to sit in an office and make money than it would be to get in front of a camera and act.''

The man was the most convincing liar she'd ever heard, Julie decided. Listening to him, she could almost believe he'd really abandoned his original idea of becoming an actor in favor of a career in finance. ''Darling, you're too modest,'' she said, her voice tinged with sarcasm. ''Most people don't find it quite that easy to earn millions of dollars.''

''Good Lord, nobody's ever called me modest before. Dearest Julie, you're so insightful. That must be why I love you so much.'' Robert gave her an impudent grin that should have been infuriating. For some reason, Julie found her mouth twitching in an answering smile.

"You're impossible," she muttered, quite forgetting her role of adoring fiancée. "I've never heard a man who lies with such splendid conviction."

"Lies?" John asked, bewildered. "What do you mean?"

"About my acting ability," Robert said quickly.

"And his modesty," Julie said simultaneously.

John looked nonplussed and was still searching for something to say when Julie pointed out the graceful medieval spire of Chipping Hill's local church. "There's All Souls, Robert." She swallowed hard, then said with determined nonchalance, "That's where Alice and John will be getting married tomorrow."

The church came more fully into view as they rounded a bend in the road. Dominating the village street from the crest of a small rise, its gray stone arches were silhouetted against the soft blue of the summer sky.

Robert looked in silence for several seconds as they drove past. "It's magnificent," he said, then added more lightly, "I think that's where we should get married, Julie dearest. My family would love an excuse to come over to England this summer."

John hunched over the steering wheel. "Your mother told me that you and Robert were getting ready to set the date, Julie."

Belatedly Julie realized she hadn't given nearly enough thought to how she would handle her mother's desire to set a firm date for their wedding. Perhaps she had no cause to worry. She'd been

procrastinating successfully for months, and with
Robert's help, she ought to sail safely through the
shoals of this weekend. She drew a deep breath and
tried to stay calm.

"Well, you know Mother sometimes exaggerates,
John. Everything's still pretty much up in the air as
regards dates. What with Robert's schedule and my
commitments to the bakery and everything..."

"Naturally we're very anxious to get things settled as
soon as possible," Robert added with infuriating
cheerfulness. "We're hoping to talk things over with
Julie's parents this weekend. They might have a few
moments to spare once you and Alice are safely away
on your honeymoon. Where are you going, by the
way?"

"The Lake District," John said, not noticing the
skillful change of subject. "We didn't want to go too
far because we can only take a few days away from
Vickie. Vickie's my daughter," he added, by way of
explanation. "She'll soon be six."

"Yes, I knew that," Robert said. "Julie's filled me
in on all the details concerning her family. I feel like an
old friend, even though we've never managed to meet
in person before this weekend." He smiled warmly,
looking so much like an eager-to-please fiancé that Julie was unreasonably tempted to shake him.

"We're here," she interjected, relieved to see her
mother and father standing on the steps of the pleasant, Georgian-style house that had been her home
since early childhood. Robert had a disconcerting trick
of making her believe in his fantasies. For a split second, she had actually started to make a mental review
of her schedule, trying to decide which date would be

best for their wedding. If she wasn't careful, she reflected wryly, by the end of the weekend she'd be discussing bedroom furniture for their New York apartment without so much as a blink of an eye.

She jumped out of the car, running up the steps to greet her parents. It was either that, or doing something disastrous like bopping Robert over the head with the nearest available blunt instrument. She wasn't quite sure why she felt so cross with him, but she *was* absolutely sure that he was overplaying his role.

Mrs. Marshall gave her daughter a swift hug. "Julie dearest, you're late, we were getting worried. But you look wonderful. It must be love. I haven't seen you look so glowing in years." Mrs. Marshall didn't give Julie a chance to speak. She rarely did. She cast a quick, assessing glance in Robert's direction and extended her hand in greeting.

"Oh, my," she said, sighing with maternal pride at her daughter's supposed conquest. "You're every bit as handsome as Julie told us. Welcome to Chipping Hill, Robert. We're delighted to meet you at last."

"And I'm delighted to be here."

Mrs. Marshall smiled approvingly. "Julie made so many excuses as to why we couldn't meet you, Robert, we began to wonder if you actually existed!"

Robert put his arm around Julie's shoulders, and laughed. "Oh, I'm very real," he said, bending down to give Mrs. Marshall a hearty buss on the cheek. "And happy to be meeting Julie's family after so many weeks of waiting. I was very disappointed at having to spend the weekend with the Governor of the Bank of England last month, rather than coming here to Chipping Hill."

"With the Governor of the Bank of England?" Mrs. Marshall repeated faintly. "You spent the weekend with him?"

"Why, yes. Harry's an old friend." Robert turned and looked reprovingly at Julie. "You did explain to your parents why I couldn't come to visit them the last time I was in England, didn't you?"

For a brief moment, Julie actually felt guilty. Then sanity returned. "I didn't specifically mention the governor," she said in her most repressive tone of voice. "I didn't want my parents to get an exaggerated idea of your importance."

Robert grinned, refusing to be repressed. "Harry's a good man to know," he said. "Much more interesting than you'd think, given the amount of time he spends worrying about boring things like interest rates and gold reserves. Next time he and I have dinner, I must take you with me, Julie, love."

"That would be nice," she said tersely, frowning a warning. Good heavens, this man didn't know the meaning of the word moderation! He was going to get them into serious trouble before the weekend was over unless he toned down his act. She'd have to take him aside and give him a stern lecture, or he'd soon be boasting about his negotiations with the Soviet ambassador or the time he entertained the President of the United States to an afternoon's fishing. Her parents might be naive, but eventually Robert was going to make some claim so outrageous that the game would be over.

"I'm Julie's father," Dr. Marshall said, stepping forward and stretching out his hand. "We're very glad you could make it up here for the wedding. It's going to be a big day for Alice and her mother."

"And for Julie, too. It's good to know you, sir." Robert took Dr. Marshall's hand in a firm clasp, then dropped his left arm to Julie's waist, drawing her against his side. The gesture was at once possessive and oddly protective. For a fleeting moment, she wondered if Robert somehow guessed that she always felt in need of protection from her family, then dismissed the thought as absurd. He couldn't possibly know how her parents' and Alice's single-minded dedication to the medical profession left her feeling totally isolated from the warmth of the family circle.

Dr. Marshall glanced at his watch. "Julie, we're running a bit late, I'm afraid. Would you show Robert where he can wash his hands? Your mother would like to serve lunch right away, because I have a couple of patients I must see this afternoon. Pneumonia and diabetes pay no heed to weddings," he added in explanation.

"I'll drive the car round the back and unload the cake straight into the kitchen," John volunteered.

"That would be most helpful," Mrs. Marshall said, bustling toward the dining room. "Now, Julie, dear, I've put Robert in the blue bedroom at the front, but for the moment, just show him where the downstairs cloakroom is, will you, please?"

On the way to the bathroom, there was no time or privacy for more than a muttered "For goodness' sake, stop inventing such wild stories! And stop kissing me!" before Julie was dragooned into the kitchen to help her mother serve lunch.

Alice, who was making the rounds of the village on an assortment of last-minute errands, didn't get home in time to share the family meal. Julie was rather glad that during lunch she had to contend with nothing more than the tension generated by John's presence and the relish with which Robert had flung himself into his role of sophisticated multimillionaire. He seemed to have an endless stream of anecdotes about the rich and the famous, all of which were slightly scandalous and vastly entertaining. Julie could hardly believe her eyes as her staid mother and stolid father drank in Robert's tall tales. She had to admit that the wretched man was a brilliant raconteur. She was forced to remind herself at frequent intervals that everything he said was either sheer invention or culled secondhand from some gossip sheet.

The nerve-racking meal finally ended. Dr. Marshall hurried out to visit the local hospital. Mrs. Marshall bore Robert off to inspect her prize roses, and Julie found herself alone in the kitchen with John, stacking plates in the dishwasher. Julie, chattering nineteen to the dozen in order to conceal her nervousness, barely saved an entire tray of coffee cups from ruin when John walked up behind her and touched her on the arm.

"You startled me," she said breathlessly, setting the tray down on the draining board and rinsing off the cups and saucers. Looking up at him, she thought how amazingly handsome he was, and wondered why his classical, Greek-statue features no longer evoked any response in her other than a vague admiration for their perfection. Her heart, she realized with surprise, was pounding with strain, not with repressed desire.

"Your Robert Donahue is every bit as wonderful as you claimed," John said. "He kept the whole table entertained at lunch, didn't he?"

"Oh...er...thank you. I'm glad you like him."

"Who could help liking him? As soon as I heard about Robert from your mother, I knew you'd found the right man. I think he'll make you happy. You're both such dynamic, successful people. I expect you'll have a stormy, wonderful marriage." John's smile contained a hint of wistfulness. "You'd have been dreadfully unhappy if you'd married me, you know, Julie."

Julie put down a coffee cup and stared at him with cool eyes. "I don't know why we're having this conversation, John. I once had a childish infatuation for you, which you quite rightly rejected. Your wife came back to you, and you tried to patch up your marriage. End of story. Now you're divorced and you're marrying my sister tomorrow. I imagine that must be because you're deeply in love with her."

John flushed. "Alice and I are well suited, Julie. We'll make a good partnership. But if I'd been free three years ago..."

Julie took a sharp, short breath. "Don't, John! The past is over for both of us, and you owe your loyalty to my sister."

"You're right, Julie. Of course you are. It's just seeing you again..." He gave a rueful little smile. "This must be what they refer to as pre-wedding jitters. Forgive me."

Julie dried her hands on a tea towel, amazed to discover that she was feeling nothing beyond mild pity. It was almost funny to think how terrified she'd been tha all her teenage infatuation would flare up again the moment she saw John. In reality, she was finding his company somewhat tedious. She scooped detergent into the dishwasher and closed the door.

"Everything seems tidy in here," she said, avoiding his gaze. "Let's go and join my mother in the garden, shall we?"

"No need, I'm here." The back door banged open, carrying a waft of flower-scented summer air into the kitchen. Mrs. Marshall entered, followed by Robert.

"I have some patients to visit," John muttered. "If you would all excuse me . . ."

"Of course, my dear. We'll see you later this afternoon." Mrs. Marshall seemed oblivious to the undercurrent of tension as John left the room. She beamed at her daughter, her bosom swelling with maternal pride.

"Well, isn't this nice? Just the three of us. What a charmer your Robert is, to be sure."

"I'm glad you like him."

"We've been having a splendid little chat, your fiancé and I. He agrees with me that we ought to set your wedding date as early as possible."

Julie cast Robert an outraged glance. He shrugged apologetically, then rolled his eyes in an obvious plea for help. Julie would have forgiven him if she hadn't been so worried. She could well imagine what Robert's tour of the rose garden must have been like. Once her mother latched onto the subject of wedding dates, a juggernaut would be easier to deflect.

"I'm glad the two of you had a chance to chat," Julie said, doing her best to redeem the situation. "But let's talk about dates again at Christmas, shall we? Summer's the best time for a wedding—''

"Summer!" Mrs. Marshall broke in excitedly. "Isn't that *exactly* what I said to you, Robert? Summer is always the best time for a wedding."

"Er, yes, you did say that." Robert, usually so well able to come up with a snappy response, seemed for once to have developed an acute attack of the mumbles.

Mrs. Marshall ignored his lack of enthusiasm and gave another happy smile. "There then, it's all settled. We'll have the ceremony at All Souls here in Chipping Hill the last Sunday in August. Does that sound convenient, Robert? For your family, I mean."

He was silent for a long minute, then he nodded slowly. "It sounds great." His sudden grin was infectious. "What do you think, Julie, darling?"

"Oh, it's perfect," she said, relieved that her mother wasn't pushing for a Christmas ceremony. At least there would be plenty of time to call off her "engagement." "We have nearly fourteen months to plan everything—"

"Fourteen months!" Mrs. Marshall's exclamation was little short of a shriek. "Julie, I'm not talking about next year! I'm talking about *this* summer, six weeks from now."

"Six weeks from now! Mother, Robert couldn't possibly manage to free up his schedule that soon. And neither could I." She shot Robert a glance that was half plea, half warning. *Protest now,* she commanded silently. *Explain that you're going to spend all of August working in Timbuctu.*

Mrs. Marshall's face crumpled in dismay. "But Robert, I thought you said—"

"The last weekend in August will be perfect," Robert interjected smoothly.

Julie's mouth dropped open and she stared at him in blank, disbelieving horror. He walked over to her side and tucked her hand through his arm. "I'm just thrilled our wedding date is finally settled, Mrs. Marshall, and I'm totally delighted Julie finally consented to name the day."

Julie wondered if Robert had inhaled toxic fumes during his tour of the rose garden. It seemed the only explanation for his sudden attack of insanity. Didn't he realize that her mother would be calling the caterers within the next five minutes? And that the vicar and all the relatives would be clearing their calendars five minutes after that?

Robert didn't seem to be aware of the enormity of his error. He patted Julie's hand, looking down at her with innocent blue eyes that gleamed with laughter. "Julie, darling, I'm so happy this is all settled. I'm going to call my mother right now and tell her the good news."

Julie, darling, tried to decide whether she was more furious with her mother or her "fiancé." Her fiancé won with ease. When she got Robert alone, she was going to murder him. Preferably by some long, slow and painful method.

Continuing to make a bad situation worse, Robert bent and dropped a swift kiss onto her cheek. "I'll have to call my brother and sister, too. Gosh, they're going to be so thrilled to hear the news."

Boiling oil, Julie decided. And thumbscrews. Or maybe death by a thousand cuts. One way or another, she couldn't wait to get her "fiancé" alone at her mercy.

CHAPTER FIVE

ROBERT, NO DOUBT aware of the danger he was in, proved to be an elusive quarry. The Marshall household teemed with the excitement of pre-wedding arrivals, and in the flurry of meeting Alice, greeting aunts, great-uncles, cousins and old family friends, he skillfully managed to avoid being alone with Julie. To Julie's fury, which was all the more intense because she knew it was illogical, he also managed to charm every relative and old family friend with whom he so much as shook hands.

"Stop smiling that seductive smile at all my aunts," she hissed when she unexpectedly found herself alone with him in the hallway for a few seconds. "I'm sick to death of hearing what a wonderful man you are! Even Cousin Jane, who used to be a suffragette and loathes men on principle, told me you were an agreeable specimen for a person of the male sex."

Robert pretended to look puzzled. "You want your relatives to dislike me?" he asked. "I thought the whole idea was to impress your family with what a great guy I am. I've been trying so hard to convince everybody that I'm not just a common or garden millionaire with nothing to recommend me but my money."

Julie gritted her teeth. "You're being *too* charming," she said, knowing she sounded ridiculous. "And there's another thing," she muttered. "Why did you tell poor Frances that you could get her a personally autographed photo of Bruce Springsteen? She's young enough to think you can really do it."

Robert stopped looking puzzled and looked wounded instead. "I didn't lie to Frances," he said. "She's a cute kid. I met good old Bruce once or twice. He's a very friendly person when you get to know him, and I'm sure he'd give me a photo. He produced a video on one of my sets, you know."

"On one of *your* sets?" Julie remarked with heavy sarcasm.

"Well, a set I was working on. You know, as an, um, as a movie extra."

"I thought this film you're making in England was the first time you'd worked as an actor for years."

Robert had no time to reply. "Your mother's coming," he murmured, and Julie wondered if she was imagining the relief she heard in his voice.

Mrs. Marshall steamed out of the drawing room into the hallway, her sister-in-law in tow. "There you are, Robert, my dear," she said with a smile of satisfaction. "Helen, I'd like you to meet Robert Donahue, Julie's fiancé. You've heard me talking about him for months, and now I'm thrilled to say he and Julie have fixed the date for their wedding. Six weeks from today!" Flushed with triumph, she turned to Robert. "And this is my sister-in-law, Helen Hattersly. I know she's longing to meet you."

Helen Hattersly merely harrumphed. Mrs. Marshall directed a thousand-watt smile in the direction of her longtime rival. Helen's daughter had been married for several years and had two sturdy, handsome sons. This weekend was Mrs. Marshall's opportunity to get revenge for all the hours she had been forced to spend admiring pictures of Helen's grandsons, and she intended to make up for every second of past frustration.

"Helen, my dear, Robert has so many fascinating stories to tell. I know you'll just love chatting with him. He's had dinner with the prime minister, you know, and he's going to be such a *distinguished* addition to the family." This was Mrs. Marshall's not-so-subtle way of pointing out that Helen's daughter had married a boring young man still struggling to make his way in a big insurance company.

Helen harrumphed again, holding out her hand to Robert and leaning over to kiss Julie at the same time.

Robert, eyes dancing, submitted to her critical inspection. "Do I pass?" he asked, returning her brisk handshake with a firm one of his own.

"I'm not one to make snap judgments," Helen countered, "but I'll say this for you. It's a pleasure to see Julie looking so lively. She's always been pretty, of course, but I knew she'd be truly beautiful if she could ever find the man to spark the fire inside her. Julie needs a man with a bit of passion in him."

Mrs. Marshall glanced at her daughter, astonishment in every line of her well-corseted body. "Fire" and "passion" were obviously not words she'd ever thought of in connection with her older daughter. Julie could feel Robert's silent laughter, although he continued to hold a perfectly proper conversation with

Aunt Helen. Julie decided she'd better speak before she exploded.

"Robert sparks my fire all right," she said. "Just being near him is enough to bring me to the boiling point."

Helen looked intrigued, Mrs. Marshall looked shocked, and Robert merely grinned. But his husky voice sounded infuriatingly sincere as he picked up Julie's hand and carried it to his lips. "I wish our wedding was tomorrow," he said softly. He pressed a tiny kiss into the palm of her hand, then curled her fingers over the spot his mouth had touched. Her legs developed a sudden, alarming tendency to buckle at the knees.

"Well, you don't have long to wait," Mrs. Marshall declared briskly. "The end of August will be here before you know it." The swirling clouds of tension had finally penetrated even her iron-clad sensibilities, and she was not at all comfortable. The sexual revolution had passed through Chipping Hill without creating much of a ripple, and it had passed over the Marshall household without leaving a trace. Mrs. Marshall sincerely believed that well-brought-up ladies simply didn't feel passion, and any evidence to the contrary left her floundering.

The arrival of a carload of cousins saved Julie from saying something she might have regretted, although it also ended any chance of a tête-à-tête with Robert.

The afternoon continued on its erratic course, with Robert charming every family curmudgeon in sight, and Julie coming closer to exploding with each remark he uttered. She was so busy observing her infuriating "fiancé" that she scarcely noticed when John returned from his hospital visits and took his place beside her sister. Even during the toasts at dinner, she was so annoyed by the wittiness and flair with which Robert proposed the health and happiness of his soon-to-be brother- and sister-in-law that she quite forgot John was the only man she had ever loved and Robert was merely the hired hand doing his best to earn a few extra pounds. In fact, if she'd stopped being enraged with Robert long enough to analyze how little time she was devoting to sad thoughts about John, she would have been amazed.

Thankfully, the evening came to an early close, with the relatives trooping off to the local inn and John hurrying home to spend a final few hours alone with his little daughter.

Mrs. Marshall, newly aware of Julie's supposed attributes of passion and fire, and alarmed that they might spill over into an unseemly display, insisted on escorting Robert up to the guest bedroom herself. Julie was left with no choice other than to retreat to the makeshift bed that had been prepared for her in Alice's room. Later, she swore to herself, mounting the stairs with her father and sister. Some time tonight, even if it wasn't until the early hours of the morning, she was going to confront Robert and call him to account for his outrageous behavior.

Dr. Marshall kissed both of his daughters goodnight. "Don't stay up till all hours gossiping," he admonished. "I want to escort a bright-eyed, rosy-cheeked bride down that church aisle tomorrow morning."

"We'll be good," Alice promised. "Actually, I'm so tired from all the last-minute errands, I think I'll be asleep the minute my head touches the pillow."

Julie smiled at Alice as the bedroom door closed behind their father. "If Dad's around, I think he'll still be fussing about our bedtimes when we're ninety."

Alice shook her head in sisterly agreement. "Just wait. Mum will probably be in any minute now to remind us to brush our teeth."

Julie laughed as she sat on her sister's bed. "I'm glad she decided to put us in here together. We haven't had a chance to talk all day."

"It's been a hectic few weeks, and today was the worst," Alice agreed. "I can't quite believe John and I have made it to the eve of the wedding all in one piece."

"And I can't believe that my baby sister is really going to be married tomorrow. And to John Farringdon of all people!"

Alice glanced up, then looked away, cheeks turning pink. "You don't mind?" she asked. "Although now that I've seen Robert, I suppose that's a silly question. Robert is obviously the perfect man for you."

Julie drew a deep breath, her throat suddenly aching with unshed tears. She had thought her feelings for John were such a well-kept secret, and yet Robert had guessed the truth, and now Alice, too, was admitting she knew of the old attraction. Her three-year dream was dying, Julie realized. Not with a bang but with a whimper of confused emotions.

"Of course I don't mind," she said, wondering if she lied. Was there any part of her that still wished she could be the woman exchanging wedding vows with

John tomorrow? The trauma of his on-again, off-again marriage to Sally had layered Julie's love for him with heavy overtones of guilt. In the years since she'd left home, she'd never really dealt with that guilt, merely covered it over with hard work and a refusal to get involved in any other serious relationship. But could she honestly say that she still loved John?

Julie swallowed the hard lump lodged in her throat and spoke the few words that she *knew* were true. "I hope with all my heart that you and John will be happy together."

Alice walked over to the big old-fashioned wardrobe in the corner of the bedroom and unfurled the protective plastic cover that hung over her wedding dress. "Do you like it?" she asked shyly. "I'm so tiny I can't wear anything too grand."

Julie stroked the ruffles of the puffed sleeves. "You'll look sensational," she said. "The style is just right for you."

Alice shook out a fold of tulle. "You don't think the rosebuds at the hem are too fussy?"

"I think they're the finishing touch the dress needs," Julie said sincerely. "You'll look like an updated version of a mid-Victorian bride. It's going to be a really pretty wedding. You and Mum have worked wonders getting it together at such short notice."

Alice flushed with pleasure, although her fingers twisted one of the rosebuds nervously. "This whole wedding is much more Victorian than you'd ever guess," she said, her cheeks darkening to scarlet. "John and I...we've never... The divorce was finalized so recently..." Alice took a gulp of air. "Julie, you'll never believe this, but I'm a virgin. The fact is,

I'm dreading tomorrow night. I'm afraid I won't be any good at all this lovemaking and stuff. I just don't seem to have a passionate nature. Not like those women you see in films and read about in books who can't wait to hop into bed with half the men they meet. The truth is, I've never really wanted to go to bed with anyone."

Not even with John? Julie thought in silent wonder. "It's different when you're in love," she said, trying to sound reassuring. This didn't seem the right moment to confess that she was just as inexperienced as her sister. "You love John and he loves you. I'm sure once you're alone together for the whole night in a glamorous hotel, everything will just happen naturally."

"I hope so." Alice's embarrassment erupted in a nervous giggle. "I keep having these nightmare visions where the hook on my bra sticks and neither of us can get it off, or something equally silly."

"I'm sure John will find lots of exiting ways to take care of any obstinate bra hooks," Julie said, wondering how in the world she had managed to get herself into the bizarre position of counseling Alice on her sex life with John Farringdon. If only her sister knew how unqualified she was to give advice on that particular topic. In more ways than one!

Alice picked up the silver filigree posy holder that had been carried by their grandmother on her wedding day and ran her finger around the lacy, curving edge. "I'm going to make John very happy, you know, even though he's not madly in love with me—"

"Oh, I'm sure he loves—"

"No. He's only fond of me. But our interests are similar and I'll be a good wife to him. I'm longing to have the chance to become Vickie's mother and to have a baby of my own.''

''You'll be a terrific mother.'' Julie managed to keep her voice light. ''I'm counting on you and John to make me an aunt before the year is out, and I promise to bake a Christening cake that will be the envy of the entire neighborhood.''

Alice tossed the posy holder onto her pillow, almost visibly seizing her courage in both hands. ''I know people think John is marrying me just because he needs a housekeeper and a new mother for Vickie. But that's not true, Julie.''

Julie remembered her conversation with John earlier that afternoon and hoped fervently that her sister was right. ''I'm sure he'll be a super husband.''

Alice smiled wryly, suddenly seeming much older than her twenty-two years. ''We're neither of us passionate people, you know. Not like you and Robert. John and I will be . . . comfortable together. You and Robert will never be comfortable, I shouldn't think, not even if you stay married for fifty years. Robert's just like you. When he's in the room, he seems to dominate it, even if he's merely standing there, not saying anything. It used to make me so jealous when I was little, the way you commanded attention without even trying. Then, when we were teenagers and all the boys started following you around, I tried so hard to be sexy like you.'' She laughed. ''Fortunately I didn't succeed, because I'd never have known what to do with a clutch of panting adolescent boys once I'd attracted them.''

''You wanted to be like me?'' Julie repeated, stunned almost beyond words. ''And to think all the time I was growing up, I wished I could be like you and Mum and Dad. I always felt so guilty and out of place because I didn't want to pursue a career in medicine.''

Smiling, Alice picked up the posy holder and carried it over to the dressing table. ''Thank goodness everything's worked out for the best in the end. I'm going to marry John, and you're going to marry Robert. We each managed to find the man who's ideally suited to our different characters. Sometimes I can't help believing in fate. I like Robert,'' she concluded shyly. ''I'll look forward to visiting you both in America. Where are you going to live?''

Where were they going to live? That was an excellent question! Julie's shredded emotions crystallized into a white-hot blaze of anger. *Robert.* The man was nothing but trouble. How dared he stride into her home, winning the hearts of her family, without a thought for the consequences? He'd been so darn charming everyone would be upset when Julie announced her engagement was over. Poor Mrs. Marshall wouldn't get a second wedding to organize. Frances wouldn't get her Bruce Springsteen photo. Alice was never going to have a brother-in-law to visit in America. Worst of all, Julie was going to look like a fool. A rejected fool, because Robert had made himself so agreeable nobody would believe Julie had willingly ended the engagement.

Julie allowed her anger to build, not pausing long enough in her mental diatribe to consider whether everything that had happened this weekend could be blamed entirely on Robert. Her emotions were in a state of turmoil, and being angry with Robert seemed far and away the most satisfactory method of coping with it. Much better than considering why Robert's announcement of their phony wedding date had made her so furious, and much, much better than asking herself why the memory of his kisses had the power to make her heart pound as if she'd just completed a fast, five-mile run.

Alice was still waiting for a reply, Julie realized somewhat belatedly. "We haven't even chosen what city we'll live in yet, much less thought about the type of house we want." She decided this might be a good moment to lay some groundwork for the soon-to-be-announced ending of her engagement. "Robert has such a busy schedule, sometimes I wonder if we could ever make a normal marriage work." She forced a laugh. "Robert probably thinks we can set up house in his corporate jet. His idea of preparing for fatherhood will be to hire a flight attendant with midwifery experience."

Alice laughed, not picking up on the broad hint. "When people love each other as much as you two, they can always work out the practical problems," she said, yawning. "Gosh, Julie, I'm sorry, but I really do need to get some sleep."

"Do you want to take the bathroom first?" Julie offered. "I still haven't finished unpacking."

Half an hour later, Alice was fast asleep. Julie lay on the narrow camp bed and listened to the sounds of the house settling down for the night. When the grandfather clock struck twelve, she could contain her impatience no longer. Getting to her feet, she pulled on her robe and walked silently to the door. Alice stirred as the door opened, but she didn't awaken, and Julie slipped out into the upstairs hallway unobserved.

The peaceful silence of a household at rest enveloped Julie, but the peacefulness didn't extend to her spirits. After an entire day of deceiving her family, her guilt and anger had simmered together long enough to produce a potent brew of emotional tension. Her self-control was poised on a hair trigger, and only a confrontation with Robert Baxter was going to diffuse her fury. Damn it! She was going to tell the man in no uncertain terms exactly what a troublemaker he was. If he didn't shape up tomorrow, she wouldn't even consider paying him the remainder of his money. That ought to sober him up into a more modest interpretation of his role.

Julie crept past the bedroom that had once been hers and that now temporarily housed Aunt Helen and Uncle Jack. She crept past the pink guest room, where regular, snuffling snores indicated that ninety-year-old Cousin Jane slept in peaceful feminist solitude. Reaching the end of the corridor and the blue guest room, Julie scarcely paused for breath before giving a perfunctory knock and throwing open the door, righteous indignation already simmering past boiling point.

Robert was awake—and unprepared for visitors. He was leaning comfortably against a pile of pillows, reading through some papers in a thick manila folder. One swift glance was all Julie needed to see that he was wearing a pair of horn-rimmed glasses and nothing else, not even a blanket. At the sound of the door bursting open, he flipped the folder closed and tossed it casually onto the bedside table.

"Hi there," he said without a trace of embarrassment, although he did make a leisurely grab for the bedclothes, hitching them into a more decent position around his waist. His tanned, muscled chest gleamed in the light of the bedside lamp, and Julie swallowed, needing to moisten her dry throat. Righteous indignation gave way to a plethora of quite different emotions.

"What an unexpected pleasure," Robert said.

His mouth curved into a warm, beguiling smile, and he crossed his arms behind his head, the picture of unconcerned innocence. Just as if he'd never made his crazy declaration that they were going to be married at the end of August. Just as if he didn't make her remember what it was like to kiss him every time he smiled at her in that special way.

He patted the bed invitingly. "Come and sit down. I'm so glad you decided to visit. I was feeling lonely."

Her heart hammered against her rib cage, doing its now familiar imitation of a long-distance runner at the end of a tough race. Her nightdress and matching robe, both sedate garments of pale green cotton, suddenly seemed inadequate protection against Robert's penetrating gaze, and she pushed the lapels of the robe higher around her neck and tightened the belt.

"I didn't come on a social visit," she said, aware that her voice sounded strained.

"Then what did you come for?"

"For heaven's sake, what do you think? To try and drum some sense into you, if that's possible. Before we have a total disaster on our hands."

Robert didn't say anything. After a long moment—an uncomfortably long moment—he reached up and took off his glasses, leaning over to put them on top of the manila folder.

Julie stared at the muscles rippling across his chest, and for a second or two she couldn't remember why it had seemed so important to have things out with him. She could only think how wonderful it would feel to rest her cheek on the taut, tanned skin of his chest, and to feel the rough curls of his dark hair against her face.

Knees shaking, she jerked her head away from the sight of him, then swallowed hard, searching frantically for what she had planned to say.

Robert patted the bed again. "I wish you'd sit down instead of hovering there in the doorway like an avenging angel." He sounded amused, although his words contained an undercurrent of some emotion Julie was too flustered to decipher. "I'm afraid I can't get up, because I'm not wearing any pajamas. I always sleep in the nude," he added helpfully—as if she wasn't all too aware of the fact that he'd been stark naked when she'd burst into the room.

Julie's stomach took a dive into her toes as her mind provided a vivid instant recall of all six feet three inches of Robert's strong, masculine body stretched out on the bed. The image was so appealing that she actually took a couple of steps forward before common sense returned.

She hurriedly sat in a wicker chair, a safe couple of feet from the side of the bed. "I didn't come here to chat," she said, trying to sound cool and dignified despite her stomach's continuing efforts to perfect its high-dive technique. She drew on the reserve of self-control she'd developed over the past three lonely years. "Robert, we have to discuss some limits for this role you're playing. Things are getting totally out of hand."

"I'm sorry you feel that way. I thought everything went rather well this afternoon."

"I'm sure you did!" Julie exclaimed, losing her tenuous cool. "But have you considered this situation from my point of view? Having convinced every relative I possess that you're my perfect mate, what do you think is going to happen when I tell them the wedding is off?"

Robert appeared to consider the question. "They'll gossip like mad for ten days, then they'll all find themselves something else to talk about," he suggested.

"My distant relatives, perhaps, but not my parents. Not my sister." Julie was finding Robert's steady gaze disconcerting in the extreme, and she pushed nervously at her hair, which seemed to be flying all around her shoulders in one of its most uncontrollable moods. She wished she'd taken the time to pin it back into its usual tight chignon. "You should never have agreed with my mother when she set a date for our wedding," she said finally. "Don't you realize she'll be marching me out to buy a wedding dress next weekend? And she's probably already put in a call to the vicar and the caterers!"

Infuriatingly, Robert seemed in no mood to provide Julie with the fight she craved. "You're right," he said, his voice contrite. "I should never have said anything that implied our wedding was so imminent. I'm sorry. We actors are taught to improvise, but I guess that wasn't one of my better lines."

Oddly deflated, and some part of her still stiff with tension, Julie accepted his apology. "I understand how it happened, I suppose. My mother has all the tact of

Godzilla in situations like this. But how are we going to explain to people that our wedding's off just when we've announced that it's on? I don't want to ruin Alice's wedding day by staging a massive argument between you and me."

"We certainly shouldn't do that," Robert agreed. "I suggest we wait until John and Alice are safely married, and then we'll decide on the best way to tell your parents our engagement's ended. We'll be able to think more clearly once the ceremony and reception are over."

He was being so darn reasonable that Julie almost couldn't remember why she had been so angry with him. "We could call my parents after we get back to London," she suggested. "That way they'll have the whole weekend to be happy about Alice before they start fussing about me."

"Great idea," Robert said affably. "And don't worry. I promise you we'll work something out. Then, if you want to, we can place the call together."

Julie's brow wrinkled in doubt. "I don't know. If we sound too much like friends, my mother will harbor secret hopes that we'll soon be engaged again."

"I see the problem. Well, don't hesitate to put the blame on me. Tell them I'm an incurable workaholic, overbearing, arrogant, never in one place long enough to make a home. Or maybe you could hint that I lost all my money."

"That wouldn't work," Julie said. "If you were suddenly poor, my parents would consider that all the more reason for me to stand by you. No, I'll tell them you're obsessed with piling up millions and millions of dollars, and I'm sick of listening to you talk about money. That should do the trick. My relatives think that the only reason to make a lot of money is to donate it to medical research.''

Robert stroked his chin meditatively. "It's kind of an interesting feeling to get rejected because I have too much money.''

Julie laughed. ''It's a shame you're not really a millionaire, Robert. What a humbling experience for you, to be thrown over because you're such a bore when you ramble on about all your brilliant investments!''

Robert grinned. "A unique experience for a millionaire, I should think." He yawned and stretched, treating Julie to another dazzling display of delectable male muscles. "Sorry, this English country air is exhausting, or else it must be the difficult role I'm trying to play. Back home in the States I usually get by on no more than four or five hours' sleep a night, but right now I can barely keep my eyes open.''

"You didn't look to me as if you were finding your day exhausting," Julie commented. "In fact, you looked as if you were thoroughly enjoying yourself every second." Somehow this fact no longer made her angry.

"I didn't know you were watching me so closely.''

"I had to be close at hand in case you made a mistake," Julie explained quickly. "After all, you're supposed to have known me for nearly a year.''

"True. Anyway, I had a good time meeting your relatives," Robert conceded. "Although I don't think I've ever been in the company of so many doctors, nurses and assorted therapists before. Doesn't anyone in your family ever pursue a career outside medicine?''

"Only me." Julie found that she was actually smiling, although until quite recently the question would have cut her to the quick. "My parents still haven't fathomed what genetic disaster caused me to become a baker."

"Your fruit pies are the result of a genetic miracle, not a disaster," Robert corrected sleepily. He scrunched down in the bed, tucking the covers neatly under his armpits. He yawned again, his eyelids drooping shut. "Please could you turn out the light as you leave?"

Julie got up from the chair, a little surprised at how reluctant she was to end their conversation. She had rarely felt further removed from sleep. Her entire body tingled with an unfamiliar energy, making her want to do something exciting, although she hadn't the faintest idea what. She got up from the chair, her movements jerky, and bent over to switch out the bedside light.

Robert's hand reached out from beneath the sheets and closed lightly around her wrist. "I need a goodnight kiss from my fiancée," he mumbled, already more than three parts asleep.

He didn't hold her tightly. There was no real reason Julie couldn't ignore him and walk away. Nevertheless, she found herself leaning down to give him a quick, sisterly kiss.

The second her lips touched his forehead, Robert's grip on her wrist tightened. He tugged—not hard, but just hard enough to pull her off balance—and she stumbled onto the bed. His arms, every bit as powerful as the rippling muscles suggested, wrapped around her waist. In two swift, economical movements, she found herself held captive.

His eyes, no longer sleepy, danced with laughter and an unconcealed gleam of desire. "Sweetheart, somebody really has to show you how a woman kisses her fiancé good-night." His hand caressed the length of her throat, nudging her chin up, leaving her unable to hide the tumble of her emotions from his gaze. His thumbs brushed gently across her eyelids, closing her eyes.

"This is how it's done," he murmured.

Julie felt the whisper of his breath against her skin, then the touch of his lips on her cheekbones. In a moment, she told herself. In a moment she would get off the bed and walk away.

"Like that, and then like this..." Robert said, seconds before his mouth closed possessively over hers.

Julie had never been kissed with such devastating expertise, never known it was possible to taste your own aching desire in the heat of a man's lips against your mouth. Some primitive, feminine part of her wanted the kiss to last forever, although common sense warned that she should call a halt now, before any real damage was done. Sternly she ordered herself to get up and walk away. Kissing Robert was obviously hazardous to her mental health, an activity to be avoided. No sensible female would ever find herself in this ridiculous situation. And Julie had spent the past few years trying to prove how eminently sensible she was.

If she could have found her voice, she would certainly have told Robert to stop. If she could have lifted her hands, she would have prevented his fingers from twining so sinuously into her hair. And if she could have moved, surely she would have pulled herself out of his arms.

But she couldn't speak and she couldn't move. All she could do was return his kisses with a hunger and an urgency that spoke much too plainly of her years of loneliness, of her sudden, inexplicable yearnings.

But even as her own control slipped, she realized that Robert's control was returning. As he slowly eased himself away from her, he gazed down with an expression of mingled regret and desire. He drew in a shaky breath and gently pushed a tangled cloud of hair away from her forehead.

"Julie, my sweet," he murmured, "I don't think this is what either of us planned to have happen when you came into this room. Much as I'd like to make love to you, we don't want to do something you'll regret tomorrow."

The thrumming in her ears faded, and Julie gradually became aware that Robert had said something to her, but for a moment she was so lost in the pleasure of being held in his arms that she couldn't grasp his meaning. Then the significance of his words gushed like ice water into her consciousness. She slid quickly to the edge of the bed, bewildered that she felt this overwhelming physical attraction for a man she had recently considered no more than a friendly acquaintance.

You don't have to be sensible, some treacherous part of her whispered. *Robert would be a wonderful, considerate lover. Why don't you just enjoy his lovemaking while you have the chance?*

But her family's values were too deeply ingrained and she quickly moved away from the bed, away from temptation. "I have to go," she said, not looking at him. She drew in a deep breath. "I'm grateful to you for...for...um...stopping things before they got out of hand.''

"You're welcome. I think." The familiar note of mockery was back in Robert's voice, and once she had the belt on her robe securely tied, Julie risked turning to look at him. She couldn't bear to think he was laughing at her. But the mockery had been directed entirely at himself, and all trace of laughter vanished from his eyes as her gaze locked with his.

"You'd better go, Julie," he said wryly. "You're so damn beautiful I must be crazy to let you walk out of here. Get going, sweetheart. My stock of surplus nobility is running very low."

Julie astonished herself with her own reply. "I wish your nobility had run out about ten minutes ago," she said, and dashed through the door before she could say something even more foolish. Something utterly insane like *Please, Robert, take me back to bed and make mad, passionate love to me all night long.*

"Julie?" Through the closed door, she heard Robert murmur her name, heard the unspoken question contained within the single softly spoken word.

She covered her ears and ran quietly down the hallway, knowing that if she stopped—even for a moment—she might give him the answer they both wanted to hear.

CHAPTER SIX

THE GUESTS ALL AGREED that Alice Marshall's wedding to John Farringdon was picture perfect. Even the weather cooperated. An early-morning breeze blew away the last of the previous week's dampness, and a warm sun smiled out of blue skies onto the radiant bride, patrician groom, tearful mother, proud father and adorable little bridesmaid. The organist played all the old favorites with panache, and the vicar had the great good sense to limit his sermon to three minutes.

Seated in the front pew between her mother and Robert, Julie found the wedding less painful than she'd anticipated. It was an exercise in willpower, but she managed to keep a cheerful smile pinned on her lips even when John slid his ring onto her sister's finger. In all honesty, Julie admitted to herself, she was having a hard time concentrating on the ceremony.

This strange but welcome state of affairs was due entirely to Robert Baxter. Not, of course, that Robert intended to be helpful. On the contrary, from his appearance at the breakfast table—bright-eyed, bushy-tailed and obnoxiously good-humored—until the moment of his arrival with Julie at church, it was as if he'd dedicated his day to the sole purpose of annoying her in every way possible. He succeeded so well that she viewed the ceremony uniting her sister with John Farringdon not through a veil of tears, but through a red mist of anger.

Despite her stern lecture of the night before, Robert had made no attempt to modify his outrageous behavior. He seemed perversely determined to squeeze every inch of mileage out of his role as Julie's suave, millionaire fiancé. He'd divided his morning between being more charming than ever to all the relatives, and conspiring with Mrs. Marshall to plan every detail of his imminent wedding. Listening to his conversation, Julie began to wonder if he'd suffered a blow to the head during the night and had forgotten that the wedding he was organizing with such enthusiasm was merely a figment of his overactive imagination.

"Are you crazy?" Julie had demanded at one point, passing him in the hallway with her arms full of roses. "Why in the world did you tell my mother that two dozen of your relatives plan to fly over to England for our wedding? Good grief, Robert, first thing tomorrow morning she'll be phoning all round the neighborhood trying to find places for them to stay!"

"Would you prefer me to take over the local inn?" he inquired solicitously. "I was afraid it might not be big enough to accommodate so many people. There are plenty of hotels in Bath, of course, but that's quite a distance away, and these English country roads are easy for Americans to get lost in."

"*Robert!* Stop this craziness!" Julie dumped the roses on the kitchen table and began tearing off the lower leaves with vicious energy. "For heaven's sake, don't you remember anything I said to you last night?"

"Oh, yes," he replied, sounding earnest and sincere. "People tell me I have an excellent memory." He grinned, eyes darkening with sudden mischief. "Besides, your parting remark was most memorable."

Julie felt her cheeks grow hot and she hastily drew a mental screen around a group of memories she didn't want to explore. "We only discussed one thing that was important," she said fiercely. "The ending of this crazy engagement of ours. Please try to remember I am *not* marrying you at the end of August. Can you get that simple idea through your thick, dim-witted skull?"

"Julie!" Mrs. Marshall chose this inauspicious moment to enter the kitchen. "Now, dear, we mustn't lose our tempers just because we're all feeling a little harassed. I'm sure you didn't mean to use that nasty tone of voice to Robert."

"Of course she didn't." Robert smiled forgivingly. He gathered Julie into his arms and dropped a tender kiss on the end of her nose. "The truth is, Mrs. Marshall, we're both feeling a little overemotional today. Sometimes six weeks can seem like an eternity."

Mrs. Marshall looked relieved that her son-in-law-to-be was proving so understanding. "Young love!" she sighed. "A lifetime of togetherness ahead of you, and you're worrying about the next six weeks." She patted Julie on the arm. "Relax and enjoy the fun of preparing for your wedding, my dear. This is a time of your life you can never recapture."

"How true!" Robert murmured. Julie saw the gleam in his eye, recognized the predatory tilt of his head and knew he was going to kiss her. And not just a peck on the cheek. She sidestepped neatly and gave him a smile that was dazzling in its insincerity.

"Here, Robert, dearest." With great care, she selected a rosebud from the pile on the table. She thrust the flower into Robert's hands and closed her fingers around the thorny stem. Hard. "This is for you," she said sweetly. "I hope it will remind you of how I feel about you."

"How nice!" Mrs. Marshall hadn't seen the half-inch thorns guarding the stem. "Oh dear, I must fly. Nobody told the caterers about the salmon." She hurried out of the kitchen, lists flapping.

Robert opened his hand, and Julie felt a spurt of guilt when she saw the dark red drops of blood seeping from the center of his palm. "I'm sorry," she said tersely.

"That's okay," he replied, his voice mild. "But I don't need any reminders of how you feel about me, Julie. I already know, because I feel the same way about you. The only interesting question is why you won't allow yourself to admit the truth of your feelings."

Her momentary guilt vanished without trace at this further evidence of his infuriating arrogance. "Have patience," she said with a smile that would have killed a cobra at twenty paces. "Once we're back in London I'll let you know *exactly* how I feel about you."

He brought his hand up to his mouth and licked away the drops of blood, his gaze never releasing hers. "I can't wait," he said softly. "Your place or mine?"

Julie made a grab for the pruning sheers, and Robert was wise enough to make a dash for the door.

But he wore the rosebud, neatly threaded into the lapel of his impeccably tailored suit, when he arrived downstairs two hours later, ready to escort Julie to the church. Julie had no idea why her stomach chose that precise moment to start its second round of practice for the high-dive competition.

THE NEWLYWEDS, faces wreathed in smiles, set off on their honeymoon in a shower of confetti and good wishes. The guests all declared that the reception had been even more splendid than the church service, and the wedding cake the most magnificent they'd ever seen. The Marshalls, not least Julie, basked in a well-deserved glow of family pride.

Only poor little Vickie failed to share in the general happiness. John and Alice had both explained repeatedly that they loved her very much and would soon be home again, bringing armfuls of presents, but the reality of their departure had failed to sink in until the last moment. Sobbing her heart out, Vickie stood on the front steps, straining to catch a final glimpse as her father's car faded from sight.

Julie, whose experience with small children was limited, began to feel really worried when offers of cake, fizzy drinks and even a ride on Dr. Marshall's shoulders produced nothing more than incoherent mumbles about Daddy and fresh bursts of pitiful sobbing.

"She's overwrought," Mrs. Marshall announced, taking Vickie onto her lap and rocking gently. "All this excitement is too much for a little girl who's not yet six."

"I prescribe a hot bath, some warm milk and a story in bed," Dr. Marshall said, ruffling Vickie's mop of brown curls. "Perhaps even two stories in bed."

"I'll take care of her," Julie offered, eager to be of help, "I love reading stories." But Vickie shrank away from her new aunt's outstretched hand and clung tightly to Mrs. Marshall's silk dress.

"I don't want Julie. She's not my friend." Vickie's face crumpled into a fresh bout of tears. "I want my daddy."

"She needs familiar people around her at the moment." Mrs. Marshall hugged Vickie tighter, totally indifferent to the chocolate smears now gracing her mother-of-the-bride outfit. "And I'm the person she knows best, I think. I'll take her upstairs and supervise her bath myself. Most of the older guests have already left, and the young ones don't need me to keep them company." She reached out in search of a table napkin and used the large linen square to wipe Vickie's soggy face. "Hush, now, sweetheart, or you'll make yourself sick. Daddy and Alice will be home again almost before you know it."

"I want them home *now!*" Each word was punctuated by a sob.

Robert bent down until he was at eye level with Vickie. "You were a great flower girl today," he told her softly. "Your dad and your new mommy were very proud of you."

Intrigued by the American accent, Vickie stopped crying long enough to sneak a quick glance at Robert, and he took advantage of her momentary silence to pass his right hand in front of her face, stopping with a dramatic flourish when he got to her ear.

"Good heavens, what's this?" he asked in exaggerated surprise, holding out a shiny fifty-pence piece. "I didn't know flower girls kept money in their ears."

"I don't...I didn't..." Vickie's sobs died away in a fragile hiccup of laughter. "My dress has a pocket...and I'm a bridesmaid, not a flower girl."

"Is that so? Well, I certainly apologize, but in America, we'd call you a flower girl." Robert repeated the previous sweep of his hand, this time stopping at her other ear. "Whoops! How amazing! Look, here's another fifty-pence piece."

This time Vickie's gurgle of laughter was stronger. "Are you a conj'rer?" she asked. "I'm going to have a conj'rer at my next birthday party. Alice said I could."

"I guess I must be," Robert said, squashing her nose with the tip of his finger. A gleaming silver coin appeared between her nose and his finger. "Either I'm a conjurer, or you have a piggy bank in your nose."

"I don't," she assured him solemnly. "Not in my ears, either."

"Well, then, there's no doubt about it, I'm a conjurer. You'd better keep the money, or maybe my magic powers will disappear." He opened her hand and pressed the coins into her small, damp fist.

"Thank you," she said, her tears forgotten as she stared at the gleaming coins. "I've never had any magic money before."

"We'd better take it upstairs and put it somewhere safe," Mrs. Marshall said. Casting a look of gratitude over her shoulder, she ushered Vickie toward the stairs.

As soon as Vickie and his wife were out of earshot, Dr. Marshall clapped Robert on the shoulder in a rare display of emotion. "Whew! That was a bit sticky there for a little while. Thanks, old chap. You helped us out of a tight spot. Now I know how you international financiers make your money. You produce it out of thin air!''

Robert laughed. ''I wish it were that exciting. Actually, we make it all by shuffling paper. Dr. Marshall, if there's nothing else Julie and I can do here to help, we thought we might go into Bath for a late dinner.''

''Good idea. Wish I could join you. I'm looking forward to a sandwich myself now that most of the guests have left. I worked so hard at being a genial host, I scarcely had time to snatch a bite of Julie's wonderful wedding cake.'' He chuckled. ''No food, and far too much champagne—that's my problem.''

And her problem, too, Julie decided. Too many glasses of champagne was the best explanation for the wonderful, floating sensation she was experiencing at the thought of going out to dinner with Robert. If she wasn't just a little bit drunk, why wasn't she protesting this latest example of his infuriating habit of organizing her life?

''Take Alice's car,'' her father suggested. ''Much better than trying to call for a taxi. Their service is so erratic these days. The keys are in the drawer in the kitchen. You know which drawer I mean, Julie?''

''Yes, Dad. But I'm not sure I should be driving.''

''I've only had one glass of champagne,'' Robert said. ''I can drive if you like.''

''Good. Have a lovely evening, and there's no need to rush back. One thing about these caterers my wife hired—they may cost the earth, but they guarantee to clean up all the mess.'' Dr. Marshall beamed benevolently and, Julie thought, just a touch tipsily. ''Show Robert how attractive Bath looks by moonlight, Julie, my dear. Perhaps he'll be so impressed he'll decide to come back sometime and make a leisurely tour by daylight. We're all hoping to see a lot more of him now that your wedding date is actually settled."

"And I plan to be around a lot," Robert said, not looking in the least guilty at this further evidence of how he had wormed his way into the affections of the Marshall family.

Julie tried to scowl. She wanted to be cross with him, but he tucked his arm casually around her waist, and something—no doubt bubbles of champagne—fizzed through her veins. Somehow, the annoyance she should have been feeling turned to a little knot of excitement in the pit of her stomach. She found herself leaning against Robert, relaxing against the strength of his supporting arm.

"I'll get the car keys," she said, aware that her voice sounded oddly husky.

Robert looked down at her, and something in his dark blue gaze made the gentle fizzing in her veins turn to fire. "I'll come with you," he said. "Good night, Dr. Marshall. See you in the morning."

Fortunately Robert kept his arm around Julie's waist as they walked to the kitchen. The champagne, she decided, was really having a disastrous effect on her muscular system. She'd never known three small glasses could make a person's knees so wobbly that standing became difficult. And why did her skin feel as if it were alive with latent electricity, right in the places where Robert was touching her? Julie could find no acceptable answers. But somehow she couldn't quite convince herself that swearing off alcohol would produce the necessary cure.

CHAPTER SEVEN

THE LONG SUMMER EVENING had not yet faded into
night when Robert drove Alice's little Toyota out of the
Marshalls' driveway, heading toward Bath. A breeze
had sprung up, and the cool gusts of air were all Julie
needed to bring a welcome burst of chilly rationality to
the overheated confusion of her brain.

Her best course of action was clear, she decided,
fastening her seat belt. She would treat this dinner with
Robert as a pleasant finale to a weekend that had
turned out to be less painful than she would have believed possible even a couple of days ago. To a certain
extent, she owed Robert a debt of gratitude. True, he
had ignored her instructions and vastly overplayed his
role of fiancé. On the other hand, Julie was honest
enough to admit that it had been easier to listen to her
relatives extolling Robert's virtues than enduring endless variations on the theme of "Now that your
younger sister has married, isn't it time you stopped
playing pastry cook and settled down with a nice doctor husband of your own?"

With this debt of gratitude firmly in mind, Julie re-
solved to keep a tight hold on her wayward emotions.
She would behave with polite, dignified friendliness
toward Robert even though things had got a touch out
of control in his bedroom last night. Julie congratu-

lated herself on being a mature woman. Instead of expressing her justifiable anger at certain aspects of his behavior, she would guard her tongue and be a model of courtesy. *She* understood how their relationship could be brought to a graceful conclusion, even if he didn't.

Putting her resolutions into immediate effect, she refrained from complaining that he hadn't consulted her about their dinner date. Glossing over his high-handedness, she turned to him with a gracious smile.

"Would you like me to make a suggestion about a place to eat? Unfortunately most of the restaurants that serve really good food are too crowded to take people without reservations. Especially on a Saturday night."

"Thanks, but I already made a booking for us at the Silver Bell. A friend in London told me it was an excellent place to eat, with great music for dancing."

"The best in Bath," Julie agreed, wondering if Robert's friend had also warned him that dinner for two at the Silver Bell would cost a very large sum of money. After a moment's silent debate, she decided not to say anything about the expense. If she chose one of the cheaper main dishes from the menu and skipped dessert, they could escape with a reasonably modest bill. And although Robert had seemed eager to earn the six hundred pounds she offered him for their weekend masquerade, she had no other reason to suppose he was especially hard up.

Robert eased the Toyota into the steady flow of traffic on the main Bath road. "That was a great wedding," he said, smiling as he glanced briefly at Julie. "If your mother ever gets bored with being a housewife, she could carve out a fantastic career for herself as a professional party organizer.''

''She's whiz at everything she tackles. When I was a teenager, I listened to her scatterbrained way of talking and never noticed how much she accomplished for various volunteer groups. She was a district nurse before she married my father, and I've heard tales that she organized the entire county so efficiently the babies all started being born between nine and five, Monday to Friday.''

Robert laughed. ''She's definitely a memorable character. I wonder how she'd hit it off with my mother?''

Julie drew a deep breath. Be calm, she reminded herself. She wouldn't leap to the conclusion that Robert expected their parents to meet. ''We're never likely to find out, are we?'' she commented. ''From what you've said, though, we already know they have one thing in common.''

''What's that?''

''They're both determined to see us safely married off to suitable partners whether we like the idea or not.''

''What a shame we can't oblige them.'' Robert's voice was as light as hers. ''I guess it's hard for mothers to realize how much energy it takes to get a career launched these days. In some ways, you and I are a matched pair. With the career goals we've set for ourselves, neither of us has had time to get involved in a serious relationship.''

''Thank goodness you realize that!'' Julie exclaimed. ''There were moments this morning when I began to wonder if you'd slipped mental gears during the night. You were so convincing in your role of devoted fiancé I didn't know whether to offer you a bonus for outstanding acting, or scalp you for driving me crazy!''

Robert grinned. "Oh, come on now, I don't think the issue was ever in doubt. You wanted to scalp me with the nearest available kitchen knife."

She laughed, settling back into the car seat. "I'm sorry I pricked you with that rose." She didn't quite know where the apology sprang from; she only knew it was heartfelt.

"That's okay. I deserved it." They stopped at a traffic light, and Robert's fingers drummed on the steering wheel. "I have a confession to make," he said. "I knew I was annoying you this morning. In fact, almost everything I did or said was deliberately calculated to make you angry."

Bewildered, she turned to look at him. "Why?"

He didn't return her gaze when he finally answered. "I decided that if you were mad at me, you would have less emotional energy for mourning the end of your relationship with John Farringdon. I hoped being angry with me might make it easier for you to get through the wedding ceremony. Was I wrong?"

"You were right," she said softly, surprised at how easy it was to admit the truth. What was the point of denying she had once loved John Farringdon when Robert had seen through her pretense from the beginning?

If admitting the truth was surprisingly easy, even more astonishing was how little she cared that—at this very moment—John and Alice were probably arriving at their honeymoon hotel. She felt no pain at the thought of them melting into each other's arms. And it was Robert, she realized, who had managed to arm her with this welcome indifference.

Julie decided to acknowledge her debt. "Thanks, Robert, for putting up with my rotten mood this morning. I'm grateful to you for making a miserable day much less horrible than I expected."

"You're welcome. I'm glad my plan worked. Am I truly forgiven, or is there a lingering danger I might be murdered if I turn my back?"

"I promise you're safe."

"Thank heaven. Now I can concentrate on life's really important problems. Like whether to order fish or meat for dinner."

"I'm afraid you can't relax just yet. We do still have one major hurdle left," Julie said.

"What's that?"

"Straightening out the mess we've created by telling all those lies to my parents. If only they didn't seem to like you so much—you were so darn charming." Robert didn't say anything, and she sighed. "Okay, your silence speaks louder than words. You're right. Explaining things to my family isn't your problem, it's mine. *We* didn't create this situation. I did. I'm the one who asked you to come to the wedding."

"But I was the one who overplayed my role," Robert admitted.

"True, and I'd love to pretend this mess is all your fault. But you can't be blamed because I didn't have the courage to come to my sister's wedding without a phony fiancé in tow. Not to mention the fact that I was dumb enough to invent that wretched Robert Donahue character in the first place. Robert Donahue, multimillionaire.'' She sighed in exasperation. "For heaven's sake! Even the name sounds fake.''

"Hey, don't talk about the guy like that! The name sounds genuine enough to me. Besides, I've grown quite attached to poor old Mr. Donahue over the past couple of days.''

" 'Poor' isn't quite the right word to describe him, is it?''

Robert raised his eyebrows, managing to look extremely pompous. "Ah, he's poor in true friends, if not in money.''

She chuckled. "What can you expect when he spends all his waking hours grinding every last ounce of labor out of his starving factory workers?''

"Julie, dearest, this is the twentieth century. There are no starving factory workers anymore, at least not in the West. Besides, we decided that this Robert Donahue guy made his millions in the entertainment industry. He doesn't have any factory workers to exploit. He makes his money coping with the outrageous egos of superstars, and the demented visions of his movie directors.''

Julie glared at him. "I invented Mr. Donahue, so I can have him grinding his workers in the dirt if I want to. You're a spoilsport, Robert. Has anyone ever mentioned that you shouldn't introduce boring facts when someone's being creative?''

For a moment, in the dimness of the car's interior, Robert's profile looked oddly stricken. "As it happens,'' he said wryly, "that's a complaint I hear all the time from my colleagues.''

Julie was surprised to find herself offering comfort. "Robert, I was being ridiculous. I'm sure that it's part of your job to quote facts and keep people down to earth.''

He grimaced. "Artists and entertainers don't appreciate having their flights of fancy pulled down to ground level. They forget that unless my, er, our company makes money on its projects, we're on a one-way trip to bankruptcy court.'' Robert steered the car into one of the few vacant spots in the parking lot at the side of the quaint, thatched-roof Silver Bell restaurant. "Anyway, right now I can't waste time worrying about how misunderstood I am. I have a vitally important mission to accomplish.''

"What's that?''

"I want to find out if the Silver Bell makes a fresh raspberry tart that's even half as good as the one you make at The Crusty Corner.''

Julie was laughing as they walked into the foyer of the restaurant. One tiny part of her mind was aware of how amazing it was that she felt so carefree when her sister had just married John Farringdon. For the most part, she was conscious only of how glad she was to be having dinner in such a pleasant restaurant with such an entertaining companion.

Their meal was delicious, well cooked and deftly, almost obsequiously, served. Robert's declaration that the raspberry tart was very good, but not quite as perfect as the ones Julie sold at The Crusty Corner, provided the crowning touch to the meal.

"I have to stop boring you with all this talk about the bakery,'' Julie said as the waiter cleared their dessert plates. She leaned back in her chair, sipping an Irish coffee, aware that she had babbled on too long about the excitement, trials and challenges of running a small business.

"You haven't bored me at all. I really admire what you've achieved with your shop. Not only are you a superb baker and pastry chef, but you've also learned how to handle the financial complexities of making your business profitable. That's not easy, especially since none of your family has the commercial background to offer any help."

"Well, thanks. Coming from you, that's a real compliment. My shop must seem small potatoes to you, but it's wonderful to talk to someone—apart from my loan officer—who understands the difficulties of getting a small business launched and operating. Your suggestions were really helpful."

Julie suddenly realized what she'd said. Eyes wide with astonishment, she put down her coffee cup and stared at Robert. "Good heavens, all the lies this weekend are beginning to unhinge me. While you were offering me that advice about how to refinance my ovens to make them more cost-effective, I completely forgot that you aren't really Mr. Robert Donahue, famous international financier!"

He laughed softly. "Well, making movies is mostly about making money, you know, and I understood what you were talking about. Besides, I'm getting kind of fond of my role. I'm flattered you think I'm convincing. Any minute now I'll get so carried away I'll slip a hundred-pound note to the band leader and ask him to play my favorite song."

"What is your favorite song, Robert?"

He cocked his head to one side, listening. The band was playing something slow and dreamy that Julie didn't recognize. "Would you believe this is it?" he said. He pushed back his chair and came around to take her hands. "Come on, we can't miss this great opportunity. We have to dance while they're playing our song."

The lights on the handkerchief-sized dance floor were dim. Even the small band was in shadow except for a single spotlight trained on the lead singer, a young woman with a mellow, slightly gravelly voice.

Julie had always loved dancing, reveling in the synergy between her body movements and the rhythmic throb of the music, but when Robert put his arms around her waist and slowly pulled her into his arms, she could scarcely hear the music over the pounding of her heart. His body felt taut and athletic against hers, and where her hands rested on his shoulders, she could feel the hard ripple of muscles, even through the thickness of his jacket.

Julie recognized the undeniable tug of physical attraction, but she was warmed even more by the sense of caring and protectiveness Robert conveyed. She thought of all the occasions during the past two days when his mere presence had given her the emotional support she needed, and realized that she would feel bereft when the weekend was over and they parted company. The possibility that she might never see him again was suddenly intolerable.

"You dance as well as I thought you would." Robert's voice was lower than usual and a little husky.

"Thank you. I like to dance." Julie shook off her gloomy thoughts about the end of the weekend and concentrated on enjoying the pleasure of the moment. "What tune is this? I don't recognize it."

"I've no idea." He looked down at her, and in his gaze she saw unmistakable desire mingled with his laughter.

For a moment, all she could think of was how much she wanted to clasp her hands behind his neck and pull his head down until his mouth covered hers. Then memory returned. "But you said it was your favorite song!"

"It was. It is. Any song would have been my favorite if it provided me with an excuse to hold you in my arms." His expression sobered as he touched the wisps of hair that had escaped from her chignon and curled at the nape of her neck. "You're so beautiful, Julie. Beautiful and passionate. And damnably elusive." He smiled ruefully. "You bring out my primitive male hunting instincts in full force. Right now I'm imagining how wonderful it would be to drag you back to my lair, throw you down on the nearest pile of bearskins and make passionate love to you all night long."

Julie's stomach swooped into a nosedive, but she smiled, determined not to let her attraction escalate out of control. "I'm allergic to animal fur. Sorry, Robert. I'd sneeze and ruin your night."

He laughed. "Trust you to destroy my favorite fantasy. But I don't really care. Having you in my arms is better than any fantasy. You fit against me as if we'd been designed to go together."

As he spoke, Julie had the impression that his eyes darkened with tenderness. Heat unfurled in the pit of her stomach as he ran his fingers over the nape of her neck, then tugged gently at the heavy coil of her hair. She swallowed, trying to keep a grip on her runaway emotions. Years ago, she had confused teenaged infatuation for John with real love. She mustn't make the mistake of confusing Robert's easygoing charm for something deeper.

"Nobody's listening to us now," she said, a little dismayed to hear the note of longing in her voice. "You don't have to pretend you love me when we're alone."

Robert didn't answer. He stared down at her, his expression suddenly inscrutable. The drummer beat out a crescendo, the singer hit a high note, and the music fell abruptly silent. Feeling slightly dazed, Julie watched the other dancers leave the floor.

"We'd better get back to the table," Robert said, his voice curt. He put his hand at the small of her back and began guiding her around the edge of the dining area. Once back at their table, Julie found that their earlier mood of relaxed intimacy seemed to have vanished.

Robert glanced at his watch. "Unless you want more coffee, I'd be happy to get out of here."

Julie stared at her own watch without seeing it. "Yes, it's late and we have a train to catch tomorrow."

Robert refrained from pointing out that their train didn't leave until late afternoon. He raised his right hand in a brief gesture and their waiter appeared almost instantly. "Yes, sir?"

"The bill, please."

"Certainly, sir. I trust you found your meal to your liking?"

"Very much so, thank you. Miss Marshall and I had a most enjoyable evening. Our compliments to the chef."

The waiter looked as gratified as if he had been praised by his most important customer of the month.

"Thank you, sir. Our chef will be delighted to hear that you were pleased. We hope we'll see you again soon?"

"Undoubtedly." Robert paused. "The bill?" he said quietly.

"Of course, sir. Immediately." The waiter scurried away, and Julie followed his departure with a smile.

"He sounds as if he took a special course in how to be ingratiating."

"What?" Robert looked vague, then seemed to focus. "Oh, well, waiters in the best restaurants like to make every guest feel special."

Two distinguished-looking men passed by the table at almost the same instant that the waiter returned with the bill. Forced to pause in their conversation in order to avoid the waiter, the older of the two men glanced at Robert and gave a start.

"Mr. Donahue!" he exclaimed in a respectful undertone. "What a pleasant surprise to see you in our part of the country. I didn't think you could ever be torn away from London."

"Mr. Donahue," the younger man repeated. "I see your unerring instinct for finding the best restaurant in any town hasn't deserted you."

For a moment, Robert's entire body went still. Then he shot a swift, oddly appraising glance at Julie. She wondered vaguely why he looked so tense. Beneath the table, he squeezed her hand, and she saw some of the unnatural stillness drain from him. He stood up to greet the newcomers.

"Graham, Henry, nice to see you," he said. "I'm relaxing for a couple of days with old friends. This is a lovely part of the country." Before either of the two men could do more than nod in agreement, Rober came around to Julie's side of the table and placed his hand on her shoulder.

"Julie, my dear, did you meet Graham Stithers and Henry Gibbon this afternoon? I don't think you did. Gentlemen, this is a very good friend of mine, Julie Marshall."

The two men looked at her with what Julie considered polite, but excessive, interest. The older man, Graham Stithers, cast Robert a glance that could only be called peculiar, before shaking hands with Julie and acknowledging the introduction.

Julie had barely managed to produce a couple of innocuous remarks about the excellence of the restaurant before Robert was saying his farewells to the two men and propelling her toward the exit.

"Sorry, wish we could stay and chat, but I promised Julie's father that we'd be back home at a reasonable hour," he said. "See you in town next week, Graham."

"I look forward to it. Tuesday, nine-fifteen." Mr. Stithers's gaze had become as avidly curious as was possible for a proper British gentleman who had been trained since babyhood in the supreme virtue of discretion. He watched, eyes rounding, as Robert tossed a pile of ten-pound notes onto the silver salver bearing the bill and ushered Julie out of the restaurant at breakneck speed.

"Sorry about that," he said when they were alone in the parking lot. "But Graham Stithers is the world's most pompous bore."

"That's all right." Julie would have had no desire to talk to Mr. Stithers or to Mr. Gibbon, even if they'd been the world's most fascinating couple. All she wanted was to be alone with Robert. Something had happened on the dance floor of the Silver Bell, she reflected, some fundamental change in the nature of her feelings toward Robert. Looking at his shadowy profile as he backed the Toyota out of its parking space, Julie wanted nothing more than to lay her head against his shoulder and leave it there forever. If he had tried to kiss her, she would have responded with all the passion he could possibly have wished.

In the past, she had often found Robert too intuitive for her own comfort. Tonight, however, he didn't seem to divine her mood. He drove fast and competently back to Chipping Hill, breaking the silence with infrequent comments on subjects as trivial as the traffic, the wedding guests or the cloudy night sky. Drawing to a halt outside the Marshall home after a record-breaking fifteen-minute drive, he switched off the ignition and turned slowly to face Julie. Her breath caught in her throat, and the world shrank until it encompassed no more than the waiting, tension-filled quiet of the car's interior.

Robert moved first. He reached out and silently traced the outline of her face. "I want to kiss you goodnight," he said at last. "But I don't think it's a good idea."

She stared at her clenched hands. When she found her voice, she asked, "Why not?"

"Chiefly because it would be unfair to your parents if we made love in their guest bedroom."

"Sharing a kiss doesn't mean that we have to share a bed."

"Doesn't it?" Robert crooked his finger under her chin and tilted up her face so that she was compelled to meet his gaze. His features were drawn tight, she realized, all trace of easygoing laughter erased as if it had never been. He ran his thumb over her lips with intolerable, aching gentleness.

"The next time we kiss, Julie, my love, our kiss will be no more than a prelude to something much more important. We both know that."

"But we're not likely to be kissing each other in the future," she said, wanting desperately for him to deny her statement. "I don't expect we shall meet again after this weekend."

"It's risky trying to foretell the future." He took her hand and held it for a second against his cheek. "Good night," he said softly, releasing his clasp. "Thank you for a wonderful evening, Julie, and for inviting me to share such a happy time with your family."

He had no intention of trying to make her change her mind, she realized with a shiver of shock. He had accepted without real protest the idea that the two of them might never see one another again after they returned to London.

Which was just the way she had planned it all along, Julie reminded herself. She had no room in her busy schedule for romantic complications, and she knew instinctively that Robert would be a major complication. He simply wasn't the sort of man who could be tucked away on the periphery of a woman's life.

Now she had nothing to worry about, nothing at all. Except the sick, empty feeling that had suddenly invaded her heart.

CHAPTER EIGHT

"NOW, JULIE, DEAR, don't forget! I'm coming to town next Saturday to help you look for a wedding dress. We'd better start early in the morning, as soon as the shops open. We'll have to buy whatever they have in stock, of course, since the ceremony's barely six weeks away. Still, we managed to find something just right for Alice, and I'm sure we'll manage with you." Mrs. Marshall beamed happily at her daughter, not in the least intimidated by the daunting task ahead.

A railway guard ran down the platform, slamming the train doors shut. Julie's stomach thudded in unison with each bang. It was Sunday afternoon, but as far as she was concerned, the weekend was already over. Reality had set in with a vengeance. The more happy and exited her mother appeared, the more selfish and immature Julie felt. She knew it would be wiser to end the deception right now, but one glance at her mother's rosy cheeks and shining eyes was sufficient to squash that notion. She was a coward, Julie castigated herself. Every action she had taken recently was the action of a moral coward.

Mrs. Marshall became impatient. "Well, Julie, can you be ready to go shopping by nine o'clock? Or do you have something more important planned?"

"Mother, you know Saturday's my busiest day at the baker—"

"My dear child, don't dare to tell me you can't take a day off from your own shop to choose your wedding dress." Mrs. Marshall smiled at Robert, not seeming to notice his unusual silence. "Perhaps you can convince Julie how silly she sounds. Children never want to listen to their mothers."

Robert turned toward Julie, his gaze somber. "Don't worry about the store," he said quietly. "I'm sure we can arrange extra help in the bakery for one day."

"I have more pressing problems to deal with next week than extra help at The Crusty Corner," she reminded him crossly.

"I know. We'll talk about them on the train. Speaking of which—" he glanced at his watch "—I wish we could stay and chat, Mrs. Marshall, but we're going to miss our train, and this is the last express tonight."

"I quite understand." Mrs. Marshall kissed Robert's cheek with matronly affection. "Thank you for making time in your busy schedule to come to Alice's wedding. All the family is so pleased to have met you."

"I enjoyed every minute of it. You organized a great party, Mrs. Marshall."

"And we'll organize something just as special for you and Julie. We've worried about her these past few months, you know. We suspected she'd broken her heart over some secret love affair!" Mrs. Marshall chuckled at her own foolishness. "I have a confession to make. Do you know, her father and I were afraid she'd turned to you on the rebound? On the phone, she never sounded as if you were truly *important* to her. In fact, sometimes your relationship didn't even seem quite real. Robert Donahue, millionaire international financier, marrying the local doctor's daughter. It sounds like something out of a silly television serial, doesn't it?'' Mrs. Marshall's cheerful laugh invited her listeners to share the joke.

Julie managed a feeble grin. ''Now that you've met him, you can see my relationship with Robert is very real,'' she said, swallowing her guilt. Having spent all weekend deceiving her entire family, she could hardly quibble at this final lie.

Robert himself didn't look entirely happy as he shook Mrs. Marshall's hand and once again expressed his thanks for her hospitality. ''I'm sure you'll find that Julie's got her life back on track now,'' he said. ''Everything will turn out for the best, you'll see.''

Mrs. Marshall's smile faded into a puzzled frown. ''Well, of course her life is on track, Robert. She's going to marry you! Unless you've changed your mind since Friday?'' Her voice rose into a worried question. ''Julie, has something happened between you and Robert? You seemed so happy—just right for each other!''

Not now. I can't handle this discussion now, Julie thought. ''Mother, we're going to miss our train,'' she said in desperation.

The shrill blare of the whistle reinforced the truth of her excuse. Thanking her lucky stars for the diversion, she called goodbye over her shoulder and sprinted along the platform with Robert, clambering on board just as the guard gave the signal to depart.

They found themselves alone in the first-class carriage, and for several minutes neither of them said a word. Robert finally broke the silence.

"I'm sorry, Julie, I feel guilty as hell. I don't usually screw up my assignments this badly."

Wearily Julie leaned back against the dusty upholstery. "Thanks for the generous apology, but the problem was caused by me, not by you, Robert. Asking you to impersonate Robert Donahue was just the final link in a long chain of deception. I spent six months creating a swamp of lies and then walked into the mire with my eyes wide open. I can't complain because I'm having a hard time getting out. Cowards always make life more difficult for themselves."

He gave her a ghost of his familiar grin. "Well, keep in mind that yanking people from swamps is one of my specialties. Shout if you need a hand." Robert leaned forward and covered her fingers, stopping their restless kneading. "We haven't reached the limit of my acting abilities, you know. I can play a mighty convincing villain if that's going to make the situation with your parents any easier. I owe you that much at least."

"Thanks, but I think it's time for the truth, or something close to it. I've learned my lesson at last." Julie shuddered. "Gosh, this is going to be a miserable week."

"Maybe it won't be as bad as you expect," Robert suggested. "Look how much you dreaded *this* weekend, and Alice's wedding didn't turn out to be so bad, did it?"

"No, but that's because you were there with me. You made me realize almost at once that I don't love...that I never loved..." Julie drew a deep breath and forced herself to finish the sentence. "That I never loved John Farringdon."

The words were out, the truth committed to words, and Julie felt an overwhelming sense of relief. With the clear vision of hindsight, she could see now that John's major attraction had been the simple fact that he was a doctor and her father's partner. She had taken that fact, added a potent measure of sympathy because his runaway wife was so selfish, flavored the brew with a dash of infatuation for his handsome features and convinced herself that she was the victim of a star-crossed grand passion. Whereas, in reality, she had been nothing more than the victim of her own immature illusions.

"If I helped you to realize that John Farringdon isn't the right man for you, then I'd say this has been a useful weekend," Robert said quietly.

She gave a wry smile. "Useful, or painful, one of the two."

It was a moment before Robert replied. "Learning the truth about the deepest part of ourselves is often painful."

"It's funny how understanding a few basic truths about myself makes a lot of other things seem clearer. John's character is a lot like my father's. Somehow I convinced myself that would make us ideal mates, even though my father and I have never really understood the first thing about each other."

"You were very young when you left home," Robert said. "Almost everyone makes the wrong choice the first time they fall in love."

In her new mood of stark self-appraisal, Julie wasn't willing to find excuses for herself. "Perhaps. But sensible people don't waste three years of their life mooning over an attraction they felt when they were too young to know any better. They get on with their lives."

"And that's exactly what you did. You started a successful business and established your own home, and generally had a great time leading your own life. Maybe you hung on to your infatuation with John Farringdon as an excuse to avoid getting involved with another man," Robert suggested.

Julie's eyes widened with surprise. "Why would I do that? I've always wanted to get married and have children."

"But maybe not quite yet. My impression is that you've spent every waking moment for the past three years struggling to establish The Crusty Corner. You wanted to prove to yourself that you didn't need to be a doctor in order to be successful. Your family didn't understand what you were trying to do, of course, so you got no emotional support from them. Convincing yourself that you were involved in a tragic love affair gave you a great excuse to avoid real-life entanglements." His eyes crinkled with amusement. "Think how much time you saved! Think of how many nights you worked late at the shop instead of going out on dates."

It was a whole new perspective on the past three years of her life. "You've very convincing," Julie said at last.

He smiled. "Pop psychology always sounds convincing. In this case, it might even be true."

The train chugged to a gradual halt as it drew into Oxford station, its only stop en route to London. Julie glanced out of the window, mulling over what Robert had said. A tall, vaguely familiar figure caught her eye.

"Look, Robert. There's Mr. What's-his-name. The man we met last night at the Silver Bell. He must be taking this train."

Robert leaned forward to look. "Graham Stithers!" With an abrupt movement, he pulled down the window shade. "Don't attract his attention!" he growled. "Good grief, we'd be a captive audience all the way to London."

Julie smiled, but her attention was not entirely on what Robert was saying. Seeing Graham Stithers had triggered a memory from the night before, a niggling memory that had lodged deep in her subconscious and now popped to the top.

"Robert! The most extraordinary thing. Mr. Stithers and that other man we met last night in the restaurant—they called you Robert Donahue!"

"What else did you expect them to call me?" Robert asked, after a split second of silence. "Actually they were extremely polite and British. They didn't call me Robert, they called me *Mister* Donahue, if you recall."

"For heaven's sake, what's the matter with you? Don't you see the problem? Your name's Robert Baxter, not Robert Donahue. I invented Robert Donahue. He doesn't exist!"

Her outburst left Robert looking puzzled. "But they don't know Mr. Donahue is an invention of yours. Surely that was the point of this whole masquerade—that the guests coming to your sister's wedding should think I was your millionaire fiancé, Robert Donahue."

"What in the world has a character I invented for Alice's wedding got to do with those two men?"

"Julie, Henry Gibbon and Graham Stithers were guests at your sister's wedding."

Understanding finally dawned. "You mean they're not colleagues of yours? They only met you yesterday? How odd! They sounded as if they'd known you for ages."

Robert got up to adjust his suitcase, which he seemed to believe was in danger of falling from the luggage rack. "I met them at the wedding reception around the hors d'oeuvres tray. I think they might be cousins of John Farringdon, or some such thing. Anyway, they latched on to me like limpets. Probably because we three were the only men in the entire wedding party who weren't doctors." He sat down again and smiled at Julie confidingly. "They seemed to think I was an expert on Common Market finances, and I didn't dare disillusion them. Believe me, after twenty minutes of hearing their views on a floating exchange rate for international currencies, a conversation about gallbladder surgery seemed like light relief!"

Everything that Robert said was both logical and plausible, and yet Julie had the oddest feeling that she was being led, gently and cleverly, right down the garden path. But how could Robert be lying? She couldn't think of any other possible explanation for the incident. After all, she was the person who'd invented the character of Mr. Donahue. It was totally irrational to suspect Robert of some obscure double-dealing.

Another cloudy memory floated to the surface. "One of them claimed to have an appointment with you next Tuesday," she said. "What are you going to do? Phone and tell him you're unavoidably detained with the prime minister?"

"Of course not," he said, eyes twinkling. "Mr. Donahue never wastes time making routine phone calls. His secretary will call and make profuse apologies."

"His secretary? An obliging actress friend of yours, I suppose?"

"Something like that. I think we'll put Mr. Donahue on a flight to Brussels. Important currency-conversion talks with leading bureaucrats from the former East Bloc countries. Sounds convincing, don't you think?"

"Amazingly convincing," Julie said, her voice acerbic. "You lie with frightening expertise."

"Not very often, I swear, Julie. Normally I pride myself on being a hundred percent honest, but this weekend..." He leaned forward and clasped her hand again, his expression rueful. "My grandfather, who's old-school, hard-core honest, would say this weekend has been a great moral lesson for me. I became involved in one big deception, and all the little lies followed on, inevitable as night following day."

Julie sighed. "Don't feel too guilty. You only got involved because I asked you to help make my crazy stories about Robert Donahue a reality."

"You say his name with such loathing."

"I do loathe him. Why didn't I just tell my parents the truth? That I was busy with my work and didn't have time or energy to find a boyfriend."

"Six months ago you weren't ready to face the truth. Now you are. My grandfather would say that we usually take longest to discover the most important truths about ourselves."

"You sound as if you admire your grandfather quite a lot."

"He's the canniest man I know. And he has the most biting tongue to go with it. I hate to think what he'd say about *this* escapade."

"He wouldn't approve of your pretending to be someone's fiancé, I gather?"

"No, he definitely wouldn't approve of that."

Robert fell silent, and Julie had the distinct impression that he was mentally reviewing several other aspects of his recent behavior that wouldn't meet his grandfather's high moral standards. When he spoke again, however, it was on a different subject.

"Are we going to see each other next week?" he asked, his tone abrupt.

"I would like to," she admitted, acknowledging that her life would seem unbearably flat if Robert walked out of it as casually as he had walked in. At some indefinable moment during the weekend he had stopped being merely a pretend fiancé and had become a man in his own right. A very intriguing and appealing man, Julie reflected. The first man in years whose presence reminded her that she was undeniably a woman. The first man in her entire life who had the power to turn her rage into laughter in the space of a heartbeat.

But this was a train of thought she wasn't yet ready to pursue to its logical conclusion. Honest appraisal of her emotions was still too recent a habit to be comfortable. "We could meet for a couple of hours and finalize the arrangements for ending our engagement," she suggested, hoping he wouldn't point out that she was free to end their mock engagement any way she wanted—and without any help from him.

Robert's expression revealed nothing of what he was thinking. "How about dinner at my apartment tomorrow evening?" he said. "Eight o'clock would be a good time for me, if that's okay with you."

Julie let out a tiny sigh, half nerves, half excitement. She might be emotionally naive and sexually inexperienced, but she wasn't a fool. Robert, she was beginning to realize, was highly sophisticated, and probably ran with a fast-living crowd. If she accepted his invitation, she would be walking straight into the lion's den.

But then, what did the danger matter when she was fatally attracted to the lion?

"Dinner sounds wonderful," she said. "I'll be there at eight."

MONDAY AT THE BAKERY was as hectic as Julie had expected after a weekend away, and it was nearly seven when she returned to her flat. The day had been muggy, with high temperatures but no sun, and she was delighted to step under the shower that had been installed in the old-fashioned bathtub by a previous tenant. The cool water washed away her stickiness, but did nothing to alleviate the anticipation that had been building throughout the long afternoon.

Wrapped in a towel, her hair already arranged in a looser chignon than usual at the nape of her neck, Julie viewed the skimpy contents of her wardrobe with a jaundiced eye. Had she really lived for three years in one of the world's fashion centers with only these drab clothes to show for it?

Logically, of course, there was no reason that dinner with Robert Baxter should provoke this flurry of discontent with her clothes. Since the purpose of the dinner was to discuss a dignified end to their nonexistent engagement, it hardly mattered if all her dresses looked dowdy.

Scowling, Julie abandoned any pretense of logic and dragged out a peacock green silk dress she had bought on sale and then never worn because the low-slashed back always left her skimpiest bra showing. After a moment's debate, she decided there was a simple solution to that problem—she would wear the dress without a bra.

She slipped on stockings, a prized set of real silk underwear, and then zipped up the dress. One hurried glimpse in the mirror was all she needed to see that the subtle, iridescent fabric clung to her front in a manner that left little to the imagination, while the back was too low-cut to cling to anything. She had never before exposed such a stretch of bare skin except at the beach.

"At least it's cool," she muttered, turning away from the mirror with a defiant shrug. She sprayed herself with perfume, snatched her bag and a light jacket from the bed, and left the room before second thoughts—or another look in the mirror—could undermine her confidence.

Anyone would think she'd been brought up in a time warp, Julie reflected wryly. A throwback to mid-Victorian prudery. A simple decision to leave off her bra and she could hardly have felt more wicked if she'd planned to perform a striptease in front of Westminster Abbey.

Her ring at the doorbell of Robert's basement flat had scarcely faded away before he opened the door.

"You have great timing," he said. "I just opened a bottle of chilled white wine. Come on in."

"Thank you." She stepped into the small vestibule and hung her jacket on a convenient coat hook. Robert's eyes widened in appreciation when he saw her dress.

"That's an elegant outfit," he commented, straight-faced. "Must be, um, cool in this hot weather."

The twinkle in his eye reminded her of the old Robert Baxter, the friendly, easygoing man who always had a special smile for her and a cheerful word for the staff at the bakery. His casualness was welcome, and she allowed herself to relax a little.

"It's great on a warm night," she agreed, glad she'd chosen to wear something so dramatic, even though Robert hadn't dressed up at all. His faded jeans and yellow cotton sport shirt made him appear very American, in contrast to his more formal appearance over the weekend.

One aspect of his personality didn't seem in the least changed by the casual clothes, Julie reflected. Despite his relaxed manner, she remained intensely aware of the force of his personality, the power that always seemed to emanate from him, as if he was so accustomed to walking into a room and commanding everyone's attention that he no longer even thought about it. Perhaps such domination was a result of his training as an actor.

"The wine's in the fridge waiting for us," he said, tucking her hand into his arm and leading her toward the back of the small flat. "I'd prefer to eat in the kitchen, unless you're offended by the informality."

"Of course not."

"I like to eat in here," he said. "It's a comfortable room. Take a seat, and I'll pour the wine. It's an unusual white burgundy from one of my favorite vineyards."

Julie followed him into a well-equipped kitchen, large enough to accommodate four cushioned chairs and a scrubbed wooden table, already set for two. The whole atmosphere of the flat was somewhat old-fashioned, as if it had been occupied for years by middle-aged people. But that wasn't surprising since the film company Robert worked for had no doubt rented it fully furnished, right down to the faded old photographs that crowded the walls.

The wonderful aroma of simmering herbs and wine floated out from the oversize oven. High windows provided a pleasant view of tubbed geraniums and window boxes full of multicolored pansies. The sun, emerging from behind its day-long cover of cloud, highlighted the geraniums in a glow of evening scarlet.

"You're right, this is a lovely room," Julie said, settling into one of the chairs. "You're lucky to get such a pleasant place to stay. London rents are horrendous."

"Glad you like it." Robert poured two glasses of wine. "And welcome," he said, handing her a glass. "This isn't quite as exciting as the Casbah, but you can see I'm already plying you with liquor. So be warned. My intentions tonight are strictly dishonorable."

She laughed, remembering their ongoing game at the bakery, which now seemed to have been played almost in another lifetime. But even as she laughed, a tiny shiver of excitement raced down her spine. She wasn't sure Robert was joking. More important, she wasn't sure she wanted him to be joking.

She took a sip of the smooth, dry wine. "Mmm. This is wonderful." She looked up at him, eyes bright with challenge, although what she challenged him with, she wasn't quite sure. "At least when you set out to ruin a girl, you go first-class."

"All the way," he agreed. "Surrender to love tonight, my sweet Julie, and billionaire Robert Donahue-class luxury awaits you in the future."

She grinned. "Right. Billionaires always eat in the kitchen, it's one of their well-known eccentricities. I suppose the chef and the butler are hiding in the cupboard so as not to spoil the intimate atmosphere?

Robert twirled his imaginary mustache. "Actually I hid them away upstairs with strict orders not to put in an appearance until tomorrow morning. When you taste my coq au vin you'll realize I don't need a chef to dazzle my prey. Beautiful women the world over have promised me nights of utter bliss in exchange for my secret recipe."

"And naturally you've rejected them all."

"Naturally."

"But I have a far better deal to offer," she murmured. "Something much more enticing than a mere night of bliss."

Robert allowed his gaze to run with slow deliberation over the silk clinging to her breasts, and she felt almost as if he had touched her. "Right now, Julie, my sweet, I can't imagine anything in this world more enticing than a night spent loving you."

Her heart jumped in a tiny spasm of reckless anticipation. She took another sip of wine, but it did nothing to ease the dryness of her throat. *This is only a game,* she assured herself. *We're neither of us serious.*

"You didn't wait to hear my offer," she said. "I'm prepared to give you my prize-winning recipe for raspberry tarts in exchange for your secret recipe for coq au vin. Face it, Robert, that's a much more exciting deal than a routine romp between the sheets."

He didn't move. No part of their bodies met. And yet when he looked at her, she felt fire leap along her veins. He spoke very softly. "Julie, my sweet love, if an exchange of recipes appeals to you more than a night of lovemaking, then I guarantee you've been making love to the wrong man. I hope some time soon you'll let me show you what you've been missing."

His words rippled over her skin, stoking the fire inside her. The urge to move closer to him was so strong that she gripped the wooden arms of the chair to prevent herself from getting up. Totally unprepared to handle the intensity of her feelings, she stepped back from the edge of the conflagration. She forced a smile.

"You didn't realize how hungry I am," she said in the lightest voice she could manage. "Right now, *nothing* sounds as appealing as food. My taste buds are all jangling, waiting to try your wonderful meal."

He didn't respond to her smile. "Maybe this dinner comes with a higher price tag than you want to pay, Julie."

She wouldn't allow herself to understand him. "My raspberry tarts are good, Robert, but the recipe for them isn't *that* spectacular. I'm prepared to pay up with a smile."

He traced the contour of her cheek with a whisper-soft movement of his hand. "I should send you home right now. You're too vulnerable to play in the big leagues, Julie, and I'm too old and too cynical to play Little League."

Her cheeks grew hot and she looked away. "I'm sure you'd never do anything I didn't want."

Robert's expression became cool, opaque. "But the thing is, Julie, I can make you want me. At least for tonight."

She swallowed. "I trust you not to."

"Don't trust me," he said, the brilliant blue of his eyes darkening to indigo. "I deserve my reputation for being ruthless. Every bit of it."

"You've never been ruthless with me."

He didn't answer. He pushed back his chair with a noisy scrape, shattering the explosive tension arching between them. He opened the oven and the wonderful, spicy aroma intensified. Julie sniffed appreciatively. She hadn't eaten all day and was feeling genuinely hungry.

With deft, competent movements, Robert placed the dish on the table, lifting the lid of the casserole to reveal golden-brown pieces of boneless chicken, clusters of dark truffles, tiny potatoes and a rich, red-wine sauce. He topped up Julie's wineglass and sat down.

"All we're missing is a loaf of crusty bread from your bakery and this would be the perfect meal," he said, gesturing to encourage Julie to serve herself. "Unfortunately I was too busy catching up on things today to stop by."

"Next time we eat together I'll bring the bread." Julie realized she was assuming they would share other meals, and she welcomed the warm glow of pleasure such a thought gave her. "But I don't understand why you're so busy. How does a film actor catch up on things? Don't you just get called to the set and either work or not?''

"Er, sort of, I guess. But there are always script changes to deal with and costume people to see—things like that. This movie is being held to a tight budget, but script writers like to rewrite everything up until the very last minute.''

Robert launched into an amusing anecdote about one of the daytime soap operas produced in New York. The script had been changed three times in the final twenty minutes, and several characters had ended up—live, on camera—reciting lines at each other from different scripts.

Lulled by the superb wine, delicious food and entertaining conversation, Julie could have denied the undercurrent of sexual awareness that cut through every glance she exchanged with Robert. Only a week earlier, she would have pretended that her pulse didn't race each time she looked into the dark brilliance of his eyes. She would have pretended that her breath didn't catch in her throat when his fingers brushed lightly against her arm. But tonight, she could find no room within herself for such empty deceptions. The tingle pricking beneath her skin, the knot tightening her stomach and the strange ache in the region of her heart all had a very simple cause. She wanted Robert to hold her, to take her into his arms, to make love to her. She wanted Robert to be the man who showed her how it felt to be a woman.

The elemental simplicity of her need scared her, and she reached for her wineglass in search of some courage. It was empty. Robert took her hand and uncurled her fingers from around the stem of the glass.

"No more wine, sweetheart." His voice was low, tender, slightly throaty. "I want you sober when I start to seduce you."

Start? Julie thought wildly. The man had been seducing her from the moment he'd first walked into her shop. Inch by inch, smile by smile, he'd coaxed her from frozen indifference into her present state of heart-racing emotion. If she wanted to avoid spending the night in Robert's arms, now was clearly the moment to leave his flat. And despite everything he had said earlier about his ruthlessness, she had no doubt that he would summon a cab and escort her home if that was what she asked him to do. But she didn't ask him, and she didn't resist when he took her hand and led her into the living room.

He flipped the switch on a built-in stereo system, and the soft sounds of an old Barbra Streisand love song drifted into the room. "Shall we dance?" he asked.

She drifted into his arms, and they swayed in unison, their feet moving in time to the music, while the rest of their bodies clung together in another, more primitive rhythm. Robert's fingers twined in her hair; he tugged gently and she heard the ping of her hairpins landing on the coffee table at the same moment as her thick, blond hair tumbled around her shoulders.

"God, Julie, you're a bewitching woman. Half smoldering fire, half beguiling innocence. Right now, I don't know which half is more enticing."

"Then you'll have to cope with all of me."

"No problem," Robert said huskily. He framed her face with his hands, drawing her mouth up to his. "I've been wanting to do this for weeks," he muttered. "From the moment I first saw you, I've had an ache in my gut that wouldn't go away."

Her lips parted in surprise at the roughness of his voice, and he claimed her mouth in hungry possession. His kiss consumed her senses, blinding her, deafening her, until she drowned in pleasurable oblivion.

Julie's hands crept up Robert's chest and reached out to touch his cheeks as she sought to orient herself in the swirling abyss. His skin felt warm and inviting, with an intriguing hint of beard stubble beneath her fingertips. He obviously hadn't had time to shave since coming home from work.

When Robert finally ended their kiss, Julie couldn't hold back an incoherent murmur of protest.

"Touch me, Julie." Robert's voice sounded unsteady, with no trace of the casual laughter she had come to expect. He took her hand and thrust it beneath his shirt, uncurling her palm until her fingers rested flat against the hard muscles of his chest. Almost instinctively, she began to stroke the taut skin. Shivers of sensation chased down her spine when he responded by giving a groan of unmistakable pleasure. It was intoxicating to realize that a simple touch from her had the power to arouse him.

Lost in the enjoyment of her caresses, she scarcely registered that the Streisand tape had ended, and that Robert was guiding her to the big, old-fashioned sofa at the end of the room. As she sat down, the prickle of the tweed upholstery against her legs brought her into sudden, sharp contact with reality. She tensed. Robert silently combed his fingers through her hair and she leaned back against the cushions, not resisting his touch, but mentally ill at ease. Twenty-four years of indoctrination by her family warned her that a nice, sensible girl wasn't supposed to feel these wayward passions. Her conscience sent out a harsh reminder that the last time she had felt attracted to a man, she had deceived herself. When she imagined herself in love with John Farringdon, only her repugnance at the thought of having an affair with a man whose divorce wasn't yet final had saved her from making a dreadful mistake. How did she know that making love with Robert Baxter wouldn't seem equally wrong three years from now?

With surprising gentleness, considering the power and strength of his hands, Robert traced the contours of her cheeks and the long, slender column of her throat.

"Look at me, Julie," he commanded quietly. "Let me see what you're thinking."

She raised her head. "I'm thinking that I ought to go home," she admitted wryly.

He took her hands and cradled them against his chest. "Julie, I think it's time for us to be truthful with each other. No more acting. No more lies. We've had too many of those already. If we make love, I want our emotions to be totally honest. Tonight, I'm not Robert-Donahue-the-millionaire or Robert-Baxter-the-actor. I'm just a man who feels something very special for you, something I've never felt for any other woman. And if we make love, I want you to participate willingly, not because I've seduced you into submission, but because you feel something special for me too."

Bereft of speech, Julie stared up at him, her heart beating in double time. She suddenly understood why her body had been playing such strange tricks on her; why after years of indifference to the male population, she had developed this acute craving for Robert's company. *She wanted Robert Baxter to be her lover because she loved him.* Some time during the weekend, when her conscious mind had been occupied with putting the past to rest, her subconscious mind had let down its barriers, and Robert had stormed into her heart.

The realization struck Julie with the force of a physical blow. She had always believed that making love and loving should be two sides of one coin, and now she saw that her beliefs hadn't changed tonight just because Robert was an expert in the art of seduction. She wanted to make love with him for the simplest of reasons—she loved him.

At some magic moment during the past weekend, her feelings for him had crystallized. In Robert's company, she laughed and felt happy as she did with no other person. In his company, she became alive, and vibrant, and *real*. With Robert, she could be the woman she wanted to be—passionate, fun-loving, and a successful business manager, instead of the cool, dedicated doctor or nurse her family had always yearned for. During the past few days, Robert had given her the most priceless gift of all. He had allowed her to become herself.

Robert obviously misinterpreted her silence. He touched her cheek with fingers that shook slightly and drew a deep, harsh breath. "If you'd prefer to leave, Julie, you just need to tell me." He smiled the endearing smile that always twisted her heart. "I'll spend the night serenading you from the pavement beneath your window and probably get myself arrested for disturbing the peace, but I won't keep you here if you want to go."

"No," she said softly, but with no hesitation. "I don't want to leave. I want you to make love to me, Robert. I want that very much."

"Dearest Julie," he breathed. "I think this might turn out to be a night we'll both remember for the rest of our lives."

Neither of them spoke again as he pulled her down to the cushions and rested his head against the soft curve of her shoulder. Bathed in the glow of his admiring gaze, Julie had never felt more feminine, never more cherished. Her inhibitions withered under the knowledge that Robert was the man she loved, and she turned into his waiting arms, eager to discover how it would feel when they finally touched, skin to skin, body to body, heart to heart.

It felt better than wonderful. Her soft curves seemed to have been designed expressly to fit against the hard angles and planes of Robert's body, a perfect joining of two disparate halves.

"You're so beautiful," Robert said huskily.

"So are you," she whispered.

The unconcealed urgency of his passion was reflected in her own mounting desire. With aching tenderness, he lowered his mouth in a final kiss. The brief moment of pain as Robert took possession of her body vanished in a crescendo of pleasure. He held her close and for an exhilarating moment she reveled in the knowledge that Robert's joy was as great as her own.

Then the world faded away into the deep, midnight darkness of ecstasy. In Robert's arms, for the first time in her life, Julie learned what it meant to be truly a woman.

CHAPTER NINE

ROBERT RETURNED to the living room wearing a short terry-cloth robe and carrying two glasses of wine. To Julie's chagrin, he caught her half-dressed and scrabbling under the sofa to find the shoes she had abandoned so recklessly a short while earlier. Hating to appear unsophisticated, she still couldn't prevent a hot scarlet blush from staining her cheeks.

Alice worried about all the wrong things, Julie thought miserably. *It isn't the before part of making love that's difficult. It's knowing what in the world to say to each other afterward.* Judging by Robert's forbidding expression, he certainly wouldn't appreciate it if she chose this moment to tell him of her love.

She cleared her throat and tried hard to produce a casual, sophisticated smile. "I'm sorry, but the zipper on my dress seems stuck."

"Don't worry about it now," Robert said, setting the glasses on the table. "We need to talk."

"But I need to get dressed first!" Her voice came out as a squeak, ruining her attempt to portray an experienced woman of the world.

Robert's expression softened. "I'll find you something comfortable to wear," he said. He disappeared out of the door, returning a couple of minutes later with a brightly flowered cotton housecoat, vintage nineteen fifties. Even in her distraught state, Julie thought what an odd garment for a bachelor to have hanging around in his flat.

"Sorry," he said, tossing it to her. "This isn't very glamorous, but it's clean, and it was all I could find."

"It's fine. Thank you." Julie pushed self-consciously at her hair, then stared at her toes. Try as she might, she couldn't bring herself to meet Robert's eyes in case the tenderness she had seen there earlier had vanished.

Robert perched on the end of the coffee table, waiting without speaking until Julie had put on the housecoat. When she was through buttoning, he handed her one of the glasses of wine. "Why didn't you tell me?" he asked quietly.

"Why didn't I tell you what?" Julie took a fortifying gulp of wine. She knew exactly what Robert was talking about, but she was finding it difficult to stick to her recent policy of honest communication. Stark self-appraisal and heart-to-heart revelations could be carried only so far by a novice recovering from three years of hard-core self-deception.

"You know very well what I'm talking about, Julie. You were a virgin. A virgin, for heaven's sake! Damn it, you're twenty-four years old and stunningly beautiful. The possibility that you were still a virgin never even entered my mind."

"I didn't know virginity had been declared illegal," she retorted, stung by the harsh beat of anger in his voice. "Even for women who've reached the ripe old age of twenty-four."

He took a short, impatient breath. "I guess virginity can be wonderful. A very special gift from a woman to the man she loves. But you gave me no clue that I should expect something so...unusual."

"You make me sound like a freak. There must be thousands of other virgins of my age."

"Outside a convent or a harem? I wouldn't bet on it if I were you." Robert ran his fingers through his hair in a distracted gesture. "We were both unforgivably careless right now. What if I've made you pregnant? Good grief, Julie, I could have hurt you, quite apart from anything else! I wasn't exactly gentle, in case you didn't notice!"

She had noticed everything. His passion, his skill, his desire and—despite what he'd just claimed—his gentleness.

"What was I supposed to say?" she asked. "And when was I supposed to say it?" She tried to make light of the situation, although she felt perilously close to tears. "'Pass the mushrooms, please. Your casserole is delicious. Oh, by the way, I'm a virgin.' Somehow that didn't seem the best way to handle the situation."

"There were other moments when you might have given me a hint."

"Maybe." Julie mourned inwardly as the glorious experience of making love to Robert began to tarnish under the acid of their misunderstandings. "I'm sorry if you feel I deceived you," she said, her voice husky with unshed tears. "But don't worry, Robert, I don't expect anything from you. This is the wrong time of month. I'm not at all likely to get pregnant."

"I just assumed you were on the pill," Robert muttered. "Seems to me, I assumed too many things where you were concerned. Darn it, I can't believe I was so careless, so insensitive! The signs were all there, if I'd only stopped to look."

He sprang up from his perch on the coffee table and paced several times up and down the room before returning to sit next to Julie on the sofa. He pushed a stray lock of hair away from her forehead and the casual, tender intimacy of his gesture made her fight back a sob. "Why, Julie?" he asked softly. "Why did you choose to take me as your lover?"

She opened her mouth to give some casual, noncommittal explanation, but the words died away unspoken. She looked into the brilliance of his dark blue eyes and realized that she owed it to herself—and to Robert—to speak the truth.

"I...like you," she said finally. Despite all her grand resolutions, in the last resort she didn't quite have the courage to admit the full extent of her feelings. "I'm grateful to you," she hurried on. "You forced me to look at myself from a different perspective this weekend, and I learned a lot about myself. I felt ready to take a new direction in my life." She forced a somewhat shaky smile. "Besides, I was smart enough to realize you would be a great lover."

He looked at her searchingly for a long time, but in the end, he didn't say anything, but simply pulled her into his arms and cradled her head against his chest.

"I have a confession to make," he said quietly. "Tonight was a first for me, as well as for you. I've never made love to a virgin before."

A thrill of pleasure rippled down Julie's spine. She was very glad that tonight had been unique for Robert, not just for her. "I'd never have guessed we were both novices. For two beginners, I think we coped rather well, don't you?''

"We were spectacular."

The tenderness in his voice caused Julie to glance up, and her gaze locked with his. Neither of them moved, but neither of them seemed able to look away. Silence grew, gradually charging the space between them with an electric, yearning tension. Robert clasped her hands and carried them to his cheek. His hands felt burning hot. Hers felt ice cold. He turned his face so that he could press a small, hard kiss into her palm. Her entire body began to burn with ice-cold heat.

Robert's eyes shaded from blue almost to black. "You know what they say, don't you?" His voice was low, teasing, and rich with the promise of passion.

She moistened her dry lips. "What do they say?"

"Practice makes perfect."

"Do you think we can improve on 'spectacular'?" Julie whispered.

"I sure as heck would like to try."

Julie drew her fingertip gently across the beard-roughened line of his jaw. Robert tensed in anticipation. "Julie," he murmured. "I think you're about to win the gold star for most improvement with least practice."

"Don't talk when I'm trying to learn my lessons," she murmured, and then there was no more need for words.

JULIE WOULD HAVE LIKED a few days of solitude to nurture the astonishing discovery that she was in love with Robert Baxter, but the demands of The Crusty Corner made that impossible. And as soon as she walked into her shop on Tuesday morning, she realized that her assistants weren't going to allow her any chance to savor her newfound love in secret.

"You look smashing," Laura said, glancing up from her task of arranging cottage loaves on a long wire rack. "What's the special occasion?" She winked in Pam's direction. "Do you think there's any chance our boss lady is going out on a date with a certain handsome American we all know?"

"Of course I'm not going out on a date," Julie said crossly. More crossly than she'd intended, because Robert had escorted her home just before dawn and then left without setting a time for their next meeting. She was certain he would phone this morning, or perhaps come into the bakery, but in the meantime, she wasn't in the mood for joking....

Julie became aware of two pairs of interested eyes fixed firmly upon her. She gave the sky blue skirt of her dress a brisk little twitch before marching in the direction of her office. "I just decided it was time to wear a new dress, that's all. I've been wearing the same old clothes to the bakery for months now. I needed a new image."

"Right." Laura smirked. "And the new hairdo must be because old Mrs. Creighton is coming in to pick up her husband's birthday cake. It wouldn't have anything to do with that smashing Mr. Baxter and the fact that you had dinner with him last night."

Julie glared at her friend. "It's a pity you're so good with the customers, Laura. I can see this is going to be one of those days when I wish I could afford to fire you."

"Aha," said Pam, grinning. "She's angry, Laura, so I think you hit the nail right on the hea— Oh, good morning, Mr. Baxter. How nice to see you." Her voice oozed smugness. "Did you come in for one of our raspberry tarts?"

"No, I came to see Julie."

"Oh, my! Are you planning to fly her off to the Casbah? I think she might be willing to go if you asked her nicely." Pam and Laura giggled, pleased with their joke.

"I'm saving the Casbah for next weekend. Tonight I'm hoping we can have dinner at Julie's flat. I've already ordered dinner for two from London's best catering service."

At the sound of Robert's low voice, Julie whirled around, her heart beating so wildly she felt sure everyone would be able to see it throbbing. "R-Robert," she said. "H-how nice...I mean, I wasn't expecting you."

He gave her a look that effectively shut out everyone else in the shop. "Surely you knew I'd never be able to get through an entire morning without stopping by."

He walked behind the counter and Julie simultaneously walked forward into the shop, so that they ended up standing mere inches apart. Robert's forehead was damp with sweat, his T-shirt clung to his broad shoulders, and his hair was blown into total disarray. She thought he looked magnificent.

"You've been running," she said. With her eyes, she told him how glad she was to see him.

"Four miles," he agreed. With his eyes, he told her how glad he was to see her.

The ping of the doorbell announced the arrival of a stream of customers. Neither Julie nor Robert stirred. Julie scarcely even heard the murmur of voices as her assistants completed the sales.

"Will you have dinner with me tonight?" Robert asked. "If you don't mind, I think it would be best to eat at your apartment. You won't have to bother with cooking or cleaning up with these caterers I've contacted. I've used them before and I know they're good."

"Yes, that would be wonderful. I was hoping you'd want us to be together again tonight." Julie found she had no room left inside herself for pretense or evasion. She wanted to spend every possible moment with Robert, and she was thrilled that he seemed to share her feelings.

"Unfortunately I have a long series of appointments to get through today, or I'd meet you for lunch. But I'll try to be at your place by seven. Does that sound good?"

"It sounds super," she said softly.

Robert glanced at his watch. "Damn! I have to go. I was supposed to be somewhere else ten minutes ago." He stared at her with an intensity that was almost frightening. "Julie, we need to talk. There are some things I need to discuss with you. Important things."

Julie's heart did a flip-flop of pure joy. Her womanly instincts seemed fine-tuned after a night in Robert's arms, and she knew with a certainty as old as Eve that tonight he would tell her he loved her. Last night, he'd been shocked by the discovery that she was a virgin. That was the reason he hadn't mentioned love. But, inexperienced as Julie was, she didn't believe that

they could have achieved that earth-shaking pinnacle
of ecstasy *without* love. She smiled, knowing her eyes
glowed with happiness.

"I'll look forward to seeing you," she murmured.
She touched her hand lightly to his arm. "Have a good
day, my love."

Robert's cheeks flushed with surprise and pleasure.
He leaned forward and dropped a kiss on Julie's forehead. "Julie—" He broke off. "No, dammit. This isn't
the time or the place. I'll see you this evening." He
turned on his heel and strode out of the bakery.

Pam whistled. "My word, I think our Mr. Baxter is
really in love."

Julie gave a contented laugh. "You know something, Pam? I think you may be right." She walked into
her office, feeling rather pleased by the stunned silence she left behind.

THE PEACOCK GREEN SILK and the sky blue cotton exhausted the high-fashion possibilities of Julie's wardrobe. Resolving to go shopping at the earliest
opportunity, she had no choice after her shower but to
get dressed in a beige linen skirt and an elegant, but
boring, black silk blouse. Sighing, she did her best to
liven up the outfit with a chain belt and some chunky
gold jewelry. Fortunately the caterers arrived from
Exquisite Dining before she had time to get too depressed about her appearance.

Julie watched with a great deal of professional interest as the two women cleared a space in the center of
her living room and erected a sturdy, portable table.
They covered this with the finest of linens, then set it
with crystal, bone china and sterling silverware. With

great artistry, they laid out an elegant variety of chilled
salads, together with smoked salmon, quail eggs in
nests of puff pastry, pâté and lobster. As a final touch,
they placed a magnum of champagne in a gilded ice-
bucket to one side of the table. A fabulous selection of
exotic fruits was put in the fridge for dessert, and the
caterers left after an interested discussion of Julie's
proposal that Exquisite Dining Service should consider serving The Crusty Corner breads and pastries
with all the meals they catered.

"We saw the write-up about your bakery in *Household Gourmet,*" the older woman said. "Write us a
proposal. Sounds a great idea to me. Here, my address is on this card."

"We'll be back to clear up the mess any time you call
to say it's convenient," added the other. "Lucky you,
having dinner with Mr. Do—"

The older woman interrupted rather rudely. "A
pleasure meeting you, Miss Marshall. Enjoy your dinner with Mr. Baxter."

Seven o'clock came and went, but Robert didn't arrive. The ice surrounding the champagne began to
melt. The endive salad began to look wilted. Julie ri-
fled through a pile of gourmet-cooking magazines trying to find a recipe interesting enough to occupy her
attention. She succeeded only in knocking the pile of
magazines onto the floor, destroying the careful order
she'd stacked them in.

By eight o'clock, she was pacing, convinced that
Robert had been in some dreadful accident. The realization that she didn't even have a phone number where
she could try to reach him was the final straw to her
lacerated nerves. When the doorbell eventually rang at

half-past eight, her overactive imagination already had
a mortally wounded Robert stretched out on a hospital operating table. She hurtled to the door and pulled
it open, convinced she would find a policeman waiting
on the other side.

Instead of a policeman, she found Robert looking
tall, dark and incredibly handsome, despite lines of
fatigue etched from his nose to the corners of his
mouth. He wore a dark business suit and carried an
enormous bouquet of roses. Julie flung herself into his
arms, crushing the roses between them.

"What a great welcome," he murmured against her
mouth. "I'm sorry I was late, sweetheart. This has
been one hell of a day." He tossed the roses onto the
hall table and swept her back into his arms. "I'm
sorry," he repeated, when they finally broke apart,
breathless from their kiss. "I was held up in a meeting
and I couldn't break away, not even to call you."

"I was worried," Julie admitted. It was easy enough
to say the words now that Robert was here—safe, and
alive, and bursting with health. "I understand how
difficult it was for you to get away. When an actor is on
a film set, I realize you can't just announce that you
have a date so it's time to go home."

Robert looked oddly disconcerted. "I wasn't on the
set," he said. "In fact, Julie, that's one of the things I
want to talk to you about tonight."

"The film you're acting in?" Julie's stomach gave a
worried lurch. She had sensed all along that beneath his
flippant manner, Robert's career was vitally important to him. She took his hand. "Oh, dear, you haven't
been fired, have you?"

"No, not at all. Don't worry, that's not the problem." Robert walked into the living room and looked around. "Good, I see the caterers have done an excellent job as usual."

"Yes, and we'd better eat quickly, because everything is turning limp and soggy."

"I think we need a glass of champagne first." Robert lifted the bottle out of its cradle of ice, wiping the moisture from its sides with a specially provided napkin. He bowed with a mock flourish and held the bottle out for Julie's inspection. "I hope the vintage meets with your approval, madam?"

"The vintage is adequate," she said, pretending to study the label. With a provocative smile, she stroked his biceps. "The waiter, however, is positively super."

Robert grinned. "Hold that thought, honey. Because this waiter always goofs when he tries to open champagne." With an expertise that seemed to belie his words, Robert removed the foil seal and twisted the wire stopper holding the cork in place. His thumbs eased the cork gently upward, but at the last moment something went wrong and the cork flew out in a froth of champagne bubbles. Julie happened to be standing in the direct line of fire and her blouse and skirt were soaked in champagne.

Robert groaned. "Oh, Lord, I should have known better than to try. I'm a walking disaster where champagne is concerned. Tell me the worst. Have I ruined one of your favorite outfits?"

"Not at all. This blouse can be washed in a machine, so don't worry," Julie reassured him.

"That makes me feel a bit less of a klutz." Robert dropped a kiss on the end of her nose. "Sweetheart,

gorgeous as you look with that silk clinging to your lu-
cious curves, I know you must feel damp and miserable. Would you like to change into something dry
before we start dinner?" He smiled ruefully. "Once
you've changed, I promise to give you complete control of the champagne bottle."

"Perhaps I should put on something else," Julie
agreed, as she felt the champagne seep through to her
skin. "I won't be a minute."

"Take your time." Robert picked up a small plate of
hors d'oeuvres and settled into an armchair by the
empty fireplace. He gestured at the stack of magazines. "Looks like I'll have plenty of reading material
to keep me entertained while you're gone."

"Happy reading," Julie said, and whisked into the
bedroom, delighted to have an excuse to change out of
her dreary outfit and into the stunning negligee that
had arrived in the afternoon post from Cousin Jane.
For a dedicated, lifelong spinster, Cousin Jane had
displayed quite amazing taste. Her brief note accom-
panying the parcel had read: "Here's a wedding present that I trust will prove more enjoyable than the
traditional silver vase, which should have been declared illegal now that nobody has butlers to do the
polishing."

Shedding her damp skirt and blouse, Julie sent a
mental apology winging to her elderly cousin. She
knew she had no right to wear something that had been
sent under the mistaken impression that a marriage was
about to take place. On the other hand, if Julie had her
way, the wedding ceremony would still become a reality, and she could tell Cousin Jane just how satisfactory the negligee had proved.

Julie sponged herself off, removing the sticky residue of champagne. Smiling, she scooped the foamy lace and satin robe from its box. Her eyes sparkled, and her heart beat faster as the midnight blue fabric fell into place against her bare legs with a delicious rustle. She slipped her arms into the loose sleeves, and the lace floated over her wrists, making them appear fragile and feminine. Fastening the long ribbon ties, she knew that she looked pretty, perhaps even beautiful, and she was glad. At this moment, she wanted to look beautiful, not just for herself but for Robert.

Excited—and a little nervous—Julie returned to the living room. Robert, a magazine open on his lap, barely seemed to have stirred while she was gone. He looked up, and she felt her excitement freeze into an icy premonition of disaster. Robert's expression, lacking any trace of warmth or laughter, was set in lines of cold anger.

Julie's stomach tightened. "Hello. I'm back," she said. Nerves made her voice sound low and throaty. "I must say you don't look very happy, Robert. Did I take too long? Are you hungry?"

His mouth twisted into a cruel sneer and he stood up, inspecting her with a gaze that hovered somewhere between mocking and downright insulting. "Only for you. I'm only hungry for you, Julie, my love. Is that what I'm supposed to say?"

She held the froth of lace at her throat, feeling suddenly exposed and vulnerable. "You're not s-supposed to say anything."

"Oh, come on now, Julie, I'd like to know if I'm still doing things according to your script. As you no doubt know, I was once a professional actor, and I wouldn't like to mess up my lines."

She shook her head in bewilderment. "We don't have any lines. This isn't a play."

"It sure isn't. This is real-life drama, isn't it, Julie, my love?"

She shivered at the loathing he poured into saying her name and watched as he tossed the magazine he'd been reading onto the floor, his eyes alight with a strange, hard glitter. "Robert, I don't understand. I just went to get changed—"

"And you did a great job, my dear. You have terrific taste." His voice dripped sarcasm. "That's the perfect negligee for seduction. Satin always works wonders for a woman's skin, but I'm sure you already know that. Tell me, what would you have done if I hadn't spilled the champagne?"

She sensed that he could barely control the massive build-up of his anger, and for a moment she actually felt afraid. "Robert, what's happen—"

"Don't bother with more lies, Julie. Sexy as you look, I'm afraid the game's up. Slipping into the negligee would have been a great tactic if you hadn't forgotten to get rid of the evidence before you disappeared into the bedroom."

Hurt knotted in the pit of Julie's stomach, caused not so much by what Robert was saying—his words made no sense—as by the cruèl, biting tone in which he was speaking. Her knees wobbled, and she grabbed the back of a chair for support. "Robert, I don't know what you're talking about," she whispered.

"I recommend that you give it up, Julie. Right now." His voice took on an edge of ice. "The innocent act doesn't play well when your audience knows it's a fake."

"But I am innocent! Or ignorant, at least. I honestly don't know what's wrong...."

He walked over and pulled her into his arms, thrusting back her head with an insulting jerk. Even now, even when Julie felt so bewildered and Robert was being so deliberately offensive, she didn't recoil from his touch. Her body hadn't quite had time to catch up with the reality of his utter rejection, and she responded to his touch with a tiny quiver of longing.

He looked down at her, eyes almost tormented, his face set into a ruthless mask that bore no resemblance to the smiling man she thought she had known. "Damn, but you do that well, lady. You certainly can command all the tricks of the trade."

"What trade? Robert, for heaven's sake, why are you behaving like this? I think you'd better go. I don't want you in my home if all you're going to do is hurl abuse." She squirmed in his arms, trying to get away from him, wondering for a fleeting moment if she might perhaps be dealing with a madman. She glanced over her shoulder toward the front door, debating whether to run and scream for help.

"It was all a setup, and I almost fell for it," he said, ignoring her question. "Well, why wouldn't I? You were a virgin, after all. That was a great touch, my dear. Calculated to bring even a jaded millionaire right to the altar. You went to so much trouble working out the perfect scam, it's hard to believe you forgot the magazine. But I guess you cheats and liars are like any other criminal—you always trip yourself up on some insignificant detail."

"What scam?" The jumble of his accusations sorted themselves into the bare outline of a pattern. "Do you mean . . . are you accusing me of setting you up for something?"

"Marriage, my dear Julie. Marriage. And you know something funny? You almost succeeded." He picked up the magazine he had tossed onto the floor and shoved it into her hands. "This is what you forgot to throw away, Julie. You left it sitting right on top of your pile of magazines."

A magazine? This terrible display of rage surely couldn't have been caused by a magazine! The most daring publication she subscribed to was a review of recipes from exotic countries. Julie blinked and stared down at the cover of the magazine, vaguely recognizing the color supplement from her regular Sunday newspaper. For a while her eyes refused to focus more precisely, and it took several long, silent seconds before she realized that she was looking at a picture of Robert. His hair was shorter, he wore the horn-rimmed glasses she had seen only once before, when she'd burst into the guest bedroom at her parents' house, but the photograph was unmistakably of him. The caption beneath the picture read: "Reclusive multimillionaire grants a rare interview."

Julie swallowed, trying to moisten the parchment-dry lining of her throat. The words "multimillionaire" beat an insistent, painful tattoo in her mind. "It's you," she croaked.

"Why, so it is." Robert's reply oozed irony.

"But why are they writing about you?"

"Turn to the article if you need to refresh your memory. Page ten, I believe."

With shaking fingers, Julie flipped through the magazine until she reached the appropriate article. Another picture of Robert, this time at a shareholders' meeting, graced the head of the page. "Robert Donahue completes his latest merger," said the caption.

"Robert Donahue!" Julie exclaimed. The smell of dressing on the wilting salads suddenly began to make her feel ill and she grabbed a glass of water, sipping frantically until the nausea faded a little. "My God, this says your name's Robert Donahue!"

"Surprise, surprise! As if you didn't know."

Wincing under the lash of his scorn, Julie started to read the article, which was dated more than a year earlier. Robert Donahue, it seemed, had made his first million producing and directing horror movies for the television and home-video market. He was a millionaire before his twenty-fifth birthday and had moved into the rarefied class of multimillionaires by the time he was thirty. He had been involved in financing all facets and phases of the entertainment industry, and the article suggested that here was a man with the vision and the financial acumen to become a second Walt Disney. Very little personal information about Robert Donahue was revealed, although the reporter did record Robert's biting comment that his major goal for the year ahead was to avoid getting sued in paternity suits brought by women he'd never even met. "The life of a devastatingly handsome millionaire," concluded the reporter, "is apparently not all champagne and roses."

Julie closed the magazine and forced herself to meet Robert's accusing gaze. "You think I set you up," she said quietly. "That I recognized you as soon as you came into the bakery and played you along until I'd piqued your interest."

"That's what I've always liked about you," Robert replied. "Your razor-sharp intellect. I'm glad you know when the game's lost beyond recall."

Julie drew her negligee around her body, tightening the belt as if she hoped that by pulling the knot tight enough, she might somehow hold the shattered pieces of her life together. "I read that article," she admitted, "but I didn't consciously remember what I'd read. I only kept the magazine because there's a long piece in it about a famous Greek pastry chef." She fumbled through the magazine and finally found what she was looking for. "See? He explains step-by-step how to stop phyllo dough from becoming leathery."

Robert didn't even glance down at the page. Tears trembled at the ends of Julie's lashes. "It's no good, is it? You're not going to believe me."

"No," he said flatly. "I don't believe you. And I'm telling you now, if you're pregnant, don't try to foist a paternity suit on me, because I'll claim entrapment."

Julie had often wondered what a breaking heart would feel like. Now she knew. She stood up, almost grateful that she could no longer see Robert clearly through the sheen of tears blinding her eyes. "You'd better go, Robert. I don't think we have anything left to say to each other."

"Oh, no, my dear. It's not quite so easy to end what you started last week. You have a sexy body, and you do a great job in bed. I'm in the mood to buy some of what you were offering so eagerly just a few minutes ago." He reached into the inner pocket of his jacket and brought out a bank book, scrawling out a check with quick, angry slashes of his pen.

"Here's a refund of the six hundred pounds you invested in landing me on your matrimonial hook, and here's another six hundred for the dubious pleasure of another night in your company." He ripped off the check and threw it toward the table. Julie watched in bleak fascination as it fluttered onto the platter of quail eggs.

"Please leave, Robert. Don't do this... to either of us."

"I want you," he said bleakly, as if he hated himself for admitting even this much. He came over and circled her waist with his arms. "I despise myself for admitting it, but I still want you, Julie."

"No!" Julie jerked her head to one side and stiffened her body, but her resistance was intellectual, not emotional. It didn't carry the ultimate ring of denial.

Robert gave a soft, triumphant laugh, the laugh of a victor who knows the game is already won, even though the race ahead may be grueling. She resisted for as long as she could, but finally, with a little sob of despair, she returned his kiss.

"You're a very satisfying woman," he murmured against her mouth. "Perhaps, if you continue to be this responsive, we might come to some mutually satisfactory arrangement. A mistress can have much more fun than a wife, and sometimes she earns almost as much money."

Julie froze in his arms, the warmth of her passion freezing into revulsion. "No," she said with grim determination. "No, Robert, I can't stand this. Go home. Please go home."

He released his grasp, holding her loosely at arm's
length, and for a moment she thought he would refuse
to accept her demand. Then he spun on his heel and
walked quickly to the door of the flat, opening it without fanfare and closing it quietly behind him. Almost
without sound, Robert Donahue exited her life.

Julie stood in the center of her living room and
wondered why she wasn't crying. Tomorrow, she
promised herself. She would allow herself the luxury of
tears tomorrow. But if she started to cry now, she was
afraid she might never stop.

CHAPTER TEN

FATE ENJOYED playing cruel jokes, Julie decided when
she snatched up the phone next morning hoping to hear
Robert and heard instead the cheerful voice of her
mother.

"I'm glad I caught you before you left for work,"
Mrs. Marshall chirruped. "How is everything going
with that handsome fiancé of yours? And have you
arranged for extra help in the bakery? I'm so much
looking forward to our shopping expedition next Saturday. Choosing wedding clothes is always marvelous
fun!"

"Robert and I aren't going to get married." Such
simple words, and yet Julie could hardly force them
out.

"Not get married! But why ever not?" Mrs. Marshall's voice quavered into a high note of distress. "For
heaven's sake, Julie, I should have thought Robert
Donahue was exciting enough even for somebody as
fussy as you. He's such a nice, *kind* man."

Right, Julie thought. Wonderfully kind. Except
when he uses a scalpel to shred your emotions without
benefit of anesthesia. She reached blindly across the
coffee table in search of a tissue, and her fingers encountered a small gold card case that must have fallen

from Robert's pocket. Probably when he pulled out his bankbook and wrote that insulting check, she thought.

Julie picked up the card case and rubbed her fingertips over the smooth, monogrammed surface. When she saw what she was doing she threw the case violently to the floor. Cards spilled out, white against gold, the neat black name staring up at her in silent accusation. Robert Donahue. *Robert Donahue.* Her imaginary millionaire fiancé who hadn't been imaginary, after all. She'd plagiarized him from a magazine article without ever realizing what she was doing. How could she have been so incredibly stupid? So totally unaware?

"Julie, what's happened? Are you all right? Are you still there?"

Julie dashed away a tear, refusing to let it fall. She'd spent the bleak hours before dawn in a storm of weeping, and when the sun rose she had vowed there would be no more tears. She reached for another tissue.

"I'm still here, Mother. I'm all right. Just busy. I need to get to the shop. I'm late, so I can't stay and talk."

"But what happened, Julie? Surely you can tell me something more than the bare fact that your wedding's off. Obviously I'm worried when you announce on Saturday that you're getting married and four days later that everything's off. You and Robert seemed so happy at Alice's wedding. Everyone commented on what a lovely couple you made...." Mrs. Marshall's outburst trailed away into mournful silence.

She could invent some excuse, Julie thought, or for once in her life she could try telling her mother the truth. Heaven knew, the truth couldn't lead to an worse consequences than her previous habit of appeasing her mother with lies. She drew a deep breath.

"Robert refuses to speak to me, Mother. He doesn't trust me. He thinks I want to marry him for his money. He thinks I tried to trap him into marriage."

She waited for her mother to explode, to bludgeon her with a long lecture on how if Julie had behaved in a more responsible fashion, Robert would still love her. The lecture didn't come.

"He thinks you want to marry him for his *money?*" Mrs. Marshall couldn't have sounded more astonished if her daughter had been accused of wanting to marry Robert because he had two left feet. "How could he possibly make such a horrible mistake about *my* daughter? Hasn't he ever spent any time talking to you? Anyone who's known you for five minutes ought to realize that you would never be interested in a person because of his wealth or his possessions!" Mrs. Marshall was puffing herself up into a healthy steam of anger. "All I can say, Julie, is that you're well rid of the man. Goodness, gracious me! Not trusting you, indeed. And all over his silly money, which is no good for anything except buying rubbish that nobody needs. His house is probably full of diamond-encrusted nutmeg grinders and platinum toothbrush holders. He doesn't sound like the sort of man who'd donate his money to useful things like medical research. . . ."

To her amazement, Julie heard herself give a tiny, reluctant gurgle of laughter. "Oh, Mother, thank you."

"Whatever for?"

"For not believing, even for a moment, that I wanted to marry Robert for his money."

"As if I could! I sincerely hope your father and I did a better job of bringing you up than that. Now, about our shopping trip on Saturday—"

"But, Mother, I just explained. We have no reason to go shopping."

Mrs. Marshall gave a snort of pure disgust. "Really, Julie. Sometimes I wonder if an alien from outer space impregnated me while your father was out making a house call."

"Mother!"

"Well, no normal *human* female would ever suggest there was no reason to go shopping. For heaven's sake, child, let's meet as we planned and buy a couple of ridiculous fun outfits. We could indulge ourselves and have lunch somewhere absolutely splendid. I'll catch the early train and meet you outside Fenwick's at half-past ten." Mrs. Marshall, true to form, hung up the phone before Julie had time to disagree. For once Julie was glad to be steamrollered into compliance.

THE OUTING with her mother turned out to be the single spark of brightness in three weeks of unrelenting gloom. At the earliest opportunity, Julie ripped Robert's insulting check into small pieces, put the pieces into an envelope, took a taxi to the flat where she had eaten dinner with him and rang the bell. An elderly man opened the door.

"Yes, miss? May I help you?"

"I'd like to give something to Mr. Donahue. Personally." She held out the envelope with hands that, despite her best efforts, shook slightly.

He took the envelope. "Who shall I say is calling, miss?"

"I'm Julie Marshall."

The man's expression shuttered into total and immediate blankness. "I'm afraid Mr. Donahue isn't available, Miss Marshall."

It was humiliatingly obvious that the man—the butler?—had been given specific instructions to bar her from the house, but it was too late for Julie to worry about pride. "Is there some time when he will be available?" she asked. "Or some phone number where I can reach him?"

The butler was human enough to allow his face to show a faint gleam of sympathy. "Mr. Donahue is out of the country, miss, and I don't know when he's likely to return."

"Well, thank you, anyway." Julie drew herself up with whatever remnant of dignity she could muster. "I'd appreciate it if you would see that my letter gets forwarded to him."

"I'll see to it myself, miss."

If Robert received the torn-up check, he made no response. He didn't phone or call at Julie's flat, and his visits to the bakery stopped as abruptly as they had begun. Pam and Laura tactfully refrained from mentioning his name. Their silence was almost as bad as their previous corny banter. Julie felt walled within the prison of her own gloomy emotions.

During a weekend visit to her parents' home, she spent a long evening with her sister and new brother-in-law. They had returned from their honeymoon looking tanned and domesticated. Alice appeared contented enough with married life, and Vickie obviously adored her new stepmother. Seeing the three of them together helped Julie to put her relationship with John

Farringdon into proper perspective. If ever there had
been a case of making mountains out of molehills, her
"love" for John Farringdon was it. Julie wished her
sister a long and happy marriage, but she herself no
longer felt even the faintest attraction to a man whose
career obviously absorbed most of his mental energy.

Miserable as she felt over her bitter parting from
Robert, there was some peace to be derived from understanding her own past actions a little better. Julie
realized that from the time she entered her teens she
had tried her hardest to fall in love with a doctor, hoping that by doing so she would make herself more acceptable to her family. John had merely been the last
in a long line of boyfriends who had all been connected in some way to the medical profession.

But how was her love for Robert any different from
these immature past attractions? Julie wondered. After all, she and Robert could hardly claim that their relationship had been based on mutual trust and honesty.
In one way or another they had been deceiving each
other from the very beginning. And yet, instinctively,
profoundly, Julie knew that her love for Robert was
real. Despite all the lies between them, at some elemental level they had touched each other's souls. That
was why his rejection hurt so much. That was why
every day since he'd left her she felt exposed and
bleeding, as if she'd been torn not from Robert but
from a part of herself.

Julie grieved for her loss even more when she realized she wasn't pregnant. Common sense told her that
a shattered relationship could never be healed by an
unplanned pregnancy, but loving Robert's baby would

have eased the terrible ache caused by losing Robert himself.

As so often in the past, work proved to be Julie's salvation. On one morning when she had woken up feeling more dejected than ever, she arrived early at the bakery to find the phone already ringing. She grabbed the receiver and mumbled a breathless "Hello."

"Is this The Crusty Corner bakery?" inquired a snooty female voice.

"It is."

"I'm Harriet Blane, personal assistant and secretary to the chairman of Brown and Associates." The snooty voice fell silent, as if allowing Julie time to absorb the full wonder of being privileged to speak to such an important person.

Julie felt a tiny grin tilt the corners of her mouth. "How may I help you, Ms. Blane?"

"*Miss* Blane," corrected the voice. "I loathe those tiresome Americanisms."

"Miss Blane," Julie amended. "How may I help you, Miss Blane?"

"Brown and Associates needs an absolutely outstanding retirement cake for the chairman of our company, and your little shop has been recommended to us." Miss Blane sounded astonished that The Crusty Corner had been recommended, and even more astonished that she was accepting the recommendation. "We need four large layers, a rich, heavy fruitcake, separated by Corinthian-style pillars, decorated with white royal icing, white scroll embellishments at the edge and sides, and pink rosebuds on each layer."

"Pink rosebuds?" Julie repeated, wondering if she had heard correctly.

"Pink rosebuds." Miss Blane's tone permitted no discussion. "Several dozen of them, scattered over each layer of the cake in a trailing pattern."

A very odd retirement cake, Julie thought in silent amusement. In fact, if the snooty Miss Blane had only known, it sounded suspiciously like a larger and grander version of the cake Julie had baked for her sister's wedding. However, far be it from her to point out the unsuitability to Miss High-and-Mighty Blane. Julie quoted an outrageous sum for the completed cake, and asked if Miss Blane would like to see a sketch of the projected design.

"That won't be necessary, thank you." To her credit, Miss Blane didn't so much as cough at the quoted price. "I'm relying on you to create something quite spectacular, Miss Marshall."

"*Ms.* Marshall," Julie corrected sweetly. "And you can count on me to produce my very best work. Brown and Associates will have a retirement cake to be proud of."

"We need the cake by next Monday," Miss Blane said. "I'll call you with delivery instructions later in the week. Good morning to you, Ms. Marshall."

Working on the cake helped Julie to keep her mind from wandering into useless daydreams about Robert. She spent long but satisfying hours creating a design that met Miss Blane's instructions, and yet contained elements of originality in the unique clustering of the rosebuds and the simple elegance of the scrollwork. She was proud of the finished cake, although frustrated that something she considered her best-ever piece of work was so unsuited in concept to the occasion it had been ordered for. However, she couldn't fault Miss

Blane without knowing the full circumstances. Perhaps the retiring chairman of Brown and Associates had a special affinity for pink roses—a prize-winning rose garden, for example. After three years of running a business, Julie was wise enough not to try second-guessing the instructions of someone as opinionated as Miss Blane.

On Monday evening, after closing the shop, Julie and Pam loaded the cake into a cab and set off for the address they had been given, an imposing square in the heart of Knightsbridge. Pam whistled in appreciation when they drew up outside the iron railings of a four-story London town house.

"Wow! Brown and Associates must be a prosperous company. What do they do?"

"I've no idea. Miss Blane didn't condescend to tell me. From her tone of voice, she implied anybody with a grain of intelligence would already know." Julie hefted the smallest of four boxes into her arms and walked toward the imposing flight of marble steps. "Wait here, Pam, will you, while I ring the bell? There's bound to be dozens of servants in a house like this who can help us unload."

The door was opened not by a butler, but by an attractive middle-aged woman dressed in a gray business suit. "I'm from The Crusty Corner," Julie said. "I have a four-tier retirement cake to deliver for Brown and Associates."

"Are you Julie Marshall?" The woman had rather a nice smile and warm brown eyes that seemed to be viewing Julie with an excessive degree of interest.

"Er, yes."

"I'm Harriet Blane." This time there was no doubt about it. The brown eyes were definitely twinkling. "How do you do, Ms. Marshall?"

"Er, very well, thank you." Miss Blane in person was not at all the dragon she had sounded on the phone. "Where would you like me to put this layer of cake? And could you please hold the door open while my assistant and I unload the other three boxes?"

Harriet Blane pressed a series of numbers into an electronic keypad affixed to the wall. "Gerald will be here in a few seconds to show you into the drawing room," she said. "Take that cake box with you. The chairman of our company would like to meet you in person and discuss his, um, retirement banquet. I'll supervise the unloading of the remaining layers and see that your assistant gets home promptly. The chairman will send you home in one of his own cars when he's finished speaking with you."

"I'll let my assistant know—"

"I'll tell her," Harriet said sharply. "The chairman doesn't like to be kept waiting." The twinkle in her eyes had faded, and her manner was now every bit as superior and unapproachable as it had been on the phone. Julie's arms ached from carrying the heavy weight of the cake, but she decided discretion was the better part of valor. Engaging in a dispute with the redoubtable Miss Blane was a waste of breath.

Gerald arrived in the front hallway a few seconds later. He turned out to be a young man in jeans and a T-shirt emblazoned with pictures of the Grateful Dead, not exactly the traditional butler Julie had imagined.

"This way, miss, if you'll follow me. The boss is in the drawing room at the end of the corridor here." The young man knocked on a pair of handsome double doors, then flung them open with a flourish. ''Mr. Baxter, the young lady you wanted to see has arrived.''

Mr. Baxter! Julie's feet seemed rooted to the ground. Then Gerald gave her a gentle push and she stumbled forward into the brightly lit drawing room. Her heart resumed beating at more or less normal speed when she saw that there was only one man in the room, an elderly gentleman seated in a brocade-covered wing chair. Dear Lord! For an agonizing, wonderful moment, she'd thought Robert might have been waiting to meet her.

The old man rose to his feet. Julie guessed he was closer to eighty than seventy—the chairman obviously didn't believe in early retirement. Despite a heavily wrinkled, lived-in face, his stance was upright, and his voice melodic and forceful, with a distinct American accent.

''Thank you for coming to see me, Miss Marshall. Gerald, would you take that very heavy-looking box and set it on the table as you go out? Thank you. Please tell everyone that Miss Marshall and I would like to be left alone for the next fifteen minutes or so. No phone calls.''

''Yes, sir.'' Gerald might not wear traditional butler's garb, but he followed Mr. Baxter's instructions with a swift expertise that would have done Jeeves proud.

As soon as the door was shut, the old gentleman smiled. ''Well, Miss Marshall, it certainly is a pleasure to meet you at last. Shall we sit down? My name's Robert Baxter, by the way.''

The blood froze in Julie's veins. Robert Baxter was a common-enough name, but after her recent experiences she no longer believed in coincidence. "Why have you asked to speak to me?" she whispered. "Wh-who are you?"

Mr. Baxter chuckled. "A very famous man. Twenty years ago, I'd have been insulted that you didn't recognize my name. I'm wiser and more tolerant now. Age at least gives us that. A small compensation, I guess, for all the other things it takes away."

"I didn't mean to be rude. I'm sorry. I meant..." Julie drew a shaky breath. "Do you by any chance know someone called Robert Donahue?"

"Intimately, for my sins. He's my grandson. And a truly horrible person to know, right at the moment."

Julie gripped the arms of her chair. "Isn't he well?"

Mr. Baxter viewed her with considerable interest, then gave an oddly self-satisfied smile. "Physically as fit as ever." He dismissed the subject of his grandson with a wave of one blue-veined hand. "You still don't know who I am, do you?"

"Well, yes," Julie said, not comprehending. "You're Robert's grandfather. His maternal grandfather, I suppose, or else your name would be Donahue."

"Delighted as I am to be so strongly identified with my grandson, Robbie isn't my only claim to fame, you know. I also happened to have directed some forty Hollywood movies. Several of them were even quite successful."

Julie felt her cheeks grow hot with embarrassment. She was no film buff, but even she had heard of Robert Baxter, winner of more Oscars for Best Picture than any other director, and a lifetime rival of John Huston. "I apologize for seeming so ignorant," she said. "I'm afraid my mind was running along its own narrow track and I just didn't make the connection. I admired *Danse Macabre* enormously, and my father, who's a doctor, once said that *Easy Street* was the best film about the medical profession he'd ever seen."

Mr. Baxter smiled. "Well, thank you for those kind words. You mentioned my two all-time favorites, which naturally makes me think you have excellent taste." He got up and walked over to a bar, concealed behind cherrywood doors recessed into the wall. "Would you care for a sherry, my dear? I only ever drink sherry when I'm visiting England. I've always thought that drinking sherry before dinner is one of the more appealing eccentricities of the British."

"Thank you. Some sherry would be pleasant." Julie bit back a sigh of impatience. Mr. Baxter was a fascinating man. In normal circumstances, she would have been thrilled to spend an entire evening chatting with him. But at this precise moment, all she wanted to do was ask a long list of questions about Robert Donahue, the most important being how she could get in touch with him.

Mr. Baxter handed her an exquisite glass of Waterford crystal half-filled with pale golden sherry. Mindful of her manners, Julie forced herself to ask another polite question. "Do you visit England often, Mr. Baxter?" *Where's your grandson?* she added silently. *Does he know I'm here?*

Mr. Baxter sipped his sherry. "I don't manage to spend as much time here as I would like. Officially I've been retired for the past ten years, but you'd never guess it from reading my schedule."

"You're already retired?" Julie asked, startled into indiscretion.

"Well, that's in the States. I run a different corporation over here, you know." Mr. Baxter sounded vague. He finished his sherry and rose to his feet. "Perhaps you could show me the cake I ordered," he suggested. "How did you become a baker, Miss Marshall?"

"At first, it was just in self-defense. Nobody in my family liked to cook and I hated to eat burned food. Gradually I discovered how much I enjoyed doing something that was both creative and extremely practical."

"Why baking specifically, and not cooking in general?"

"I originally started training as a chef." Julie lifted the lid from the cake box and carefully removed the layers of packing, answering Mr. Baxter as she talked. "Then I found out that baking gives me the ultimate chance to combine creativity and practicality."

"Why is that?"

"Most people eat bread every day, and I've enjoyed experimenting with various recipes to make multi-grain breads that provide the health benefits of whole-grain flour and still taste delicious. Then, at the opposite end of the scale, baking cakes and pastries gives me the chance to create foods that are sheer indulgence, or part of a special celebration. Such as your retirement cake, for example."

"Hmm." Mr. Baxter stared at his cake in silence. "You're very talented," he said. "At my age, a man's had more cakes baked for him than he cares to remember. This is exquisite. Hopelessly unsuitable design for a retirement cake, of course.''

Julie frowned. ''I followed Miss Blane's instructions most precisely—''

''She's a wonderful woman, Harriet. She can look down her nose at a bishop and make him feel guilty.'' Mr. Baxter resumed his inspection of the cake. ''However, this is a wedding cake if ever I saw one. Guess I'll just have to stick with my job a bit longer and see if I can't find some other use for the cake. Cost me enough. I don't like to see it go to waste.''

''Wouldn't it be easier to order a different cake rather than change your retirement plans?''

The old man made no attempt to answer Julie's question. ''Robbie's been in the States for two weeks,'' he said reflectively. ''He came back yesterday morning looking as foul-tempered as he did when he left. What the devil did you do to my grandson, Julie Marshall?''

Julie's voice was tinged with sadness. ''Loved him,'' she said.

Mr. Baxter snorted, a snort that sounded highly reminiscent of Julie's mother at her most impatient. ''Damn fool romantic nonsense. Tearing each other apart and calling it love. In my day, a sensible man looked for a woman who could cook and have strong babies, and left it at that.''

''I can cook,'' Julie pointed out, with a ghost of a smile. ''You could say your grandson got it half right.''

''Probably tried to make a few strong babies, as well, if I know anything about him. Ha! You're blushing. After fifty years in Hollywood, I'd forgotten there were

any women left who knew how to blush off camera."
Mr. Baxter removed the largest of the pink roses from
the cake and popped it into his mouth, crunching with
evident enjoyment.

"Robbie's working in my study right at this moment," he said, swallowing sugar petals. "Third door
on the right, if you should happen to be interested.
Can't think why you would be, of course. From what
I can make out, the damn fool boy has made a total
donkey's rear end out of himself from the moment the
two of you met. Do you think you could knock some
sense into him before he sends his entire office staff
crazy? Not to mention driving me into an early grave."

Julie took the old man's outstretched hand. "Thank
you," she murmured. "Thank you for giving us a
chance to work things out."

Her whole world suddenly seemed light and full of
color, as if she were Dorothy stepping out of the
whirlwind and into the Land of Oz. "Don't you ever
go to the movies, Mr. Baxter?" she added with a teasing smile. "All the best love stories are about women
who fall in love with a damn fool of a man."

She found the study without difficulty. Robert was
seated behind a massive desk piled high with papers.
He wore the horn-rimmed glasses that he obviously
needed for reading, and his face was set in hard lines of
concentration. Something about his posture, though,
spoke of a bone-deep weariness.

Julie's heart jumped into immediate overdrive. She
had missed him intolerably over the past few weeks,
and seeing him again, she realized just how empty and
colorless her life had been recently despite all her hard
work at the bakery. The thickly padded carpet ab-

sorbed the sounds of her footsteps, and Robert didn't notice her until she was well inside the room. She stopped as soon as he looked up.

"Hello," she said softly.

For one unguarded moment, she saw delight flare in his eyes. Then the shutters fell and he gazed at her from behind a mask of cool indifference. "I don't think we have anything to say to one another."

She understood him far better now than she had done on the night he left her. "Are you that scared, Robert?" she asked quietly.

"Of course I'm not scared." He paused for a split second. "Scared of what?"

"I don't know. Maybe of finding out that you made a fool of yourself by leaping to conclusions. Maybe of discovering that you still feel something for me, even though you're convinced you ought to despise me."

"That magazine was pretty conclusive evidence that you must have known who I was."

"I suppose so, if you insist on ascribing the worst motives to people. I don't suppose the flat where you gave me dinner is really where you live in London. But I'm not leaping to the conclusion that you're a scheming person who deceived me for totally evil reasons."

"The flat belongs to my housekeeper, and I own the rest of the house. I planned to tell you the truth about that and a lot of other things the night I discovered the magazine." Robert took off his glasses and pinched the bridge of his nose, then rubbed the back of his neck in an effort to ease muscles that obviously ached with fatigue. "How did you know where to find me?"

"Your grandfather invited me here."

"I can't imagine why my grandfather would take it upon himself—" Robert broke off abruptly, and his face whitened beneath its tan. "Of course," he said flatly. "You're pregnant and you want me to pay for the baby."

His stubborn refusal to see her for the person she really was hurt more than Julie would have imagined possible. "I'm not pregnant," she said wearily. "And if I were, I wouldn't want my child to have anything to do with such a money-obsessed father. You're a rotten judge of character, Robert."

She had hoped so much that the time they'd spent apart would have made him understand that she'd never marry any man for his money, least of all him. Obviously she had deluded herself. She started walking toward the door and turned to speak sadly over her shoulder. "You were right, after all. We don't have anything to discuss. Goodbye, Robert. Have fun making your next billion dollars."

Out of the corner of her eye, she saw a blur of movement and when she tried to open the study door, Robert was in front of her, barring her exit. He shook his head, almost helplessly, then reached out and with infinite gentleness caressed her cheek.

"I can't let you walk out of my life again," he said unsteadily. "I'm a fool and a coward, but please don't go."

She closed her eyes. "I love you, Robert, but sometimes love isn't enough. There has to be trust, too. And respect. If you don't trust me, why would you want me hanging around? Except that you enjoy making love to me. That's not the sort of relationship I want."

He winced. "'Enjoy' is hardly the right word. When we make love... when you're in my arms... it's like nothing in the world I've ever experienced." A faint flush of color stained his cheekbones, and when he spoke again his voice was dry, almost clinical. "In other words, the physical attraction between us is utterly spectacular."

"Then let's have an affair," she said quietly, although her heart twisted in such anguish that she had no idea how she would follow through if he took her up on her suggestion. "Physical attraction would make a great basis for an affair. No depth. No emotion. No strings. And no hurt feelings when it's over."

"I don't want an affair," he muttered. He looked up, eyes glittering. "You could teach me how to trust."

"By proving that I didn't set out to trap you?" Julie shook her head. "I can't prove that, Robert, and what's more, I don't even want to try. If you know me at all, you'll know I didn't set out to deceive you. And if you don't know me, how can you say I'm important to you?"

"Because when I'm apart from you, it seems as if the light has gone out of my life." Robert looked stunned by his own answer, and Julie felt a fragile flower of hope blossom inside her. Reaching out her hand, she stroked the hard, tense line of his jaw.

"I feel the same way," she murmured. "It hurts to be apart, doesn't it?"

"It hurts like hell. Oh, God, Julie, I've ached for you these past few weeks." Robert clamped his hand over hers, then drew her to him in a convulsive embrace, his grip so tight she could scarcely breathe. She felt his lips on her mouth, feverish with the need to be close to her.

Julie's response was immediate, but curled somewhere inside the passion, a dawning sense of wonder began to stir.

In his professional life, Robert was the masterful, all-powerful businessman, but in his feelings for her he was as uncertain—and as vulnerable—as any other man. From what she had read in the infamous magazine article, Julie knew that he had ample reason to be cynical about the power of his money to attract false protestations of love. For Robert, even the ultimate joy of fathering a child had been reduced more than once to the sordid level of lawsuits brought by grasping women he had scarcely known, let alone taken to bed.

Early in their relationship, Robert had set her free from the bonds of her past and her immature fixation on John Farringdon. Now she could return the gift. Simply by loving Robert freely and without conditions, she could show him that he had much more to offer a woman than the depth of his bank balance.

She clung to him, wondering how to make him understand her insight. Then she realized how few words she needed. "I love you," she said, looking up at him "I love you for richer, for poorer, for better, for worse, in sickness and in health."

He met her gaze and his blue eyes glowed with a dawning sense of wonder. "I love you, too." He spoke the words carefully, testing their truth. Then his face broke into a delighted grin and he hugged her tight. " love you, darn it! I love you!"

"I wish you didn't sound quite so surprised."

"I love you," he said, his voice suddenly sober and full of promise. "Will you marry me, Julie?"

She smiled, so full of happiness, she felt light-headed. "Of course I'll marry you. How could I say no? I already baked our wedding cake, although your grandfather had me fooled into thinking it was a cake for his retirement."

Robert gave a crack of laughter. "His retirement cake? That conniving old so-and-so will never retire. He'll be directing the crowd scene on the way to his own funeral."

"We'd better not let him get together with my mother, then, or we'll find ourselves in the middle of a wedding for a thousand guests, with a brass band to lead the procession."

"Sweetheart, sometimes a wise man knows when it's time to bow to the inevitable. By the time my grandfather and your mother have spent ten minutes together, the only issue up for grabs will be whether it's a fifty-piece brass band or a hundred."

Julie laughed. "Shall we go and tell him the good news?"

"He's probably listening at the keyhole."

"Then let's give him something worth listening to." Julie reached up and framed Robert's face with her hands. "I love you," she said, her voice almost fierce.

"And I love you."

Julie rested her head on his shoulder, a faint echo of her anxiety returning. "But you have no more reason to trust me now than you did ten minutes ago."

He held her a little tighter. "I have the best reason of all," he said softly. "I looked into your eyes and allowed myself to believe what I saw. When you told me you loved me, you gave me the confidence to trust the truth of my own feelings."

"All I did was return your gift," she murmured. "You made me understand myself and my family—for the first time."

A loud knocking at the door interrupted their kiss. "Are you two ever going to come out of there? Damn fool youngsters. In my day, you could have arranged the wedding, the honeymoon and planned the furniture for your first house in the length of time you've been closeted in that study."

Robert and Julie broke apart, exchanging reluctant grins. Robert swung open the door. "Actually, Grandpa, we were kind of anticipating that you'd plan the wedding for us. With some help from Julie's mother, of course."

"I already have her waiting on the phone," Mr. Baxter said.

Robert rolled his eyes heavenward, "Now why aren't I surprised to hear that, I wonder?"

Julie chuckled. "Darling, if you have any preference in brass bands, I think you'd better speak now or forever hold your peace."

Robert put his arm around her waist and pulled her close. "The biggest and the best," he said softly. "I want the whole world to know I'm in love."

Mr. Baxter snorted, but his eyes were suspiciously moist. "Damn fool nonsense. I'd better go and talk to your mother, Julie. Now there's a sensible woman for you. Reminds me of my own dear wife."

"Which one?" Robert inquired.

Mr. Baxter looked pained. "Julie, do an old man a favor and keep your fiancé quiet for five minutes while I talk to your mother."

"With pleasure." Julie stood on tiptoe and locked her hands behind Robert's head. "Kiss me," she commanded.

Mr. Baxter's conversation with Mrs. Marshall lasted for nearly an hour. Neither Robert nor Julie noticed.

THE LADY AND THE TOMCAT
by Bethany Campbell